Wyrm Lord

The Cloven Land Trilogy, Book 2

Simon Kewin

Wyrm Lord – The Cloven Land Trilogy, Book 2

Copyright © Simon Kewin 2015

STORM
CROW
BOOKS

ISBN: 978-1-9993395-3-1

For Ellie, the second part of my own magical trilogy

CONTENTS

1 - CROWHAUNTED

Cait plummeted toward the spitting pit of lava. The heat from it was like a solid wall. She screamed as visions of burning alive consumed her. Nox had tricked them all. The portal was already sealed. They had the wrong cave. The whole thing with the undain and the chase was a mad joke to get her to throw herself into a pool of molten rock.

She only hoped, when she hit, it would be a quick end. No more than a few moments of agony.

Then she thumped into solid ground. Instead of raging heat, the air was cold on her cheekbones. She held Ran's hand in hers. His skin was rough. Her other hand was empty. What had happened? She'd tried to grab her mother for the leap through the portal, but they'd fallen before they were ready. Nox had fallen, too; she'd heard his cry as they fell. She replayed the moment in her mind but couldn't decide who had jumped or fallen first.

She opened her eyes. Wherever they were, it wasn't a lava pit in Iceland.

She, Ran and Nox lay on a plain of hummocky grass inside a circle of jagged standing stones that rose from the ground like pointed teeth. The portal from the other side. The circle sat in a wooded valley surrounded by the slopes of steep hills. Frost gilded the ground, Cait's breath billowing into the air as she exhaled. A thin, early morning light infused the scene, casting long shadows from the standing stones. Dewy cobwebs covered the tussocks of grass like frozen smoke in the sunlight. A ghostly mist drifted from the ground.

They were alone. Apart from the stone circle, the only sign of human activity was a stone archway in the distance. Whether it was the remains of a bridge that had once spanned the valley or something else entirely, she couldn't tell. It was clearly ruined now.

"What happened?" she said. And then, an even stupider question, "Where are we?"

Without replying, Ran released her hand and sprang to his feet. He spun around, assessing threats from any direction, then sprinted to one of the stones. Vaulting on top, he balanced there to get a better view of their surroundings.

Nox sat on the ground behind her, a broad grin on his face, like all his plans had worked perfectly. And, OK, he *had* escaped Genera for the moment. But given where they were it surely wasn't much of an improvement.

"Well," he said, some of his old self-assurance returning. "Here we are, Cait. You and me together in the mythical land of the undain."

She scrambled to her feet. "That's not how it is, Nox." She thought about everything he'd done. The way he'd hunted them. The pleasure he'd taken in her distress at the refinery. Danny. "Just leave me alone."

She strode toward Ran, feeling a little ridiculous. She

wished the others were there. Not only Danny. Fer and Johnny, too. Her gran or her mother. Wishing for her own mother, how pathetic was that? But she felt suddenly so alone without them. Helpless.

Childish tears swelled within her. She couldn't do this. She couldn't do any of this. She wanted to go home, back to her old life.

Out of habit she pulled out her mobile, thinking she could speak to one of her friends, text them at least. Feel closer to them. But, of course, she couldn't. No signal in the other world. How could there be? She was such an idiot. The bookwyrm was there, installed as an app. Its icon was an illustrated dragon entwined about a gold and crimson letter *D*. But without an internet connection it would be of little use. Besides, the phone's battery was down to 10% with no way to recharge it. She switched it off.

Ran atop his stone peered into the east. Nox, now standing, brushed mud from his waterproofs, the swishing sound loud in the dawn calm. She didn't really know either of them. At least *they* knew what they were doing. Ran wasn't afraid of anyone, and Nox was smart, knew things about Angere, knew people here. What chance did she have? She was just a girl who'd worked a bit of witch-magic without really knowing what the hell she was doing.

Except, she wasn't alone, was she? There was the fourth companion. The one no one knew about. The ghost or echo of the dead witch-girl inside her. There was her hope, a thing she could cling to in this terrible place. A much-needed friend. Cait shut her eyes again and reached within herself, seeking the faint presence.

No reply came. Dread seeped through her. Maybe the possession magic, or whatever it was the girl had worked back in Manchester, didn't survive the leap between the worlds. Maybe Cait really was on her own.

She tried again, yearning for the girl's presence. That cool mountain pool. This time there was a stir, like brittle leaves drifting in a breeze. The girl was there. Distant, but definitely there. Relief flooded through Cait.

Can you hear me? she said.

The reply was faint when it came, like a winter wind shaped to form words. *I can hear you. But everything feels so strange. Where are we?*

We've left our world. We jumped through a gateway to Angere.

The land of the masters? The horrors? Say it's not true. Why would you do such a thing?

I'm sorry. We had no choice. It was the only way to defeat them.

It's no way. You will never defeat them. Not like this. They always win, always... She sounded fainter and fainter, as if fading there and then.

No! said Cait. *Don't go. Don't give up. I need you. You're the only one here that can help me. Promise me you won't go.*

There was a pause, a long moment that stretched. Then, finally, came the reply. *I won't give up on you. For better or worse. But I won't be enough. We won't be enough to defeat them. You know that?*

"Yes," replied Cait, speaking out loud. "Yes, I know that."

Ran glanced at her with a puzzled look on his face then returned to scanning their surroundings. But the girl was right. They wouldn't be enough. They could only try. What else could they do?

"We should get away from here," she called out to Nox and Ran. "They'll find us easily."

"No hurry," said Nox, grinning as if she was amusing. "We're a long way from the White City. Hundreds of miles. They probably think we're still somewhere in our world. I kept the details of the Iceland portal very secret."

Anger swelled within her. "Yeah. Or maybe you want to wait here so your undain friends can come pick us up."

Nox shook his head. "You're not making sense. Why would I do that?"

"Because if you could get back in their good books you would. I bet you'd jump at the chance if they offered it."

Nox regarded her thoughtfully. "You know what, Cait? Perhaps I would. But that's not going to happen. I've failed them and I've betrayed them. Trust me, Menhroth is not the forgiving type. He doesn't do grey areas. And ironic as it is, my only hope for revenge lies with a few witches and their ridiculous plan to get both halves of the book to Andar."

Cait met his gaze. Maybe Nox did want revenge on the undain. But it was just as likely he wanted revenge on *her*. His fall was her fault. He wasn't going to forget about that.

"We have to head for the White City," she said. "Find the other half of the Grimoire. And then somehow make it across the An."

It sounded ridiculous as she spelled it out. How was any of it going to be possible? She didn't mention the thing that was uppermost in her mind: Danny. Would the undain take him to Angere? If they did, she had to rescue him as well. Another impossible task. They'd been an item for, what, one day before he'd been captured by an army of undead freaks. It was typical of her luck.

"We should work out where in Angere we are first," said Nox.

"I thought you knew about the portal?" said Cait. "I thought you were all, like, *I make it my business to know what's going on.*"

"I knew about the gateway in our world, not this side. We should assess the situation, gather facts before deciding what to do. It could be weeks before they think to look for us out here."

"No," said Cait. "We have to move. They could be here at any moment."

"I don't think so. I told you, I'm very good at keeping secrets."

"I'm sure you are. But I don't think Danny is."

"Danny?"

"Danny. Didn't you notice he wasn't with us? They took him in Manchester. We tried to rescue him, but we couldn't." She stopped for a moment, fighting back tears. She had to get a grip on herself. "Don't you see? The undain have him and that means they'll soon know *everything*."

Nox looked startled. This was clearly news to him. He really was cut off from Genera and everything that had happened recently. "That changes matters. We have to leave now."

"Yeah. Like I said."

Ran jumped to the ground, landing beside Cait with cat-like grace. He said a single word in his language, nodding toward a clump of trees that crowned a nearby hill.

"What did he say?" asked Cait. She needed to learn some of Ran's language. She hated being dependent on Nox to translate for her. Problem was, she wasn't much good at languages. She'd barely scraped a *D* in French.

"He said *crows*."

"Crows?"

"Crows," said Nox. "Look."

Above the trees, a great flock of birds wheeled around in the dawn like a cloud of black smoke from some raging fire.

"They're rooks," said Cait.

"What?"

"Rooks, not crows. Crows are solitary birds." Her mother had explained it on one of their holidays. Strange the things that stuck in your mind. "And why are we even talking about it? You think there's time to do some bird watching?"

"Rooks or crows," said Nox. "What matters is they might be looking for us."

Cait turned back to the shifting cloud of black dots. One or two were peeling off from the flock, flying in different directions. Fanning out.

"Which way is the An?" asked Cait.

Nox studied the sky. "We're west of the river, so we

need to head toward the rising sun. Which takes us directly past the crows."

"Rooks."

"Whatever."

She longed to ask Ran what he thought they should do. His people were from here. Long ago, sure, but he might know something useful. She didn't know the words. And she didn't want to ask Nox to speak for her. She didn't trust Nox not to misrepresent her. In any case, she needed to seem like she knew what she was doing, even if she didn't have a clue.

The seeing stone. Maybe it would help. She had to do *something.*

"Wait here," she instructed, trying to sound like she was used to giving people orders. It sounded ridiculous even to her. She marched out of the circle. Maybe they'd think she was working some terrible magic. Communing with the whatever-the-hell-it-was you communed with. When she was far enough away, making sure they couldn't see what she was doing, she squinted through her gran's glassy green stone at the rooks.

It was impossible to identify individual birds in the flock. They swooped and circled, and by the time she'd picked one out with her right eye, she'd lost it through the stone. She turned her attention to the lone birds. One flapped toward them, calling out with a grating *caw.* She eyed it through the stone. Its body glowed with a yellow light. It was natural; it was just a rook. It glided overhead, black plumage shining in the slanting rays of the sun, wings splayed wide into fingers. It didn't stop.

Another approached, this one much lower, flapping hard to stay in the air. It landed on one of the standing stones and regarded them with shiny eyes, head cocked as if trying to understand who or what they were. It, too, glowed with an inner light through the seeing-stone. She studied three other birds and each time it was the same.

"Come on," she called to the others. "They're birds.

They can't harm us. We'll head into those woods. At least we won't be out in the open. Then we'll decide what to do."

She set off walking. Ran immediately caught up with her and raced on ahead.

Nox shouted to her. "Are you sure?" He sounded doubtful, like she couldn't possibly know what she was talking about. She ignored him. After a moment she heard him muttering to himself and setting off to follow them up the hillside.

The ground sloped more steeply as they ascended. They walked in shadows, the sun not yet high enough to illuminate this flank of the valley. Cait said nothing. She needed to try and think of a plan. She'd assumed her mother would know what to do when they got there, but now it was up to her. Which was ridiculous. She didn't have a clue where to start.

She tried again and again to see a way to defeat the undain, save the world. Save the *worlds*. But all she could think about was Danny. What was happening to him? What were they putting him through? He'd try and be brave. Crack stupid jokes instead of telling them what he knew. They'd get everything from him sooner or later.

Half-way up the slope, she stopped to catch her breath. A stitch already pulled at her side. That wasn't good. There were hundreds of miles to cover. Nox reached her and stopped. He was breathing hard as well, which made her feel a little better. Ran, of course, looked ready to race up the hill.

"How do you know the birds aren't undain?" Nox asked once he could talk.

Cait shrugged. "I just do."

"Some spell?"

"Maybe."

"Well, be careful. If they can detect the use of magic you'll alert them to us."

"I know what I'm doing."

"I hope so," said Nox.

So did she. She changed the subject. "So the sun rises in the same direction in this world?"

Nox nodded. "Angere is different from our world, but in some ways it's very similar."

"So the seasons? Back home it's the end of the summer."

"It's a month or so later here, but the worlds stay more or less in sync. That's why the portals work. So I was told."

She nodded as if that was what she'd suspected, and looked away, up to the trees. The rooks still thronged the branches. The leaves up there were definitely turning to yellows and reds. The grass beneath her feet was crisp with overnight frost. How long before the snow came? Time was short. She set off walking again.

She'd thought vaguely the frozen river would be a way to reach Andar. But, no. That was no good, was it? By then it would be too late. If they could walk across the ice so could the undain, and Andar would already be lost. Everything would be lost. Somehow, they had to find another way. And do so before winter struck.

She was still thinking these troubled thoughts when she came upon the dead rook. Or maybe it was a crow. She nearly trod on it. She stifled a shriek of horror. The ruined carcass lay on the ground beside a rock as if it had simply fallen off its perch. It was little more than fine white bones and sinews held together with tatters of flesh and feathers. Its head was just a skull. It moved and, for a moment, she thought it was alive, impossibly alive. But it was only flies, fat and purple, crawling through it. The bird was long-dead. Tiny white maggots wriggled and writhed through its eye-socket. The cloying smell of decay filled her nose.

She recalled a holiday, a day when she and her mother had come across a dead sheep in a field, little more than a bag of wool stretched over a gaping frame of bones, buzzing with fat flies. The sight of it had filled her with shivering horror. But her mother had pulled her away, held her close, told her it was OK. It couldn't harm her. That was how it went. Life and death. She wished her mother was there now to repeat her words. She glanced at Ran, watching her with his wary eyes. No comfort there. She sighed, stepped around the dead bird, and carried on up the slope, heading for the safety of the trees.

The ground rose more steeply the higher they climbed, and it took another twenty minutes to reach the tree line. Darkness lingered under the eaves of the great branches as if reluctant to yield to the daylight. The cacophony of the rooks' calls filled the air. Cait turned to look the way they'd come. The standing stones were unexpectedly distant, a perfect circle in the centre of the valley, like the pupil of an eye. Nox toiled up the hill toward her, his chest heaving. They were both going to have trouble crossing Angere, even without the undain pursuing them. Only Ran was unaffected by the effort of the climb. He stared into the trees in case some unseen danger lurked within.

A rook flapped awkwardly into the sky from down the slope. It was injured; it climbed as if one of its wings was damaged. She watched it, wondering how it had hurt itself. How they hadn't noticed it. It must have been feeding on some carrion. Then, for the briefest moment as it laboured and flapped, she saw daylight through its body. Alarm pounded within her. She thought of the dead bird on the ground, the maggots swarming in its broken skull. The eye-socket staring up at her.

Was it the same bird? The broken rook struggled into the sky, wings ragged. It shed feathers on each flap, as if it was only the memory of how to fly that kept it in the air. A rasping croak came from it. She thought it would fly east, toward the White City, but instead it jerked away from them, heading down the valley.

Nox arrived. "What is it? What have you seen?" He peered around in clear alarm.

Should she tell him? Maybe she'd imagined that

glimpse of light through the rook's body. It had been such an insane few days. "It's nothing. Just … thinking. I'm in another world. I mean, it's amazing isn't it?"

"Yeah," said Nox, pushing past her for the cover of the trees. "Amazing."

When he'd gone she lifted the stone to her eye. But the bird was only a speck of black, too far away for her to tell if it was natural or not. It flew underneath the stone arch and disappeared from sight. She waited for it to emerge from the other side, hoping to discern some clue about what it was doing, where it was going. But there was no sign of it.

Frowning, she turned to follow Nox into the trees.

2 – A NATION OF SLAVES

An hour later, they sat on the other side of the hilltop copse, eating the supplies they'd brought with them from Dublin: dry biscuits and some sickly, sugary cake that Cait could only nibble at. They sipped at water from plastic bottles. They didn't have enough of everything to get them very far; some time soon they'd need fresh supplies.

Loose boulders lay scattered around, half-buried in the ground, as if someone had attempted to erect a building long ago but it had fallen into ruin. They sat on them, each alone with their thoughts. The rooks racketed in the treetops, but their calls were less harsh. It sounded more like they were chortling with laughter. A wind had come up, gusting strongly enough to send the branches swaying and lashing. Autumn leaves – lime-green, blood-red, honey-gold – fell around them, gliding to the ground like dying butterflies.

Angere lay stretched out before them, flooded with white sunlight. Nox glugged back water and handed her the bottle. "So, does Angere surprise you?"

"A little," Cait replied, not looking at him. In truth, it surprised her a lot. It wasn't what she'd expected at all.

She'd imagined a scarred, ruined landscape: grim metal buildings, raging fires and the air heavy with smoke. But Angere was *beautiful*, there was no other word for it. It looked more like a vast garden than a wilderness. A carefully tended patchwork of lawns and avenues and meadows stretching in all directions. Even this late in the year, swathes of colourful flowers were everywhere. The air was thick with their heady scents.

Dotting the landscape were shining white houses: palaces with towers and domes and steeples. They looked like the stately homes her mother dragged her to on weekend trips to the country. But those had been old and crumbling, their oak-panelled corridors carpeted with fading rugs, their walls hung with the blackened portraits of stern former owners. These houses sparkled in the light of the sun, their white stones glowing.

"Are you sure this isn't Andar?" she said. "Maybe we ended up on the other side of the An by mistake."

"This is Angere," said Nox. "Things aren't always as they seem here."

"So you know this area?"

"No. I've only ever visited the White City. Never this far west."

She shaded her eyes as she gazed across the landscape. One or two other hills rose from the plain, also crowned by copses. Upon one she discerned another of the stone archways like that in the valley. This rose above the trees like the legs and body of some vast beast. Definitely not a bridge, then.

"What is that?" she asked, pointing at the distant hill. "Something to do with the undain?"

"No, the arches predate the undain. The dragonriders built them, scattered them over the land. No idea why; they don't *do* anything except slowly crumble away into dust. Maybe Ran knows what they were for."

Between the hills there was only open countryside. She'd hoped for dense forests, but there was little cover in the wide, rolling landscape.

"I don't see how we're going to get to the An," she said.

Nox shrugged. "Perhaps we shouldn't try. Perhaps we should seek help in one of those palaces."

"That's a mad idea."

"Coming here was a mad idea, Cait. Trying to defeat the undain is a mad idea. The truth is we don't have much chance either way. We're exposed out here and we need help."

"From the undain. Right." It made no sense. Their only hope was to avoid being detected, however unlikely that was. "If they spot us they'll throw us into their dungeons or eat us alive or something."

"Maybe. Maybe not." He held up his right hand to show her the gold ring he wore. "Do you know what this is?"

It looked expensive. Probably not the sort of thing you bought in *Bling Thing*. She shrugged. "Just a ring."

"I was given this by Menhroth himself when he made me a Baron of the Undying Land three years ago. Anyone here would recognize it and know its meaning. Unless they were an earl or a duke or a lord, they would be duty-bound to do what I tell them. That's the way it works here. We could go and demand food and shelter and whatever help we need."

"You're not one of them. You're not an undain."

"That doesn't matter. They do what they're told by those higher up. This society is basically feudal. Damn good system if you ask me."

"But even if they were to accept you, which seems pretty unlikely, what about me and Ran?"

He'd clearly been thinking about this. Making plans. "You at least are OK, Cait. Children only go through the Ritual of the Seven Ascensions when they reach seventeen. It wouldn't be odd for you to be ... normal."

"And Ran?"

"Ran is more of a problem. There are still dragonriders here and they're still the king's personal guard. But they're all undain. They're very different from our friend. Ran would have to stay out of the way."

"You've got this all worked out, haven't you? Sounds to me like you're trying to split us up."

He shook his head. "We need help, Cait. It's the only way."

"It's too dangerous. Once they learn from Danny we're in Angere, they'll come looking for us. They won't care if you've got a hundred stupid rings."

"Perhaps, but I've been thinking. Did Danny know where in Angere the portal led? Did you talk about it?"

She thought back. The details were already hazy. Too much had happened. The bookwyrm had said something about the portal being a long way from the White City, hadn't it? "We knew it wouldn't take us anywhere near Menhroth."

"But not which direction?"

"No. I don't think so."

"There you are, then," said Nox. "The undain will be scouring the banks of the An. That's where I'd look. That's where most things happen. This place is a forgotten backwater."

"No, it's too dangerous. I'm not going anywhere near one of those houses."

Nox scowled and said nothing for a moment. He wasn't used to being argued with. Well, he'd have to *get* used to it. And there was more to this than he was letting on. She waited. If he had something more to say he should say it.

After a few moments' silence he spoke again. "The thing is, Cait, when I was here before – in the White City I mean – I heard some rumours. Very vague. But I've learned it pays to listen out for things like that. You never know when they might come in useful."

"What rumours?"

"Rumours of battles being fought within Angere. Factions opposed to Menhroth. The Revenant Army being dispatched to suppress uprisings. I heard the name *Phoenix*, too. Some kind of rebel leader."

"Seriously?"

"That's what I heard."

She took another sip of water. "But, why? Why would they fight each other?"

"Oh, it's the same everywhere. People see power and want it for themselves. Trust me, I should know. And here it comes down to Menhroth. He's responsible for the ascension of every other undain, either directly or indirectly. And there are people who don't like that, his control over everything. They don't like the way he does things. So I heard."

"But we can't walk up to one of those houses and ask if they're secretly fighting the King," she said. "That's insane."

"Obviously. But maybe we can make contacts. Win their trust. Network. It's no different to negotiating a contract or manipulating politicians back home. It's all about striking up a relationship. Finding weaknesses you can exploit. You'd be surprised what people let slip when they're relaxed and not concentrating. I wouldn't expect you to understand, but that's how the grown-up world works."

"Really? Is that right?" She could have punched him. She very nearly did, but she restrained herself. "Well, I told you. I'm not going anywhere near the undain. I'm heading to the An to get Danny and the book. If you want to go and alert the enemy you're on your own."

Nox shrugged. "OK, Cait. Whatever you say."

She caught the frown on his face. She thought about the first time she'd seen him, outside Central Library. The day he let both her and the Grimoire slip from his grasp. He'd scowled at her then, too. It was like seeing the real him for a moment beneath the mask.

"What was it like?" she said.

"What was what like?"

"Back home. Running Genera. You must have been incredibly powerful. You must have been able to do *anything* so long as you kept your masters here happy. You could go anywhere, have whatever you wanted."

Nox nodded. "You want me to say it wasn't like that? Actually, yes, it was wonderful. A lot of fun. Like you say, I could do pretty well anything. The world was my playground."

"And losing all that because of me?"

It took him a few moments to reply. "Don't exaggerate your role, Cait. I made plenty of mistakes on my own."

"But you do blame me?"

"Not really. Maybe a little. You were only doing what made sense for you. In your position I'd have done the same."

She nodded. Could she believe him? Time would tell. She glanced back at Ran, sitting a little way back in the shadows. He was busy hacking off his pony-tail, his black hair falling to the ground around him. When he saw her watching he spoke words of explanation that she didn't understand. Cait asked Nox what he'd said.

"Oh, so now you want my help?"

"Just tell me."

"Says short hair is better for fighting. His braids get in the way."

She turned back to the dragonrider. "Ran? Which way to the An?" She spoke slowly, nodding her head in the direction of the plains in front of them. "Which way would you go?"

Ran considered her words. He appeared to understand at least some of them. He rose to his feet, regarding the wide land before them. He wore only a thin shirt while Cait was bundled up in several layers of fleece. The tattooed blue spirals on his arms seemed to swirl as he pointed. Not east. North. He said something more.

Again, Nox translated. "He said *the mountains*. And some words I don't know."

Cait gazed that way. In the far distance, beyond the patchwork of green and lime and gold fields, she could see a line of mountains in the haze: jagged peaks, their tops merging with the clouds.

"You think we should go that way? Head north?"

Ran nodded, although whether he understood her words or not, she didn't know.

"The farther north we go, the longer it will take," said Nox. "And the sooner we'll hit the winter."

"Still," said Cait. "I'd rather go around than try to walk across these plains unseen. What's south of here?"

Nox shrugged. "As far as I know it's like this all the way to the deserts."

"Which are nearer? Mountains or deserts?"

"I don't know, Cait. I generally had more important things than geography lessons to worry about when I came here."

She considered. The truth was she didn't have a clue what to do. But Ran and Nox didn't have to know that. What would her mother do? Or her gran? They always knew what was for the best. Except, maybe they didn't? Maybe they made everything up as they went along. Maybe they pretended to know what was right and then, because everyone went along with it, that *became* the right thing to do.

It was like with teachers. You assumed they knew everything. But then if you asked them an awkward question they'd have to go and look up the answer. It was like they were only pretending to be teachers. Perhaps that was what everyone did. Maybe you only had to pretend to be something long enough and hard enough and you *became* it. Even someone like Nox: how could he have known how to run an organization like Genera? Maybe he'd had to play-act the role until everyone – including him – accepted it.

It was all she had. It wasn't quite magic but it was close enough. She'd play the part of someone who knew what they were doing. Perhaps she'd believe it herself eventually. Fall for her own trick.

So, east or north? She was tempted to try south to spite them both. But north made more sense. The An ran through those mountains judging by the stories she'd heard. Perhaps they could reach that, then head south to the White City. Get a boat, maybe.

In truth, she didn't want to leave the haven of the woods. She felt safe, like she had on the roundabout back in Manchester. Perhaps this copse, the remnant of some vast wildwood, was another magical place. Maybe the undain feared it and left it alone. It would be good to think so. But they couldn't stay.

"These *factions* you mentioned," she said to Nox. "Do you know where they are?"

"I don't know anything about them. I don't know if they even exist. That's why I wanted to find out. We need more information, we're in the dark."

"We'll head north," she said. "Cut east when it looks safer. There are palaces that way, too, but not so many by the look of it. The wooded hills might give us safe places to sleep. Maybe we won't be seen."

She stood up. It was weird making the decisions for two grown men. She kept expecting them to laugh at her or ignore her. Well, let them try. They might not like the fact, but she was the key to all this. Not them. She felt a little better at having decided, whether or not it was the right thing to do.

Ran stooped to pick up his backpack. Nox shook his head but said nothing.

They walked around the hilltop, staying in the shadows of the tree-line as much as possible. Nox trailed along behind them, occasionally bashing rocks and trunks with a stick he'd found. Cait conversed with Ran, trying to learn some words of his language or teach him some of her own. The dragonrider picked things up quickly, needed to speak words only a few times before getting the shape of them right in his mouth. They soon had *tree* and *hill* and *sky* and other easy words in each other's language. But then she wanted to ask him about Andar, and the undain, and his people, and the stone archways, but didn't know where to start. It was going to be a long time before they could talk properly.

Still, she found herself warming to him. She was grateful to him, of course; he'd rescued her from the refinery and was doing everything he could to protect her. Something to do with the ancient history of his people. She did find it just a *bit* creepy. If he grumbled or complained or argued at least he'd seem more human. As she laughed at his attempts to pronounce *hedgerow* or *dragonrider* he did grin, very slightly. He looked a lot less fearsome when he grinned.

They reached the northern edge of the hill after an hour. In the distance another mound rose from the landscape, but in between lay an expanse of open country, only the occasional hedge or tree to provide any sort of cover. They'd be visible for miles. Not far away, half-hidden behind a rise in the ground, the white spires of one of the palaces rose into the sky.

There were people down there, too: stick-figures in the fields. A line of them worked their way across one meadow on hands and knees like the police doing a fingertip search.

Ran had picked up a branch as well, and he'd cut and trimmed it to make a heavy staff. He gazed down the slope, swinging the staff around as if weighing it for use.

"There are too many of them down there," said Cait. "We'll never get past."

"No need to worry about them," said Nox.

"Why?"

"They're slaves. Undain, but lowly ones, made to follow orders and not think for themselves. They strong and tireless but they'll ignore us."

"You didn't think to tell me before?"

"There didn't seem to be much point. You weren't listening to anything I said."

"And you're sure of this?"

"Of course. Most of the undain are like that: useful machines. That's how this place functions. The higher undain, the lords and ladies of the Holy Court, have incredible powers. But most people are like *that*, slaving away to make everything beautiful. Like I said, it's an excellent system."

"Not if you're one of them."

"But I'm not, am I? And they don't know anything about it. They don't mind. When they went through the ritual they were changed into creatures that were happy to slave away, so where's the harm?"

Cait shook her head. "It's horrible. I mean, who are they? Where did they come from?"

"From all the places Menhroth has invaded. They take prisoners as well as Bone and Spirit."

"So you mean ... people from our world, too?"

Nox shrugged. "Some."

"And Genera sent people through the portal to be turned into these ... zombies? *You* sent them through?"

Nox at least looked thoughtful for a moment. "I did, I admit it. But things are different now, aren't they? Now I'm on the other side."

"Yes," said Cait. "So you say."

In the end they had no choice but to descend the hill. Cait kept a close eye on the figures working in the fields, ready to turn and run if any pointed or shouted. None did.

They approached the line of undain she'd seen from the hilltop. What Nox had said appeared to be true: these were mindless slaves. They were nearly skeletons, shocking to see, their eyes sunken and hollow as they laboured, skin stretched over stark bones. Most were swathed in rags and tatters, impossible to tell which were men and which were women. Judging by the size, some were children. Each had a pair of metal clippers which they were using to trim the grass to a perfect length, blade by blade. They crawled backward so they didn't mar the perfection of their work. Each had a basket on their back into which they dropped the slivers of cut grass.

Others worked at tall lines of bushes that had been planted in swirling shapes around the edges of the meadow. From up on the slopes, their patterns had reminded her of the tattoos on Ran's skin. The bushes were ablaze with red and purple blooms, but frosts had burned them and now they were dying. The air was thick with their scent: sickly and cloying with an overtone of decay. The undain plucked the blooms and dropped them into baskets at their feet. They worked at amazing speed, arms almost a blur, kicking their baskets along every now and then. None of them, whether on their hands and knees or plucking away at the bushes, glanced up as Cait, Nox and Ran crept by.

She'd expected a different kind of ugliness. She would almost have preferred the shattered, grim landscape she'd imagined. That at least would have seemed more honest.

The nearest undain to her was definitely a woman, her age impossible to tell. She worked at the hedge, eyes staring without blinking. Unable to stop herself, Cait reached out and touched the yellowing, wrinkled skin on the undain's arm. It felt more like leather than something alive.

The woman paused, briefly. A look of confusion flashed across her features. Cait stepped back, terrified she'd woken the undain, terrified they'd turn and attack, like something from a horror film. The woman gazed around as if trying to understand what had happened or chasing an elusive memory. Then she simply resumed her activity, picking endlessly at the flowers.

"Come on," said Nox. "This isn't going to help us."

They moved on toward the next hill that rose upon the

horizon. They might, Cait thought, be able to get there by the evening if they hurried. She hoped so. The thought of spending the night in the open filled her with dread.

The lines of hedges around them were a maze. She'd studied them as they descended, seeing a path through easily enough. Now their curves and loops were disorientating. She pressed on, refusing to admit she wasn't sure of the way, keeping the sun to her right as much as possible. The cloying smell of rotten flowers thickened.

She was about to stop and ask Nox or Ran which way they thought they should go when they emerged through a gap in the hedgerow onto a wide, open meadow. Its grass was perfectly manicured, smooth enough to dance on or play some ballgame. A solitary scarecrow stood in the middle of the field. The hills lay beyond it, their slopes closer now.

It was only when they neared the scarecrow that Cait saw it was another undain. Its eyes were shut but its head lolled from side to side as if it had been made to keep moving to scare off the birds. It was lashed to a crude cross of poles. It was impossible to say how long it had stood there. Its clothes flapped in tatters and its tanned skin was creased from its years of weathering storms.

Its brown eyes opened wide at their approach. There was a dim light of understanding in them, a glimmer of intelligence. The creature called out with a dry, rasping voice, shouting words Cait didn't understand.

"What's it saying?" said Cait.

"No idea," said Nox. "It can't harm us. Keep going."

They walked in a semicircle around the solitary undain, not wanting to get too close. Ran kept his staff held ready as if it were a sword. The undain tracked them with its eyes, twisting its head round as they walked past, continuing to rasp its babble of syllables. When they were far enough away, the creature stopped speaking and its head drooped forward.

"I hate this place," said Cait. "I wish we'd never come

here." Neither Nox nor Ran replied.

They marched on in silence after that, across the springy grass. A bank formed a solid line at the edge of the field. Ran peered over it then leaped on top, turning to help pull Cait and Nox up. On the other side was a single-track lane, its surface packed stones, running in a straight line in both directions. Judging by the wheel-ruts, it was much used, but nothing was visible on it in either direction.

"So," said Nox, clearly enjoying seeing what decision she'd come to. "Which way?"

The problem was neither was right; the lane ran east-west and they needed to head north. They could cross it and continue across the lawns and gardens. But maybe it curved north, in which case it might take them to the next hill more quickly. If only her phone worked so she could download a map.

She peered along the lane in both directions. To the east, spires visible in a dip, was the palace. Clearly the lane led to it. The obvious answer was to go the other way. If the lane didn't turn north after a few miles they'd have to cut across the gardens again.

"This way," she said, jumping down into the lane and turning west.

"You do realise the An is in the opposite direction?" Nox asked.

"The An and that house."

"We can't just wander around here forever. Sooner or later they'll find us."

She didn't stop walking. She called over her shoulder. "We aren't wandering. We're making our way to the river without being seen." Hopefully she sounded confident. Perhaps he was right and she was leading them nowhere. If only Ran would say something, offer an opinion. Once again, after a pause, Nox followed.

The hedgerows on either side grew taller. Ran occasionally vaulted on top to scout out the land ahead.

They reached a point where the lane was lined with trees, their branches reaching overhead to form a shadowy tunnel. The trees' roots writhed around and through the bank, but the branches were leafless and dead, like trees in the depth of winter. Then she saw tiny black buds sprouting from the tips of their twigs, as if the trees flowered through the winter and lost their leaves in the summer. Maybe they were transplanted from a distant land and kept alive by magical means. She didn't like the look of them. The air beneath them was colder, as if they hoarded the damp and darkness. Their branches were long fingers clawing at the sky. The crows seemed at home though; several were perched among the branches, mere shapes against the light.

She was about to slip the stone to her eye to study the birds when Ran stopped, head cocked, his eyes narrowed.

"What is it?" she said.

Ran waved her quiet, frowning. She looked at Nox, but he only shrugged. The lane stretched out empty in front and behind them.

"Hide," said Ran. His accent was strong and it took her a moment to grasp his meaning. He leaped onto the bank next to one of the skeletal trees and reached down to offer them a hand. Cait could hear nothing. She scrambled up, grabbing hold of Ran's outstretched hand and the roots of the tree. On the other side lay another perfect green lawn, no undain in sight. She jumped down, Nox and Ran landing beside her. They peered through the tree roots onto the lane.

She could hear something. A distant thunder, growing louder each moment. She tried to still her breathing, keeping as low as she could behind the bank.

Something appeared over the crest of a rise in the lane, moving quickly. A carriage, careering along at speed. At first she thought it was hauled by horses. But no, not horses. *People*. Undain pulled the cart.

They surged down the lane, the cart's iron wheels just

fitting between the high hedges. A boy stood in front of the cart, golden hair streaming behind him. He held thin ropes in his hands: reins to steer the undain. A look of exultation lit up his face as he urged them on, faster and faster. He shouted something but Cait couldn't make out what it was. Metal containers of some sort clanked and rattled in the cart behind him.

The carriage thundered under the trees but didn't slow. The crows in the branches scattered. Steam rose off the undain as they surged forward, eight or ten of them in two lines. Each had a leather harness wrapped around their torso by which they pulled the cart along at breakneck speed. The reins the boy held passed through metal collars around their necks. Their bodies were powerful, thick with muscles. Their pumping legs were a blur and their eyes were wide, full of alarm, like those of panicked horses.

Then, moving before Cait or Ran could stop him, Nox leaped up. He clambered onto the bank, shouting something. Ran grabbed his ankle, pulling him back and pinning him to the ground, covering his mouth with a hand. But it was too late. The nearest undain, spooked by the sudden noise, tripped.

For a moment she thought the creature was going to regain its footing. But it had lost its rhythm. It stumbled, and the other undain, powering along behind, had no chance of stopping. They ploughed into the fallen creature, only to be overrun by those behind. In a moment, the rushing team of undain had become a tangled mass of limbs and bodies.

Her hopes of slipping across the fields without being seen were gone.

3 – A HARVEST OF BONES

The boy screamed as the cart collided with the fallen mass of undain. The impact threw him into the air. The metal churns he'd been hauling, five or six of them, flew after him. The boy's landing was cushioned by the mass of undain bodies, but the metal containers cartwheeled, clanging onto the road. Their caps were jarred free and a clear liquid glugged from them.

On the ground next to Cait, Nox struggled and fought, but Ran was too strong for him. Ran raised his fist, threatening to beat Nox if he didn't stay quiet. Nox got the message and stopped trying to call out.

Back in the lane, the boy had hauled himself to his feet and was wading through the tangled team of undain. He surveyed the wreckage around him, combing his hands through his long hair in a gesture of desperation. He appeared to be oblivious to Cait and the others. The trees had hidden Nox from him. Ran's quick thinking had saved them for now.

The boy screamed, the fury and frustration in his words clear. He hurled furious abuse at the tangled mass of undain. None uttered a sound in reply. Some tried to rise, attempting to struggle free from the mass of bodies, the compulsion to carry out their instructions too strong to resist. One crawled forward to lap at a pool of the spilled liquid, licking it from the road. The boy started kicking this one, an edge of panic in his voice.

Cait reached toward the boy's mind, as lightly as she could. His fury was a mask for something else. Outright fear. He was filled with terror at what he'd done, what was going to happen to him. The metal churns; it was all to do with that. They'd been full of some precious cargo and he'd smashed them. He was supposed to be going carefully but he'd driven the undain too fast and now he'd lost everything. He was in terrible trouble. His fear blotted out everything else.

She could hit him with freezing ice while he was preoccupied, perhaps dash him to the ground to knock him out. Then they could flee and no one would know they'd been there. If anyone found the boy they'd think he'd been injured in the crash. She closed her eyes, readying herself for the pain that would come, focusing on the cold well of magic within, trying to recall how this was done.

She felt a hand on her arm. She opened her eyes. Ran. He shook his head, telling her *no*. She pulled her arm free but the dragonrider persisted.

"No," he whispered. He struggled to find the right words. "Not this."

With an effort she let the magic ebb away. He was right. She wasn't thinking. They had to stay hidden.

Nox struggled again, trying to break free of Ran's grasp, but Ran held him down with a single muscled arm.

On the other side of the hedge, the boy pulled a knife from his belt. He began to saw at the leather straps that tethered the undain to each other and to the cart. He was in tears as he worked. More than once he glanced around as if terrified someone would see what he was doing.

One by one he freed the undain who had hauled the cart. She expected them to flee but instead they stood and waited in a quiet line, oblivious even to their broken limbs sticking out at bad angles.

One of the undain, perhaps the one that had first stumbled, was too badly damaged to rise. It tried again and again, but each time its legs buckled and it crashed to the ground. The boy kicked the creature repeatedly but it made no difference.

The boy turned away in disgust. He shouted words and the standing undain shuffled across to right the cart and collect the spilled churns from the road. When everything was loaded, they lashed themselves together, threading the leather straps through their belts and tying the cut ends.

Within a few minutes they were ready. The boy stood over the fallen undain, who was still trying to rise, hauling itself up by the tree roots on the bank. The boy kicked the creature aside and took a thin tube about the size of a pencil from an inside pocket. He put it to his mouth and blew. A high-pitched whistle screeched from the instrument. The boy blew three times, gazing into the sky as he did so.

Then he climbed into the cart and urged the undain forward. They lumbered down the lane in the direction of the white palace, the empty churns clanging and clanking like broken bells.

Ran took his hand from Nox's mouth when the cart had gone, finally letting him speak.

Cait stood over him. "What the hell were you doing? What were you thinking?"

She'd been so wrong about him. She'd trusted him. Despite everything she'd trusted him, and he'd betrayed her at the first opportunity. Bringing him had been a terrible mistake. *Her* mistake.

"I told you," said Nox, making a show of freeing himself from Ran now that the dragonrider had loosened his grasp. "We're not going to survive out here. We can't stroll around Angere as if we're on holiday. It doesn't work like that."

"So you decided to let them know we're here? That's your brilliant plan?"

"No," said Nox. "You don't understand. The boy wasn't one of them. Use your brain, Cait."

It was a phrase more than one teacher had used over the years. It really didn't help her mood. "What difference does it make he was a boy? That's not going to make him our friend, is it?"

"It's very unlikely he'd know anything about affairs in the White City," said Nox. "The undain wouldn't include him until he became one of them. They don't trust the young until they're converted. He'd see I was a Baron and do what I said. We could have extracted information from him. Then escaped before he told anyone."

She glanced at Ran, wondering how much of this the dragonrider was understanding. "That makes no sense, Nox. They'd know we were out here when the boy told them about us. They'd find us easily."

"Perhaps, perhaps not," said Nox. "I decided to take that chance. He might have helped us. Someone has to do something."

She had to suppress the urge to kick him. Kick him like the boy had kicked the undain. "You decided? You're not in charge any more, Nox. People don't obey your every word now, don't you see? You're here because I agreed to it."

She turned and walked away, shaking with fury. What were they going to do with him? She'd hoped he'd be able to help, use his knowledge of Angere. Clearly that wasn't going to work. They had to get away from him. Leave him. Or was even that no good? He could still tell the undain where they were. Buy Menhroth's trust with their betrayal. So did that mean they had to silence him permanently? *Kill* him. Could they do that?

She threw a glance at Ran. Perhaps he was thinking the same thing: put an end to Nox while they had the chance. Ran would do it if she told him to, most likely. He probably knew a hundred ways to kill someone with his bare hands.

She shook her head, pushing the thought from her mind. Evil as Nox was she could never do anything so vile. She hated to kill anything. She was the one who insisted on capturing and releasing insects rather than swatting them. Which, OK, meant she was going to be a fat lot of use in a terrible war to save two worlds. But there it was. Somehow, they'd have to get by.

Without glancing back at Ran and Nox, she climbed over the hedge into the lane. The undain had crawled a little way along beyond the last tree, where it now lay in a broken heap. It was still alive, if alive was the right word. It watched her with wide grey eyes as she crept near. She expected it to lunge for her at any moment. But it was too broken. It tried to rise but once again its legs buckled and it flopped to the ground.

She hated to kill anything but sometimes it could be a mercy. Once when she'd been young, on a family trip to Wales, a rabbit had run into the road under their car. She could still recall the faint bump as the wheels went over it. They'd stopped to see what had happened, but her parents had told her to stay in the car while they went to see. She'd only been small and had to peer through the rear window to watch what her mother and father did. They stood in the road for a time, as if debating, then her dad crouched down. Cait thought he was going to pick the rabbit up, bring it with them to look after. Instead, her parents returned empty-handed and got into the car without saying anything.

"Was the rabbit OK?" she asked.

"No, love," said her mum. "It was very badly injured when the car hit it. It wasn't going to survive. It was suffering, you see and…"

"Did you kill it?"

"Yes," her dad replied. "We had to, Cait. I'm sorry."

"How did you kill it?"

Her dad didn't want to say, but he couldn't avoid her question. "I broke its neck."

"With your hands?"

"Yes, love. With my hands. It was the kindest thing to do."

She remembered the conversation clearly. The hot plastic of the car seats on the back of her legs. The taste of the fruit sweets her mum gave her as they drove off. And her dad, suddenly very silent when, only a few minutes earlier, he'd been singing along to the radio. He was sad because he'd killed the rabbit, she understood now. He was a gentle man, yet he'd made himself do this thing with his bare hands.

She looked down at the undain. She had to do the same. The creature was little more than a beast of burden, resurrected as a slave. A thing. Could it still feel pain? Perhaps. There was something in its eyes. Fear, maybe. Even a glimmer of understanding, like the scarecrow, as if it knew what it had become and what was about to happen. Because once it had been a man, a man like her father. And she couldn't let it lie there in the road, suffering like the rabbit.

Without stopping to think she closed her eyes and let herself sink into the icy waters that lay within her. The other girl was there, somewhere in the blue depths, but she stirred as Cait approached, offering her help. The dead witch-girl understood, approved. They would do this thing between them. It was the kindest thing to do. They would unleash a storm of ice and put an end to the creature's misery.

"Cait!"

She was working the spell when Nox shouted from somewhere behind her, alarm clear in his voice. At the same moment she was aware of Ran's pounding feet. She turned even as he dived at her, knocking her to the ground with a sickening jar. She banged the back of her head hard on the ground. At the same moment, a rush of cold air swept over her, along with a shadow that cast the whole world into brief darkness.

Then it was gone. A stench of decay lingered in the air, as if something long-dead had flown by. She thought of the crow, although this was much larger.

Ran rolled to his feet and pulled her up. Her vision whirled for a moment, then cleared. "What was that?"

"It's coming back!" Nox was perched on the bank, holding onto one of the wintry trees. In the sky, a ragged shape flew in an arc, banking steeply toward them.

"Is that a dragon?" she said.

It wasn't what she'd expected. She'd imagined vast, noble beasts with proud heads and jewelled skin. She'd seen the films, read the books. But this creature was a mess. It wasn't even symmetrical. One of its wings was noticeably shorter than the other as it flapped toward them. Instead of smooth, flowing lines, its body was all lumps and angles. Instead of a roar of flames it made a sound like a load of bones being blended in a mixer.

Ran, standing beside her, shook his head. "Undain," he said. She thought she caught a glimpse of something in his eyes. It was gone in a moment, but it was a thing she'd never seen in Ran before. Fear.

"Kill it," he said to her. "Kill it now."

The creature swept by again, calling its grating call, its head all teeth and bones, its body tattered flesh and claws. Once more it almost knocked Cait over with the rush of its ragged wings. The nearby trees were preventing the creature from getting at her. The stench of its passing hit her again and she had to resist the urge to run.

"What the hell is it?" she said.

"Bone Harvester," said Nox, still up on the hedge. "One of the undains' attempts to spawn creatures like dragons. The boy must have summoned it with that whistle. To collect the body and take it away to be ... recycled."

The creature banked again, more steeply this time, then

half-landed and half-fell. It filled the lane as it limped toward them, mouth gaping wide.

"How do we stop it?" said Cait. "What do we do?"

Ran tried to find the words, then gave up and broke into a stream of his own language.

Nox translated. "He's saying you have to kill it. He said Fer managed it and now you have to do the same."

"But why don't we just run?" she shouted. "It's come for the undain, not us."

Nox jumped down into the lane to stand with her. "No. It doesn't work like that. It's been summoned to collect bones and that's what it'll do. I've seen them in operation before. They're very … single-minded creatures. It'll try and take all of us, and it won't care if we're alive or dead."

Great. Just what she needed. She studied the creature, trying to see into its mind, understand its intentions. But there was only a blank, a void, impossible to read. Was it something like the beast that had flown across the An? The one that had set in motion everything that had happened? Fer *had* defeated that creature, it was true. But even she'd had no idea how she'd done it.

Working magic wasn't like in books, where all you had to do was shout a few words in Latin and incredible things happened. It *hurt* and it was difficult. And she had about five seconds to come up with something. She tried to think of a plan. Think of *anything*. All that came to mind was the urgent need to flee.

The creature stopped when it reached the stricken undain on the floor. It sniffed, nuzzling with its long, bony snout, almost gently, as if the undain on the ground were one of its young. The fallen undain tried to crawl away, understanding on some level what was about to occur. With a sudden snap, the Harvester struck. It picked up the fallen undain and held it, body sagging loose on either side of the creature's mouth. The Harvester shook the undain then dashed it to the ground where it lay, unmoving.

The Harvester croaked its broken roar and turned its attention to Cait and the others.

Ran leaped, his staff whirling. He shouted some battle-cry. The creature lunged at him, mouth snapping, but Ran was too quick. The dragonrider threw himself to one side, swinging his staff at the same time to connect with the side of the creature's head.

There was a cracking noise as Ran's blow broke bones. But the creature wasn't slowed. It roared as it twisted and raked a claw at Ran. Once again Ran danced aside, and once again the staff crunched into the creature's head.

He was playing with it. Distracting it so she could work her magic. She had to do something. Even Ran couldn't keep this up for long, the creature was too powerful. She felt stronger under the shadows of the trees, the cold air making the magic easier somehow. And she'd be safe whatever happened, wouldn't she? The undain wouldn't dare harm her because of her precious blood. She'd be OK.

The creature opened its mouth to lunge at Ran. Instead of leaping aside, the dragonrider waited and then thrust his staff into the gaping maw, hoping to wedge it open. It didn't work. The creature closed its jaws and the heavy staff snapped like a straw.

There was a loud tapping noise from behind her, like three or four strikes on a small drum. Confused, she spun around to see Nox, holding a pistol and sighting along its barrel. He fired at the creature. Each shot missed the dancing Ran and struck the undain. The creature appeared not to notice. It continued to flail at the dragonrider, as if bullets couldn't harm it. Maybe it didn't have vital organs. It was just an assortment of parts lashed together and magically animated.

Ran, meanwhile, had drawn a knife from his belt: a pathetically small hunting knife that Danny and Johnny had bought in the shop in Dublin. It didn't look like it would be able to inflict much damage, but Ran didn't let that stop him. He began to slash at the creature's limbs.

Cait stepped forward, holding her hand forward as if the simple act would make the magic work. The creature lashed out at her with a claw, sending her crashing into the bank. For a moment she was winded, confused, some stone or tree root digging painfully into her back. The creature had attacked her. Tried to hurt her. That wasn't supposed to happen.

Rage flared within her. Anger at being struck. Anger at everything damn thing that had happened to her. She didn't want any of this. There was a moment, a brief moment, when she knew she could control the rage. Set it aside. But instead she channelled it, let the fury take her. She'd pay for it with the agonies that would follow, but the foul creature would pay a higher price. And it wasn't only *her* rage. The witch-girl from the tower-blocks was there too, her quiet voice guiding her, showing her the way.

Like this. Do it like this.

The vile creature towered over her, jaws wide, the stench of decay enough to make her gag. It had to be now. The creature wasn't going to spare her. In a voice that was partly her own and partly that of the dead girl from the ground beneath Manchester, Cait screamed.

Cold magic like a winter wind flared from her hand. The pain cut through her immediately, sharp as if she'd been cut, but she carried on, refusing to relent. Welcoming the pain, almost, because it meant she was harming the creature.

The Bone Harvester shrieked and writhed in the icy blast. It pushed forward, struggling against the gale. With one final effort it lunged and Cait ducked, covering her head, stemming the flow of magic.

She crouched there, expecting the creature's jaws to seize her. Nothing happened. The creature loomed over her, but like the guards outside the factory, blue frost covered it. It wasn't frozen solid, though. It was too big, too bulky. Instead it writhed and twisted, as if being attacked by countless invisible insects. What had she worked? The magic had a shape, a form in her mind and this time there'd been something different about it. Some new spell the witch-girl had worked.

A patina of ice coated the creature's flesh, blooming like the fronds of ferns. The ice crackled as the cold intensified. The magic was still working away, seeping into joints, opening up fissures. Ice crystals gleamed in the creature's startled eyes. It writhed and twisted as if bugs were burrowing inside it.

It grated a single, agonized shriek and exploded.

Cait threw herself to the ground and covered her head. Shards of ice and bone clattered into her, cutting into her arms and back and legs, each prick sharp and freezing at the same time. At the same time, cramps tugged at her insides from the magic she'd worked.

When the hailstorm stopped she looked up. The Bone Harvester was no more, shattered to mismatched fragments of bone and flesh. She'd done it. Incredibly, with the help of the witch-girl, she'd done it. She rose to wobbly legs, hauling herself up by the tree roots in the bank just as the broken undain had.

The pain inside her was still intense, blotting out the cuts on her skin from the ice. Despite this, she felt the weird urge to laugh out loud.

We did it! We did it! The voice within was gleeful, girlish.

How did we do it? said Cait. *What did we do?*

Evil magic held it together, gave it strength, said the girl. *But the ice. The ice broke it. Broke the magic and broke the creature. We did it!*

The pain was subsiding slightly now, the tearing sensations in her insides fading. Would there ever come a time when it didn't? If she went too far? She had to be careful. The danger of working magic was terrible. She had so much to learn.

Ran lay a few yards away, his face and the backs of his hands bleeding from the fragments of bone that had hit him. But he was alive, his eyes wide at what he'd witnessed. Nox was OK, too, cowering behind the hedge, gun still in his hand.

"It attacked me," she said, as if this was the funniest thing in the world. "I didn't think it would, but it tried to kill me. Why did it try to kill me?"

"Why wouldn't it?" said Nox.

"The blood," said Cait. "They need me alive, remember?"

Nox jumped into the lane, slipping his gun back into his backpack. "Actually, it's a good thing it tried to kill you."

That stopped her laughing. "What do you mean?"

"The undain in Manchester were instructed to find you, you or someone from your family, and bring you in alive. This creature clearly wasn't. You were just bones to it. Which means they have no idea you're out here."

"I suppose you're right. Still, it doesn't make me feel much better. On balance I think I preferred it when they weren't trying to eat me alive." She crossed the lane to offer Ran a hand, hauling him up as he'd done so often for her.

"It wouldn't eat you, Cait," said Nox. "It…"

He stopped, staring up into the sky at something. She tried to follow his gaze but could see only the swaying branches. Ran sprang onto the bank and up one of the trees to get a better view.

"Cait?" said Nox.

"What is it?"

"That magic you worked. Can you do it again?"

She couldn't. She was spent. "Why?"

Nox pointed at something. "Because I think you're going to have to."

She caught a glimpse of it: another Harvester, wide wings flapping unevenly as if it were a broken toy. It circled around them. The grating cry from it echoed through the air, deeper and coarser than the first one.

"You think it heard the boy's whistle as well?"

"Either that or it caught the death-call of the other and now it's come for all the bones."

She looked from Nox to Ran. What could they do? She'd thrown everything into the magic to destroy the first creature. Perhaps too much. The agony had faded but she felt limp, weak. She should have held something back. She couldn't manage it again. Deep inside, a faint whisper in the fog, the voice of the witch-girl said, *No, no, oh no…*

"We have to run," said Cait.

"Run where?" said Nox. "I told you we needed to find shelter. We've got nowhere to run *to*."

"We have to try." All her amusement had leeched away. She barely had the strength to walk. But they couldn't just stand there and wait. She set off, backing away from the ruined monster in the road. Perhaps between the two destroyed undain there would be enough bones to satisfy the new creature. Perhaps it wouldn't come for them. Perhaps they had a chance.

The shadow of its wings swept over them, darkening the lane. The stench of its decay was sickening. The croaking call came again, much nearer, like a metal bucket full of rocks. The ground shook as the creature landed. It was even bigger than the first one, its skin a tattered patchwork of greens and greys, the talons of its claws like swords skittering on the lane.

Ran attacked, vaulting onto the hedge, running along a short way and then leaping onto the creature's back. He sat there as if he were riding it, plunging the knife into the creature's body again and again. Nox had his gun out and was firing shot after shot. Neither had much chance but they tried anyway. She had to do the same. The creature strode toward her, mouth gaping in a roar. Somehow she had to do this.

Help me, she said to the dead witch-girl. *You have to help me. Please.*

Distantly, the cold fury within awakened. It swirled

sluggishly, but then whirled a little faster. The pain of it was already sharp, as if old wounds were being opened up and rubbed raw. The storm grew until it howled and raged.

There was a moment, a brief moment, when the pain was too much. Dizziness and disorientation made her stagger sideways. She was losing it. She caught a glimpse of an impossible vision: buildings and cars from back home. A strange sensation seized her, as if a ghost were passing through her mind.

She forced it away. She had to fight. With a scream that was part rage and part agony, Cait unleashed a second bolt of blue cold. It poured from her and slammed into the Harvester. The creature charged at her in the same moment.

Cait threw everything she had into it. The world about her faded, like the curtains closing on a stage at the end of a play. She was losing consciousness, too exhausted, racked by too much pain. She seemed to be outside her own body, staring down at herself on the lane. Her blue hair and the blue ice arcing from her hands and the lumbering undain horror about to reach her.

Then came a moment of dizziness, a sensation of falling. The world went dark and she knew no more.

4 – THE GATES OF HELL

Genera, Inc.

Clara Sweetley stood in the cavernous hall at the heart of the refinery, her pulse beating with a delicious fear. The great day was finally here. Her moment of triumph.

This close, she could make out the words upon the rock-face above the waterfall: *The Gates of Hell*. They'd been carved there three hundred years ago, before the refinery had been built to enclose the waterfall, before Genera existed. Local folklore had given this outcrop of rock a dark reputation. There were plenty of old tales of the nightmare creatures that emerged through the curtain of water. Of screams in the night and stolen children. All true, of course, all true. It might not be *hell* the gateway led to, but Angere was close enough. And Clara was going there. She smiled to herself at the prospect.

Cold spray from the cataract misted her face. She paid it no attention. Today she would step through that cascade and enter into the presence of the Witch King himself. Menhroth the First and Last. Menhroth the Undying. Her careful plans over so many years were bearing fruit. So much time spent trotting along in Nox's shadow, obeying his orders, vying with his other lieutenants for promotion.

All of them *men*, of course. That was how it went. She'd had to battle her way up from the bottom, twice as smart, twice as ruthless. She'd made enemies, sure. Done things she might regret if she stopped to think about it. She didn't stop to think about it. It was all worth it. Today, finally, she'd be anointed Executive Director of Genera, the King's eyes and hands in this world. And who knew where that might lead? She'd heard whispers of the undain's immortality. That must have been Nox's prize, one that had been snatched away from him. Really, she had to smile. She'd smile all the more when *she* became one of the undain instead.

Oh, she'd taken risks. The part she'd played in helping the schoolgirl escape the refinery, for example. A few security systems distracted at the right moment. One or two guards assigned to bogus tasks. It was surprisingly easy. Quite why Angere considered the girl so important she didn't understand. Something to do with a prophecy. Or a spell. Some fantastical nonsense. It didn't really matter. All she knew was Angere wanted this Cait Weerd badly. Which made the girl a valuable commodity. Ensuring Nox lost her had been very good for Clara Sweetley's career.

She glanced aside at Williams, her Chief of Security. "Any word of Nox yet?" She had to shout over the roar of the waterfall and the deep thrum of the machinery in the walls. She didn't mind. She was used to shouting; she found people responded to it. They liked clear instruction.

"Nothing," said Williams. His bald head and face were covered in a sheen of spray. His expensive suit was soaked through. He wouldn't dare complain. "Nox was in the Forest of Dean when our riders encountered the renegades there, but he didn't accompany them to Manchester."

She scowled, pretending to be angrier than she was. Much better to track down Nox once she was established and could take all the credit. "And have you worked out where they jumped after Manchester?"

"No. They seem to know a lot more about the portals than we do."

"How is that possible?"

"We don't know."

"And Nox? How is it *he* knows where all the gateways are?"

"We don't know."

"You don't know very much, do you?"

Williams' glum expression became a notch glummer. "We're doing our best to find out, Ms. Sweetley, I assure you."

"And this book Nox took? Any news of that?"

"Nothing. I think Mr. Nox has it with him. Perhaps as a bargaining chip."

"Is that what you think?"

Williams nodded but didn't reply. He looked worried now. He was in her debt, and he knew it. She'd saved him after the girl escaped. He should have lost his job. His job and a *lot* more besides. But she'd insisted they needed him and so Williams had stayed. He'd be loyal for a while and then, if the security lapses did come to light, he could take the blame. She'd make sure of it.

She turned away from Williams to her personal assistant standing at her other side, appointed to her when she'd taken over from Nox. What was her name? Diane? Diana? Whatever. "How much longer before we can go through?"

"A few minutes, Ms. Sweetley," replied Diane or Diana, consulting an iPad in a waterproof case. "There are three Bone containers and then you."

Ms. Sweetley nodded. She thought about expressing her impatience at being made to wait, but decided against it. No point doing anything to upset Angere. Not now. Despite her successes she had to be careful. In this game, you always had to be careful. Nox was still at large, and there were those within Genera loyal to him. Or, at least, who disliked *her* more. A word from one of them to their masters in Angere could ruin everything. She would keep her impatience to herself. She was good at that.

The bound figure kneeling on the ground beside her, his arms tied behind his back, his mouth gagged so he couldn't cry out, made her feel better about everything. Strictly speaking, the boy had been captured by the undain, not Genera. But she'd offered to escort him through the gateway into the presence of the Witch King, and the undain had agreed. She had to laugh. They were good at being superhuman undead horrors, but they had a lot to learn about politics. She kicked the boy with one of her expensive shoes. He groaned and looked up at her, his brown eyes wide. Her gift for the Witch King. One way or another the boy would tell the undain everything. She almost felt sorry for him. Except he was a pawn, a playing piece. He wasn't important.

In front of them, the last of the containers lumbered into the waterfall on the tank-track conveyor belt. Another lorry-load of Bone. It had taken time to undo Nox's little acts of sabotage. Once they'd got the network fully functional, she'd increased throughput by a couple of percent. A simple matter of draining global stockpiles. Nothing they couldn't sustain for a week or two. Enough, hopefully, to please Menhroth and calm any fears he might have about her. She'd upped Spirit extraction levels a few points, too. The great silver pipe that led through the waterfall was running at 80% capacity. She'd explain how Nox had made mistakes, let things slip. Make it clear they could rely on her. Then, when her position at the top of Genera was secure, she could address the other problems. Nox and the girl. How hard could it be for a globe-spanning corporation that controlled just about everything to track down two people? Their capture was only a matter of time. When she handed the fugitives over to Angere, she could take credit for everything.

The prospect was delicious. It would take time, years maybe, to win the ultimate prize, but today she was taking a big step forward.

"We're ready, Ms. Sweetley," said her PA. "Would you like an umbrella?"

"No, that won't be necessary. A bit of water never harmed anyone."

"When should we expect you back?"

"Hard to say. Cancel my other appointments. If anyone gets in touch tell them I've gone to Hell."

"Of course, Ms. Sweetley."

She nodded to the guard standing over the boy. "Untie his legs so he can walk. He can follow me through."

"Yes, ma'am," said the guard. "Shall I accompany you to ensure he complies?"

"There's no need. But if he tries to run away, do shoot him, won't you?"

"Yes, ma'am."

She marched forward, not looking back, holding her head high. She was in a position of strength, that was the thing to remember. The undain needed Genera and she was the best person to run Genera. So long as she gave them what they wanted all would be well.

Sheets of water gushed from the rock face that the vault, the whole refinery, was built around. She could hear and see nothing but the roaring of the cataract. She kept walking, without checking if the boy was behind her. She couldn't be seen to hesitate. She reached the solid wall of water and strode through. The force of the downpour hammering onto her head almost knocked her down, the noise through her skull like the beating of metal drums. The soaking cold made her gasp. She sucked in water and for a moment couldn't breathe. Spluttering and coughing, she pressed on. How far did she have to walk to get through to Angere? And why did it have to be a damn waterfall anyway? Nox had told her they could do nothing about it. This was how the gateway worked. The magic.

Well, she'd see about that. It was complete nonsense, like something from a children's book. When she was in charge she'd make changes, drag them kicking and screaming into the modern world. Assuming she reached Angere without drowning. It was a good job she'd put waterproof make-up on.

Then, suddenly, it was over. A white light blinded her. She gulped air in great, ragged breaths and squinted, one hand shielding her eyes. Her sight began to adjust. She forced herself to stand upright. She was completely dry. Nox had told her the water didn't follow you through the portal. More fairy-tale nonsense, she'd thought, but that, at least, turned out to be true. She smoothed the lines of her skirt and made sure her hair was back in place.

The whole world gleamed white. She stood in the middle of a wide square, bordered by walls and towers and spires, dazzling sunlight glaring off every surface. It was an incredible sight. Buildings the colour of the full moon on a winter's night. Although, of course, she knew what she was really seeing. Knew what those domes and towers and steeples were made of. They shipped vast quantities through the portal, just as they had for nearly two hundred years. And this was where it all went. The glory of the White City. Countless millions of carved human bones. It was more beautiful than she'd ever imagined.

Off to one side, a small gathering of dishevelled people watched her warily. They were little more than skeletons wearing rags. The stench of their filthy bodies almost made her retch. At first she thought they were some sort of undain, like zombies from a film. But the wariness in their eyes told her they were human: half-starved, broken people. They stood before a pair of carts with spoked iron wheels, clutching thick ropes. Of course; this was a slave society. Creatures like these would do the hauling, the lifting, all the backbreaking work. When a container came through they'd move it to a new building site. They'd work until they were nothing but skin and bone. And then, here was the beauty of it, when they died they'd be resurrected as undain slaves to labour away for the rest of eternity. Or else their bones would be used to extend the city where they fell. Such a marvellous system. They could do with something similar back home. She made a mental note to herself.

She turned to see the portal from this side. It was a huge, square frame, like a cinema screen with no film showing. It was formed from femurs and skulls, interwoven with ribs and phalanges and bones she didn't recognize. A huge skull crowned it, the size of an elephant or larger. The skull was pointed and snouted: the head of a predator, with rows and rows of sharp teeth. Were there really such creatures here? A fossil of some dinosaur perhaps. The Spirit pipe led directly into it, the skull sealed up, air-tight. Two red gems glinted from its eye sockets. The horns on its head had been extended into wide, branching tubes like antlers, all fashioned from gold metal. Smaller pipes fanned around the frame, subdividing into ten, a hundred, a thousand smaller ducts. These sprawled like the roots of a tree to distribute the Spirit around the city.

At that moment, the boy flopped from the portal to land in a heap on the ground. He squinted at her and made a little animal whimpering sound. She ignored him. The slaves dropped to their knees and bowed their heads. Good to see they'd remembered their manners. Except that wasn't it; they weren't looking at her. Someone behind her. She turned to see three figures striding toward her.

She'd encountered several undain during her time as Nox's underling, and she'd heard much more about them. The forms they adopted. Their inhuman powers. Still, she wasn't prepared for what she saw.

Two of the undain were giants, twice as tall as she was. Their bodies were mountainous, broad and powerful. They had no skin. Or, if they did, it was transparent. Light shone from within them as if they were hulking machines. But they were clearly flesh and blood; she could see their muscles bunching and flexing as they moved. Where their skin should have been, black lines wound about them in whorls and spirals, something like tattoos. Whether they were like this out of choice or as some sort of punishment she couldn't tell. The patterns twisting about their bodies were beautiful. Each of the giants bore a sword: a snaking blade a metre long.

A normal-sized man stood between them. He was ancient, his hair grey and his skin wrinkled and blotchy. A large iron key hung around his neck on a chain. He stooped forward, as if the weight of the key pulled him down. His face was expressionless, his eyes white. Yet he could clearly see her; he worked his way directly to her.

Ms. Sweetley stood her ground. She wished she'd worn taller heels.

"You are the human?" The old man's voice quavered. It was a ridiculous question to ask, although she chose not to say so.

"I am. And you are?"

"Lord Charis, Holder of the Keys, Guardian of the Aether, Prince of the Holy Court of Menhroth the Undying."

She struggled not to show any shock. She knew all about Lord Charis. Why he chose to adopt the form of this ancient wretch she had no idea, but he was one of the original undain, converted by Menhroth himself five hundred years ago. He had the strength of a hundred men. A necromancer, too, if Nox was to be believed. Was that why he adopted this deathly appearance? No one and nothing passed through the portal without his consent. He was the King's most trusted courtier.

"You speak English well," she said.

Charis's blank eyes bored into her, as if he was studying her. "Yes. Obviously. This surprises you?"

"No. No, not really."

"And that is the witch-kin?"

For a moment his words puzzled her. He had to mean the boy. He was on his knees now, staring up at Charis and panting heavily.

"Yes," she said. "This is the one we captured before Nox helped the others flee."

Charis's eyes narrowed for a moment as he considered her words. Of course, Nox didn't really have much to do with the renegades' escape. But the undain didn't know that. Did they?

"Very well," said Charis eventually. "We will take him now."

One of the giant guards stepped forward. This wasn't how it was supposed to go. She'd imagined the look of appreciation on Menhroth's face as she handed the boy over.

She moved aside. "Of course, Lord Charis."

The hulking undain picked up the boy with one arm, dangling him in the air like a sack of something unpleasant. When the undain turned and walked away, she could see the suggestion of a creature in the black lines of its skin. A winged creature. What it meant she had no idea. Something else to discover. The boy struggled and shouted muffled cries through his gag as the undain carried him across the square. She put him out of her mind. He didn't matter. She would never see him again.

"Now you will follow me," said Charis. "I shall escort you to the Capitol to meet the King."

"Thank you," said Ms. Sweetley, trying to sound calm. "I'm very much looking forward to it."

Charis seemed surprised at her words. Then he shuffled off. The remaining guard waited for her. Clara shrugged and followed the stooped old man.

They crossed the wide white square toward a distant gateway flanked by two towers. The scale of the place confused her; she found it hard to judge distances and sizes. How tall were those towers? She didn't appear to be getting any nearer. Back at the portal the slaves had resumed their work. They were already hauling another container of bones onto their cart. Such inefficiency. She made another mental note. Perhaps she could earn some favour by persuading the undain to adopt modern technologies. Did they even *have* electricity?

The towers loomed above her as they approached, the arch easily a hundred feet tall. Why did it need to be so large? A single black bird, stark against the gleaming white, stood atop a gargoyle's head carved into the wall. Some sort of rook with tattered feathers and ragged wings. It watched her with one eye, head cocked, as she passed underneath.

Beyond the arch lay another vast expanse of white, flanked by more spires and domes and towers. The White City was endless. There were many more of the rooks here. They really were a *mess*. Why did the undain tolerate them? They marred the pristine whiteness of the walls. Some clearly had broken wings and legs, and one or two even lacked a head. None of it appeared to trouble them. They perched about the walls, framed by gothic arches or atop finials. Always watching. Or, if they had no eyes, listening.

One tall tower, in particular, was thick with them. Hundreds of tiny entrances had been built around its peak, and a constant stream of birds flapped in and out. Many carried small metal cylinders on bands around their necks. She thought she knew, then, what this was. The sorcerous crows were a communication system, carrying messages from across Angere. It was incredible. The place was *medieval.* They really needed her to come in and sort everything out. First things she'd arrange were some phone masts. Then they'd thank her. This witchcraft was no match for technology.

Something in Charis's empty eyes expressed disapproval. Was it possible he could read her thoughts? She hadn't heard they could do that. She hadn't heard they couldn't, either.

"You haven't been to An before, have you?" asked the undain.

The question puzzled her. This was Angere. Was that the same thing? "I'm sorry. I don't know where *An* is."

"Here. This is An. The Cloven Land."

"I thought this was Angere?"

"Yes. An, West-of-the-river."

"So Andar…?"

"Is An, East-of-the-river. You do not know this?"

She couldn't afford to appear ignorant. It was all about impressions. "It's familiar now you mention it. Once the land was called An. Before it was … cloven." It was a stab in the dark. Fortunately she appeared to get it right. Charis nodded. He led her toward a broad sweep of steps that climbed to some higher level of the city.

The flight of stairs was at least fifty metres wide and maybe a hundred high, the whole thing crafted from thousands of interlocking bones. Each step was steep, and she soon felt the effort of it in her calves and thighs. Charis didn't slow at all, didn't even run short of breath. She longed to stop for a rest, the muscles in her legs burning, but she forced herself to press on. They passed a line of slaves, scrubbing the stairs with something like toothbrushes, carefully cleaning and polishing the bone an inch at a time. They paid her no attention. She wondered how long the creatures had been there, labouring away on their knees. Decades and decades by the look of them. At least the tang of the soap they were using masked their reek. Were they still alive or were they undain? It was hard to tell.

Placing her foot deliberately onto a patch that had already been cleaned by one of them, she climbed onward. At the top, another wide plaza opened. An ornate palace stood directly before her, all twisting towers and carved figures, like some gothic cathedral from back home that had melted and dripped slightly. The Capitol. More of the giant guards, twelve of them, stood before the doors, swords held forward.

She paused for a moment to calm her breathing, steel herself for the meeting. She covered it by turning to admire the view of the city. The year was more advanced here. Nox had mentioned that to her. The low sun suggested it was autumn, although there were no trees visible by which she could properly tell. Away over the steps, beyond the tops of the walls, lay a vast expanse of water: the An, presumably. It sparkled in the cold white light. They called it a river, but that seemed wrong. She could see no far shore. It looked more like a lake or a sea.

Between her and the river stood a flat expanse of land, curving along the edge of the water. Something like an old pier had been built a short way upstream, striding out into the river to end abruptly after a hundred yards. She'd never seen the point of piers. They were like bridges to nowhere.

Black dots stood upon the bank around it. Many, many of them, all arranged into regular squares. What were they? Trees? Stone pillars? Again, the scale was hard to discern. Then she saw movement. Another square marched into place. People. It was an *army* standing there, unmoving in its massed ranks. A vast, silent army. The sun glinted off rows of weapons.

"Come. The King will see you now." Charis stood behind her. The impatience in his voice was clear. She wanted to ask him about the figures near the river but dared not.

They walked toward the grand gateway. The carvings around the doors – life-sized figures engaged in some battle – were exquisite. They were warriors, knights in armour, all rendered in delicately carved bone. Some rode horses, others dragons. The twelve guards with their transparent black-veined skin stood as still as the carvings, serpentine swords held at the ready. She knew they would stop at nothing to protect their King. Long ago in their history there had been some betrayal, some failure of security according to Nox. It would never be allowed to happen again. She had to admire the way Menhroth had everything set up. He was their father as well as their king and their god. He'd created all the other undain – directly or indirectly – and in doing so had tied their existence to his own. That way he ensured their absolute loyalty. If he died, so did they. It was a beautiful thing.

"You will enter King Menhroth's audience chamber now," said Charis.

She tried to order her thoughts. "Tell me. How should I address the King?"

"You shouldn't."

"No, I mean what do I call him? What is the protocol here?"

Charis peered at her, as if he were examining some interesting insect crawling on the floor. There was disquiet on his face, as if he thought her audience wouldn't go well. "There is no protocol. You do not call him anything. You do not speak. You nod your head to indicate you have understood your instructions."

"I see."

"You may walk as far as the third arch. Thereafter you crawl on your hands and knees into his presence. Do you understand?"

"I do." She did. She understood *very* well.

"So be it," said Charis. "If you are returning to your own world I shall meet you here."

He shuffled off toward the steps. Ahead of her, the line of guards parted. She walked forward, heart hammering once more. She strode into the audience chamber of the Witch King, wondering what Charis had meant by *if* she was returning.

A cavernous hall stretched in front of her. In the distance she could see its far end, maybe half a mile or more away. A series of archways processed down the hall, four or five of them. Light slanted from high windows, illuminating the carved splendour of the interior. It was bone, all bone. Overhead, the vaulted ceiling looked impossibly distant, higher than the sky. The whole thing was incredible. It was meant to awe, of course. It was damn well working.

Her steps echoed as she marched forward. It was going to be a long walk. She was glad she hadn't worn high heels after all. She studied the statues that lined the sides of the hall. Hundreds and hundreds of figures, each different, each in a warlike pose. Who were they? They couldn't be former kings; Menhroth had been on the throne for five hundred years. Most looked like normal soldiers. It was as if someone had carved bone statues of the entire undain army.

After ten minutes she reached the third archway. She paused for as long as she dared, then got to her hands and knees. The other end of the hall was still some distance. She crawled. The bone floor was smooth to her touch but sharp on her knees. Her tights would be laddered in no time. It was a good thing no one at Genera could see her. Was this what Nox had done whenever he came here? Another detail he'd neglected to mention.

She crawled on, studying the polished whiteness of the floor. The way each individual bone had its own grain, its own unique beauty. She'd never noticed that before. Occasionally she glanced up. A raised platform stood ahead of her. She didn't dare look high enough to see who or what was there.

Finally she reached a step. She stopped and kneeled, head bowed. Her bruised knees burned. She didn't move, awaiting instruction. Instruction from another man. It was like Nox all over again. It was the same everywhere, wasn't it? She waited, filled with a mixture of terror at where she was and rage at what she'd been made to do. Who the hell did they think they were? Well, she would play the game for now. But one day she'd turn the tables. One day she would sit up there while people crawled into *her* presence. She'd make damned sure of it.

"Clara Sweetley."

She raised her head to the Witch King. She expected another desiccated old man like Charis but Menhroth was *beautiful.* Young, tall, strong, he sat upon his throne gazing at her with a look of benign amusement. His long blond hair flowed down his shoulders. She could do with a few underlings like him at her beck and call. Only his solid black eyes, shiny as polished obsidian, gave away his true nature. He wore clothes of the purest white, inlaid with gold thread. On his head was the crown of Angere, crafted, so Nox had said, from the finger bones of ancient enemies. Two golden tubes snaked out of the throne directly into his neck. She knew how precious even a drop of Spirit was to the undain, but Menhroth was mainlining a constant supply. She could only wonder what godlike powers it gave him.

She nodded, acknowledging her name, remembering not to speak.

"And you are to replace Nox?"

She nodded again. Perhaps it would be as easy as that. She wondered how well-informed this King really was, sitting there all day being told what he wanted to hear, far removed from events. Perhaps there would be ways to manipulate him. Subtly, of course.

"And you have made a good start," he continued. "Artificially increasing the supplies of Bone and Spirit by a few percent in order to demonstrate your worth. Doing your best to ensure Nox gets the blame for the recent setbacks."

His words hammered through her. Did Menhroth know everything she'd done? But if he was aware she'd helped the schoolgirl escape, surely Clara wouldn't be there now? She'd be either dead or in some long, drawn-out process of dying. She had to be careful. Very careful. Masking her alarm as best she could she nodded once more.

Menhroth held her gaze for a moment, assessing her. When he finally unleashed his smile on her it felt like a light being switched on. "You have only done what any sensible person would. I will allow you your little deceptions since you have had no direct orders. But from now on, I will give you my instructions, and you will carry them out immediately and to the letter. If you do not, you will be replaced. Do you understand me, Clara Sweetley?"

She nodded her assent at Menhroth's words.

"Excellent," said the King. "Firstly there are some wicca – witches – in your world that I require you to locate. One was held by you but managed to escape. Bringing them to me is your most important task. You *will* succeed in this. Do you understand?"

Another nod. The request was ridiculous, of course. How could a few new-age nutters who thought they could do magic pose any threat to all this? She'd seen it before: individuals so rich and powerful they'd lost sight of reality and became obsessed with some nonsense. Well, so be it. She could use that to her advantage. This so-called witch, Cait Weerd, was just an unremarkable schoolgirl. Once they found her, they'd hand her straight to Menhroth, a gift a thousand times more valuable than the boy.

"Secondly there is the book," said the King. "This, too, was recently held by you. I require its immediate return. Stop at nothing to make sure this happens."

Nod. So the King was as obsessed with this spell book as he was with the girl. More craziness. It barely mattered. Once they tracked down Nox she would take great pleasure in handing both him and the book over as well.

"Finally there is the matter of Spirit. You may ignore our need for Bone for the moment. There will be plenty of time for extending the White City in the future. But I have ambitious plans, and it is Spirit we need."

She nodded. There were many rumours of an invasion. She thought about the army, waiting motionless on the banks of the An. She pitied anyone standing in its way. It was of little concern to her. As to the Spirit, an increase by another few percent was sustainable for a month or so.

"I require you to triple the amount you send us."

For a moment she blinked up at him in astonishment. She very nearly spoke, very nearly shouted, *No!* Tripling the amount was impossible. Milking humanity for its Spirit was a delicate process. Extract a few percent too much from people, and you risked a collapse of their mental state. You'd lose Spirit in the long run as people gave up hope, became angry and depressed. Fought and killed. Tripling the rate would have terrible global effects. Smouldering resentments the world over would break out into wars. Suicide rates would soar. The international economy would slump into depression. Banks would collapse and countries would go bankrupt. Still she kneeled, trying to take it in, visions of what it would mean flashing through her mind. It was utterly insane. What had been the point of all her delicate calculations in the face of this?

"Clara Sweetley? Do you understand me?"

He sat there, calmly awaiting her response. She couldn't object. There was only one thing she could do. Because if she refused him someone else would crawl there and agree.

She nodded her assent and lowered her eyes to the white ground.

"Very good. Return to your own world and begin work."

Back outside the audience chamber, at the top of the broad sweep of stairs, she stopped to take it all in. A wind had picked up, cold on her face. Her heart fluttered in her chest, from the long walk and the shock of the King's demands. How could she possibly hope to do this thing? The effects on the world would be calamitous.

But still, but still. If she *could* do what was asked of her, her position in Menhroth's favour would be assured. The price would be terrible, it was true. But it wasn't a price she'd have to pay personally. Genera would have to make enormous changes. Add a second or even a third pipeline.

The whole global extraction network would have to be reconfigured. But perhaps, somehow, they could achieve it.

While Charis descended ahead of her, Clara Sweetley gazed out over the walls. The army still stood unmoving, massed on the banks. Beyond them, the waters of the An glistened and winked. Somewhere there lay Andar. The land east of the An. That was the target of the invasion if the rumours were to be believed. That was why the undain required so much Spirit. Well. If that was what they wanted that was what they'd get. One way or another.

She stared into that distance, making plans, until Charis called for her to hurry up and follow.

5 – THE FIRST FROSTS OF WINTER

Andar

Hellen Meggenwar gazed west over the waters of the An. Curtains of mist hung above the sparkling waters. There would be no visions of gleaming towers and spires today. Still, she didn't need to see the White City to know the undain were there. She could *feel* them. Or rather, feel where they weren't. Living beings danced like lights to her inner eye, but the undain were the opposite. An absence. A blotting-out. Unseen clouds in the night sky that covered the stars.

Sound travelled farther over water. The splash of a leaping fish or the call of a bird in the mist sounded near at hand. Perhaps it was the same with the inner eye. Beyond the ravenous minds of the river serpents, over the wide waters, that great *wrongness* was clear. It had the same feeling as the discordant drone she'd heard in the Song on Islagray. Every day a little louder, like the approach of some vast swarm. Standing beside the waters the sound seemed to thrum in the air. Its deep power sent a shiver through her old bones.

But that wasn't why she'd returned to the water's edge. She tried once again to put it out of her mind. She sought another presence, farther west. She'd thought coming here, to this precise spot, the place where the winged abomination had landed, might help. Give her a touchstone, a place of contact. But it wasn't working. She was a fool for even trying. It was just that she had to do *something*.

Fer had it bad enough, pursued by the horrors of that other world. But it was much worse for Cait, across the waters in Angere and quite possibly alone. The faint message through the aether from the wise man, this Lizard King, had been clear enough, whispering in her dreams. *Cait has left this world for Angere.*

The girl would be a great witch one day, if she lived that long. Right now she was a girl: brave and clever and resourceful and surprising, but also inexperienced and ignorant. And no doubt terrified. And with all the undain of Angere standing between her and the waters of the An.

Hellen sighed. It was her fault. She had set these things in motion. Sent Fer off through the Tanglewood. Got Cait caught up in the whole business. She was to blame. Here she was on this sunny riverbank while Cait and Fer and the rest were out there facing horror and death. Oh, you could point the finger at others. Menhroth. Ilminion. Or you could pretend Cait was some sort of chosen one, that fate had picked her for this role. But that was nonsense, a way of avoiding blame. She, Hellen Meggenwar, had chosen to do these things. She could have sent someone else. She could have gone herself. But she hadn't.

Out of fear? She didn't think so. In truth it was hard to be sure. But if she had gone, who would have stayed to deal with everything else? Ariane could mutter all she wanted about keeping your feet on the ground. The plain truth was that peaceful, beautiful Andar lay slumbering, and someone had to try and wake it up. Hellen had done what she'd thought was best. Maybe she'd got it wrong. Trying was always better than giving in and doing nothing.

She sighed again, slumping to the ground with her scuffed boots dangling over the lip of the bank. This early in the day, frost gilded each blade of grass like slivers of delicate glass. At least the remains of the winged undain were gone. The dragonriders had seen to that. She smoothed her hand over the ground, watching the ice crystals disappear with the warmth of her touch. The first frosts of winter. Ice was coming as the days shortened. It wouldn't be long before it crept down the An, freezing it from bank to bank. Unwittingly building a bridge for the undain army.

A tiny spider, little more than a speck, crept its way among the grass, traversing with difficulty its vast forest. She watched it work. If the undain came and Andar fell, would this tiny spider notice? Or would it and its children be here for the rest of time, oblivious to larger events? She almost envied its ignorance.

She reached out with her mind again, pushing with all her strength toward that distant void. The effort of it made her gasp out loud as sharp pains shot up her arms and across her chest. Nothing. She gave in, her breathing rapid and ragged. She wasn't powerful enough. She would never be powerful enough. The great Hellen Meggenwar, eldest of Andar, could do nothing.

She hauled herself to her feet. Sitting there and feeling sorry for herself wasn't going to help anyone. She had her part to play, and she would play it to the best of her abilities. She owed it to Cait and Fer, at least, to do what little she could. The magic the witches could wield was ill-suited to the task of defending Andar. Witchery was weak, it was a craft of coaxings and cajolings, of working with things as they were. They did the things people needed doing even if the people didn't realise they needed it yet. They could ease a woman through childbirth and take away the pains of ailments and agues. At a pinch they could work the weather, persuade wind and water to behave themselves, and they could commune with living plants and animals. It would all be of some use, perhaps, but none of it would be enough. They needed others.

Half a mile north, the uppermost tower of Caer L'dun jutted through the mists. It was the tallest building in all of Andar, it was said, taller than the Wycka, taller than the Sun Tower in Guilden. It was modelled on the riders' original fortress in the far north of Angere. Now that tower, Caer D'nar, was abandoned, and the remnants of the riders lived here in its replacement. Today she would go there. There was someone she had to meet, but she also had to learn more about the dragonriders' intentions. They were not all like Borrn and Beltaine. Different individuals bore their guilt in different ways. She needed to understand their minds. Discover whether they were as willing to help as she hoped.

She walked north, following the curve of the bank. Flying was all very well, but the simple act of putting one foot in front of the other let her think. Ariane would approve. *Keep your feet on the ground, down here with the rest of us.* Hellen wished her oldest friend were with her. But Ariane lay in the infirmary, recovering from their efforts to heal the woman in the other world, Cait's grandmother. The effects on both Hellen and Ariane had been hard, but it had been worse for Ariane. She'd given everything she could.

A line of twelve dragonriders stood at the arched entrance to Caer L'dun. This was how their ancestors had guarded the rulers of Angere five hundred years ago. The dragonriders liked their traditions. Or perhaps they did it as another reminder of what they were, what they'd done. Their betrayal. She could well believe it of them.

The sun had burned off the mists, and the ancient stones of the fortress glowed like the red embers of a fire. The soaring building looked immovably strong, as if the blocks had stood so long they'd fused back into mountain.

Perhaps there *was* hope here, in the stones' strength and the watchfulness of the dragonriders.

The peninsula of Forness jutted into the waters of the An, making this arc of land the nearest point to Angere. That, of course, was why they'd built their fortress there, reusing the stones from the shattered bridge. A watchtower for Andar. For five centuries the dragonriders had gazed over the An, ready to defend the land from the nightmares they'd helped create. Defend the land or die trying.

It would be a good place to talk, a place for perspective. She spent too long cooped up in Islagray, hatching plans. The summons from Beltaine was unexpected, but welcome. Late the previous evening one of the dragonriders' ensorcelled falcons, darting low over the treetops of Islagray, had landed on her windowsill, drawn to her like a moth to the flame. Around its leg was a metal ring. The falcon had regarded her with a predator's disdain as she gently unclasped the message. Then the bird had ruffled its feathers as if shaking itself from a dream and flew away. Hellen had unfurled the slip of paper and read.

Come to Caer L'dun. There is one here you should meet. Beltaine.

Now, the twelve guards stood unmoving as she approached. Six women and six men. They were stationary, but in the tense way a cat about to pounce is stationary. Their serpentine blades were held ready. For a moment she thought they'd refuse her entry. That this was all some deception and they'd attack with those cruel blades. Twelve of them together might be a test.

But then another emerged from behind them. The red tattoos winding up his arms glistened with sweat. For a moment she thought it was Borrn, finally returned to them from the far north.

But, no. It was Beltaine bowing low to her. "My Lady. Thank you for coming."

He looked as sombre as before. His chest heaved in his leather armour. Did the dragonriders ever let their hair down? Did they even smile? Probably not. Too busy maintaining their state of grim readiness. She didn't approve in the least, but perhaps it was something they'd all be grateful for, sooner or later.

"And I told you to call me Hellen, dragonrider. I have no claim of lordship over you."

Beltaine dipped his head in acquiescence. "Forgive me. Hellen."

You couldn't win with them. That damned guilt of theirs. Children couldn't be held responsible for the mistakes of their forebears, but the dragonriders revelled in it.

"Are you going to allow me entrance into Caer L'dun? Or must I stand here until I die of old age?"

Beltaine looked mortified. "No, please, come in. You are always welcome here. My apologies."

They couldn't take a joke, either. Which only made goading them more irresistible. "And this mysterious visitor? Has Menhroth himself come to surrender to us?"

"No, My Lady. Not that. It is someone from Andar. He awaits in the Watchtower. I will take you to him. We can talk there."

Hellen sighed. Goading people without a sense of humour was no fun. "Very well, *My Lord*. Show me the way."

Beltaine led her through echoing stone passageways and up numerous winding staircases. She was soon disorientated. Perhaps that was intentional. Caer L'dun had one purpose: to withstand an onslaught.

Ranks of dragonriders drilled in the courtyards, shouting and moving in perfect synchronisation, their actions somewhere between a dance and combat. Elsewhere, wooden seats like outsized horses' saddles had been set up. More dragonriders sat astride these, wielding their weapons in choreographed sequences of thrusts and parries. After all this time they still practised the arts of fighting from dragon back. Though only a ritual now, their single-mindedness was impressive. Even the lack of actual dragons didn't deter them.

Hellen and Beltaine strode on, past rooms filled with racks of serpentine swords and long, barbed spears. Past the individual cells where the riders slept: plain, square rooms empty apart from a raised wooden cot. Everything was plain stone, bare wood, hard surfaces. Nothing comfortable or decorative or beautiful.

Except for one thing: the great tapestries that covered the walls of the larger halls. Hellen stopped to consider one. Red and blue dragons twisted and curled in the air. Whether they were dancing or fighting she couldn't tell. On their backs sat riders, each wielding a sword and one of the spears. In that gilded, vibrant scene, the dragons flew again.

"You brought these cloths with you from Angere?" asked Hellen.

"The originals. These are copies."

"I have read of them. And the dragons? Do they still exist? Must we fear them, too, when the attack comes?"

"They are long-dead," said Beltaine. "Even great Xoster, the mother of them all, must have succumbed to age and grief by now. But there would be no need to fear them. The dragons despised the undain and would never have allowed one to ride them."

Hellen studied the tapestry, picking out more and more detail. She had no eye for such things, but she could admire the craftsmanship. The thread used was very fine, silky smooth as she brushed her fingers over it. She must show Ariane, if there would ever be a chance, now.

"How do you decide your colours when you have no dragons to bond with?"

"We take those of either our father or our mother."

"Never both?"

"No. A choice is made when the boy or girl comes of

age."

"There are none of you with black markings any more?"

He looked puzzled at her question. "No. Black was reserved for the King's personal guard."

"So there were black dragons, too?"

"No. The black tattoos were added to the normal markings when a rider was chosen."

"Those who remained in Angere. What colour dragons did they ride?"

"All colours. There was no one Wing that remained loyal. Now, if you will follow me to the Watchtower?"

Another long flight of winding stairs spiralled upward, rotating sunwise, the better to defend against right-handed attackers. Beltaine sprang ahead of her. Hellen took her time, thinking, listening. The curving stones of the narrow stairwell were smooth to her touch. The air was close, but a breeze breathed from above, bringing with it scents of open air and river. She could hear raised voices, some fierce argument. She tried to make out words but couldn't.

At the top, the stairs opened into a light, airy room, its narrow windows open to the wind. They were in the highest tower. From this room the dragonriders had watched for five centuries for the coming of the undain. Three riders stood with their backs to her, one at each window, staring west, northwest and southwest, out over the flowing waters.

But it wasn't the watchers who'd been arguing so fiercely. A square wooden table filled the centre of the room at which five others stood. A map of Andar covered the table, the whole land laid out, with the An taking up the western edge. A memory of a dream flashed through her mind: a dream of flying over the patchwork landscape of Andar. She thrust the thought away. Old fool. She had to think straight, now. She looked around at the five faces that had turned to regard her.

Four of them were dragonriders. A woman with red

tattoos like Beltaine, a man with blue like Ran's, a younger woman with green and finally a second man with bronze-gold tattoos. Each had five silver studs in their ears, compared to Beltaine's three and Ran's one. It was the fifth figure that drew her attention, though. This was no dragonrider. Instead of a grim scowl, he grinned at the sight of her. A tall mancer from Guilden, decked in his finest robes. His hair was a dishevelled mess, as it always was. Hellen crossed the room, and threw her arms around Ashen Meggenwar, her son.

"Ah, it's been too long since I saw you, boy."

"I should have come south sooner," he said into her ear. "I've been lost among the books of Guilden. Don't know where I get *that* from."

She held him at arm's length to drink in his features. He was his father's son, no doubt about it. She remembered that same roguish smile on Borrn's face. Her old heart quickened at the memories.

"How long have you been at Caer L'dun?" she asked.

"Three days now. I came down the coast road as quickly as I could."

"You should have come on to Islagray."

"I had to pass my tidings to the dragonriders. I am theirs as much as yours."

She hesitated. "And that was well done. But why have you lingered here?"

Ashen looked sheepish. "The truth is I was no longer sure of my welcome on the Witches' Isle."

"You grew up there. Why would you not be welcome?"

"I am a mancer now. Not everyone on Islagray feels as you, I think."

"Perhaps," said Hellen. "There are fools everywhere, even on Islagray. *Especially* on Islagray, come to that. But it's far too late to worry about such petty differences."

"Yes."

"You'll return with me?"

Ashen grinned the winning grin that had got him out of trouble many times as a boy. "I will."

She turned to the calculating gazes of the four dragonriders. She had never met any of them before. Their simmering anger filled the room like a smouldering fire. An anger driven by suppressed fear. Ashen's news had stirred them.

Beltaine cleared his throat. "My Lady, these are the chiefs of our people. This is Barion, First Rider of the Or Wing, the gold dragonriders. This is Axana, First of the Crimson Wing, the red dragonriders. Here is Jenath, First of the Verdant Wing, the green dragonriders. And here is Den, First of the Azure Wing, the blue dragonriders."

The four chiefs bowed to her, some more enthusiastically than others.

She knew each of them by report. "Do, please, continue your argument. I am keen to join in."

Barion spoke first. He had been a chief longer than anyone else. If the dragonriders had a leader, it was him. His head was smooth. The tattoos threaded across his scalp like a shining golden vine.

"We were debating tactics for the defence of Andar," said Barion. His tone suggested that he didn't think Hellen would have much of use to add. From what Borrn had said, Barion rarely valued the opinions of others. He had all the dragonriders' usual guilt but very little of their humility. In him, the burden of their past had given rise to a barely-concealed rage.

Hellen raised an eyebrow and crossed to the map. There was Islagray, a green island in the middle of the Silverwater. There was Caer L'dun, north and west. Then the cities and towns of Andar, Hyrn's Oak and the rest, strung along the banks of the An up to Guilden in the north. Beyond that, the jagged teeth of the mountains and the white wastes.

"You were debating where and therefore *when* the undain will attack," said Hellen. "Will they cross in the far north as soon as the first ice descends from the mountains? Or will they wait deeper into winter, until the ice freezes here and they can march directly on Caer L'dun and Islagray." She looked up to meet Barion's eyes. "And what have you decided, First of the Or Wing? March to the defence of the northern cities or sit and wait in your fortress?"

Barion's eyes narrowed. His nostrils flared slightly. He hadn't suspected she knew about the ice, and his mistrust of witches and mancers – of any magic – was well-known. And, perhaps, understandable.

"It seems you already knew what Ashen has hurried south to tell us," he said, his voice low. "It is a pity, Hellen Meggenwar, that you did not think to share the tidings with us."

"I've come here in part to do that. We only learned the truth of it recently ourselves. And since then we've been busy making our own arrangements for the defence of Andar."

"Is that so? I wasn't aware you had an army."

"We each fight as we can."

"That is very reassuring to know," said Barion, his voice mocking.

"And what of Ran?" said Den, the Azure rider. "He was sent to you nearly a week ago. We have heard nothing from him since."

"Ran consented to join a group crossing through the aether to another world."

"Oh?" said Barion. "Has he gone to seek aid? Will he be returning with reinforcements?"

"He will not. If he returns it will be with a book. Or part of a book," said Hellen.

"A book," said Barion, his voice thick with disdain. "And that is all? How will a book help us now, Hellen Meggenwar? How will *part of a book* help us?"

Hellen considered him. Could she trust him? His commitment to defending Andar was absolute. But his mind was full of battle tactics and military formations. He would never understand about the Grimoire. He knew its history, knew more than he was pretending. But in his mind it was simple. Magic had caused their problems. Magic would make matters worse. Only strength of arms would save them. Still, somehow, they had to find a way to work together.

"The book might be our salvation," said Hellen. "Without it we are doomed. With it we only *might* be doomed."

Barion snorted and shook his head. "You think so little of us. You think we won't be able to stem the onslaught when it comes?" Even under his tattoos his face reddened. Curiously she found herself warming to him. This anger was preferable to the fawning deference of Beltaine and the rest. Borrn had shown some of that, too. His humanity. Although it had taken some teasing out.

"Tell me, Barion," she said, "how many dragonriders are there in Andar? How many who can pick up a sword and fight?"

"Enough."

"How many?"

"Over a thousand."

"How far over a thousand?"

Barion at least looked sheepish now. "A few over a thousand."

"I see. And you think that a thousand dragonriders, for all their skill and bravery and devotion, can fight off the undain? When we don't even know where and when they will be attacking?"

"Caer L'dun has never been sacked by an enemy," said Barion.

"Caer L'dun has never been *attacked* by an enemy, as you are well aware," said Hellen. "Tell me, how many undain do you think there are over there?" She nodded her head toward the western window.

"It's impossible to say."

"Would you like to know the number I have in my head?"

"If you wish. It can only be a wild guess."

"Perhaps. But I can feel the undain massing even if I can't see them. And I can count. The undain are born, but they don't die. Not properly. How many do you think there are after all this time?"

"Many," he conceded, glancing at the map.

"Yes," said Hellen. "Many. Tell me, can a dragonrider fight a hundred foes?"

"Of course not."

"Then that is a shame. Because I think each of you will have to."

"A *hundred thousand* undain? Are you mad?"

"I don't believe I am, no. Of course, if you still had your dragons the odds might be closer. If you had even one it would be something. But as things stand it looks hopeless. The undain will slaughter you. They will slaughter us all."

"And what help may we expect from you?" said Axana, speaking for the first time. Her eyes were an intense blue, contrasting with the red swirls of ink across her skin. "What real help? Five hundred years ago the witches and mancers unleashed the great flood that swept away the bridge. Can we rely on something similar this time?"

Hellen shook her head. "I wish we could. But unleashing a flood is one thing. Holding back the winter is quite another. And there are fewer of us now. Then there were witches and mancers on both sides of the An."

"So why are you here, if it is so hopeless?" asked Axana.

"Because it isn't hopeless," said Hellen. "I didn't say that. I said we couldn't defeat the undain in battle."

"But why trouble us if you think our numbers so worthless?" asked Barion.

She shook her head. They were making this

deliberately hard. "We must fight them, of course. And we must hope it buys us time. But that is all we can hope for. Force of arms will not be enough. They will win in the end."

"Unless we acquire this book," said Den. His hair was long and thick, but silver-grey over his blue tattoos. There was an intelligence in his eyes, his mind, she hadn't noticed at first. He had been watching her closely, assessing her. "You do not name it but we all know to what you refer. The *Shadow Grimoire*, Ilminion's book of necromancy."

"That is correct."

"And so your plan is to use the undains' death magic against them," said Den. "To turn us into those nightmares so we can fight back. That would be no victory, I think. That would be worse than death. Perhaps using this evil knowledge is precisely what they want. To do their work for them."

"There is dangerous knowledge in the book," said Hellen. "There are terrible things in it. But we need all the help we can get. And knowledge is neither evil nor good. It becomes one or the other when it is put to use."

"I do not see how necromancy could be put to a *good* use," said Barion.

"It may if it is used to counter necromancy," said Hellen. "But that aside, what matters is that the undain hunger for this book. I do not fully know why, but there must be a reason. They need it urgently. And that is why we must make sure they don't get it."

Barion snorted. "Books and legends! By the horns of Hyrn, they mean nothing, old woman. It is swords we need. Swords and spears. If we have to fight a hundred undain to a man we will do so."

"Oh, don't be ridiculous," said Hellen. "And if you call me *old woman* again I'll strip your finely tattooed skin from your bones where you stand, First Rider of the Or Wing or not."

Barion glowered at her. A prickly silence filled the

room. Their guilt and rage seethed within them, and for a moment she thought it would boil over. That she'd lost them. Their willingness to make the ultimate sacrifice was an almost solid presence. That was their choice, but she wanted to live. Somehow, against these terrible odds, they had to survive. Either with the dragonriders help or without it.

It was Jenath who spoke, her quiet voice filling the silence. She was the youngest of the four chiefs and the most favourable to working with others, if Borrn was to be believed. Her easy smile dispelled some of the tension crackling through the room. "It would be a shame to slay Barion. Then there would be one fewer dragonrider and the odds would be even worse. We have a common enemy. We may disagree over the means, but we must fight together."

The words were directed at Hellen, but meant for the other chiefs. Hellen studied their faces as she replied. "You are right, Jenath. And I promise you we of Islagray will do what we can to help you."

"As we will for you," said Jenath. "Barion?"

Barion took several moments to find his reply. "Of course. So long as it doesn't take more riders from us we will do what we can."

"Excellent," said Hellen. "Then, since we are being so helpful, I do have something to ask of you."

"Go on," said Den, the suspicion clear in his voice.

"You dismiss ancient books as unimportant and yet you keep one here," said Hellen. "Akbar's Journal, brought by your forebears across the An with the Grimoire. I have seen mention of it in our own ancient texts. His account of those events and of the necromancy he read in the book before he clove it in two. I would like to read his journal. There may be something useful in it."

"That book is useless," said Barion. "No one has ever been able to make any sense of it."

"Then you won't miss it if I take it with me. I know of

someone who may be able to read it."

"And if we give you this treasure, what will you offer in return?"

"The only thing we can give," said Hellen. "The promise that we of Islagray will fight beside you to defeat the undain. That we will fight and die at your side."

Barion studied her for a moment and then looked through the westerly window. "Very well. Take the book if you think it will help you. Then we may return to forming our battle plans."

Hellen dipped her head in thanks, although Barion didn't see.

"I am grateful," she said. "But on that matter you still haven't answered my question."

"Question?"

"Will you march north or wait here?"

Barion shrugged. Looks passed between the four dragonriders. Clearly this had been the source of much debate.

"The cities have their own watches and militia," said Barion. "They must defend themselves. We can not be everywhere. We are strongest at Caer L'dun."

Hellen nodded. The city watches were capable of handling a few drunken revellers on a 'tweenweek night. They would not be able to fend off an approaching undain army and they all knew it.

"Much that is fair and beautiful will be lost," said Hellen.

Barion nodded but didn't reply.

"Very well, then," said Hellen. "I must return to Islagray. There is much to do. And perhaps either there or here will see the final battle for Andar when the undain come. Then we will stand together and fight."

She nodded and turned to leave. Ashen, grinning once more, bowed low to the dragonriders and followed her.

At the foot of the spiral stairs she halted and waited for him. Really, the meeting had gone as well as could be expected. She knew now how matters stood with the dragonriders. And the conversation had helped her to come to a realisation. What she had to ask of Ashen. And Ariane. It seemed she was forever sending people into danger and trouble. At least this time she would go, too.

"Would you really have skinned Barion alive?" asked Ashen as he joined her.

"What do you think?"

"I don't think you know any such magic."

Hellen smiled. "True. I know little of the terrible arts of the mancers. But thankfully he didn't know that."

"But what you said about us being slaughtered. You meant every word of that, yes?"

She put her hand on his shoulder. He was taller than her, as tall as his father. "I did. Nothing is certain, but that's the most likely outcome. You were one of the mancers who measured the winter ice on Howl Hill, weren't you? You know what's coming. That's why you're here and not in Guilden."

He nodded. "How did you know that? Some powerful farseeing magic?"

"Johnny told me."

"The minstrel? He's at Islagray already?"

"You met him leaving Guilden didn't you? Told him about the ice. He was at Islagray, but now he isn't. There is much to explain. Much we need to say to each other. I must return to the Isle. We can talk as we make our way there."

"But surely you'll be flying? I'm afraid my terrible powers don't extend to such things. I have to tramp along on my blisters."

She was in a hurry. Time was running out. Still, events had conspired to give her this time with her son. Her only child. Perhaps it was unwise, but she would seize the opportunity. The beauty and glory of Andar could look after itself for a while.

"Let's walk together," she said. "We may not get

another chance in what is to come."

"My Lady!" Beltaine arrived, racing down the spiral stairs three at a time. "My Lady, my apologies for what happened. You are our guests, and we should have treated you better. The Wings have been arguing for many weeks over what we should do. We would not normally be so unwelcoming."

She waved away his apologies. "We have more to worry about than a few angry words."

"We haven't even offered you refreshment," said the dragonrider. "Will you at least take food and drink?"

"And the Journal?"

"I've been instructed to give it to you. I will retrieve it while you eat. Also, I thought you should know, both of you, that there is no news of Borrn."

It was as she'd expected. There's been no news of Borrn for a long time. Ashen looked troubled, although it was mostly worry for her. He'd barely known his father.

"Are they still arguing up there?" asked Hellen.

"They are. You might like to know that some want to abandon Caer L'dun and put our strength into defending Islagray. The Songroom. That is the true heart of Andar, not this stone fortress."

"Jenath?"

Beltaine nodded. "Yes. But another of the Wings wishes to march north and meet the oncoming army."

"Which?"

"The Azure. Den."

"But he was persuaded?"

"He was. For all we know the entire undain army may wait until Midwinter and attack us here."

"Well," said Hellen. "For what it's worth I think you've made the right choice. You will be harder to defeat in the Caer."

"Perhaps. And perhaps the undain will pass us by and slay everyone else while we sit watching from our walls."

"I don't think you need worry about that. The undain

aren't going to leave you alone. They aren't going to leave anyone alone."

Two days later, Ashen sat with his mother and Ariane on the soft grass of the orchard on Islagray. The sun gave them light but little heat. A thin breeze blew about the hill, occasionally sending withered leaves spinning to the ground from the wizened trees. The damp air smelled of rotting leaves and wood smoke. Ashen gazed around, remembering adventures from his childhood. He'd had the run of the Isle. Climbing these particular trees had been strictly forbidden, of course. That hadn't always stopped him. The ancient spirits of the dead witches had whispered and creaked their outrage, but he'd climbed anyway.

"So," said Ariane, "you've finished telling the dragonriders what to do and now it's our turn, is that right? I know that look in your eyes, Hellen Meggenwar."

"Only if you've finished hiding your head in the sand and hoping Angere goes away," said his mother.

Ashen looked between them but didn't speak. Ariane had been an aunt to him growing up, had looked after him nearly as much as his mother had. The two of them always sparred. It was what they did. Their fighting brought more fond memories flooding back. In a weird way it made him feel safe. They loved each other dearly.

Ariane didn't look well, though. She'd been through some ordeal, and now her chestnut skin was pinched and drawn. There was silver in her black hair, although her smile at seeing him had been as wide as ever.

"But you do have some dark and secret plan for us, I'll wager," said Ariane. "Or did you drag us up here to admire the view?"

"This isn't a game," said his mother. "We'll all die if we don't act. Most likely we'll die even if we do."

"Aha, so you do have a plan. Then you had better give us our instructions."

His mother sighed. "Very well. If you can be bothered to listen I'll tell you what I have learned. Cait has gone to Angere. I didn't foresee that. It changes everything. The risk to her is terrible, but the risk to us is terrible, too. She is of the blood. If Menhroth discovers she is there, he will send his entire army to capture her."

"She's gone for the book?" asked Ariane, disbelief clear in her voice.

"I think so. I don't know for sure. Who imagined she would attempt such a thing?"

"Very inconsiderate of her, not following orders," said Ariane.

His mother ignored her. "I've been searching for a way to get the book from Angere. Now we have to help Cait, too."

"But it's impossible," said Ariane. "No one can cross the An. No one apart from those vile abominations."

"Unless we head north and cross the ice," said Ashen. "It won't be long before the waters freeze."

"No," said his mother. "There's no time to wait. We have to act now."

"So what miracle do you plan to bring about?" asked Ariane.

"First, we need to get a message through to Cait," said his mother. She turned to look at him. Here it came. They'd had only a few days together. A few precious days. He'd been lucky to have that.

"Ashen," she said. "Will you help?"

"Since when do you ask people if they're willing?" asked Ariane.

"I thought I'd try it out."

"Well, stick to just giving orders," said Ariane. "Then we'll all know where we are."

Ashen held up his hand, laughing at the two of them. "Enough! Of course I'll do what I can."

"Very well," said his mother. "There is one in Andar who might be able to send a message across the An. A wise man of sorts. You have heard of the Blind Mapmaker?"

"Heard stories," said Ashen. "He's real?"

"I believe he is. I've tried to speak to him many times, but he always refuses to talk."

"Or he doesn't exist," said Ariane.

"Or that, yes. But if what I've read is true he is powerful enough to converse with those on the other side of the An. He might be able to reach Cait."

"But why would he listen to me?" said Ashen. "I'm the one who turned his back on Islagray to become a mancer. I'm the one who pursued the dark arts of drawing magic from spell books and artefacts and the aether rather than from myself. I'm the one who works sorcery without *paying the price*."

"Some people aren't so tangled up in these petty differences, as well you know," his mother said. Ariane snorted in amusement but didn't comment. His mother, ignoring her, carried on. "He's a wise man, yes, but I've read he also uses a seeing sphere to help him peer through the mists, like any good scryer from Guilden."

"And where does he live?" asked Ashen. "Do you know that?"

"South, far down the An on the borders of Azandia. And then east up the Meander, the river that runs from the Azend mountains. There's a tower on a hill from where he stares into the aether with his mind's eye and draws his maps. If you take Johnny's boat and don't stop for food or sleep, you can be there in a week."

"Assuming he exists," said Ashen. "And assuming I don't get swallowed whole by curious river serpents, why would this mapmaker help us?"

"Why wouldn't he?" said his mother. "The undain won't make an exception of him. And we have certain items you can take as gifts. Old maps stored in the tunnels that he might appreciate. They say he has the largest collection in the land."

"And what message should I ask him to send if I find him?"

"Tell him Cait must make for the bridgehead near the White City with all speed."

"The bridgehead?" said Ariane, shocked. "But that's madness. That is where the undain are massing. It's the one place she should avoid."

"Perhaps," said his mother. "But I'm hoping there will be one or two others there. Others who can help."

"Who?" asked Ariane.

"Isn't it obvious? You and I, of course."

6 – PALACES OF THE UNDAIN

Cait awoke in cold water, spluttering and struggling as she was sucked down into purple depths. She fought and broke the surface for a moment, gasping, inhaling as much water as air. She sank again, mountains and sky becoming a shifting blur of colour through the waters. Sounds were muffled and distant. She struggled and thrashed, fighting for the light. But it was too far away. There was only water. Her lungs and her blood were ice, and the distant mountains faded to darkness. The only sound was her heart, beating like a bell.

A hand grasped hers, the grip strong, hauling her upward. She broke into air. For a moment she couldn't remember how to breathe. She struggled and spluttered, but another hand cradled her head, supporting her. Finally she gulped hungry mouthfuls of air.

Sound returned. Vision returned. She floated in the freezing waters of the mountain lake, and the dead witch-girl was beside her, supporting her.

The undain. The Bone Harvester. She must have used up all her strength trying to defeat it. "Am I dead?" she asked.

The other girl laughed. "No, silly. How can you be

dead and still talking to me?"

Her lips were blue and water streamed off her hair as if she'd just emerged from the depths herself. It was hard to see where dark hair stopped and the water began. A ragged doll floated a short distance away, bobbing on the ripples.

"You're dead and I talk to you all the time," said Cait.

"It's not the same, is it? You do know where we are, don't you, Cait? You do know where this pool really is?"

She could see only the ring of jagged mountain-peaks and the deep blue of the sky. For some reason there was no sun, although bright light illuminated the scene.

"The mountains somewhere," said Cait. "I don't remember exactly."

The cold throughout her body was intense, but she wasn't shivering. She felt more alive each moment.

"It's inside *you*," said the girl. "In your head. Your memories. Your mind. This is how you picture magic working. That's all. This isn't a *real* lake, although it must be based on one you saw once. But you can't be dead otherwise we wouldn't be here, would we? Not you. Not me. Not the lake."

Cait worked her way to her feet. The waters were suddenly shallow enough to stand in. Here eyes were level with the witch-girl, who still held her hand.

"So does that mean you're not real either?" said Cait. "I'm making you up?" The thought was terrible. The witch-girl was her only friend in Angere. The only one she could talk to.

The girl giggled again. "Of course I'm real. I came with you from Manchester. A part of me did, anyway."

"So part of you is still there?"

"Oh, yes," said the girl, shrugging as if this was the most normal thing in the world.

"But how is that possible?" asked Cait. "How can you be alive in my mind?"

Her blue lips curled into a smile. "Isn't it obvious? Haven't you worked it out?"

"What?"

"That we're related."

"We are?"

"Of course, Cait. How else could this work?"

"I don't know. Magic?"

"You know," said the girl, "you haven't even asked me my name."

She hadn't, it was true. The girl was a ghost, a spirit, a long-dead memory. But she was also a child, a year or two younger than Cait when she died.

"I'm sorry," said Cait. "Will you tell me your name?"

The girl smiled brightly. "It's Bethany. Bethany Weerd. My sister was one of your mother's mother's mothers. Many cold years ago."

"So you're my … great great great aunt or something?"

"I am. Or I would have been. We're the same blood. I knew it as soon as I saw you by the towers."

It made sense. Her great great great great grandmother had come from Andar in 1819, so her mum had said. They were *Weerds* because the family tradition was for the husband to take his wife's name, not the other way round. Something her dad had gone along with. He'd pretended to complain, but had secretly liked it. Perhaps doing names like that was how they did it in Andar, and her forebears had brought the tradition with them.

"And let me make sure I have this completely clear," said Cait. "I'm definitely not dead."

"Trust me. I know what it's like to be dead, and you're not. You blaze far too brightly. It was close, though. When we attacked that second monster it almost finished you. You and me. It was a good job I was there, showing you what to do. Showing you when to *stop*."

"So I'm unconscious?"

"The pain was too much."

"But how long have I been asleep?"

"I only see the outside world through your eyes. I've been alone while you slept. Minutes, days, weeks, I don't know."

"But where am I? What happened to the Bone Harvester? And Ran and Nox?"

"The only way to find out is to wake up. I think you're ready now. You'll ache something terrible for a few days, but you'll survive. You're not one to give in. My mum always said the same about me."

"OK," said Cait. "So what do I do? How do I wake myself up?"

The girl lifted an arm, water cascading off it as she pointed. "There's a path there, leading out of the valley. It's very steep. Steep and slippery. I've tried to walk it, but I can't. I get so far and fall back. I think only you can take it."

The path was a zig-zagging line up the side of one of the mountains. "I have to go that way?"

"You can do it. And I'll still be here when you leave."

Cait hugged the girl. Bethany's flesh was cold but her heart pounded in her chest.

"Go on," said the girl.

Cait waded ashore, hauling herself onto the soft grass. She stood and looked back as Bethany retrieved her doll and clutched it.

"You're younger than me," said Cait. "But you're also a lot older. What should I call you?"

The girl shrugged. "Call me Bethany. Everyone else does. Now climb that path so we can find out what's going on."

Golden light filled Cait's eyes as she surfaced into the real world. She'd climbed the mountain path, each step an effort. Now there was light and warmth and softness. Where was she? Not the lane, that was clear. There was no sound, no breath of air on her face. For a moment she let herself hover on the edge of wakefulness, enjoying the sensation of floating, of hovering between worlds.

One by one, aches and agonies prodded her, as if she

were repossessing her own body with all its bruises and cuts. The pains in her chest were sharp as she inhaled. She tried to take in shallow breaths. She felt like she'd been beaten with sticks. Not that she'd ever been beaten with sticks, but it had to feel something like this.

It was tempting to drift away, back to sleep. Back to the safety of the mountain lake. Instead, she let her eyes flicker open, the world an indistinct blur through her eyelashes.

She lay on a bed in a cream-coloured room, a pearly light suffusing everything. Sunlight filtered through the shades, making the air in the room glow. Specs of dust like tiny fairies thronged and danced in the beams. Someone had carried her to the big house, the palace they'd glimpsed.

She hauled herself around to sit on the edge of the bed, an act that seemed to take all her remaining strength. She sat with her head in her hands while the room lurched. The walls took several moments to decide which way round they should be.

She tried to understand what had happened. She must have killed the second Bone Harvester, she and Bethany. She'd passed out. And now she was a prisoner, a prisoner with barely enough strength to stand.

Great. She was doing a fantastic job of saving the world, wasn't she?

The room was weird. Gold edging and touches of rich scarlet highlighted an otherwise white bedroom. Walls, floor, even the furniture: it was all a polished white, translucent where the sun caught it. For some reason it put her in mind of her mum's bone china tea set, the one she kept for best in a cupboard and never actually used.

As prisons went it was pretty luxurious. Maybe they'd locked her in while they sent messages to the White City, which meant she might not have much time. They could come for her at any moment. She had to get away.

And where were Ran and Nox? She had to find out what was going on. She forced herself to stand. The floor canted, as if she were aboard a boat upon a lurching sea. Her stomach heaved, and she fell to her knees, retching. A bitter taste filled her mouth, but she wasn't sick. How long was it since she'd eaten? Since she'd drunk? Too long. She retched again dryly, then kneeled there, panting.

The floor beneath her nose was smooth and white, a mosaic of tiny fragments cemented into swirling geometric lines. Wood, maybe, or some grained stone. She tried to follow the pattern but couldn't. For some reason staring at the floor made her feel worse, made her stomach flip. She turned to lie on her back.

She needed water. Cold water and cool air. There were two doors in the room, one shut but the other half-open. She crawled that way, glad none of her friends were there to see her.

As she'd hoped, the door led to a bathroom. More polished white tiles covered every surface, but at least there was a basin, with ornate gold taps. Kneeling, she found the cold, then thrust her mouth into the stream of water.

She gulped, feeling the water sliding to her stomach. She'd read somewhere not to drink too much if you were parched. She couldn't resist. The water was crisp and clear. She'd never tasted anything so wonderful in her life.

She tried standing again. This time the world decided to remain stationary. That was good. She held on to the side of the large, rectangular bath. How long was it since she'd washed? Or brushed her hair? She didn't like to think.

She came to a decision and turned on the bath taps. Maybe the Witch King himself would turn up and cart her off to the White City. Maybe the undain hordes were about to enslave everyone she knew back in Manchester. But one thing was clear. She'd find it all a lot easier to deal with if she were out of her filthy clothes and clean. It felt like she'd been wearing the same things for weeks.

As the water gushed into the bath, she peered into the bedroom. Someone had laid out a long gown on the bed. White, inevitably. It wasn't the sort of thing she'd normally wear, but it would have to do.

She peeled off the clothes she'd been wearing since the day at the library and sank into the waters of the bath. It was five minutes or more before it occurred to her what the white walls were, what the building was constructed from. A vision of metal containers travelling through the waterfall at the refinery came to her, and she retched again. They carved it with such delicacy, such care. Such craftsmanship. She had to get away. They were sick, all of them.

When she was dry, she pulled the flowing white robes over her head, the material silky on her skin. She studied herself in the mirror. The clothes weren't her style at all. She usually went for the goth look, not hippy angel. The blue dye in her hair was fading, too. Still, perhaps it would all help her fit in. Disguise her as she tried to escape. She slipped on the white shoes they'd provided, too.

The dizziness had faded a little. She could walk, although she doubted if she was up to much magic. Her muscles ached like they did after she'd run a cross-country race at school.

She was preparing to leave when shouts sounded outside her window. Her heart raced. They'd come for her. She'd waited too long. Fearing what she'd see, she peered around the shades.

She was on the second floor of the palace, overlooking a wide courtyard. Intricately carved spires jutted around the yard, white walls gleaming in the rays of the sun. Down on the ground, three figures posed upon horses. The beasts were tall, their white flanks powerful. Two had six legs and one – it took her a few moments to count – had eight.

As a young girl, Cait had once clopped along on a docile pony as a birthday treat. These beasts, by contrast, looked as though they could run like the wind. They bridled, eager to be off. Around their legs jostled a pack of animals, something like hounds but with larger mouths full of too many sharp teeth.

The riders shouted to each other, laughing at some joke. One of them was clearly a lord of the undain. He sat tall and proud in flowing white robes trimmed with scarlet and silver. His hair, also, was silver, flowing down his back as he controlled his eight-legged steed with a gloved hand. He turned his horse, revealing a face that was striking in its beauty. Ancient and young at the same time.

Nox was there, too, riding a six-legged horse. It was Nox the undain lord was laughing with. She saw how it was. Nox had brought her there after all. It was what he'd planned all along. He'd handed her to the undain and now he was enjoying a ride with his new friends while she was kept prisoner.

The first inklings of anger arose within her. The first stirrings of that cold fury that she could bend to her will to fuel her magic. Soon she would be stronger. Soon she would be able to fight back. And when she did, it would be Nox she'd deal with first, she promised herself. To think she'd trusted him, believed he was trying to help them. How could she have been so stupid?

The third rider was the boy from the cart. He stood apart from the other two, astride his own six-legged horse. He sat unmoving, sullen, staring into the distance. He clearly didn't want to be there. Servants wearing white veils offered drinks to Nox and the undain lord, holding the delicate glasses on silver trays, but no one offered the boy anything.

Shouts went up from the opposite side of the courtyard and another group of servants appeared. A huddle of them, hauling a prisoner along by the arms. A man, struggling and screaming as he fought his captors. The servants brought him to the undain lord.

The lord broke off his conversation with Nox and glanced down at the prisoner, assessing him. The hounds milled around in a frenzy of excitement, sniffing at the man, jumping and snapping at his face. The undain lord nodded to the servants, and they released the prisoner. The man stood for a moment, gaze darting around, terror bright on his face. He stepped backward, and the boiling mass of hounds followed. A word from the undain held the beasts in check.

It was the man's chance to escape. He didn't need to be encouraged. He turned and sprinted through an arched gateway and out of the courtyard.

After he'd run a few dozen paces, the undain lord lifted a silver pipe to his lips and blew. A metallic wailing noise blared. Cait understood, then, what this was. A hunt. A man hunt.

Beyond the white walls she could see the prey fleeing through the palace's grounds, leaping low hedges, racing toward a distant copse of trees. Was he an undain, altered to run fast like those that had pulled the cart? Was that how this sport worked?

She still had the seeing-stone about her neck. She pulled it to her eye. The spark from the darting figure was just visible; this was a living man, not an undain.

She wondered where he'd come from. Her own world? Did Genera supply victims for the undain lords and ladies to hunt? She wondered who the man was, what he'd been. Someone like Tom outside the library, perhaps. Someone homeless and friendless who wouldn't be missed.

Revolted, she pushed open the doors that led onto the balcony and stepped into the sunlight. She wouldn't stand by and watch while they hunted this man. She knew all-too well what it was like to be pursued. And this was no sport. Between those magnificent, magical horses and the pack of snarling dogs, what chance did the man have?

She stood dazzled for a moment. The cold magic coiled within her. But it was faint still, barely a whisper. It wouldn't be enough. What exactly was she going to do? Call down politely? Ask them to stop? The thought was ridiculous.

She grasped the handrail and stood there, impotent,

shaking with fury. She had to think of herself. Giving herself away wasn't going to help anyone. And perhaps, somehow, the man would survive, evade the dogs and those incredible horses. Although she knew, also, it wasn't true and that she was only trying to make herself feel better.

As all this passed through her mind, the sullen boy looked up at her. Nox and the undain lord were distracted, watching the running man, readying themselves for the chase. But the boy wasn't interested in that. And now he'd seen her in the bright sun, gazing down upon them.

There were bruises on his face, and one of his eyes was black. Had he been injured in the cart crash? She didn't recall his face being hurt. She thought he'd call out, tell the others she was awake. Instead he stared at Cait, something like a smile playing across his damaged face. She still held the stone in her hand, and she put it to her eye. The boy blazed with red light. He was as alive as she was.

The undain lord blew another blast on his pipe and spurred his eight-legged mount into motion. Nox followed, apparently as comfortable on a horse as he was on a motorbike. The boy, however, stayed where he was, watching Cait. His hair shone gold in the sunlight.

The undain lord called over his shoulder to the boy, some harsh syllables Cait couldn't understand. The boy delayed a few moments more, then nodded his head at Cait. He turned and plodded after the other two, making no effort to catch up.

Ahead of him, Nox and the undain lord spurred their steeds into a gallop. They clattered through the gateway and into the palace's grounds in pursuit of the fleeing man, now a distant dot in the fields.

Cait retreated into the shadows of her room. She'd been foolish to reveal herself. She couldn't make any more mistakes. Ran must be dead and Nox had shown where his true allegiances lay. Now it was all up to her. She didn't have much hope. But she damn well wasn't going to give in. And perhaps she could flee while Nox and the undain were off hunting.

She wished she could turn herself into a crow as her mother had done. Become a bird and fly away. She had no idea how to attempt such a thing. Perhaps she could climb down to the courtyard and escape that way? There had to be plenty of handholds in all that ornate cake-icing carved bone.

No. She was too weak for anything like that. Dizziness whirled inside her. She'd succeed only in falling and breaking her neck.

In the end she tried the other door and found, to her surprise, it wasn't locked. She expected there to be guards outside, armed undain of some description. But there was nothing. A long corridor stretched in both directions, the polished white walls decorated every few yards with tapestries. The ceiling was delicately carved into organic swirls. There was no one in sight.

She picked up her phone and a few other essentials and set off, keeping to one side of the corridor, ears straining for a sound of someone approaching. Apart from the croaking of birds from somewhere she could hear nothing.

She reached the top of a sweep of curving stairs. Two figures knelt part-way up, polishing the steps. The seeing-stone told her what she'd suspected. Undain. They hadn't noticed her. As with those in the courtyard, these had lacy white veils covering their faces, obscuring their features.

Would they react if they saw her? She thought about retracing her steps. But there might not be any other way down. This might be her only chance.

She peered over the banister. The floor was a long way down. For a moment the dizziness lurched through her. She gripped the handrail. She had to do this.

She descended, warily watching the two undain on the stairs. They didn't look up. As she approached they moved aside to let her pass. Then, when she'd gone past, they carried on again, polishing and scrubbing silently.

Several times as she descended the nausea overcame her and she had to grab the banister to stop herself toppling forward. Once she had to sit on the stairs with her head in her hands and wait for the world to stop spinning. She passed more slaves toiling away, men and women and children, but none bothered her. None even dared look at her. Once or twice she tried the seeing-stone, but there was no spark there, no life.

Finally she made it to the foot of the stairs. The floor was another mosaic of bone fragments, white and cream and sepia, this time forming a picture. Some battle scene of dragons whirling in the sky, breathing white fire upon a cowering army. Distantly, she could hear kitchen sounds, the clank and clang of pots and pans. The smell of cooking meat was in the air, making her stomach heave again.

Across the floor stood a high set of double-doors, gold metal with white inlay. She stepped across the ancient battle, wary of being visible down side-corridors, sure some alarm would sound. From gold frames about the walls, painted figures stared down at her with disapproving frowns.

Again, she expected the doors to be locked, but the large brass handle turned as she pulled and the doors swung open. No one cried out. No footsteps came running.

It didn't make sense. Were they really going to let her walk away? Or was there some magical barrier to keep her inside? Some sorcery she didn't understand?

Only one way to find out. She stepped over the threshold.

The light was blinding, reflecting off the relentless white walls and terraces. Squinting, she set off across a paved level to another flight of stairs. Beyond, the manicured gardens stretched toward green fields and distant woods. Perhaps she'd be able to get far enough away before they discovered she'd escaped.

She weaved between delicate fountains and bone

statues set among formal flower-beds. Many more of the undain tended to the plants. Again, none of them paid her any attention.

The gardens filled the air with their sickly scents. Huge flowers with rubbery, fleshy petals leaned over her as she stumbled by. Ahead, a gate set in a square hedgerow led into the fields. She was nearly free.

Then she tripped over a low line of stones edging one of the beds. She tried to right herself, but her legs had turned to rubber. She fell. A sharp pain thudded through her head and then the world went dark again.

She came round to the sound of horse's hooves clattering nearby. Her head throbbed. She must have struck something. She put her hand to her scalp, feeling carefully. Her fingers came away wet, the pain sharp where she touched the wound.

She peered into the blinding sky. A tall figure sat astride a horse, an indistinct shape against the light. She tried to rise but couldn't.

The figure leaned forward and his face became visible. That ancient, beautiful face, that long silver hair. His eyes shone like polished steel as he studied her.

"Hello, Cait," said the undain lord on his eight-legged horse. He spoke with an odd accent, the vowel-sounds twisted, but his words clear. "Did you decide to go for a little walk?"

7 – FEASTING

Two hours later, Cait sat at a grand banqueting table in a hall of the palace, wondering what was going on. The sumptuous room about her blazed with light. Gold-framed mirrors decorated the walls, breaking up the relentless polished white, their reflections of each other making the space confusing to the eye. Enormous chandeliers filled the air above her head, each holding thousands of tallow candles. Their bobbing flames provided a quiet chorus of hisses.

Her head throbbed from where she'd struck it. Between the nagging pain and the light it was hard to think straight. She didn't appear to be a prisoner. She hadn't had chance to talk to Nox yet, but it didn't look like he'd betrayed her. The undain lord – introduced to her as the Duke of Greygyle – had been treating them as though they were honoured guests.

Still, while Nox may have been right about the local undain nobility, she wasn't actually safe was she? When Danny talked, when the undain found out the truth, things would be very different. They had to get away soon, without attracting attention.

The Duke sat beside her at the head of the table. Nox

was opposite her while the golden-haired boy – called simply Lugg – was next to him. The boy was, so she'd been told, the Duke's son. The table was enormous, easily fifty feet long, but no one else was there, apart from more servants hovering in the background and occasionally swooping in to fill a glass or deposit a dish.

More food than they could ever eat was being laid out on steaming silver platters. Cait's stomach growled. Although, in truth, there wasn't actually much she could eat. It didn't look like the undain were big on vegetarianism.

The dish in front of her contained four whole piglets, their bodies baked brown and arranged in a tableau of playful fight. Steam billowed from them, heavy with the scents of burned flesh. Next to them was a whole swan, cooked and painstakingly re-feathered so that it resembled the living bird once more. Upon its back sat five cygnets, also cooked and re-feathered, laid out in another mock still-life scene. Their eyes were all black gems, glinting in the candlelight. It was like one of the hideous stuffed-animal scenes they had in museums. Only this one she was expected to eat.

She wasn't brave enough to tell the fearsome undain she didn't touch meat. Somehow she didn't think he'd understand.

Nox, meanwhile, clearly had no such qualms. He lifted an entire roast piglet onto his plate and carved at it, the crisp flesh crackling. Cait looked away and reached for a dish of something that might have been fine threads of pasta.

Nox nodded in approval at her. "Spiced peacock tongues. Delicious." Juices from the piglet dribbled down his chin as he spoke.

The boy dropped a few slices of meat onto his own plate, but he wasn't eating. He sat with his head bowed, idly pushing the food around and occasionally nibbling at a morsel of it. The bruise around his eye was livid purple, the whole side of his face swollen. Occasionally he glanced at them, but a scowl from the Duke quickly cowed him, and he lowered his gaze.

The Duke wasn't eating at all, watching over them in silence. A pallor the colour of ash had come over his features. He'd been film-star beautiful just a few hours ago, but now he looked sunken and weary as if he'd been through some terrible exertion. The lines of his bones showed throw his skin, making the raw shape of his skull visible.

A large silver contraption, something like an ornate tea-urn, was carried in by four veiled servants and set on the table in front of him. The device was highly polished, with battle-scenes like those on the mosaic engraved upon it. Distorted images of the room were reflected in it. No one spoke and the Duke closed his eyes, licking his lips as if relieved some long wait was over.

The servants turned little wheels on the contraption, and a louder hissing noise began within it, along with a faint bubbling. Finally, one of the servants unwound a rubbery tube connected to the urn and handed it to the Duke with a bow of her head.

The Duke's hand trembled as he took the tube and sited it onto a silver band around his wrist. He nodded, and the servants turned more wheels on the shining urn. The hissing sound increased and the rubber tube pulsed as liquid flowed through it. Neither Nox nor Lugg said anything or even watched, as if the whole thing was utterly normal.

After a few moments the Duke sighed from combined relief and pleasure. His features were suddenly handsome once more. His wrinkles faded as Cait watched, his skin smoothing over as the deathly grey was replaced by a youthful glow. Only his silver eyes retained a hint of his age and former decay.

The Spirit pumping into his body had brought him back to life. The Spirit leeched from people in her own world, most likely. She had to stop herself from standing and yanking the tube from his wrist or smashing the urn to the floor. She had to continue their subterfuge. It was their only hope.

Finally, Greygyle disconnected the tube from his arm and the veiled servants removed the Spirit paraphernalia from the table.

Greygyle licked his lips and sat forward. "So, Cait, I hope the food is to your liking?"

"Yes," she said. "Thank you. It's … good."

"Excellent. It's rare the servants have to produce a feast for guests. If their efforts are not to your liking I'll have them replaced."

Replaced. She suppressed a shiver. "No, it's fine, really," she said. "I'm still getting my appetite back."

"Of course," said Greygyle. "And tell me, what news is there from the City of Ghosts? Is everything in the capital prepared for the invasion?"

The City of Ghosts? What was that? Another thing she'd never heard of. "Uh, *The City of Ghosts*?"

"Forgive her," said Nox, jumping in. "Sometimes she is a little slow." He turned to Cait, an indulgent smile on his face. "Duke Greygyle is referring to the court of King Menhroth of course. The Bone Palaces. The White City."

"Of course," said Cait. "The City of Ghosts is fine. Everything is … just as white as ever."

The Duke nodded but didn't reply. His eyes narrowed as he studied her for a moment.

"You speak English well," said Cait to change the subject.

A flicker of amusement crossed the Duke's face. "Many of us take pleasure in learning tongues from the other world. From your world, I mean. You could say I'm rather an aficionado of your culture. I have an extensive library of English literature. I must show it to you."

Great. Now he sounded like one of her teachers trying to convince her reading a book would somehow be good for her. "Oh yes. You must. What books do you read?"

"Oh, you know. The classics. Anything and everything I can get my hands on. Although I prefer real life stories. Not all those *fantasy* tales people write. I fail to see the point in such rubbish. They make it all up."

"I thought all books were made up?" She was engaging in polite conversation with one of the undain nobility. How had it come to this?

"I visited your world once," said Greygyle, ignoring her question. "Many years ago. A sightseeing trip. Fascinating. The way people live. Of course, this was long before the Baron of Albion was in charge of our lands there."

"The ... Baron of Albion?"

"I mean your father, of course."

She flicked a glance at Nox, who smiled warmly, nodding his head slightly in encouragement.

"Of course," she said. "It's just I don't ... I don't normally call him that."

"My apologies for my daughter," said. Nox. "It's so hard to foster the necessary respect in the young, don't you find?"

So that was his story. He was her father. Great. He was a bit young wasn't he? Maybe the undain weren't good at judging age by appearance any more. And she couldn't contradict him. She had to go along with the story, maintain the pretence.

Nox was loving it, though. OK, so he hadn't betrayed her, but still. The thought of *him* as her father made her flesh crawl almost as much as the cold stare of the Duke.

"Your father tells me you two are looking for a place to build a villa?" the undain lord asked. He still wasn't eating. Presumably they didn't need to eat.

His gaze sent another shiver through her. She hoped it wasn't obvious. She put all her effort into trying to sound light-hearted. "Yes. We're looking for somewhere to live. That's right."

"Well, plenty of space out here," said the Duke. "Lots

of land. We're a long way from the An and all its distractions, but there is much beauty to be found in our hills and valleys. These lands are at peace now. My advice would be to stay in the south. The farther north you go, the wilder the country becomes. Here we have good connections to civilization. There's even talk of building a Spirit pipeway so we don't have to rely on deliveries by cart."

She caught the brief look of malice the undain lord cast toward his son as he spoke. Lugg didn't meet Greygyles's gaze.

"But I must apologise for our poor welcome," the Duke continued. "Our household is much reduced. Normally all the seats at this table would be filled."

"Are the rest of your family away?" Cait asked. "Will they be returning soon?"

"Oh, no. They're all still here."

"I'm sorry, I … I don't understand."

A spark of fury blazed in those grey eyes, just for a moment, and Cait thought she knew how Lugg had ended up with his swollen face and blackened eye.

"My kin and household rest in the family crypts," said the Duke. "Lying in torpor to survive the dearth. I'm afraid our supplies of Spirit have been temporarily interrupted. You receive our hospitality at a fallow time. We are honoured you made this diversion in your itinerary, of course, but it is fortunate you are both *as you are*. I fear we would struggle to be the welcoming hosts were you ascended." The words were polite, apologetic. None of it fooled Cait. This was simply the latest punishment meted out to his son. The boy had been beaten and now he was being humiliated.

"Your welcome is most generous, Duke Greygyle," said Nox. "We are truly grateful to you. Aren't we Cait?"

"Oh, yes," she said, chewing on something rubbery that she hoped wasn't an animal part. "Truly grateful."

Nox picked up one of the dishes and passed it to her,

the grin still wide on his features. "Buttered mouse livers, beloved daughter?"

The banquet lasted for days. So it seemed. Nox ate enormous amounts, intent on sampling every dish set before him. Cait managed to find a few things that hadn't recently been running or swimming or flapping around. The undain clearly liked to have meat with everything. Even the dessert – fragments of crushed ice in some sort of cream – had little balls of jelly floating around in it. Balls of jelly that might have been the eyeballs of some unfortunate creature.

When they were finished, Nox and the Duke headed off together to sample some of the undain's collection of red wines. Cait caught Nox by the arm and pulled him aside for a moment.

"If we get out of this alive, I'll kill you," she whispered.

"Cait, Cait," said Nox. "I told you. We need all the help we can get."

"Don't be ridiculous. There is no help here. We're in one of the palaces of the enemy. If they knew who we really were…"

"But they don't, do they? Just pretend you are my daughter and do as I say and all will be well."

"In your dreams, Nox. Or is that why we're really here? So you can play at being a Baron for a while longer?"

Nox glanced at the Duke, waiting for him in the doorway. Nox inclined his head in a gesture of acknowledgement then turned back to Cait. "I'm doing everything I can to help us, stupid girl. It was me that saved you when you blacked out on the road. Without me you'd have been picked clean by carrion crows days ago. You and Ran."

"Ran's alive?"

"Thanks to me. He was trying to fight that Harvester with a stick. A stick! It was just as well I had my gun."

"Then where is he now?"

"He couldn't come here, could he? He's obviously from Andar. I needed to bring you here to get help. Ran is out in the wilds somewhere, fending for himself."

"We need to find him. It's not safe out there."

"Oh, come off it. He's loving every minute of this. A chance to sacrifice himself at every turn."

"And what happens when they come for us from the White City? No doubt you'll explain it was you who captured me and turn me over, yes? Is that your plan?"

"I told you, these people live in the middle of nowhere. They have no idea what's going on in the real world."

"Look," said Cait. "We have to leave. As soon as we can. Stay if you like but I'm going."

He studied her for a moment. "Wait until the morning at least. It's dark now."

"Dark's good. I'm less likely to be seen."

"Less likely to see what's chasing you, too."

"I'll manage."

"Are you sure about that?"

"I'll take my chances. What are you plotting? Why do you really want to keep me here?"

"Because you're ill. You look like death. You need to rest, not storm off into the night."

She did feel pretty rough, it was true. Her stomach was cramping with the sudden glut of food. Although it might be her period about to start. She'd lost track of what day it was. Another thing she had to worry about. Heroines in books never had to stop to contend with the joys of menstruation while they were saving the world, did they?

"I don't trust you."

"Yes. You mentioned it. But if I'd wanted to turn you over I could have done so while you were unconscious. Do try to think."

She restrained herself. "We'll leave first thing tomorrow. And if you're too busy networking with your new zombie friend I'll go without you."

"He's not a zombie, he's…"

She turned away. "Yeah, yeah. I know exactly what he is."

She had to stop twice as she climbed the stairs back to her room, the cramps in her stomach sharp. She resisted the urge to bend over to ease the pain pulling at her insides. She wished her mum or her gran were there. When she whimpered from the pain, she was glad she was alone after all.

She reached the landing and slipped gratefully inside her room. She was about to close her door when she saw movement farther down the corridor. Someone emerging from another door. One of the veiled servants? No, Lugg.

The boy glanced around, wary. He didn't see Cait in the shadows of her own doorway. He moved away from the staircase, into a part of the palace she hadn't visited. He crept rather than walked.

She paused, her hand on the door handle. She wanted to curl up on the bed and groan quietly to herself. But the boy intrigued her. What was he up to?

He'd said nothing during the meal, but she'd sensed the burning resentment in him. He'd almost lashed out at his father more than once but he'd managed to keep it in check, grimacing with the effort of holding his tongue. But he was up to something, and she wanted to know what.

Lugg disappeared around the far corner of the corridor. Cait set off after him, pulling her own door quietly shut behind her. Her stomach was still cramping, like a fist grasping her insides and squeezing. She tried to ignore it.

She crept along the corridor, keeping to the walls just as Lugg had done, not really knowing why. No one had said she couldn't go there.

She slipped past the door the boy had emerged from and peered around the corner. Up ahead was another stretch of corridor: more white walls, more doors. Hundreds of candles in holders had been lit along it, giving everything a shifting, illusory quality, like a scene from an old black-and-white film. There was no sign of the boy.

She continued, listening at each door she came to, terrified of someone bursting out and asking her what she was doing. Perhaps she could claim to be lost. Put on an act of being dizzy and confused. Actually, it wouldn't be that much of an act.

She came to a door that was open a crack. A draft of cold air streamed through it onto her face. Had he gone that way? No way of telling. But the corridor was a dead-end.

She listened and, hearing nothing, pulled the door open. A flight of wooden stairs spiralled upward. There were no candles. A thin, iron handrail ran around the outside wall. Cait grabbed hold and climbed.

In only a few steps the light from the corridor faded, and she was left in total darkness. She carried on ascending, feeling for each step with her foot. The air smelled of dust, tickling her nose. She peered upward, but there was no sign of any light. Perhaps he hadn't gone this way.

She was already panting, but still there were more stairs. Endless stairs. If you fell on a spiral staircase would you tumble all the way down or would the turn stop you? She hoped she wouldn't find out.

She was about to give up and retrace her steps when she discerned a faint glow from above. There was a noise, too. A rustling accompanied by a pattering, scratching sound. Something was scrabbling around up there. Several things maybe.

She clutched the seeing stone in her spare hand. It made her feel better. A little better. She thought about her gran. Her gran wouldn't turn around and run. And she, Cait, wasn't going to either.

She climbed a little higher and peered over the top step. A faint light from the full moon filtered in through a series of small, arched openings in the walls. They were large enough, maybe, to put an arm through. It was a circular room, and the openings went all the way around. The air smelled of feathers and straw, overlaid with the faint tang of decay.

She knew where this was. She'd spied this spire from her window, watched as birds flapped in and out through the openings. It was the tallest tower in the palace. The undain appeared to use the birds for communication: instead of carrier pigeons they had carrion crows. Greygyle had called it *The Rookery*.

The rustling sound came from the centre of the room, where a tower of little boxes stood, each open at the side. Roosts for the birds. Occasionally one hopped down in a flurry of feathers and skittered around on the wooden floor, searching for a better perch or pecking at food. With a jolt of alarm she saw that one of the flapping birds was little more than a patchwork of bones and flesh, just as the bird by the standing stones had been.

It took her a moment to see that a shadow beside the roosts wasn't a shadow, but a person. A person quietly sitting there, watching her. Two sparks of moonlight pinpricked his eyes.

"You followed me," said Lugg. His speech was a little slurred. It had to hurt to talk.

"Sorry, yes," said Cait. "Not in a creepy way, obviously."

"Obviously." His voice was heavily accented like the Duke's, but he spoke good English. Someone had schooled him well.

"Mind if I sit down?"

Lugg shrugged. "Can't stop you, can I?" He was little more than an outline as she sat beside him. She could hear his faint breathing. Night air streamed in through the archways, wonderfully cool, bringing with it the faint scent of cut grass and night-blooms.

"What are you doing up here?" she asked.

He didn't reply for a moment. "Nothing. I come up here to think. To look. You can see for miles up here, all the way to the mountains."

"But it's dark. You can't see anything."

He shrugged again. "I like it here. No one else ever comes here. Until tonight, anyway." He glanced aside at her, his features catching the light. Underneath his swollen features he was a good-looking boy. Not in the glossy-magazine way Greygyle was handsome: there was something vulnerable in Lugg's features. Perhaps it was the bruising that marred half his face.

"I'm sorry for what your father did to you," she said. "Was it because of the Spirit?"

"How do you know about that?"

"I just heard some had got lost."

"Lost, yeah. You could say that. I was bringing the whole month's supply and the cart crashed."

She decided not to tell him she'd been there. "Not good. And now you're in big trouble?"

Lugg snorted in amusement. "You have no idea. The entire family apart from *him* will have to slumber in the catacombs until our next delivery. The others are just as bad. When they wake up they're all going to take it out on me."

"But he – the Duke – there's enough Spirit for him?"

"Oh, of course. Anything else is unthinkable. The rest of the household can go without, but not him."

"But the servants?"

"Tiny drops. Enough to keep their limbs moving."

"But you can't just let him beat you. It's wrong. It's abuse."

Lugg didn't reply for a moment. His breathing became a note louder in the twilit room.

"I'm not stupid, you know," he said at last.

"What do you mean?"

"All that talk about looking for a site for a new palace. All this concern for me. It's complete nonsense isn't it? You're not here for that at all."

Was it that obvious? How much had he guessed? And

if he did know the truth, what should she do? Silence him somehow?

"I don't know what you mean," she said. It didn't sound convincing even to her.

"Oh come on. It's obvious. Your father is a Baron from the *other* world. He has to be someone the king really trusts. Yet here he is, wandering around in the middle of nowhere, without any plans for places to stay. I don't think so. And then you happen to faint near *our* palace and have to be brought here."

"Actually, that is all kind of true."

"Whatever you say."

She dreaded to hear his answer, but asked anyway. "OK, what do you think we're doing here?"

"You're obviously spying for the Holy Court."

"*Spying?*"

"Obviously. But don't worry, I have no idea where the Smouldering Fire are or who Phoenix is."

Relief flooded through her. Lugg didn't know who they really were and why they were there. "You think we were sent by Menhroth?"

"There's a war coming. Everyone knows it. The last thing the King needs is a rebel army marching on the White City while his soldiers cross the An. He's afraid of the Smouldering Fire, and he's sent you to find them. You and others, no doubt."

"I've no idea what the *Smouldering Fire* even is," said Cait.

"Of course you haven't."

"Are you saying it's a rebel army? How big? Enough to defeat Menhroth?" A faint hope awoke within her. Nox had been right, although she wouldn't admit it to him. They did need help. The thought of having allies – a whole army of them – was delicious.

Lugg shook his head. "You're not a very good spy, you know. I think you're supposed to subtly trick me into revealing what I know. Not just *ask* me."

"Perhaps it's a clever double-bluff." She grinned, hoping to show him she was joking. It didn't seem to work.

"Look," he said. "I really have no idea. I've heard the same rumours you have. The Smouldering Fire has been growing in strength for years. Phoenix is simply awaiting the right moment to attack. Some even say they've got dragonriders among them; that the wild wyrms of the high north have returned to Angere. Who knows? All I know is Phoenix doesn't live anywhere round here."

"But this army exists?"

"So people say."

This was getting her nowhere. "I'm not working for the White City, I promise. I'm not spying on you. I'm not going to tell them about you."

"Whatever you say. Actually I don't care if you do. By the time you're back east I'll be long gone."

"You're leaving?"

"I'm going to join them. Join the rebels. Try and find them, anyway. There you are, I've told you. Feel free to inform your masters. Frankly I don't care any more."

"But your father. Your family. They're all undain. You want to fight them?"

"I despise him and all the others." The boy spoke freely now, in a sudden rush, the pain in his face forgotten. "I was brought up by monsters, Cait. Monsters who survive by sucking the life from others. Do you have any idea what that's like? I would destroy them all if I could. I'd do it right now. You know what I want? I want to live a normal life. I want to fall in love with a girl and watch my children grow up. I want to grow old. And some day I want to die. After a long and happy life, with my family gathered around me. A family who might actually miss me."

She touched his mind, very lightly. There was an edge to it, a hardness that made her think of his father's steely eyes. The rage within him was clear. He *did* hate the undain. Hated them with a burning fury. What must it have been like growing up there? Give her Manchester any day.

"Do you know what the worst of it is?" he asked.

"What?"

"It's the way they assume I want the same as them. They talk so happily about the rituals and how wonderful it will be. My own family want to kill me and resurrect me as one of those vile *things*. And I'm supposed to be delighted at the prospect."

Silence filled the round room at the top of the tall spire. Even the birds had been quieted by his outburst. She took a decision. Maybe it was the right thing to do and maybe it wasn't. But there was no one else to take it.

"My father isn't really my father."

"What?"

"The Baron. Nox. He's not my father. Actually, I kind of hate him, too. But the truth is we're here to try and destroy Menhroth. Destroy the undain."

"How could that possibly be true?"

"We came through a portal from our world. A portal Menhroth doesn't know about. There's a stone circle in a valley."

"You've been to the stones? The wyrm road?"

"That's where we landed when we jumped through."

"Why would I believe you?"

"I can prove it." She pulled her mobile from her pocket. It was still switched off to preserve the battery, but she carried it out of habit. "This is called a *mobile phone*, Lugg."

He leaned over to look at it. "Pretty lame. You should upgrade."

"You know what mobiles are?"

"Obviously. What do you think we are? I have whole *lessons* in your culture. Pretty boring a lot of it is, too."

"OK, fair point. But I have pictures on here that will prove what I'm saying."

"Pictures of what?"

"It's a long story. But you know about the book, right? The Grimoire?"

"Obviously."

She held up the picture for him to see. Danny's hands were visible as he held the book up in front of his face. She'd taken it that day in his room, just before they'd tried to burn the book. "See? Here it is. It was hidden in our world. There are others who are taking it to Andar right now. To fight Menhroth."

Lugg didn't speak for a moment. "It's just a book. The cover of a book. It could be anything." He didn't sound completely sure. He wanted to believe her. He took the phone to study the picture more closely.

"It's the Grimoire, I swear. I mean, look at it, all the skulls and skeletons. We're here to get the other half. To take it to Andar to reunite it and…" she'd spoken before she'd thought what she was saying. The look of astonishment on the boy's face was clear in the glow from the mobile.

"I shouldn't have said that," said Cait. "Seriously, forget I mentioned it."

But that wasn't what had stopped him. He turned the phone round to show her. He'd been flicking through her pictures. He'd stopped on one she'd taken in the Forest of Dean as they hacked through the undergrowth. A lake sparkled in the distance between slopes of trees. At first glance they looked like any family out for a pleasant walk.

"This," said Lugg. "This man standing beside you. He's a dragonrider."

"Ran, yes. He came from Andar and then to Angere."

"He's *here*?"

"Sure. Somewhere outside. I don't exactly know where. He's sort of protecting me."

Lugg's hand was shaking as he studied the picture. "You're speaking the truth," he said. "You're actually speaking the truth."

"Obviously. Thanks for doubting me."

"A dragonrider," continued Lugg, as if the idea was too incredible to grasp. "From Andar." He looked puzzled for a moment. "Why is he protecting *you* specifically?"

"That's part of the long story I mentioned."

A look of suspicion crossed Lugg's face. "This isn't a fake is it? I know you can alter these pictures. Is this all part of your plan to lure Phoenix into the open?"

"No. Trust me, I'm really not big on plans. I'm basically making this up as I go along. It didn't even occur to me you knew what a dragonrider was."

"Of course I do! They're our legends. Our heroes and heroines. And here's a real one. Don't you see? This changes everything. This is ... wonderful."

"But you have riders here, too. The ones who stayed behind. I heard the story."

Lugg shook his head. "No, no. They're no longer what they were. They're corrupted, monsters. This Ran is a true rider. He could open up the wyrm roads. He could... He could..."

A coarse grating sound interrupted him as a large grey bird clattered in through one of the archways. In a flurry of wings it landed on the ground and cocked its head on one side to regard them. It was a tattered mess. A faint alarm wormed through Cait as she saw the bones jutting from its feathers, smelled the stench from it.

"That's odd," said Lugg. "That's not one of our birds. It must have flown through the night to get here. It may even have used the wyrm roads. They have some that can do that now, scraps of dragon bone spelled into them to awaken the old magic."

Cait's throat had gone dry. "Is there a message?"

"Around its neck."

Carefully, Lugg reached out to unclip a metal ring from the bird. The crow watched his hand with beady-eyed malice, ready to strike at any moment.

"It's from the White City," read Lugg. "For the eyes of Duke Greygyle only."

"We have to open it."

"Why?" Lugg sounded suspicious again. "Is it a message for you?"

"No. But I think it might be about me."

Lugg considered. "Guess I can't get into any more trouble." He pulled out a little curl of paper and unfurled it, holding the message to one of the archways to catch the light. Finally he looked up at Cait.

"Oh," he said.

"What is it?" said Cait. "What does it say?"

He looked up at her. "It says they're coming for you. West from the White City, travelling with all speed. A host of them. Imperial Cavalry, two squadrons of Bone Dragons. We have to look out for a girl and two men. Renegades, enemies of the undain. You're to be seized if seen."

It felt like her blood was crystallizing into ice in her veins. "When will they be here?"

Lugg was about to reply when a drawn-out screech cut through the night air. As it faded away it was answered by more screeches, rising and falling, coming from all sides of the palace. Some were distant, some very near. Bestial shrieks that were also, clearly, the calls of communication. The look of horror on Lugg's face told her everything she needed to know. "I'm sorry, Cait," he said. "They're already here."

8 – THE ICE HOUSE

Shrieks filled the night air, a wailing that seemed to scrape across Cait's bones, striking discords over and over. Bestial growls joined the cacophony, like some of the more *death metal* bands Danny listened to. The sounds grew louder all the time. Closer.

On her knees, Cait peered through one of the little archways. Banks of lights glowed all around, as if an army was encamped out there.

Lugg scrambled to his feet. "We have to leave. We have to leave right now."

She looked back into the darkness of the loft. "What do you mean *we*? They haven't come for you."

"I can show you a way out," said Lugg. "I can help."

"No. It's not safe. You can't risk it. This is your home. They won't harm you."

"You think? You know what will happen to me if I stay. There's nothing for me here. I told you, I'm going to try and reach the Smouldering Fire. With a dragonrider we might have a chance."

Cait stood, one hand on her stomach, the tugging pains inside her still sharp. She had a headache coming on too, a thick blanket creeping over her brain. She tried to ignore it all. She could think only of getting away from this terrible, beautiful palace and the monsters living in it.

They clattered down the spiral staircase. She expected to find a ring of undain horrors waiting for them at the bottom, all swords and snarling teeth, but the corridor was deserted. They had a few more moments before the Duke found out the truth. A draught of air from somewhere made the candles flicker and dance in their sconces.

"Is there a back door?" asked Cait.

"They'll be watching it," said Lugg. "We'll go to the kitchens. There's a tunnel that leads to the Ice House. It's only used by the servants."

They ran, past Lugg's room, past Cait's room, to the top of the grand staircase. As they reached the landing, the tugging pain in her insides flared up again, making her gasp and stumble to her knees, clutching the carved bone of the banister.

"What is it?" asked Lugg. "What's wrong? We have to hurry."

"Easy for you to say, I…"

She stopped talking. The wrenching pain rose to a crescendo, sharp as knives, as if she were being pulled apart … and then suddenly, gloriously, it was gone. In its place a rush of euphoria filled her, like a golden light switched on inside her body. She gasped with the wonder of it.

There came something else, too: a vivid awareness of her surroundings. She saw everything about her in incredible detail, as if looking through a telescope and a microscope simultaneously. The veins in the back of her hand as she clutched the banister. The gem-like patterns in Lugg's blue eyes as he watched her. The dancing flames of the candles, writhing as if alive. She could hear the beating of her own heart and the pounding of the blood through her arteries. She saw it all with crystal clarity. And, as in the fight outside the factory, when Nox had come for her and Danny, she was within it but above it all, too, gazing down, seeing everything.

This time it went farther. Her senses expanded, an inflating bubble that soon covered things and places she couldn't possibly see. The veiled servants on the floor below scrubbing the mosaic floor with their tiny brushes. A spider scuttling along the edge of the hallway, its tiny mind thinking only of the hunt. Nox and Greygyle in a cellar below that, still unaware of what was happening outside. The drop of red wine that slipped from Nox's mouth as he sipped at the chalice offered to him. The nod of Greygyle's head as he encouraged Nox. The dead eyes behind the lace veil of the servant who stood with them, holding dusty wine bottles on a tray.

On and on she saw, farther and farther, her perception passing through the walls of the palace and into the darkness. Her gran had shown her the undain at the roundabout in Manchester, tried to make her see the emptiness, the void where there should be light. The seeing stone had helped. But now she found she could see them without holding the jewel to her eye. The creatures were perfectly clear: an emptiness in the world where there should have been the mothy teem of the night-time air.

She picked her way among them. Some were brute animals, beasts of burden or ravening attack-dogs clamouring to be unleashed. One or two, commanders and nobles perhaps, loomed with the depths of their intelligence. One, in particular, was a deep well of darkness, threatening to suck her in as she drew near. Surely the commander of the army. With an effort she pulled herself away from him.

The majority of the undain were sentient creatures, but with minds that were limited and enslaved. Soldiers intelligent enough to take orders but not to think for themselves, not to question.

Her mind skipped across them. She caught a glimpse of something in one or two: a flicker of movement in their minds. A flicker that slipped away as she tried to focus on it, like a moth flittering off in the darkness. What was *that?* It was like a little light, a spark of colour.

"Cait? What is it? What's happened?" Lugg was kneeling beside her, an arm on her shoulder, the worry on his face clear despite his swollen features. "We have to hurry."

"The undain," said Cait. "They're out there. I can see them. There are *thousands* of them, Lugg."

"That's why we have to run, remember?"

"Yes," she said, her attention still half-caught by the surrounding horde. She had to get a grip. "Wait, I mean no. We have to get Nox. The Baron. My father."

"You said he wasn't your father."

"He isn't! Look, it doesn't matter. He has to come with us."

Lugg cast a worried glance down the stairs. "Why? You said you hated him."

"Yes. I do. It's complicated. I thought he'd betrayed me, but now I don't think he has."

"You don't sound very sure."

She wasn't sure. But if he *was* an enemy of the undain and they captured him, his fate would be terrible. She'd already let them take Danny. She didn't want to be responsible for anyone else going through ... whatever it was they would go through. Not even Nox. If he was on her side she couldn't simply abandon him.

She closed her eyes and found him again, laughing with the undain lord over some jest. Cait touched his mind, seeking for answers. It felt wrong. Intrusive. She had no right to do this. Still, she had to know and there wasn't much time.

He was slightly drunk from the wine. That made it a little easier. His mind was always a glass wall, like he had some magical protection or was very well trained. Probably both. She managed to slip beneath his woozy surface thoughts, a knife slicing through fog, searching for the real *him* beneath.

For a moment, the briefest moment, she saw him. It was like flicking the light on and off in a room and having that instant to take everything in. She caught only that glimpse, but there could be no doubt. Beneath his calm, cold exterior, his self-control, Nox was terrified. Terrified of Greygyle even as they joked and laughed together. Terrified of what would happen to him. Terrified of the undain.

Then, seeing her intrusion, Nox reacted. His mind snapped shut, closing itself off from her.

Was he filled with terror that Greygyle would learn the truth about what they were doing? Or was it something else, a fear that other schemes wouldn't unfold as he wished? His mind was a network of plans, layers of deception, bluff and double-bluff. He was a spider in its web, legs feeling the threads for signals. There were depths there. Subterfuges she couldn't discern.

This was the Nox that had run Genera. Had he really changed? She couldn't be sure. But his terror was clear, the scale of it boiling away inside him.

Her connection to him was severed as he threw her out of his mind, furious at her invasion. She clung on a moment more. She had this brief chance to save him. To save him or to fall into his trap.

She chose. *Nox, we're leaving. The undain are here. They know. Get away. Down to the kitchens. Now.*

She fled from his mind, back into her own body. She stood, hauling herself up by the banister. She was slightly out of breath, but there was only the faintest discomfort in her stomach at the magic she'd worked. The light glowed within her still. She felt strong. For the first time in a while, she actually felt great.

"OK," she said to Lugg. "He'll find us. Now let's get out of here."

A bell began to toll: a deep clanging from one of the high spires. It echoed off the white walls. A moment later, knocks thundered on the door.

The army from the White City could have bludgeoned down the door, bludgeoned down the *walls* if they wanted. Deference to Greygyle and his house stayed them. It gave her a few precious moments. On the ground floor, a veiled servant floated toward the main doors to admit the soldiers.

"This way," said Lugg.

They fled from the staircase, farther down the corridor. It looked like another dead-end, but Lugg cut through a doorway from which a flight of steep steps led downward. These were plain and narrow, the walls undecorated and yellowing. The stairs and corridors used by the servants. She'd seen something similar back home, when she and her mother visited country houses on Sunday outings. The stately homes that were, in fact, two separate houses intertwined. Two sets of rooms with two sets of inhabitants who only rarely met. The grand, decorated chambers of the lords and masters. The plain, cramped quarters of the servants. They had their separate floors and their separate doors. And their separate staircases, like this one.

Cait and Lugg raced along a bare corridor and arrived in the kitchen. It was a cavernous room filled with shelves and jars and copper pots and dead game birds hanging blank-eyed by their broken necks. The steamy air was layered with smells of spice and cooking meat and the delicious aroma of baking bread. One entire wall was occupied by a towering iron stove, a fire raging away behind its grill. The heat coming off it reminded Cait of the furnace back in the factory. The furnace whose fire had taken her father and into which she and Danny had hurled the book. That already seemed like a long time ago even though it was only a few days. A few insane, terrifying days.

Seven or eight undain servants drifted around the kitchen like ghosts, carrying pots and pans between the oven and a large wooden table in the centre of the room.

Why were they cooking? What did they do all day? Of all the inhabitants of the palace, only Lugg ate food as far as she knew. It was like the undain were going through the motions of running an aristocratic house from back home. Greygyle aping the ways of the other world he appeared to be fascinated by. But it was a pantomime. A sham. It wasn't like that back home any more.

Lugg pointed to a low wooden door in the corner. "Go that way. It runs underground for fifty yards then emerges in the Ice House."

"Now you're not coming?"

"I'll follow. I've thought of something we might need."

"What?"

"I'll only be a few minutes." He hared off without replying, back to the stairs they'd come down.

Could she trust him? Was he really trying to help her? She was beginning to doubt everyone. The place was getting to her.

As she waited, a clock on the wall whirred into life and chimed the hour with a cracked, metallic ring. As one, the servants stopped what they were doing and looked up. Silently, they began to move. Some of them carried *serious* chopping knives. Cait stepped back, thinking they were coming for her.

Instead, they filed toward a wooden rack on the wall beneath the clock. Hundreds of small glass ampoules stood on the rack, tiny bottles of a bright blue liquid. One by one, the servants picked an ampoule, snapped off its glass neck and, lifting their veil, drank a few drops.

She watched their faces as they sipped. For the briefest moment, their lifeless eyes flared as the liquid trickled into them. Then their expressions faded to drab lifelessness. They lowered their veils and returned to their duties.

She thought about smashing the bottles there and then. It would be easy. They probably wouldn't even try to stop her. But what would become of the creatures? Without their infusions they'd die, fade away, crumble to dust.

Would they know anything about it? Would they feel pain? Maybe. Even if they were mindless machines now, they'd been people once. She couldn't do that to them, deprive them of the Spirit that kept them moving. Although, wasn't that the point of all this? Putting an end to the undain? Which meant putting an end to these slaves as well as the high and mighty lords and kings.

She couldn't bring herself to do it. Instead, watching the servants warily, Cait edged around the room to the wooden door. A rusting iron bolt kept it locked, but she slid this back easily enough. None of the silent servants tried to stop her.

Through the door, a tunnel led into the darkness, the air cold and smelling of mud. It seemed like she was forever having to creep or crawl through tunnels since this whole thing with the book had started.

She'd wait a few moments for Nox and Lugg. What was going on up there? If they weren't there soon she'd go without them. A line of bells hung on the opposite wall of the kitchen, each with the name of a room underneath on a little brass plaque. Each bell pivoted on a coiled spring and was attached to a chain leading through the ceiling. Two of the bells clanged as she watched. She couldn't read the words beneath, but she didn't need magic to know what was going on.

Greygyle had learned the truth and was summoning his servants to find her. The veiled servants turned to see which bells were ringing. A third and then a fourth bell shuddered into life and jangled.

She was about to back into the tunnel when footsteps pounded down the corridor. It was Nox, alone as far as she could tell. He emerged into the kitchen and for a moment, the fear she'd sensed in him was clear on his face. Then his old swagger returned. He strode toward Cait, ignoring the servants.

"The kitchen," he said. "Why are we in the kitchen?"

She could smell the wine on his breath. She ignored his

question. "We should never have come to this house. It was an insane thing to do."

Anger flushed across his face for a moment, but he kept himself under control. "What was I supposed to do? I wish I knew how the White City found out about us. Greygyle was beginning to open up to me."

Was it the dead bird she'd seen at the stones? Maybe. She wasn't going to admit that to Nox.

"We have to get away," she said. "Lugg showed me this tunnel. And he says he knows something about Phoenix."

"Lugg? You think you can trust the boy?"

"Not particularly. About as much as I trust you."

A smirk passed across his face. He probably practised it in the mirror. "So now you're saying it was worth coming here after all? Just like I said?"

She was thinking of a suitably scathing reply when Lugg clattered down the corridor, running at full tilt. He burst into the kitchen. "They're here. Searching the rooms."

In his arms he cradled a sword: a vicious looking weapon with a snaking blade. It was far too heavy for him; he was barely able to lift it.

There was no time for further questions. Cait turned and stepped into the darkness of the tunnel. A thin light from the kitchen revealed a sloping floor paved with smooth cobbles. Nox shut the door and darkness consumed them.

"I have a torch on my key ring," said Nox. "Or we could wait around while you try and witch-up one of those little lights?"

She didn't rise to it. Maybe sarcasm was how he coped with fear. And maybe it wasn't. "Yes, shine your torch," she said. "That would actually be useful."

Stooping in the cramped, damp tunnel, they shuffled forward in the bubble of shifting light from Nox's torch. She reached out with her mind to find the massed undain. Perhaps they were only a yard or two above their heads.

The mind-expanding moment of clarity she'd experienced had receded. She could sense only a blurred mass of undain. Perhaps the thickness of the ground above them muffled her senses. She needed to know where the tunnel would take them. What they would face when they reached the other end.

"What is an Ice House anyway?" she asked over her shoulder.

"It's a house for ice," said Lugg. His voice was strangely intimate in the enclosed space, as if he were whispering in her ear,

"Why do you need a house for ice?"

"To keep it cold. Obviously. We don't have fridges or electricity like you. We prefer to stick to stylish, old fashioned technology that doesn't actually work."

"So you put ice into a damp cave to keep it cold?"

"Just as people used to in your world. We have big blocks of it delivered from the north. There's not a lot of it left by the time it gets here. That's why it's so precious."

The air was certainly freezing enough to make her toes go numb. They splashed through pools of water. Nox's torch showed stone walls coated with green. Here and there, sconces for candles had been set into the walls, the algae thick around them as if it clustered there for warmth. Cait waded through an ankle-deep puddle and then the floor sloped upward again. Her felt squelched unpleasantly in her shoes.

"What's with the sword?" said Nox from the shadows. It sounded like he didn't trust Lugg at all. "Are you planning to take on all the undain when we get out there, boy?"

"Not me," said Lugg. "This is a dragonrider's sword. We have a collection of them from the old days, but this is the best. It's very old. The Duke will be furious when he sees it's gone."

"I think he's going to be fairly furious anyway," said Nox.

"Why do you even have it in the house?" asked Cait. "Shouldn't the dragonriders have it?"

"I told you, they're not true riders," replied Lugg. "When they submitted to the Ritual they lost everything they were. The dragons would no longer allow themselves to be ridden. All the riders' ancient magics failed or turned against the corruption. The riders couldn't even wield their ensorcelled blades any more."

"Their what?" asked Cait.

"Their magic swords," said Nox.

Fer had told her about Ran's sword. He'd used it to wedge a grille shut in the cellar of the library in Manchester. Their swords were precious to them, made for each individual. And he'd thrown it away without a thought to save Fer.

They emerged into a square room, the walls stone and the floor mud. A cube of ice stood on a stone plinth. Shards had been chipped off it by the servants and a puddle of mud surrounded it as it melted and dripped. Beyond it lay a low wooden door. Cait walked past the ice and gripped the handle.

Lugg stopped her with a hand on her arm. "It's going to be dangerous out there, Cait. Best I go first."

"You?"

"I'll protect you."

"Lugg," said Cait. "When you studied our world, did you cover sexual equality at all?"

"Huh?"

"You know, equal rights, all that stuff?"

"Uh, yeah. I think so. I may have skipped a few lessons."

"Good. Well, here's the thing. It's sweet of you, but you don't have to protect me because I'm a girl. And you don't get to tell me what to do, OK? That's how it works in our world."

He looked genuinely confused. "But ... I've got a sword."

"A sword you can barely lift."

"And I know the ground out there. I know the best route to take."

"Sure. But I know where the undain are. More importantly I know where they *aren't*. Do you?"

"Well I was hoping they wouldn't see us."

"Then it's best I go first, isn't it?" said Cait. "And don't worry, I'll protect you."

She caught a glimpse of Nox, grinning at her. She ignored him. Lugg looked like he was about to reply then thought better of it.

Cait turned and reached out with her mind into the night beyond the stone walls of the Ice House. The undain were there, some only becoming visible when they moved. She stood for long moments, studying the visions in her mind, looking for a safe path through. It wasn't going to be easy. Most of the undain were behind them, thronging around the palace walls. But there were sentinels dotted around out here. Lugg might need to use his sword after all.

"Is your gun loaded?" she said quietly to Nox.

"I've got a few shots left."

"Don't fire unless you have to," said Cait. "That will bring them all running."

"What a good job you mentioned it," said Nox. "I was about to race outside firing."

She ignored him. "Walk quietly and follow me. The undain are everywhere but we might be able to thread our way between them. If we can get far enough without being seen, maybe we'll have a chance."

"But if you can sense them can't they sense you?" asked Lugg.

In truth she had no idea. "Perhaps. Perhaps not. Depends how powerful they are."

Without waiting for further objections she pulled the door open. It was fully dark outside. The Ice House lay in a steep-sided dell in the ground. Black trees encircled them, leafless branches silhouetted against a starry sky. Cait crept forward, feeling her way through the night with her mind's eye, trying at the same time not to trip over a root and sprawl in an embarrassing heap on the ground.

There was an undain presence about twenty yards away in the trees. She could feel its seething hatred, but it didn't appear to be aware of them. A foot-soldier. She was about to move on, search farther afield, when she caught the flicker of light in the undain's aura. This time she glimpsed a rapid blur of faces, sounds, colours. She saw what they were. *Memories*. Echoes of the life the undain had once lived.

She turned aside and stepped carefully away. Nox and Lugg followed. They worked their way up the sloping side of the pit and weaved between the boughs of the trees. She caught a glimpse of the undain she'd sensed, a distant shape between the trees, impossible to say which way it was facing. It made a snuffling, snarling sound, like some hungry beast.

She moved on, treading as lightly as she could, terrified of snapping a twig like people always did in the movies. She counted seven or eight of the undain in the immediate area, arranged in a rough arc. She headed for the biggest gap in the ring.

Could any of them sense her? Nox kept his mind closed off, guarded. She needed to do the same, although she had no idea how to go about it. Another thing she should have been taught. She tried to imagine glass windows and walls, anything that represented a barrier, but had no way of knowing if it had any effect.

Like this. Hide from them like this.

The tiny voice from within her was unexpected. Bethany. Bethany was showing her how to work the magic. Bethany who'd spent so many years hiding beneath the cobbles of Manchester.

Cait let Bethany guide her. There was a brief pinch in Cait's insides as the witch-girl worked the magic, but it faded immediately. The spell put up a wall of thin fog around her mind, obscuring her. It was like looking at the world through frosted glass. Standing up close she could see through it, but anyone looking at her would see only vague shapes. It wouldn't hide her completely but it would help. This was clearly something she had to practise, get a whole lot better at if she were to have any chance of surviving in Angere.

Thank you, she said.

Just get away, said Bethany. *Get away from here as fast as you can.*

They crept from tree to tree, moving as quickly as they dared. More snuffling grunts came from here and there in the darkness, but no alarms were sounded and no one came running. They reached the last of the trees without being seen. Beyond lay a sea of darkness, fields and lawns by day. There was one undain nearby, the last guard in the ring, but it appeared to be unaware of them. Behind them, the house blazed with candlelight and lamplight, beautiful as a fairy palace.

Cait shivered, peering into the darkness ahead, deciding which way to go. And her mobile chose that moment to sound its *low battery* bleep.

"No. Damn. No."

As she fumbled to turn the device off, the nearby undain snarled. It stamped forward, snuffling the air, a deep growl in its throat. She could see the shape of it moving toward them between the trees.

Nox raised his pistol while Lugg struggled to raise the sword. Cait's mind spun. What had she done? What should they do? The monster was coming straight for them. There was no way they could hide.

Then she saw it. The glimmer of memory in the void of the creature's mind. Could she use that? Was it even possible? She could think of nothing else.

She reached into the approaching undain's thoughts. It was like diving into a pool of freezing water in a lightless room. For a moment she was lost, drowning, the void sucking at her. Then she saw the light again. It bobbed and danced away. It was such a thin, weak flame, barely there at all. She willed herself toward it.

She caught an echo of something from it: confusion mixed with fear. Again and again it was eclipsed by the all-encompassing hunger of the undain's mind, the yearning to snuff out all the light in the world.

Then she saw the speck again, nearby now. It was beautiful up close: all oranges and reds and swirling yellows. As gently as she could, she reached out to touch it. The light dimmed but stayed where it was, allowing the contact.

Help me, she said to Bethany. *Help me do this.*

Hurry, hurry, said Bethany. *Here, like this. And this.*

Between them they peeled away the layers of the light, teasing it open like the bud of a flower. More and more colours flashed. There were sounds, too. Shouted words, brief bursts of laughter. A woman's kiss. Cait carried on peeling, revealing. Then with a blinding flash the speck of light exploded. The whole of the undain's mind was flooded with colour and light. A jumble of sensations rang out: faces, voices, cries, more laughter.

Cait fled the undain and looked through her own eyes again. Their attacker lunged at them, a snarling beast that was all teeth and claws. It was carrying a sword big enough to slice through all three of them in a single stroke. But the creature stopped as if it had struck an invisible wall, a look of shock twisting its features. It dropped the blade and studied its own hands as if seeing them for the first time. It began to scratch and scrabble at its own flesh. It sank to its knees then crashed to the ground, writhing and mewling in agony, thrashing around as if a swarm of wasps were attacking it.

For a moment, no one spoke.

"What did you do?" said Lugg. The horror in his voice was clear. "How did you do that?"

The undain continued to flail on the forest floor, oblivious to them, seeing only the visions filling its mind. What would her gran say to what she'd done? That she'd freed the poor creature from its fate or subjected it to terrible torment? Cait watched the creature lashing around and didn't know what the answer would be.

"I showed it what it had become," said Cait quietly. "I let it see itself."

"Dear god," said Nox, staring at the writhing creature on the ground.

"Let's get away from here," said Cait. "Even if no one else heard, something might have sensed the magic being used."

She turned and had walked one step when a sudden blur of movement flashed through the night air. Where a moment before there had been only darkness, a figure now stood before her. An old man, bent over, frail looking. A large key hung about his neck, seeming to weigh him down. His eyes were milky white as if he were completely blind.

She wasn't deceived for a moment. She could sense the seething malevolence of his mind. This was no foot-soldier or mindless beast. She could do nothing to defeat or trick this one. This was the howling presence she had felt before.

The leader of the army.

The old man bowed his head to them. "Welcome back, Lord Albion. And welcome to you, Cait Weerd. My name is Lord Charis, Holder of the Keys, Guardian of the Aether, Prince of the Holy Court of Menhroth the Undying. Truly I am delighted to meet you."

9 – WYRM ROADS

Nox stepped toward the ancient undain and kneeled. "My Lord Charis. As instructed, I've brought you the witch from our world. I've brought you the heir of Ilminion."

The undain sent a white light above his head, illuminating the scene with a harsh glow. The branches of the trees loomed over them as if leaning in to listen. Distantly, Cait was aware of Bethany screaming. She'd walked into Nox's trap after all. He'd manipulated her, brought her to this palace and summoned the undain to come and take her. How could she have been so stupid?

But Charis was shaking his head, looking down at Nox with indifference, apparently able to see him despite his opaque eyes. "Still playing your games, Lord Albion? Do you think you can manipulate me? That you can buy your way back into the King's favour even now?"

Nox stayed where he was, staring at the ground. "I've only done what I had to, to find the witch and bring her to you. What alternative did I have? She escaped with the help of others and I was thrown out of Genera as a result. The only way I could bring her here was to pretend to befriend her. Surely you see that, my Lord?"

Charis laughed a dry, humourless chuckle as if he had stones in his throat. "And now you wish to accompany me to the White City, yes? To resume your place as our trusted agent in your world?"

"I do, my Lord."

"And why would I agree to this?" asked Charis. "We have the girl now. You offer us nothing. And another now acts as our eyes and hands among your kind."

"Who?"

"I think you know."

"You mean Clara? Ms. Sweetley?"

"Just so. Your former underling now runs Genera. So you see, we have no further need for you and your games, Lord Albion."

"But I think you do," said Nox. "The shadow path we used to come here. I can show you it. It is a threat to Angere. Only two of us came through this time, but others could follow. A whole army could march upon you while you gaze east across the An."

Chris shook his head, as if disappointed. "Oh, I intend to find out all about this gateway, seal it or make use of it. These western lands are riddled with the ancient wyrm roads. But I don't need your help for any of that. I don't need you for anything."

Charis waved a hand. Three giant soldiers appeared from the darkness. They wore silver and brass armour, but their heads were bare and the skin of their faces was like glass: completely transparent, like some classroom anatomy model. A light glowed from within their tissues, illuminating the workings of their muscles. The white orbs of their eyes swivelled within their sockets. Dark lines decorated their skin – if it even was skin – the patterns similar to the spiralling tattoos on Ran. Each of the three held a serpentine blade, although they were far larger than the one Lugg carried. They could only be wyrm lords. Dragonriders. Or what the dragonriders had become in Angere.

"Inform the Duke of Greygyle his spawn has been located in the company of the renegades," Charis said to them. "Bring him to me now. When I am finished with him you will take these three to the White City with all haste. Kill the males if you must but the female must be kept alive. Winter is drawing on and time is short. I shall take the army west to this stone circle in case more have come through. Inform the King I shall return to the An as soon as possible."

One of the dragonriders bowed and hurried away.

"Lugg has done nothing," said Cait. "He didn't know about us. I asked him to show me around, show me a way outside and he did. There's no need for him to be taken, too."

Lord Charis's parched little laugh sounded again. "Oh, I think there is, daughter of Ilminion. He is well-known to us: a sick, deluded child, imagining rebellions and revolutions where there are none. Strictly speaking he is too young to undergo the Ritual of the Seven Ascensions, but I think we can make an exception in his case. It will do him good to be ritually slaughtered."

"Never," said Lugg. "I'll kill myself first."

"Oh, no need, my young friend," said Charis, delighted with himself. "We do all that for you."

The ancient undain stepped forward and studied Cait, seeming to sniff at her. Something about the pallor of his weathered skin made her want to retch again. "So, here you are at last, Cait Weerd. You have caused us much difficulty, you and your brood. Rest assured when we kill you there will be no ascension, no eternity for you. It is your blood we want, nothing more. You are the carrier, girl. The container. The vessel. Once we have what we want you will be discarded. Do you understand?"

She tried to summon some terrible magic to strike back at him. Tried to find the ice within her to blast at him, hurl him away from her. But there was nothing. The presence of this ancient creature numbed her utterly, stilling her power. Bethany was only a silence inside her.

Instead she spat at him. Futile, but it made her feel a little better. "You're a creep, you know that?" she said. "You're hideous. You're sick, all of you."

Charis simply smiled. "I believe the boy said something similar. Just before the end."

"Wait, Danny? You saw Danny?"

"Of course. He lived for a while. But he refused to answer our questions or he couldn't answer our questions. It amounted to the same thing. He mewled and begged to be saved. I imagine you will, too."

She threw herself at him then, thinking to punch him, kick him, hurt him. She didn't get close. Some barrier stopped her and she could only stand there, flailing uselessly at thin air.

"We may meet again at the White City," said Charis. "If you live that long. If not, farewell. And thank you for bringing us what we needed."

Charis stepped away to give the other two dragonriders their orders. Nox rose from his knees and, not looking at Cait, stepped backward to stand beside her, head bowed.

"What the hell was that?" she spat at him. She was furious now, didn't care who heard. "You turn me over to them as soon as you can?"

"Don't be an idiot," replied Nox in a conspiratorial voice. "I was trying to gain an advantage. I wasn't turning you over."

"Really? It damn well looked like it to me."

"Do I really have to keep explaining this to you?"

"No, Nox. You don't have to explain anything."

The Duke of Greygyle appeared in the half-light, pushed forward by the rider who had gone to fetch him. He stumbled toward Charis, then bowed low and stood with his head down. Charis completed giving his instructions to the riders then turned his attention to the Duke.

Cait couldn't understand the words Charis spoke but

the venom in his voice was obvious. He clearly blamed Greygyle for harbouring Cait and Nox. The tirade lasted several minutes, during which time Greygyle continued to stare at the ground, unmoving.

Eventually, when Charis was complete, Greygyle bowed as if agreeing with everything that had been said. Charis cast a final glance back at Cait, then strode away into the night, not looking back.

When he was gone, Greygyle flared a light of his own. His face was ugly with fury. Not speaking, he walked directly up to Lugg and struck him hard with the back of his hand, dashing the boy to the ground.

Lugg sprang up and prepared to launch himself at his father. But one of the riders intervened, putting himself between Lugg and Greygyle, one hand on the pommel of his sword.

Greygyle turned away from Lugg. "And you, Lord Albion. You betrayed my hospitality. You betrayed *me*. You've placed me in a very difficult situation."

"Not as difficult as my situation," said Nox.

"Even so. I hope they take you to pieces when they get you to the White City. I hope they do so slowly in payment for what you have done here."

Greygyle glanced at Cait. He looked like he was about to say something to her, too, but then thought better of it. Scowling, he left for the palace, the dragonrider who had brought him following closely behind, sword drawn as if shepherding a prisoner who might bolt at any moment.

The two remaining guards stood in discussion for a moment, one giving instructions to the other. Cait kneeled beside Lugg. Blood flowed from the side of his mouth. Another wound to add to his collection. She tore a strip from her ridiculous white gown and handed it to him to press onto the cut. He thanked her with a nod of his head.

"What were they saying?" she asked Nox. "What will happen to Greygyle?"

"Difficult to say," said Nox. "He may survive. He may

be stripped of his land. He may simply be denied supplies of Spirit and left to wither and fade."

"He blames us."

"He's right to," said Nox. "Isn't that why we're here?"

"Of course. Yes. What else did Charis say?"

"He's commandeered Greygyle's prize horses. They're to take us back to the An with all speed. The dragonriders will run and only those horses will be able to keep up. The King wants us in the White City tomorrow. Wants *you*, specifically."

"Right. Great."

"What's the problem?" said Nox. "We are trying to get to the White City, aren't we?"

"Not like this."

The rider giving the instructions nodded his head to the other and marched off into the night, heading for the fairy-lights of the house. The other planted his feet and stood, sword drawn as if expecting them to flee at any moment.

Could they escape with only one rider left to watch them? Somehow she didn't think she could work magic powerful enough to freeze or destroy the creature. She tried searching into the rider's mind for a speck of memory she could work with, but got nowhere. There was no mote of light in that void.

"I really wasn't betraying you," said Nox quietly.

She didn't reply for a moment. "I know."

"You do?"

"You said *two of us* came through. You didn't tell them about Ran. I was just mad at you. Mad and scared."

Something of Nox's cockiness returned. "Well, as long as you admit you're mad, I'm happy."

Cait ignored his sarcasm and extended her senses into the darkness. She could feel the army beginning to mobilise. Groups of undain were sweeping away from the palace with unearthly speed, heading west. She felt the raging void that was Charis departing with them. Without him, the darkness of the night seemed almost bright. Did

Charis really believe some army was about to come through the stone circle? It wouldn't take him long to discover there was no threat.

"We have to do something," she whispered to Nox, "We have to get away."

Nox hadn't moved. He still spoke in a low voice, always watching their dragonrider guard. "We'd have no chance against him. Bullets, magic, nothing can touch them. Believe me. Perhaps once we're on the horses we can get away somehow. Await our moment."

Cait frowned. The urge to fight, scream, do *something* was overwhelming. But she was also aware that the rider would happily kill Nox and Lugg if he had to. She couldn't endanger them, not again.

In that moment of indecision it was Lugg who acted. He'd been lurking in the shadows, nursing his wound. But suddenly he sprang forward, screaming with fury. He charged at the dragonrider, the ancient sword held forward as if he'd put all his strength into this one, desperate act.

For the briefest moment the rider didn't react, and Cait thought Lugg might hit home. Then the rider swung his great blade, scything it through the air. She thought he was going to kill Lugg with that single blow, but instead the rider hit the boy with the flat of his sword, swatting him sideways.

Lugg landed in a crumpled heap. The rider stepped over to him, kicking the boy's legs to see if he got a reaction. Lugg didn't move. The rider knelt to push Lugg onto his back. Cait expected to see a wound, pooling blood on the ground.

Instead, Lugg came to life. With a cry of desperation he swung the sword he still carried, aiming it at the dragonrider's head. She knew it was futile. The rider's magical defences, his superhuman reactions, would protect him. Even if Lugg struck, he surely wasn't strong enough to do any real damage.

But, incredibly, the blade bit, and the dragonrider flew

backward through the air, like some superpowered kill in a computer game.

The rider shrieked in agony. As he crashed to the ground, the swirling lines on his face burned a furious red, a fire raging through them. Smoke coiled off his head and a sickening smell of singed flesh filled the air.

Cait stepped backward in horror. The rider clawed at his skin as he flailed, flames licking him. He managed to rise to his knees, features invisible in the fire, then crashed to the ground. He twitched once and lay still. The red fire about his head faded and died but dirty smoke coiled off him.

For a moment no one moved. Lugg, still lying on the ground, seemed as astonished as everyone at what had happened.

"How did you do that?" asked Cait.

"I just hit him with the sword," said Lugg. "I didn't think it was going to work."

A light of hope flared within her. Charis, clearly, hadn't even considered it possible they could defeat one of the riders. Now they were alone. Now they could get away.

She was about to haul Lugg up to his feet when she heard the sound of horses approaching at speed. She readied what threads of magic she could muster, expecting Charis to materialise from the darkness at any moment. But instead it was the other wyrm lord riding Greygyle's eight-legged steed, the two six-legged beasts pounding along behind. All the horses were saddled, ready to whisk them eastward to the An.

The rider, taking in the scene, pulled the horse to a halt and slid to the ground. Not even breaking stride he leaped toward Lugg, sword swinging. Once again, the boy raised the ancient blade. This time the tip was visibly shaking as Lugg struggled to hold its weight.

She had to do something, the rider would surely kill the boy. She could think only of unleashing more ice. She had to at least try. She summoned the cold from inside herself, preparing to hurl it at the undain. Working the spell was easier than it had been. Each time she tried it was easier. Was that good or bad? No time to consider now. She put all her strength into the magic, desperate to stop the rider before he reached Lugg.

The cold storm raged within her. The pains in her stomach grew but they were bearable. When she could contain the fury no more she hurled it at the rider. At the same time, Nox fired his gun, two shots and then a third.

The icy blast struck the rider square in the back. He staggered, but regained his balance. The black lines around his head flared as if they were absorbing the magic. Channelling it. Then they returned to normal. The undain glanced backward, creamy eyeballs rotating horribly in their sockets. Whether Nox's bullets had struck him or not she couldn't tell.

The rider turned away, clearly not considering her or Nox a threat. He towered over Lugg. With a swift movement he kicked away the sword Lugg held with an armoured boot, sending it spinning into the darkness.

Lugg tried to crawl backward, away from his attacker. The fear on his face was terrible, his eyes wide and panicky. Nox fired again, aiming for the rider's head. Once again it had no effect. The rider held his sword over Lugg and prepared to deliver the killing blow. His great sword arced downward.

There was a flash of movement in the shadows to Cait's left. For a moment she thought Charis had returned after all. Then she glimpsed a tattooed arm and it was Ran, hurling himself at the giant undain dragonrider. In his hands he wielded Lugg's sword.

Ran dashed the undain's sword-blow aside with his own blade, a jarring metallic *clang* ringing in the air. Ran whirled away. He danced around the giant undain, blade darting in and out, seeking an opening. Where Lugg's movements had been clumsy, Ran's were sure and elegant. But the undain rider was twice Ran's size and many times stronger. His reach was far greater, too, and suddenly it was Ran on the defensive, jumping and wheeling out of the way as the undain rider scythed his blade from side to side.

For a moment the two dragonriders, human and undain, circled each other, testing each other's defences. Then the undain struck, blade moving too rapidly for Cait to even see. Ran's back arched like a cat's to avoid the blow. Not quickly enough. The blade caught his side and he crumpled to all fours, all grace suddenly lost. The undain lunged immediately to finish him off.

A shout of warning rose in Cait's throat as the great blade came down. Only then did Ran's intention became clear. As the undain swung, Ran rolled aside and in a single fluid motion leaped to his feet. The manoeuvre placed him inside the arc of the undain's sword, too close for it to hit him. Ran's own blade jabbed upward.

The undain flinched backward but it was too late. With a sickening crunch, Ran's sword struck.

As before, the undain was hurled backward with explosive force. The lines on his head flared livid red and burst into flame. The rider screamed and crashed to the ground, beating at his own face to extinguish the sudden fire. In a moment he stopped moving, no more than a smoking lump on the ground.

Everything went dark as the fire died. Cait worked a small, pearly light while Nox switched on his torch.

Ran, crouched in a cat-like stance, sword held at the ready, unfolded and stood. He nodded to Cait and Nox as if he'd simply bumped into them in the street, then reached down to offer Lugg a hand.

Astonishment lit up the boy's face. Astonishment and something else, too. He looked at Ran with something like awe. Cait had seen that look before, usually when one of her friends got within touching-distance of a pop star.

Ran pulled Lugg to his feet and murmured words to him, holding him by the arm as he did so. Whatever Ran's words were, they made Lugg glow with delight.

"We have to get away from here," said Cait. "They'll know magic's been used even if they didn't hear. That demon will be back for us."

"The horses," said Lugg. "We'll take the horses. They can run like the wind. You don't want to know how many real horses my father butchered to create them."

The horses bridled and reared at the smouldering bodies of the two giant undain. Despite their nature they clearly retained normal horse instincts.

Lugg took their reins, stroking their bucking necks. The horses calmed at the familiar touch but their ears continued to swivel. Lugg led them forward, talking to them all the time.

Like horses back home, their muscled bodies and huge hindquarters ended in delicate ankles that made them look almost awkward. It would surely be different when they ran. They were creatures of speed: beasts that only *made sense* in full gallop. Especially the nearest one with its eight powerful legs. The magnificent animal towered above Cait. It stamped on the forest floor to be away, eyes as pure white as the rest of it. It could have torn itself away with ease and thundered off, but it tolerated Lugg's reassuring presence.

"Can you ride?" Nox said to Cait.

The fabulous horse was a long way from the plodding pony she'd once sat on. "I'll manage."

She heard a shout of rage, and it took her a moment to understand that it wasn't a normal sound. None of the others had heard it; she'd felt it with her mind. *Charis.* He'd realised what had happened. Realised his mistake. He'd return at any moment in a blaze of fury. Half the army were continuing to race westward, but the other half, Charis at its head, was flying back to the palace.

Ran put his hand to the eight-legged beast's muzzle, stroking the creature's head, murmuring to it. Then he stepped around and leaped onto its back, sitting tall and proud. Nox took one of the six-legged horses, perhaps the one he'd ridden in the hunt. Lugg hesitated. They had only three horses for four people.

"Ran," said Cait, "Can that horse carry two?"

They didn't have to know she couldn't ride. She gesticulated to him to convey her meaning. Ran nodded and reached down a hand for her. The horse's back was wide and smooth, easily big enough for both of them. Ran gave her the saddle and positioned himself behind her, feet sharing the stirrups. She clutched the reins and the scratchy hair of the horse's mane, the ground scarily distant. Lugg climbed on to the other horse.

"They're coming for us," said Cait. "We have to get going."

"Which way?" said Nox.

"North," called Lugg. "Follow me."

The horses leaped into motion, racing from the lights of the undain palace. Air streamed into Cait's face as the horse's eight legs clattered faster and faster, rattling her and making her bite her tongue. You had to move with the horse, she remembered that much from her brief lesson. It was better for rider and mount. She tried to relax, let her body flow with the creature's movements. It didn't help much; she kept getting the rhythm wrong and falling when she should have been rising.

They picked up more and more speed, trees and hedges flashing by in the darkness. Her gown gave her little insulation from the rush of cold night air. She no longer bothered to maintain the werelight. As well as their extra limbs and their prodigious speed, the undain horses seemed to have been imbued with some extra sense that allowed them to run in the dark. More than once they flew over an invisible hedge or ditch, Cait struggling to suppress a cry of alarm as she was lifted from the horse's back. Ran, saying nothing, took hold of her robe to help keep her on the horse. If it had been Nox she'd have objected, but the dragonrider's reassuring grip was welcome, as was the warmth of his body behind hers.

The world became a blur of speed: glimpses of trees and hedges and walls as they thundered forward. She quested with her mind into the darkness, seeking for the pursuing undain. She didn't have to look hard. They were a vast shadow behind them, like storm clouds massed on the horizon, rolling forward with terrible speed. Could the horses outrun them? Even if they could, where were they going to run to? They couldn't keep going forever.

"Where are we heading?" she shouted, but her words were whipped away by the streaming wind. She switched to using magic, finding the little lights in the darkness that represented Nox, Ran and Lugg. She called to them, repeating her question.

Nox, glancing over at her from atop his lurching mount, frowned, as if resenting the intrusion. But Lugg replied. He was probably used to magical communication.

The wyrm roads. Perhaps with Ran here we can make them work.

The wyrm roads? she asked. Where are they? What are they?

You've seen them already. The rider's ancient pathways. They're our only hope.

How far?

Several hours, even at this speed.

Ran did something with his legs and the horse accelerated even more, surging forward across the landscape with dizzying speed.

The journey seemed to last forever. Pain jarred through her seat and back with each stride, despite all her efforts to move in time with the horse's gait. She gritted her teeth and clung on, the world filled with the *huffing* of the horses, the thunder of their hooves and the sweet smell of their sweat. After an hour or so a full-moon rose, impossibly large on the horizon. It shone like a vast spotlight picking them out. The white flanks of the horses glowed. It seemed they flew through a sea of moonlight, the hard surfaces of ground and trees vague and distant.

The undain were still out there, their massing fury clear, but they were getting no closer. For the moment there was nothing she could do.

At one point she heard a whispering presence in her mind, very weak. She'd felt something similar before, when the Bone Harvesters came and she'd had the weird sensation of a ghost passing through her mind. Was she under attack? Was this Charis or one of the other undain lords creeping into her thoughts? With an effort she cast the presence away, refusing to allow it inside her. She waited for it to attack again, for its tendrils to come creeping through the night to find her. But there was nothing. Perhaps she'd banished it, or perhaps she was exhausted and imagining spectres that weren't there. She put it out of her mind, and concentrated on moving with the lurching horse beneath her, trying in vain to ease the agonies pounding through her.

The sun was lightening the eastern sky when they finally stopped. Ran slid from the horse and offered her a hand. The drop to the ground was alarming. The three horses steamed in the dawn light, veins bulging, great limbs twitching at the effort of their gallop through the night.

Her legs were as stiff as wood and her back and bottom were raw with pain. It felt like she had a whole collection of bruises that had joined up into one enormous *throb*. She tried not to let her discomfort show as she worked some life into her body, stretching her back and rubbing her legs.

She reached out with her mind to find the pursuing undain. They were there, but more distant than they had been. The horses had bought them a little time.

Five of the vast stone archways stood in a ring around them: one complete, three half-ruined, and one little more than two crumbling stone pillars. Ivy wound about them, covering them, slowly picking them apart with their patient tendrils. Stone carvings adorned each column, although the shapes were weathered into obscurity now.

So *these* were the wyrm roads. The archway she'd seen back near the stone circle. And again on the hilltop. Somehow the dragonriders had used them to travel around. *These western lands are riddled with the ancient wyrm roads.* Lugg had said something about the carrion crows doing the same thing to carry messages across Angere.

Ran was staring up at the ancient stones, eyes narrowed. Lugg stood beside him, pointing out details, explaining something.

"What are they saying?" asked Cait.

"Lugg is explaining he's come here often, to try and make the gateways work," Nox replied. "Once he thought he saw something, like a mist in one of the archways, but nothing happened when he walked through."

"Then how do they work?"

"I think they just *did* for the ancient dragonriders. That's why the archways are so vast, they're big enough for dragons to fly through. But they stopped working when the riders underwent the Ritual. When the dragons and everything turned against them."

"So with Ran with us we just walk through one of the archways and escape?"

"That's the theory. The problem is they don't know which. From what they're saying, Ran's people have no memory of where the roads led. Once there were maps, but they're long lost. The people of Angere now know only one or two of the pathways."

"So if we take the wrong one – if they even work – we could end up in the White City or something?"

"Yes."

She considered. The horses had bought them these few moments, but the undain were closing in rapidly. Charis must know they'd stopped. She had to do something.

"I'll go and see if I can work out which archway to take then, shall I?" she said.

"You?" said Nox. It was clear from his voice that he

didn't think she'd be able to do any such thing.

"Me," she said. "You can, I don't know, stand guard or try and think of something useful to do while I'm working."

Without waiting for a reply she strode toward the complete archway. It towered above her. A rook had nested on top of it among the matted ivy. Through the arch, the grass plain upon which they stood stretched toward a line of low hills. There didn't appear to be anything magical about the ancient stones. Was this really going to work? She shivered in the dawn air.

When she was sure no one was near enough to see, she pulled out her phone and powered it up. The battery was down to a couple of percent. For a moment it seemed it didn't even have enough electricity to start.

Finally the familiar screen with all her apps appeared. With trembling fingers, expecting the device to shut down at any moment, she scrolled to the icon of the stylised dragon and touched it.

The screen went black and for a moment nothing happened. Then the bookwyrm appeared, strolling across the screen, its body lines of gold and purple and red, like something from a medieval manuscript. An *archaeon* Fer had called it, a creature that dwelled within books. Or within the ideas written in books. Fer had brought it from Andar, and in Manchester it had discovered the delights of the internet and uploaded itself, replicating itself as it infiltrated servers and devices the world over. Cait had downloaded this avatar during the car-chase into Manchester with Johnny Electric. She was glad she had, now.

Keeping the phone's volume low, she began to talk. "Can you hear me, noble Archaeon?" She tried to adopt the tone her mother had used back in the Forest of Dean. It wouldn't do to upset the creature. There was no time for games.

The creature slowly turned its head and let out a plume

of stylised red flame. A cartoon dragon breathing cartoon fire. "Hmm, no phone signal, no WiFi. Not even any GPS satellites. So you're stuck in Angere, are you?"

"Yes, noble Archaeon, We…"

"And let me see. You've awakened me because you urgently need my help, is that it?"

"Yes, that's it."

"And you do realise that without a connection to the net I am cut off from the world's data? That even I may not be able to tell you what you need to know?"

"Yes, yes, I get it. Still I hoped…"

"Also you do know your battery is down to 1%, don't you? You do know this device is going to shut down at any moment?"

"Yes, that's why I need you to answer *now*." She had to resist the urge to shout into the phone.

"Then why don't you stop beating about the bush and ask your question?" said the bookwyrm. It lay down on its belly and snorted out puffs of smoke, as if utterly bored.

"When you travelled from Andar with Fer," said Cait, "the other witch, Hellen Meggenwar, lured you into a book."

"Ah, she did," replied the dragon. "She knows my weaknesses that one. All the countless books in the tunnels beneath Islagray Wycka and she chose…"

"Yes, yes. A book mapping the shadow paths. Fer explained it to me. The thing is, do you have that data with you? Did you download it when you installed, or is it only on the internet back home?"

"Such a rare and precious tome. All the pathways mapped out, with notes in so many hands on the exact means of opening and closing each. A book I've been wanting to explore for years. Centuries. As Hellen Meggenwar well knew. It…"

"Do you have that information with you?" Cait hissed.

"Of course I do," said the dragon. "What do you think I am?"

"OK. Good. And did the book map out the dragonriders' wyrm roads?"

"The ancient network of pathways criss-crossing Angere that allowed the dragonriders to fly instantly across the whole land?"

"Yes. Those. Tell me!"

"It did. So you're planning to use one are you? Interesting. And Ran is still with you is he?"

"He is. But the thing is, we don't know which archway to try. There are five of them in a circle here. We want to go north, but for all we know the northern archway goes east or something."

"Fiveways, yes. One of the main crossing-points in the wyrm road network. Very well, to go north you want to take the north-western archway."

"The north-western one? You're sure?"

"Of course I'm sure, little witch. I'm always sure. But whatever you do…"

The voice from her phone cut off as the battery finally died. Cait slipped it back into her pocket then turned to face the others, wondering what it was the dragon had been about to say.

"This one," she said, pointing to the ruined archway that stood opposite the rising sun.

"That one?" said Nox. "How do you know? How can you possibly tell?"

"Didn't I say?" Cait replied. "I'm a witch. We know these things."

She reached out with her mind to find the approaching undain as she strode toward the archway. For a moment she thought the army had vanished completely. Then she saw why she'd missed them. They were no longer in the distance.

They were there.

The monsters flowed over the ground with phenomenal speed, or appeared to simply materialise from nowhere. They surrounded the ring of arches in a few moments. There were hundreds of them. Thousands of them. Wyrm lords, soldiers, snarling beasts of war she couldn't begin to identify. And, at their head, framed by the archway they were supposed to pass through, Charis. The elongated shadows from the archways reached out to touch them.

For some reason the undain weren't coming any nearer. Perhaps some ancient warding magic kept them back, as it had on the roundabout back in Manchester. Perhaps she and the others were safe within the ring of ancient archways.

Then Charis worked some magic she couldn't identify. She could feel the depth of power to it, although Charis didn't appear to be at all inconvenienced. A white lightning arced from his outstretched hand, passing from arch to arch in the ring about them. In a moment, the light faded. It seemed nothing had changed. But then Charis walked forward. As he moved, the entire army moved with him.

"Run!" Cait shouted.

She sprinted *toward* Charis. It felt like an utterly insane thing to do. Was anything really going to happen? The land on the other side of the stones looked no different from the ground inside the circle. There were no magical lights, no distant realms visible through the archway. There was only the undain horde, closing in on them.

The bird on top of the other archway croaked.

"Ran! We have to go through together!"

Ran appeared beside her, loping along to match her pace. Lugg and then Nox hurried forward next to him. In a line, they sprinted toward the ruined stones of the ancient archway, toward Charis and the waiting undain army.

10 – THE SMOULDERING FIRE

There was a moment of disorientation that felt like tripping and falling, then Charis and his clamouring horde winked out of existence. In their place stood a mountain range Cait had never seen before. Snow-capped, jagged peaks massed higher and higher as they marched into a far distance. The air was cold, grasping her in an icy grip.

She wheeled about, expecting to see the undain come flooding through after them. A low sun shone directly at her through the archway they'd emerged from, limning the tall pillars with gold, making detail beyond hard to discern.

Ran, Lugg and Nox stood beside her. Lugg glanced at her in triumph at what they'd done, but Ran, dragonrider's sword in hand, stood as if preparing to fight the entire undain army. Nox was frowning, troubled by something. No one spoke. There was a moment of utter calm as they waited for their pursuers to arrive. But nothing moved in the whole world, save for a distant bird flapping its way through the glowing dawn.

"We have to keep going," said Cait. "They'll follow us. Charis worked some magic, broke down the barriers so he could enter the ring of arches. I felt it."

"No, no, we're safe here," said Lugg, his breath billowing in a mist as he spoke. "The wyrm roads only opened for the dragons and their riders. That's how the ancient magic worked. To be honest, I wasn't completely sure jumping here would work, but…"

"You weren't sure?" she replied. "You didn't think to mention this?"

He grinned like it was all some great joke. "We didn't have much choice. It was this or be taken to the White City. And I've read everything there is to read on the riders of old. All the lore and legend. The roads had to open because Ran is with us."

Cait hugged her arms about herself. She was already shivering. The white gown they'd given her was useless, offering no warmth. She wished she'd thought to fetch the outdoor clothes they'd bought in Dublin, but they were somewhere back in Greygyle's palace. She wouldn't see them again. Still, the chill was strangely refreshing, making her thoughts sharper.

"We should have brought the horses with us," she said.

"No point," said Lugg. "They needed their infusions of Spirit."

"But where will they get that back there? They're miles from home."

"The undain might supply them. If they don't, the horses will sag and crumble into dust before the day is out."

The thought of that was hard to take. They were such beautiful creatures, fabulous beasts that had borne them safely across Angere and stayed ahead of Charon all the way.

"We can't just let them die."

"They're undain, too," said Nox. "Letting them die is the whole idea."

"Yes, yes. Still, they didn't ask to become what they did. They're victims, in a way."

Nox shook his head as if pitying her. "So perhaps we

should stop trying to defeat the undain and befriend them, is that what you're saying? Understand their problems? Respect their rights?"

She forced herself not to reply. Instead she turned to Lugg. "We're still in Angere, though, aren't we? Even if Charis can't use the wyrm roads he can move at incredible speed. He can get to us."

"Caer D'nar," said Ran from beside her. He nodded toward the jagged mountains.

Lugg said something back she didn't understand, but she heard the same phrase repeated several times.

"What are you saying?" asked Cait.

"Caer D'nar," said Lugg. "The ancient fortress of the wyrm lords. The old stories say it lies in these foothills, on the edge of the Northfang Mountains. Or, looking at it from the perspective of the dragons of the high north, on the edge of the inhabited lowlands. Ran says he recognizes the scene from some old tapestries he's seen. And the rumours all say this is where we'll find the Smouldering Fire."

"But that makes no sense," said Cait. "If there were a rebel army here, Menhroth would have come long ago to destroy it."

"The Dragon's Tongue," said Nox, as if he'd just worked something out, too. "We've crossed the Dragon's Tongue haven't we? That will protect us."

Cait looked from Nox to Lugg to Ran. "None of you are making any sense, you know that? What the hell is the Dragon's Tongue?"

"A river," said Nox. "Just a tributary of the An, but still huge. It flows out of the Northfangs and cuts east, flowing for hundreds of miles. And Caer D'nar lies north of it."

Cait shielded her eyes and squinted south, through the archway. It was still impossible to see any detail in the blinding light. The land that way appeared to be flat, with only a few indistinct hills here and there. But something sparkled in the far distance, something that might have been a river.

"These lands are where the riders of old lived," explained Lugg. "They're part of Angere but separate, too. From here the dragons flew along the wyrm roads, defending the land from anyone who threatened it."

Lugg walked up to the stones of the archway and touched them. The carvings were cleaner up here, the details sharp. Flying dragons had been cut into the stones, bodies entwined around runes she couldn't begin to read. Frost gilded them as if they sparkled with diamonds.

"The sagas describe scores of dragons soaring around these peaks," said Lugg. "Vaster than a flock of birds, to turn the air to thunder. Wings eclipse the moon and sun to rule the wide lands under." He sounded like he was quoting some poem or story. "Imagine seeing that, Cait. Imagine the blast of their passing as they roared through this gateway."

"Sure, it would be cool," said Cait. "But it's ancient history, it doesn't help us."

"History doesn't just stop," said Lugg. "The story is still being told. Five hundred years ago Ran's ancestors fled to Andar, leaving everything behind. Leaving even their dragons behind. And now things have come full circle. A dragonrider has returned to Caer D'nar, in the company of a witch who carries the blood of Ilminion in her veins. Who knows what's possible now?"

He looked like he really believed what he was saying. Surely he didn't think life was that simple? A few coincidences, a few old stories and everything would work out fine? He was a dreamer, his head caught up in his ancient stories. And that was something she admired in a way. But they had to face facts.

"Look, fine," said Cait. "Perhaps you're right. But we can't just stand here talking about it."

"We should head north," said Lugg. "Try and find the tower of Caer D'nar itself."

"Yes. Let's do that."

Nox shrugged as if it didn't matter one way or the other. Which, quite possibly, it didn't.

They set off from the archway, past the ruined remains of an ancient guard tower, its walls mostly collapsed to strewn stones, its doorway an empty archway leading into shadows. Cait half-expected someone or something to come flying out to attack them. Ran strode on ahead, apparently eager to reach the mountains. He studied the peaks as he went, like he was expecting to see creatures soaring around them.

Nox caught her up. "Here, Cait. Wear this. I can see you shivering from here."

Nox didn't have his outdoor gear with him either, but he'd at least thought to bring his black jacket. He put it around her shoulders.

"It's leather," said Cait. "I am a vegetarian you know."

"I'm not asking you to eat it."

"And I'm not some damsel in distress who needs looking after."

"Oh, I know," replied Nox. "Trust me, I know. Just take it, OK? When I start going blue you can give it back to me."

The jacket was still warm from Nox's body. She tried not to think about it. "Tell me about the Dragon's Tongue. How exactly does a river protect us?"

"You don't know?" said Lugg, walking on the other side of her.

"We don't have many magical rivers or mythical beasts in Manchester."

"You're sure of that are you?" said Nox.

"Look, just explain to me. I don't see how a river gives Andar or us any protection. I don't see why the dragons couldn't fly across the An with Ran's ancestors, for that matter."

"Magic can't cross flowing water," said Nox. "When I asked Genera's finest scientific minds why, they basically shrugged and said *because*."

"It's because running water leeches magic away," said Lugg. "Flying over a river is not like flying over solid ground, even for a dragon. Magic flows *from* the earth, and running water stops that working. That's why the undain can't reach Andar. That's why the riders' dragons couldn't either. Not even the ancient ones could achieve such a feat."

"But that can't be right," said Cait. "A witch from Andar, Fer, told us two undain flew across the An to reach them."

"Across the An?" said Lugg. "That's impossible."

"So they all thought. Until it happened."

"She's right," said Nox. "One of the undain entered our world from Andar. It had flown across the river."

"When was this?" asked Lugg. He sounded shocked.

"About a week ago."

"But that's…" Lugg tailed off. He frowned, like he was trying to do calculations in his head. "I mean, the amount of Sprit needed would be incredible. It would be enough to supply Angere for years, all used up at once."

Cait thought about the great pipeline in the refinery. The global network of collectors and pipes Ms. Sweetley had described. And she thought about how many people there were back home. Billions of them. And the screens she'd glimpsed in the refinery, scenes from all over the world of fires and wars and riots.

"The Spirit you receive," she said. "Those metal churns in that cart. You do know where it all comes from, don't you?"

He didn't reply. She could see from his eyes that he did.

"Menhroth has been collecting Spirit from our world for centuries," she went on. "That's how they were able to cross the An. All that suffering and pain piped in from our world." She glanced aside at Nox, but he was looking down at the ground and didn't catch her eye.

"But why?" said Lugg. "Why would they go to so much effort? Two undain is hardly an invasion."

"The book, of course," said Cait. "The half that was taken to Andar and then to my world. They wanted it before the main assault."

All Lugg's earlier delight at the opening of the wyrm roads was gone. "And did they get it?"

"Not yet," said Cait. "Not when I left, anyway. Although the undain were there, pursuing those with it."

Lugg didn't speak for a moment as he thought about what she'd said. "They say these mountains go on forever," he replied eventually, looking beyond Ran. "Maybe Menhroth doesn't know where Caer D'nar is. Maybe he won't be able to find us up here. Maybe we'll be safe."

"Menhroth has dragonrider guards," said Cait. "Of course he knows where this fortress is. Or at least where it was. He'll guess we've come here and come looking, however much it costs." She glanced at Nox again. He would know more about a lot of this than she did.

"She's right," said Nox. "Most likely they already have more flying undain constructed as part of the invasion. They call them dragons, you know. Some time very soon they'll come for us."

"How long?" asked Cait. "Hours, days, what?"

Nox looked thoughtful. "Necromancy that powerful takes time. Power has to be dripped slowly into the creature's bones so they have a chance of surviving the crossing. But a few days, a week maybe, and they'll be here."

"So, wait, you knew?" said Cait.

"Knew what?"

"About the undain they created to cross the An. You knew where all that Spirit was going. You knew what Menhroth intended for Andar."

"Of course," said Nox. "Although it was a surprise when the undain turned up at the Central Library. But I could hardly run Genera without knowing what Angere wanted. We had to make plans, build infrastructure, recruit the right people."

"You sound like some company executive building a chain of factories or something."

Nox shrugged. "That's what I was, pretty much."

"You didn't stop to think what you were actually doing? All that suffering?"

"Look, Cait, I'm sorry. No, I didn't. I told you. Running an evil empire is actually a whole lot of fun. It's an absolute blast. You get to do whatever you like. Of course I didn't question what I was doing. I was having the time of my life. I'm sorry, but that's the truth."

They trudged along in silence for a while after that. The ground rose slowly toward the slopes of the mountains. At least the effort made her a little warmer, although her toes were tingling into numbness.

Every now and then she stopped to peer back the way they'd come, but there was no sign of pursuit. Nor could she sense any undain anywhere. Up ahead, the peaks grew taller and taller, as if they were only then being pushed up from the ground. She couldn't pick out any towers or fortresses among them. Most likely this Caer D'nar had crumbled to dust centuries ago.

She thought about Danny, and Charis's words. *The boy said something similar just before the end.* The thought of it was too much to take in. It was this terrible weight in her mind she kept creeping toward and then fleeing from. Danny was dead. Stupid, funny Danny and his stupid, funny jokes. How could he be dead? She never should have gone to his house, never should have asked him for his help. His parents would be going crazy by now, and that was all her fault, too. The icy air froze the tears she cried as she stumbled forward. She almost wished the undain would find them again, so she didn't have time to think about him.

She returned Nox's jacket after a few hours. Despite Ran's fast pace, Nox was shivering slightly, his teeth gritted. He hadn't said anything. Lugg was marching on ahead with Ran, engaged in some long conversation she couldn't understand. She stopped while she slipped the jacket off. The cold was immediately intense, sucking the warmth from her.

"What do you think we should do?" she asked Nox.

"You want my opinion?"

She wasn't in the mood for more confrontation. "Yes. I have no idea where we should go next. We have no food and no warm clothes. Perhaps we should have let those riders take us to the An. We're farther away than ever. It seems hopeless."

Nox pulled the jacket on. "We might as well see if this Smouldering Fire exists. If it does they may be able to help. If not, then we know we can use the wyrm roads now. We can come back here with Ran and use them to get to the White City."

"I suppose."

"You can work out the route, can't you? Use your inner eye or whatever it is?"

Somehow she doubted she'd be able to find a recharge point for her phone in the frozen wilds of a magical land. But Nox didn't have to know that. "Of course. If I have to."

"And while we're talking about it, why don't you spooky up some heat? You can do lights, surely a fire can't be much harder?"

"It's not as easy as you think, Nox. Whatever you do there's a cost. A price to be paid. We're not like the undain, burning Spirit stolen from others."

"No, I know. And think what you could achieve if you did. We wouldn't have to *walk* for one thing."

He was joking. At least, she preferred to think he was. They started moving again, trying to keep up with Ran and Lugg.

"How did Lugg kill that rider?" she asked. "He could barely lift the sword."

"I don't think he did kill it," said Nox. "I think the

sword did that all by itself. Because it's a true rider blade and it reacted when it came into contact with an undain wyrm lord. Like it was angry."

"Magic swords. Great."

"It doesn't help us much, though," said Nox. "Not even Ran can defeat an entire army on his own. Although he'd probably try if you told him to."

"The riders who stayed, then. The ones who became those monsters. They lost everything too, in a way. Dragons, swords, the wyrm roads."

"Oh, sure. In return for immortality and superhuman strength. You have to feel sorry for them."

"And what's with their weird transparent skin? They look hideous."

"You know how fanatical they are," Nox replied, keeping his voice uncharacteristically low. "You've seen how Ran is."

"But transparent skin? I don't get it?"

"Apparently there was some doubt about their allegiances in the old days. To demonstrate that they had nothing to hide, they adopted this see-through skin when they underwent the rites."

"That's insane."

"A lot of things here are insane. Their skin became a mark of their devotion so they all ended up doing it. Instead of different-coloured tattoos they have those glowing lines."

"And their dragons. What do you think happened to them?"

"All I know is they flew into the north, away from people," said Nox. "Some reports said they were so broken by the loss of their riders they went to die among these peaks. We'll probably never know. Old stories. They don't make much difference to us."

"No, I suppose not."

"Come on, let's keep up. If you really can't summon up a horse or something we'll have to walk faster."

That evening they sat around a crackling fire of twigs and scrubby branches, gathered by Ran as they walked. There was more smoke than heat to the flames, but Cait was glad of the warmth, however faint. She'd lit the fire herself, after Bethany had quietly shown her how to work a flame. Cait hadn't mentioned to Nox he'd given her the idea.

The dead witch, meanwhile, had sounded more like a little girl again when they'd talked. She'd laughed and giggled as if her dread had lifted in the cold north, away from the undain. Cait had tried to discuss plans with her, decide what they should do next, but she'd got nowhere. Bethany was happy to be away from the undain and simply wanted to stay that way.

Now, Cait sat staring into the smouldering fire, seeing faces appear and disappear in the glow. Ran was off somewhere in the darkness, no doubt patrolling. Nox lay on the ground, eyes closed, possibly asleep. They'd eaten what few supplies Ran and Lugg had been able to forage: bitter, fibrous roots pulled from the hard ground and a few bright red berries that screamed *poison* to look at but which were actually very sweet. She'd eaten them, but in truth she wasn't very hungry, despite the long march.

Lugg came over and sat next to her. He poked the fire for a few moments, rousing it into a little more heat. He looked more sombre than before. Older, somehow. There was something else, too. Like a light in his mind. A secret that almost glowed through his eyes. She had to resist the temptation to delve into him to see what it was.

"I'm sorry for what Charis said," he murmured at last, not looking at her. "About Danny."

Cait didn't reply. She watched as sparks from the fire danced and swirled in the line of smoke rising through the air. The night sky was clear, a swathe of cold stars scattered across the sky. The sparks seemed to rise and join them.

"He was your beau?" Lugg asked.

"My what?"

"Forgive me, I don't always remember the right words. Your … boyfriend?"

"He was. Yes. Just about."

"Such a terrible thing. One of many terrible things. We have to make them pay, don't we? That's all we can do."

He sounded earnest. Deadly serious. He was right, of course. The price had to be paid. Even so, she wasn't interested in revenge. How was that any better? She just wanted this madness to stop. She wanted to go home.

When she didn't reply, Lugg carried on. "Was he a witch, too? A … warlock, I mean?"

"Danny? No. Nothing like that. He was just a boy. He was always pleased to see me, you know? And the thing is, he only got involved in all this because of me. I'm to blame."

"No, I don't think so, Cait. The people from my world are to blame. The necromancy is to blame. You didn't ask for any of this to happen any more than he did."

She sighed. If only it was that easy. "If it wasn't for me he'd still be alive, sitting at home playing computer games or watching football or trading stupid videos with his mates. And instead of that he's lying dead somewhere inside a sick city built of human bones."

Lugg looked like he was about to say something else, then thought better of it. They sat together for a time, neither speaking.

"And what about you?" asked Cait at last.

"What about me?"

"You've lost everything. This morning you lived in a palace, knowing you faced the prospect of eternal life as an undain lord. Now you're on the run with a bunch of renegades from another world."

Lugg grinned. "Honestly? This has been the best day of my life. Admittedly there haven't been many other good ones, but I wouldn't have missed any of this for the world."

"Seriously?"

"Seriously. I told you. I always meant to run away and find the Smouldering Fire. Doing so with you and Ran is more than I could ever have wanted. I don't even know anyone else who isn't one of *them*. Especially not, you know, anyone my age."

He glanced across at her as he spoke. She could feel the excitement flaring inside him. The thrill at what he was doing. She'd touched his mind more than once on the long walk, panicking that she couldn't trust him, that he was still, somehow, in league with the undain. She'd found no hint of deception in him. But there was this *thought* he kept returning to, rolling it over and over in his mind, too deep for her to see.

"You've been talking to Ran a lot," she prompted.

Lugg nodded. "His language is different from that spoken by the ancient wyrm lords, but we can understand each other."

"He said something to you, didn't he? Something important."

He narrowed his eyes as he studied her. "How do you know that?"

"We witches know things."

"Is that how you knew about the cart, when I crashed and lost all the Spirit?"

Cait smiled to herself. Probably best not to tell him they were to blame for that. "Like I said, we witches have our ways."

"So you can see into my mind? Find out what Ran said?"

"Maybe, if I really wanted. But if I did, you'd never trust me again, would you?"

"No, most likely not."

She thought he wasn't going to tell her, but then he spoke again.

"It was that sword, you see. The ancient blade that I brought for him."

"What about it?"

"Their blades were sacred, bound to them. One that old would have been forged in actual dragon fire. And I killed an undain with it."

"Which was amazing. I still don't get it."

"The blades are like the wyrm roads. They only operate for the riders. Don't you see? Only a rider can use one of their swords, and I killed that undain with one. I don't know how I did it, but I did."

"So that means…"

"Exactly. I'm a rider, too. Or I could be. I have the potential. You know I said I once thought one of the archways started to work? When I saw a mist through it? Ran said that was my rider blood stirring. Then when I was faced with that undain it woke within me."

That was it. That was the glowing light of excitement filling his mind. It was everything he had ever wanted, something he had dreamed about for years.

"Were there riders in your family all that time ago?" she asked.

"There were riders in every family. It wasn't a matter of blood. It was a thing some people were born with. Girl, boy, rich, poor, no one could tell who would have the seed within them. Everyone was tested when they were young and those who could bond with a dragon became a rider. To do so was the greatest honour of the ancient world."

"That's great. Incredible. So the wyrm roads will open for you now?"

"Maybe. Ran said I need training and discipline. My powers will wax and wane, so I shouldn't go off on my own or anything. Isn't it wonderful, Cait?"

"It is. I'm happy for you. Only, well, there are no dragons any more, Lugg. You haven't got a dragon and you haven't got a sword and you don't even have the tattoos. Don't take this the wrong way, but what will you be able to *do*?"

Lugg waved all this aside as if it were mere detail. "I

don't know yet. But one way or another Menhroth and Greygyle and Charis and all the others had better look out. A few days ago there were no wyrm lords in Angere. Yesterday there was one. And now there are two. And a witch. Pretty soon we'll be unstoppable."

She didn't contradict him. In his mind there was some great army up there in the frozen wilds. An army big enough to sweep the undain away. It was a crazy fantasy, but she wasn't going to spoil it for him.

She lay down on the hard ground, lying as close to the fire as she dared, and tried to get some sleep. Thoughts of Danny drifted through her mind. After a while she stopped telling herself he was gone, and let herself succumb to her own fantasy.

Some time later, she was dimly aware of Nox putting his leather jacket over her. She stirred and turned over, but didn't fully awake.

11 – CAER D'NAR

That night Cait dreamed of shadows.

They were birds at first: the angular, flapping shapes of crows and rooks and ravens flocking above her. They circled, shadows merging into a whirling black mass, darkening the ground around her like ink. Their wing beats filled the air, loud as the wind roaring in the trees. Every time she looked up to see what they were doing one dived at her, wings tangling in her hair and slapping at her face. More and more birds came. Soon she was the eye of a storm of black feathers, pressing her to the ground.

She waited for their twig-like claws to scrabble at her, for those sharp beaks to peck at her neck and back. But they didn't attack. Their raucous cries were of alarm, not fury. They were trying to rouse her, trying to tell her something. Danger approached, some terrible danger that she had to wake up and face.

Then, as if swept away on a gale, the birds were gone.

In their place came a cold silence: the quiet of a winter's night when nothing moves and the ground is ice. Cait lay on the frozen ground and the cold was a white mist drifting over her. She tried to peer through the mists, make sense of what was happening, but the miasma thickened as if blown in on a wind she couldn't feel. In a moment she could see nothing else. Her world was reduced to a cocoon of white.

The fog moved over her then seeped into her, passing effortlessly through her flesh and bones to freeze her thoughts. Her body stiffened as if she were turning to ice.

Then Bethany was there, a looming face, a hand stroking Cait's hair. Worry creased the witch-girl's features. "The crows, Cait. You must listen to them."

"What's happening?" Cait managed.

"The fog claims you. You have to wake up or you'll never wake again."

"I don't understand."

"You're turning to ice in your sleep. Some cold is too much. You have to wake up."

Cait tried to rise, but her numb limbs refused to respond. "Help me, Bethany."

The witch-girl bent down and breathed into Cait's mouth, as if resuscitating her. The trickle of warmth was welcome. It revived her a little and she tried to struggle to her feet.

"Cait, wait. There's something else." Bethany looked confused, staring into the fog.

"What?"

"Nearby. Very nearby. There's a friend as well."

"Ran?"

"No, no. A different friend. He's real! He's here. All this time I thought he was like me."

"Wait. What? Who's here?"

"Just a whisper in my mind for all these years. But he's here. Come to help. But you need to act, too, Cait. Wake up, now. Wake up. Hurry, hurry, hurry."

With an effort she forced herself from sleep, expecting to find Charis and his undain nightmares surrounding them in a ring. Instead she lay in a pearly white glow. The mist was real, lit by the first light from an invisible dawn. It had crept over them in the night as Bethany had said, snuffing out the fire, sending its tendrils into them.

With a cry Cait scrambled to her feet, limbs awkward and sluggish. She could see nothing beyond the fog. There was no sign of Nox or Lugg or Ran. She had no idea what was out there, what monsters lurked just beyond her vision.

She spun in a circle but it made no difference. Had their attackers crept up under cover of the mist, or had they conjured it? She felt something within the fog. A deep, slow movement. An *intent*. Then she understood. The mist was their attacker. The mist or the thing that looked like a mist.

There was a cold, slow intelligence to it. Slow but vast, as if the whole of the fog was its thin mind. She caught glimpses of the core of its being. Endless and ancient, it drifted over the land, craving the warmth and intricacy of those that fled from it, those who shut it out with doors and windows, or held it back with flames. It had roamed the darkness for countless aeons, its hunger for the heat of life, limitless. And when it found that life, as it had now, it fed. It would drain the warmth from their bodies and minds and offer only ice in payment.

Desperately, Cait tried to find the others in the mists. Rouse them before they succumbed. But perhaps they already had succumbed. She could feel no spark of life anywhere near. Not even Ran, endlessly wary of attack. Perhaps he had seen only a winter's mist and had lain down by the fire to find what warmth he could. Lain down and never stood again.

With a cry of fury and fear, Cait reached for her magic. Ice and cold was how she worked magic, how she understood it, but what use would that be here? She needed fire, not ice. She needed to balance the cold, dispatch it rather than seek it out. She feared fire, everyone knew that, but sometimes you had to use your weaknesses, your fears, rather than your strengths.

She found the remains of the campfire by smell as much as anything: charring wood, the faint scent of burning leaves. She took two steps toward it and could discern, dimly, the glow of its smouldering ash. She worked her magic, sending out whatever power she could muster to fan the flames.

The fire roared blue, burning brightly and driving away the creeping fog. It recoiled as if injured. In the widened circle of light, Ran, Nox and Lugg were huddled lumps on the ground, unmoving.

Then the fire faded. The flames needed something to burn and there was nothing left. The mist closed in again. She felt the slow hunger in it mounting inexorably.

She tried again, fuelling the fire with the strength of her own body, the raking pains pulling at her muscles. The fire flared, but dimly this time, and in a few seconds it was gone. The mist closed about her once more.

She crouched to the ground, holding her stomach against the cramps. She had to fight. Could the mist survive in the daylight, or would it dissipate? If she could hold it off for a few more moments, perhaps the rising sun would come to her rescue. She called on Bethany, and between them they stoked the flames a third time.

It was futile. Even with Bethany's guidance and help she could summon only a brief flicker. Then the mist was upon her, seeping into her, finding her mouth and nose and ears, feeling its way into her mind.

She had come all this way to die in the freezing wastes. The unfairness of it made her weep. People had depended on her and she'd failed.

Then red lights flared around her. Roaring flames swept backward and forward, burning into the mist, brushing it away like an artist repainting the hard details of the world. The fires were torches and hands held them, whirling around to banish the mist. Figures. Men or women, swathed in thick furs.

Cait cried and tried to rise, but the world swam and she

lurched back to the ground. She was spent. All her strength was gone, given to the flames. And something else: perhaps something of that cold fog had seeped into her, numbing her. She didn't know. She fell. But it was darkness, a welcome darkness, that consumed her, not the limitless hunger of the white mists.

Her last conscious thought was that she had to stop passing out like this. It was starting to get embarrassing.

The full warmth of the sun on her face roused her. She sat up with a gasp of surprise. Figures stood around her: the swathed figures she'd seen with the torches. They were all normal people like her. She could sense the presence of no undain nearby. Although, in truth, she felt too groggy to concentrate properly. She studied the figures, trying to understand. She was sure she'd never seen any of them before in her life.

Someone had placed furs over her. Animal furs to keep her warm. Back home she would have recoiled in horror, but she let it pass. Nox and Lugg, a few yards away on the other side of the rekindled fire, were covered up too. Only Ran was awake. He stood stretching his muscles, running through the moves of some exercise regime that was part-dance, part sword-fight. He nodded his head when he saw she was awake but carried on with his routine.

One of their rescuers knelt beside her. An old man, his face lined with deep wrinkles. He was bald, and a gleam of sweat slicked his scalp. There was a clear look of concern in his eyes as he studied her.

"Hello, Cait. It is good to see you."

How come people knew who she was all the time? Did everyone in Angere know about her?

"Uh, hi."

"Are you feeling well after your ordeal? Sun and fire will warm you back to life. You will be as good as new in an hour or two."

That was good to know. She hadn't felt *as good as new*

for a long time. "What was that thing? That mist? Was it some sort of undain?"

"No, no. Something far older. It has drifted around these mountains for years uncounted. It was here before the first men came, and it will be here when we are all dead and gone."

"I felt its hunger. Such a terrible hunger."

"Yes. It is a being of the aether. You have heard of such creatures, have you not? The one Fer summoned into the Tanglewood? This was one of them." The man sat beside her, groaning slightly with the effort of getting to the ground. "Somehow, long ago, it found a crack in the walls and seeped into our world in search of sensation and warmth. Perhaps the wyrm roads attracted it here, summoned it from more distant lands. I don't know. But it's here and there's nothing we can do about it but dispel it when we must. Fire is too much for it. It craves the heat, but it recoils and burns from direct flame." He glanced aside at her, as if aware of the weight those words would carry with her.

Cait, head still full of wool, tried to make sense of everything. "Wait. How do you know all this stuff? How do you know about Fer? And how come you can speak English? Who *are* you?"

"Forgive me. Let me introduce myself. People call me Phoenix. Not my real name, you understand. My real name is actually rather dull. Phoenix is more of a title. Actors come and go but the role remains."

"Actors?"

"I'm the ninth or tenth Phoenix, I think."

"And you're the leader of the rebels?"

The old man smiled to himself as if she had told a joke. "Yes, that's me. This is us. You see about you the mighty warriors of The Freeborn. The Last True Men. The Smouldering Fire."

She couldn't stop herself counting. Apart from the old man there were seven of them. A couple lay on the floor as if exhausted. Others watched over Lugg and Nox. Some were younger, but most were nearly as old as the man. They each had a wiry strength to them, though, as if used to hardship. Were they all people who had fled the horrors of the Ritual to live freely in the cold north? They weren't much of an army, but the sight of them warmed her heart. There were normal people in Angere. Normal, mortal people living out their days free from the Witch King and the undain.

"Not very impressive, are we?" the man said. "Hardly a threat to Menhroth." He seemed saddened by his own words.

"This is all there are of you?"

Amusement twinkled in his eyes. "Oh, no. There are *several* more back at the fortress who weren't well-enough to travel. We saw you approaching and hurried to meet you. It was fortunate we reached your camp just as the aether-being found you. Another few minutes and you would never have awoken."

"But how did you *see* us? And you still haven't explained how you know about Fer. And about me."

He looked a little troubled by her question. "I will tell you. But you must understand I do not like to intrude. I only do so when it seems important. To follow events. I know it's no defence, but I don't ever feel comfortable about what I do."

"I don't get it."

"You remember when Fer explained about the man she met in Manchester. The Lizard King?"

The wise man. He could see what other witches were doing but was powerless to act. "You're like him?"

"I am. Seeing across the aether is much harder. The visions are flickering and confusing, but I have been watching you, off and on. You and your mother and your gran. And Fer." He leaned a little closer so no one else could hear. "And Bethany, come to that."

"Bethany?"

"Oh yes. It is harder with her. She is well hidden. Buried deep. But I see glimpses of what she sees. I know you carry a part of her within you."

Cait nodded. "She mentioned you. Said you'd been a whisper in her mind for years and years. She thought you were a ghost haunting her."

The old man smiled at that. "She thought *I* was a ghost? That's pretty funny when you think about it."

"Actually it's a relief to know you've seen her."

"It is?"

"Well, you know, people who hear disembodied voices in their heads. It's good to know I'm not completely crazy."

"I can assure you Bethany is real. A ghost, a memory, a pattern in the mists, who knows? But sometimes I see through her eyes. See that cold pool in those high mountains. Sometimes I see you there, too. But don't worry. I won't tell anyone your secret."

"Wait, so, you can see back home? You can tell me what's happened to mum and gran and Fer? And Johnny?"

The man shook his head. "Not for some days. The aether is more than usually turbulent at the moment, something I think we can thank Fer for. Seeing across to worlds such as your own is like trying to see through rippling waters. There are broken snatches of sound, disjointed images, but it is hard to make sense of anything. I'm sorry."

"And what about the witches in Andar. Hellen and the others?"

"Glimpses only. I have spoken to Hellen Meggenwar more than once over the years, but not for some time. The An is between us, of course. And all the undain. Perhaps we are both too old and feeble." The sparkle in his eye returned, suggesting he thought they were no such thing.

"But how come you're even here? Why hasn't the Witch King destroyed you?"

"The Dragon's Tongue is part of the reason, as Lugg

there thought. Caer D'nar is another reason. The stones are mostly ruined, now, but there is a lingering power about the place that would keep out all but the most determined foe. But I rather suspect," and here the old man sighed, "that the main reason is that Menhroth couldn't be bothered. We're hardly a danger to him. In truth, I think it suits the Holy Court to have a beacon of hope for disaffected younglings like Lugg. Menhroth and Charis and the rest watch to see who stares wistfully into the north dreaming of the Smouldering Fire, and they know who they can and can't trust. Sometimes I think we should put an end to ourselves to rob Menhroth of our use."

"You shouldn't. You should never do that. You give people hope. You gave Lugg hope."

The old man nodded. "Yes. But sometimes I wonder if that is a kindness or a cruelty. Perhaps people would be better knowing the truth. I'm afraid it is hopeless."

"But Ran is here now," said Cait. "A true dragonrider. That has to count for something. And Lugg, too. He has rider blood in him, so Ran said."

"Is a dragonrider without a dragon truly a dragonrider?" the man asked.

"Well, no. I suppose not. So the creatures are really gone, then? There are none up in these mountains? I thought maybe they'd still be there and we could … wake them. Or whatever it is you do with dragons."

She sounded crazy even to her own ears. A few days ago she'd have said dragons only existed in stories and games. Now she was discussing them quite happily, hoping they existed.

The old man was silent for a moment. He seemed to be deciding how best to reply. "I've never seen any, certainly."

"But you suspect? You know something?"

"No. Not really. Come to Caer D'nar and I will explain what I know. It is little enough. But we are not safe in the wilds. It will be nightfall in a few hours. We can talk properly with the windows shuttered and a fire keeping the cold at bay."

Lugg and Nox were both stirring now, groaning as they stretched stiff limbs. Lugg, opening his eyes, looked around in sudden alarm.

Cait called over. "It's OK. We're not in danger. This is Phoenix. We got close, but in the end he had to come and find us."

She could see that Caer D'nar stood in ruins as they approached. A tall spire of stone remained, jutting up as if to compete with the mountain-tops. But there was ruin all around, the stones of walls and buildings scattered and cracked, as if desperate battles had raged there long ago. The sky was darkening as they approached, but she could see, at the top of the tower, a ring of archways or windows from which a yellow light flickered. A beacon in the darkness, a lighthouse in a sea of mountains. Even from this distance, she could tell that this was no magical werelight. Someone had lit a fire.

Phoenix led them around huge boulders that might once have been sections of massive walls, and approached a steep staircase cut into the rock. It was narrow and rose steeply, twisting around and up the rock-face to reach the foot of the tower. The steps were uneven, and many were so worn that Cait had to scramble upward. In many places there were no steps at all, just the bare rock. It seemed a strange way to reach such an impressive and grand tower. Then it dawned on her. This was not how the dragonriders of old had reached Caer D'nar, they'd flown through those high openings in the tower. The staircase had been cut into the rock some time in the five hundred years since.

It was fully dark when they approached the top of the stairs. Phoenix and his men carried sputtering torches, but these were only bright enough to outline each step in wavering shadows. A gulf of darkness gaped on the party's left, and Cait stayed as tight as possible to the rough rock-face on her right, grasping what handholds she could find when the whistling wind threatened to pluck her off the mountainside.

The long climb had taken its toll on her thighs, the burning in her muscles even distracting her from the raw pains inflicted by the horse. In the darkness, she had no idea how high they'd ascended, but the air was bitterly cold and at one point as she'd toiled upward her ears had popped.

She'd felt the lingering power of the tower's old stones like a hum in the air. Now, touching the massive blocks at its base, the iron magic worked into the stones was clear. There was something about it that reminded her of Ran: that same obsidian impenetrability. There could be no doubt this was the ancient fortress of the dragonriders.

Inside it was in ruins. Huge caverns had been opened in the hillside, leading off from the base of the tower. The carved archways must once have been impressive, like the interior of some great cathedral back home. But more than one of the stone pillars holding up a part of the roof had crashed to the ground, and there were many mounds of rubble.

There were others there, as Phoenix had promised. Nine or ten of them: some standing, most huddling on the ground beneath furs. Old, weary faces. The pinched expressions of those suffering the rigours of some illness.

A whispering passed among them as Cait and the others arrived, and Cait saw they weren't looking at her. They were looking at Ran. They glanced at her but their gaze moved on immediately. What did they see when they saw her? Just a girl. Young, exhausted, in need of a bath. Perhaps Phoenix hadn't told them who she was, why she was there. And she was glad of that, but she couldn't help resenting all the wide-eyed stares that followed Ran as he strode past the prone figures.

In Ran they saw hope.

The halls were cold, and icy draughts blew in from every angle. But in one, as promised, a log fire had been lit. The draughts made it roar with an orange flame. They sat around its heat and ate wedges of dry bread and some sort of stew. It tasted wonderful. Only afterward did Cait wonder whether it contained meat or not. Darkness gathered around them, and the ancient walls seemed to recede into the shadows. Low voices murmured. She wondered how many Angere people, how many generations of people, had trekked north to sit and shiver and be free in these ancient buildings.

She tried to catch Lugg's eye but he was staring into the flames, lost in his own thoughts. He had barely spoken since emerging from sleep. She understood why. He'd imagined a great army up here, and instead there were only these ragged few. What would he do? Become another like these, living out his days? Perhaps. But she caught something in his eyes as he stared at the flames. A spark. Perhaps it was just the reflection of the fire.

Later they climbed to the top of the tower. Phoenix led the way, followed by Ran, Cait, Lugg and then Nox. The ascent up the winding staircase seemed endless, and she soon lost count of the steps. Her muscles were soon burning again. There were no lights apart from the occasional small window open to the night sky, through which a faint starlight shone. The only sound was the scuffing of their feet on the stairs and their laboured breathing. It felt like they'd been climbing forever, the same few steps repeating over and over, when finally an orange light glowed from above. She heard the crackling of another fire. A few more turns, and they emerged into a wide, round room, the night air sweeping in through tall archways. The fire they'd glimpsed burned brightly from the middle of the floor.

"We like to keep it burning up here," said Phoenix. "A beacon, even if there's no one out there to see it."

"The smouldering fire?" said Cait.

Phoenix nodded. "Just so. Although, in fact, we were originally given the name by a witch called Fyr. A play on words, I suppose. She was one of those who unleashed the flood that swept the bridge away five hundred years ago. She found a sanctuary up here in the north, she and the few other survivors."

"What happened to her?"

"Oh, she died of old age."

He crossed to one of the archways. There was no wall or barrier to stop someone falling to the distant ground. Cait held back, afraid the wind would gust and hurl her into the air.

"The riders used to mount their dragons here," said Phoenix. "Each of the great wyrms had a cave carved into the mountains, and when it was time to fly the riders summoned them with brass horns. The tradition was for the riders to run and leap into the air for their dragons to catch them."

She thought about the number of steps they'd climbed. The yawning drop to the stony ground. "Why would they do that?"

"Because they could, I suppose," said Phoenix. "There were many traditions like that. Then the wars came and the riders left. Some to Andar and some to the Witch King's side. But the riders who went to Andar built another tower, modelled on this one. *Caer L'dun*. Its tower is exactly the same height as this. Although it was built to watch over the An for the coming of the undain, not for dragons."

Cait glanced at Ran, who was looking around at the walls and archways. He looked like a kid at Christmas. His eyes were wide and he was breathing deeply. At the phrase *Caer L'dun* he looked at Phoenix and nodded. She couldn't follow the words he uttered, but Phoenix translated. "He says he is glad to have finally seen Caer D'nar. The first rider to do so in five centuries. And I believe he's also the first person ever to have visited the top of both towers."

Cait stepped a little closer to the open archway. The sky was fully dark, and a dazzling tapestry of stars shone down. She knew a few of the constellations from back home. Not that they were visible from Manchester with the orange glow of its night skies. But her dad had pointed some out to her on a long-ago holiday trip to the coast. None of these constellations were familiar. Different stars shone upon Angere and Andar. They seemed brighter, too.

"My friends," said Phoenix, "I've asked you here so the others can't hear what I'm about to say."

"Why?" said Nox, suspicion clear in his voice.

"I don't wish to trouble them."

"Go on," said Cait.

The old man paused for a moment, staring out into the deep darkness. "I only wished to say this. The Witch King leaves us alone because we are no threat. Or because we are useful to him. But with you four here that will change. He can't ignore the presence of a witch of Ilminion's line, two wyrm lords and a renegade Duke. He will come and come soon, there can be no doubt."

He turned to face them, the red glow from the fire lighting up his face, making his features dance. "If you choose to stay here, we will fight alongside you. Fight and die. Perhaps it is time we finally did something. But we have to face the truth: if you remain here, Menhroth will come."

"You want us to leave?" asked Nox.

Phoenix shook his head. "Truly, no. Events are moving quickly across Angere and Andar. And beyond. This is the turning point, when everything changes, for better or worse. We won't run from that. The four of you are at the centre of it. We of the Smouldering Fire will play our roles, do what we can to help. Caer D'nar is the safest place in all of Angere but in truth it is not safe at all. If Menhroth wants to grind it to dust, he will."

"But where else is there to go?" said Cait.

"You planned to reach the An? To try and cross to

Andar?"

"We did," said Cait. It seemed pointless to hide anything from him.

"Then that is one option. The wyrm roads are open to you. You can travel anywhere within Angere."

"Are there other options?"

He shook his head. "Stay and fight. Escape down the wyrm roads. I can see no other courses. But you have a day or two's grace, I think. And we can talk more tomorrow when you are rested. I simply wanted you to know how things stand."

Ran and Lugg stayed at the top of the tower, staring out into the darkness together, while Cait descended with Phoenix and Nox. Back at the bottom of the tower, the old man showed them where they could sleep: simple rush mats on the floor covered with more furs. As Nox fussed around trying to make his bed comfortable, Cait touched Phoenix on the arm and drew him to one side.

"You mentioned something about the dragons, too? What did you mean?"

The old man looked troubled. "It's nothing. A wild idea, nothing more."

"Tell me."

Phoenix glanced around to see who was listening. He relented. "It is just an old man's foolishness. But ... there is something. Something I didn't want Ran to see. Or Lugg come to that. In truth I don't know what it means."

"What is it?"

"You wish to see now?"

"Might as well."

"Very well," said Phoenix. "Come with me to the crypt and I'll show you what I've found."

12 – WYRM LORD

Cait and Phoenix walked through the shadows of a damp, dripping corridor, deep beneath the halls of Caer D'nar. They'd descended staircases lined with stone, but now they were in a rough tunnel cut through the natural rock. Phoenix carried a torch but its flame barely burned, as if there wasn't much air. Cait peered into each side-passage they passed but could hear and see nothing. The air was cold and damp on her face and smelled of earth.

"What is this place?" she asked.

His voice sounded hollow as he replied over his shoulder. "A mine, originally. This is the reason Caer D'nar stands where it does. There was a rich seam of wyrmfire here."

"I don't know what that is."

"Forgive me. It's sometimes called brimstone. It's what the wyrms of old consumed to give them the power to breathe fire. Tiny, precious flecks of the glittering stone can be found all over these mountains. It's why the wyrms lived here, in fact. Although extracting wyrmfire is terribly dangerous. If you're not careful it explodes in a huge fireball."

"So how did the dragons get it?"

"Certain streams high up in the mountains carry specks of wyrmfire in their waters. But the wyrm lords offered the dragons the plentiful supply they mined, and that helped forge their relationship. With all the brimstone they needed, the wyrms were truly formidable creatures."

Phoenix turned a corner and stopped at an arched iron doorway, brown with rust. He fished out a key from a pocket. Cait tried to sense what was through the door but got nothing. Iron seemed to block her mind's eye for some reason.

"What's through there?" She'd seen things like it in castles back home. Damp, dark dungeons they threw people into and then forgot about.

Phoenix seemed to be aware of her unease. "There's nothing to fear down here, Cait. Let me show you."

He pushed the key into the lock and turned it with an effort, using both hands. The door squealed as if complaining at being disturbed. Phoenix went first. Cait closed her eyes for a moment and worked a werelight. She barely noticed the twinge of pain it cost her. She sent the flame bobbing on ahead of her before following Phoenix inside.

They stood in a low, wide room with a vaulted ceiling supported by massive round pillars. The walls were cut stones once again: massive square blocks that must have weighed tons. And all around the floor, in great piles, were bones. Mountains of bones. But, she saw immediately, not human bones. Many were vast, like the remains of dinosaurs from some museum, but all cluttered together in random piles.

"Dragon bones?" she said.

"Dragon bones," said Phoenix. "People say the wyrms flew away when the riders abandoned them, headed north into the distant peaks never to return. And perhaps that did happen to some. But the truth is most of the creatures ended up here."

"I don't get it," said Cait. Some of the bones were as big as tree-trunks. And some, she saw, had been neatly cut into sections by saw or knife. "What happened here? Who would do this?"

"The undain. Who else? You've heard how the dragons fled in horror from their former riders. The truth is the riders – or the things they'd become – wanted them back. But no dragon would let an undain ride them. So instead the undain fought and slaughtered the riderless beasts one by one in a series of terrible battles.

"Why?"

"So they could resurrect them. So they could use necromancy to fashion the wyrms' remains into revenant dragons bound to the undains' will."

"You mean like that creature Fer said flew across the An?"

"Something like that. And you've seen the Bone Harvesters, too, although they're poor imitations. But perhaps after all this time the Witch King has worked out how to perform the necessary rites. Or perhaps he simply accumulated enough Spirit to force it to work."

"It's hideous," said Cait. The room reeked of an ancient decay. Her stomach writhed. "There must be hundreds of them down here."

"Many hundreds, yes. But it was all such a long time ago. Eventually the undain stopped coming and in truth, we thought they'd given up trying to fashion dragons of their own centuries ago. Our predecessors spent many years gathering up the ancient bones scattered around the plains and mountains to bring them here. They could think of little else to do. I've often thought we should try to match them up, reform the skeletons of individuals. But where would you start?"

Cait stepped forward, weaving her way between the mounds that towered over her. She was glad Ran wasn't there to see this. Ran or Lugg. She tried to imagine what it would have been like to see the dragons in flight. Glorious, just as Lugg had said. And now they were here, long-dead, ancient remains jumbled up in these piles.

She turned back to Phoenix, who still stood by the door. Her voice boomed as she spoke. "But there's more, isn't there? You didn't bring me just to show me this."

He stepped toward her, stopping to pick up one of the smaller bones as he did so. It was thin and twig-like, from a wing, perhaps. "I come down here sometimes, you see. To look at the bones. It seems wrong to leave them in the dark. I like to imagine the creatures still flying, up there in the sky where they belong. Does that make sense?"

"Yes. It does."

"The thing is, sometimes, I get a flash of something when I touch the bones. A vision."

"A vision of what?"

"I don't know. It's a bit like when I see through the eyes of another witch. Except, it's not really like that. When a normal vision comes to me through the aether I know what sort of mind I'm contacting. It's vague and sometimes confusing, but I have some idea who, or at least what, I'm in touch with. This … this is different. I catch a glimpse of something … huge. Huge and terrible. And not at all human. And I have no name for the person, the being, I'm in touch with."

"You think it's the Witch King?"

"Perhaps. Except it doesn't feel like any of the undain. There isn't that gaping absence. This is something alive, something very alive. There is rage there, a burning rage, and I wondered…"

"You wondered if it was a dragon?"

Phoenix looked directly into her eyes and nodded. "It's wishful thinking, I know. But there are all the old stories, you see. Tales of how the really ancient wyrms lived in the far north and never came to Angere, never met their end at the hands of the undain. I thought that perhaps they might still be there. I thought, maybe, it was one of those minds I was touching."

He held out the bone for Cait to take. "And then it occurred to me you might be able to sense something, too, if you touched one of the relics. I know you're new to all this, but you're far beyond me already in what you can do. Look how easily you worked that light. Something like that would defeat me completely."

Cait hesitated, then took the bone. It felt dry and dead, like stone, although it was surprisingly light. She closed her eyes and, not really knowing what she was doing, tried to seek for the presence Phoenix had described.

She stood for long moments, eyes closed, peering into the darkness. She was aware of Bethany stirring and joining in, offering her strength to the search. Between them they scoured the shadows.

She opened her eyes. Phoenix was watching her expectantly. "Anything? Did you feel it?"

She shook her head. "I'm sorry. No. There was nothing."

Phoenix nodded, as if this confirmed all his fears. "Ah, well. Just an old man's foolishness then. Now we know, at least."

He took the bone from her and, carefully, as if returning it to its correct position, laid it down on the floor. "Well. There we are. Now you know all my secrets. Let's go back up. Perhaps in the morning everything will make more sense and we can decide what is to be done."

They locked the iron door behind them and left the ancient bones to their darkness.

The following morning, Cait toiled her way back up the stairs to the top of the tower. She'd slept late, lost in dreams she couldn't recall. Her head felt like it was still full of fog but at least it didn't hurt so much to walk. Bread had been laid out for her, along with a simmering kettle of some tea-like drink. She ate in silence, enjoying the moment of peace and solitude.

Nox was already at the top of the tower when she

arrived, studying huge maps unrolled on the floor. The fire was grey ash, a faint coil of smoke coming off it. Three people stood by one of the archways, hauling up something heavy with a rope running over a rusted winch. Phoenix was one of them. He nodded a welcome at Cait. They were lifting up logs for that evening's fire.

Through the arch it was a bright, clear day, the sun already high in the sky. Cait made her way around the circle, well away from the edge, taking in the view. She could see for miles.

To the south, the plain of Angere stretched into a hazy distance. The sparkling ribbon of the river – the Dragon's Tongue she supposed – was quite clear. To the east and west were the wooded slopes of the foothills. Northward lay the mass of towering peaks, their flanks purple and their sharp tops white with snow.

She crept a little nearer the openings than she had the night before. The icy wind streaming into her face was exhilarating. The ground seemed so remote it felt like she was flying.

She knelt on the ground beside Nox.

"Awake at last are we?" he said.

"Yes. Well spotted. What are these maps?"

"They're the riders' ancient maps of the wyrm roads."

"They've survived?"

"Drawn onto dragonskin, apparently. Very hard wearing."

"Lovely. Can you read them?" The maps were yellowed and cracked from age, their ink faded.

"This is obviously the An," said Nox, indicating a blue strip filling the right-hand edge of the map. "And up here, this tower is clearly Caer D'nar. Other towns and fortresses are marked, but they're places I don't recognize."

"Where's the White City?"

"I think it's here. I don't think there was even a town there in those days, but the bridge is clear."

"The bridge to Andar?"

"This map was obviously drawn before it was swept away. The Witch King founded his city near the bridgehead."

"And these long lines zigzagging across the map? They're the wyrm roads?"

"I think so. See here, this must be the one we took. You can see the point where five of them meet."

Cait bent down, tracing the fading lines with her fingers. Dragons had been drawn onto the map, flying along each wyrm road, red, green, blue and gold. It was like looking at a map of the tram network back home. They could get to the White City by taking the road to Fiveways, and then another of the archways across to the An. One change. It looked easy. There was writing along each line, too, but the letters were faded and the script completely unfamiliar. She really wished she could decipher it. For all she knew it was saying not to take that particular road under any circumstances.

"Do you think they have a map like this? The undain?"

"I never saw one. But I think we have to assume they do."

"And did you see any kind of archway in the White City? Something that might have been the end of this wyrm road?"

Nox considered then shook his head. "Never, no. But the place is vast and I didn't see it all. I saw the portal through to the refinery often, of course. That was sort of an archway. But never anything like those stone ones. I don't suppose they'd go out of their way to look after it."

"So maybe they won't know about it? Maybe it won't be guarded."

"That seems pretty unlikely, Cait. I'll bet Charis has them all watched."

"Actually, he may not," said Phoenix, coming over to study the map as well. He was sweating from the exertion of hauling up the logs, wiping his brow on an old red rag.

"Why?" said Nox.

"The arch at that end was destroyed in antiquity. During the dragon wars, the battles at the bridgehead. And without archways to anchor the wyrm roads they … flap around."

"Flap around?" said Cait.

"So the ancient texts say. All the riders' old books and scrolls are here. Most have crumbled, but some have survived like this map. The ones written on dragonskin. I've deciphered all I can. They say the wyrm roads flow and twist over time. That's why the riders built the archways, to fix the roads into place."

"So this one might emerge anywhere now," said Cait.

Phoenix nodded. "It might have shifted tens of miles. Hundreds even."

"Then we could use it and they'd never know."

"Perhaps," said Phoenix. "Although it could also drop you right in front of the Witch King and his court."

"Or in the middle of the An," said Nox.

Phoenix considered this with a frown. "That's possible, too, although less likely. The running water would deflect the roads, I think."

Cait studied the map for a few more moments. It was so tempting to remain at Caer D'nar. It felt peaceful and safe. But, of course, it wasn't. "We need to talk to Lugg and Ran, decide what we're going to do. We don't want to wait here and draw Menhroth's army down on us."

"Perhaps that will happen anyway," said Phoenix. "As I said, it's not important. What matters is what you do. Everything is finely balanced. One misstep and it will fall apart. You're at the centre of everything, Cait."

"And Ran. Without him we'll have to walk to the An."

"Ran, too," said Phoenix.

"Where is he anyway? I haven't seen him or Lugg this morning."

"I'll show you." Phoenix's knee joints cracked as he pushed himself to his feet. "They're down on the ground.

Fighting."

"Fighting?"

"Come, see."

Nox returned to studying the map while Cait edged as close to the lip of the archway as she dared. They were facing south toward Angere. Somewhere in that distance sat Greygyle's palace. And the White City. And, quite possibly, the army preparing to cross the Dragon's Tongue and come for them. She searched with her mind but could detect nothing.

Rusting iron handrails had been set all the way around each arch. Cait grasped hold of one and leaned over as far as she dared. The wind, whipping about the tower, lashed her hair as she peered down. She picked out Ran and Lugg on the ground, tiny figures circling each other, Lugg occasionally darting forward to attack, Ran leaping effortlessly out of his way.

"What are they doing?" asked Cait.

"Like I said, fighting," said Phoenix. "It looks like Ran has taken Lugg under his wing."

"I think Lugg's a bit in awe of Ran."

Phoenix sat on the lip of the drop, as if he were simply dangling his legs over the bank of a river. "It's understandable. Ran is training the boy, showing him how to move, how to fight. When I found them early this morning at the foot of the tower, Ran was using a needle to cut ink into the skin of Lugg's arm."

Cait, clutching the ancient iron railing with all her strength, sat warily beside him. "He's giving Lugg dragonrider tattoos?"

"He's made a start."

"Where did he get the needle from? And the ink?"

"Carries it with him, I think. So he can add to his own from time to time."

"That means Lugg will have blue lines, too."

"Azure Wing, yes. I believe they get more tattoos as they progress. They're a sort of badge of rank as well as a magical defence."

"A magical defence? Is that why I can never see Ran's mind?"

"I thought you knew. Disconcerting isn't it? It's impossible to know what he's really thinking."

"I'm used to not knowing what people are thinking," said Cait. "Seriously I don't know what *I'm* thinking most of the time."

Phoenix nodded. "Of course. But I've spent my life glimpsing the world through other people's eyes. With people like you I can see much farther and clearer but just about anyone is open to me if they're near. With Ran, there's nothing."

"Like the undain."

Phoenix glanced aside at her, a puzzled expression on his face. "Why do you say that?"

"You can't read them, either. They're an emptiness. Like … the opposite of a living mind."

"Yes. But Ran is most definitely not an undain. I can sense his mind, burning brightly. I just get no detail from him. No colours, no faces, no thoughts. He keeps it hidden away. It's a vital skill, and one you must master, but none do it like the wyrm lords."

"So the tattoos … they somehow deflect magic."

"In a way. From what I've read they originally had them because of the dragons."

How come she didn't understand any of this? She felt like such an idiot. "Why?"

"Dragon's minds were vast and terrible. Their appearance was obviously fearsome enough, but there was more to it than that. They emitted a baleful aura that made people cower or run screaming when one was near. The fire they breathed was terrible, but it was the burning in your mind that was their greatest weapon. In battle they often didn't even have to do anything. Just by being there they defeated their foes. But somehow the patterns of the riders' tattoos protected them. Like a magical armour."

Cait sighed. "There's so much I don't know. So much I don't understand. I'm supposed to be saving everyone, saving the world, and I haven't got a clue about any of it."

"I know. They were only trying to protect you, you know."

"Who?"

"Your mother and your gran. They wanted to tell you everything but feared doing so. Feared exposing you. I think they hoped it would pass you by and you could live a normal life."

Cait snorted. "Not much chance of that, now, is there?"

"Perhaps. Who knows what the future will bring? It may be they were wrong to keep you in the dark, and it may be they weren't. But I do know they agonized over it, and I know they were only doing what they thought was best for you. When I touch their minds their love for you burns even across the aether."

"Have you … seen them today?"

"I'm sorry, no. I tried to reach them again last night but got nothing."

"Will you keep trying?"

"Of course."

"Phoenix." It was one of the other Smouldering Fire members, a woman who'd helped haul up the logs. She stood behind them, one hand on Phoenix's shoulder.

Phoenix looked up at her. "Demara. What is it?"

"A messenger from the outpost."

A look of concern clouded Phoenix's wrinkled face. He turned to Cait. "We should see what this is."

He pulled himself up and followed the woman. A black bird was perched on the lip of one of the other archways. It looked like a crow except its beak was bright red, as if dipped in blood. Another member of the Smouldering Fire was scattering grain on the ground for the bird to peck. Around the bird's neck was a tiny metal container.

"You use messenger crows, too?"

"Something similar," said Phoenix. "Come see."

Cait followed him to where the bird was hopping around, stabbing at the food.

"They're choughs," said Phoenix. "Like crows but more common around these cliffs. We use them to send messages to our watchtowers."

"Where?"

"You saw the remains of one at the archway. We haven't manned that one for many years. But we have three others, spread out across the northern banks of the Dragon's Tongue."

Phoenix knelt and, moving very slowly, held out a flat hand toward the chough. The bird regarded him with a suspicious eye. It croaked once, then hopped onto Phoenix's hand. Carefully, Phoenix unhooked the message from the bird's neck. He stood, angling the piece of paper he'd unfurled to the light, and read.

When he was done he handed the message to Demara. Cait didn't need to peer into their minds to see how troubled they were. The looks passing between them were enough.

"What does it say?" she asked.

"It's from the southern watchtower. I'm sorry, Cait. We may not have as much time as we thought."

Phoenix peered through the archway, southward into the distance. He looked suddenly very old and weary. "The undain are massing to cross the river and march on Caer D'nar as we speak."

13 – VOICES IN THE AETHER

Phoenix unhooked a curling brass horn from the wall and, standing in one of the open archways, sounded a deep, blaring note into the open air. A few minutes later Ran and Lugg arrived up the spiral stairs, Ran first, both of them breathing heavily. Lugg had cuts and grazes to add to his existing wounds. His forearm, where Ran had begun work on the tattoos, dripped blood freely. He didn't appear to be troubled by any of it. In truth, he looked happier than she'd seen him. He stood close to Ran as they gathered around the wyrm road map and Phoenix repeated the news from the river.

"We must decide where to go," said Nox. "If we stay here they'll kill us all, sooner or later." Nox glanced at Phoenix who nodded his assent, a frown deepening the lines on the old man's face.

There was a moment's silence. Cait glanced around the ring: Nox, Ran, Lugg, Phoenix, Demara. She realised they were waiting for her to speak. As if she had all the answers. As if she had *any* answers. It seemed clear they should try and reach the An, somehow get the book as they'd agreed, but that meant heading *toward* the enemy. Even if the gateway at the White City wasn't defended, the arches at

Fiveways most certainly would be. How could they hope to use the wyrm roads without being attacked? It seemed utterly hopeless.

Frowning, she leaned over the map as if some answer, some secret way they hadn't noticed before, would be revealed. She found Caer D'nar, a sketch of the tower they stood within, at the edge of the great range of triangular mountains. The wyrm road they'd used headed to the south, crossing over the meandering blue line of the Dragon's Tongue to the ring of archways.

"If we can get back to Fiveways then we can take this road east to the river."

But as she pointed out the line, she brushed the cracked surface of the ancient map with her finger…

…and she fell into sudden darkness, as if a trapdoor had opened in the floor of the tower, plummeting her to the ground. She screamed, but there was no sound. She flailed around, confused, disorientated. If she was falling why was there no rush of air on her face? And if she wasn't, why couldn't she feel hard stone beneath her feet? Where had the tower gone? Where had Nox and the others gone? What the hell was happening?

Bethany!

The dead witch-girl's voice quavered as she replied. The fear there was clear. *Something has come for us, Cait. Oh, Cait, get away. Get away now.*

Cait twisted around, trying to understand where she was, see what was coming. The darkness was absolute. She could hear nothing but her own panicky breathing. None of it made any sense.

She only realised she wasn't alone when two red eyes opened in front of her. Two vast red eyes. She sensed the other presence clearly then, its mind filling the void like a sun, its bulk making up half of the world. There was a towering rage to it: a fury that seethed and boiled, barely contained, as the eyes regarded her.

Involuntarily, Cait took a step backward. It made little difference; the eyes moved no farther away. Their gaze bored into her, filling her vision. Cait threw her arms over her face to keep them out. The eyes were in her mind, picking through her thoughts and memories with ease.

She fell to the ground – if there was a ground to fall to – and writhed as the attack continued. She tried to fight back, tried to hurl the invading mind out of her own. Distantly she was aware of Bethany doing the same. But neither was strong enough. Not nearly strong enough. And the red eyes shone on everything in Cait's thoughts: every event, every face, every terror. There was nothing she could do. She could only writhe, exposed, vulnerable, in that red glare.

The rage in the invading mind burned clearer with each moment. In desperation, in her own anger, Cait threw herself outward, flinging herself at the red eyes, trying to reach through them to her attacker. Perhaps she could find some weakness. Perhaps she could hurt the invader in some small way.

It was useless. She was hurling herself against glass walls, impossibly thick. But she did sense a word. A word intimately entangled with the being's thoughts. A *name*, perhaps. Not knowing what else to do she shouted the word, screaming it out loud even as her attacker delved deep into her oldest memories. Cait caught glimpses of her father and her mother from when she was young, the intruder seeing it all at the same time, tinting everything flame-red.

Cait screamed the word again and this time the being reacted. It recoiled and began pulling itself out of her mind. Its fury was unabated, but whether she had repelled it, or whether its curiosity was simply satisfied, she couldn't say. The malevolent eyes burned into her for a moment more and then blinked off and were gone.

Cait lay alone in the utter darkness, exhausted, sobbing. She hurt in ways she didn't know she could hurt, her brain raw from the intrusion. Bethany was a distant, wordless moan in her mind. So this was what it was like to have your mind invaded, your memories and thoughts pulled apart and rifled through. Had it been like this for Nox when she'd looked into his thoughts? Perhaps. She would never do that to anyone again. The brutality of it. The violation. She would make sure, also, no one could ever do it again to her. Her anger flared once more and she struggled to her feet…

…and she was back in the watchtower of Caer D'nar, faces with concerned expressions all round her. She was still standing, leaning over the map.

"What is it, Cait?" said Nox. "What's wrong? You just stopped talking. You look like you've seen a ghost."

Phoenix walked around the map and put a hand on her arm. "Cait? Did you see something? A vision?"

She tried to speak but couldn't for a moment. She looked into the old man's eyes and nodded.

"Who, Cait? Who was it? Was it Menhroth?"

She looked at the map. Her fingers were still stretched out to touch the parchment. She'd touched the bone in the crypt and felt nothing. But then she'd touched the dragonskin of the map and been engulfed by darkness and those red eyes.

"Not him," she said. "There was a name. I heard its name."

"What was the name?"

"Xoster."

Silence filled the room once more as if she'd worked some spell. Cait's legs were shaking, threatening to buckle beneath her. Phoenix's eyes were wide, as were Ran's and Lugg's.

Only Nox looked confused. "Xoster? Never heard of him. Will someone tell me what is going on?"

"An ancient name," said Phoenix. "A name from the old stories."

"OK, so who is he?" said Nox.

"*She*," said Phoenix. "Xoster was the first dragon. The mother. The wyrm whose children the undain slaughtered five hundred years ago."

"There was ... such rage in her," said Cait. She could see the red eyes in her mind. "I tried to keep her out but there was nothing I could do. She was filled with fury at what has been done to her. Even now, after all this time, she burns with it."

"Xoster," said Phoenix, as if tasting the word. "Xoster, alive. It's incredible. It changes everything. I thought, I mean, I hoped. Even one dragon could make all the difference. And Xoster..."

Ran spoke then, a steam of syllables she couldn't follow, although she picked out the name several times. Lugg replied and the two of them conversed excitedly, both speaking at once. Phoenix joined in occasionally, dropping in and out of English as Nox threw in questions.

Cait tried to understand what they were saying but couldn't keep up. Numbness overcame her. Her legs shook. She slumped to the ground and held her head in her hands, shutting everything out for a moment. Were they talking about *finding* this creature?

Phoenix crossed to a low table, where a metal urn had been set. Steam coiled from its spout. He poured a drink into a battered metal cup and crossed back to hand it to her. His voice was gentle, sympathetic. "This might help."

Her hand shook as she took the drink. She sipped it gratefully. It wasn't as good as the tea her gran made, but it was good enough.

She let Nox and the others talk, their excitement obvious. She heard something about the *Wyrm Way*. Whatever they were saying their intent was clear. They planned to head north. They planned to track down this dragon. This mad, raging dragon.

It had been a mistake to come to Caer D'nar. They'd had little choice, it was true, but she'd been too hopeful of finding friends here. Too desperate for help. But it wasn't going to work out like that. There was no army, and now Lugg and the others wanted to go chasing off into the mountains.

"No," said Cait.

Nobody noticed, and she had to repeat herself, shouting to make herself heard. "No! No, you mustn't do that. I told you. She was … terrible. It was like drowning in a sea of anger. She *hurt* me. We can't go anywhere near her."

Glances passed between the five of them. They had it all arranged, all agreed between them. A few minutes earlier they'd looked to her for answers and now they were ignoring her.

"We have to get to the An," she continued. "Try and reach Andar. It's our only hope. We didn't agree anything about chasing after crazed dragons."

"We didn't know there were dragons any more," said Nox. "Menhroth has no idea Xoster is still alive. That anger you described could be turned on the undain. *Unleashed* on them."

"Or it could be unleashed on us," said Cait. "I'm not sure she sees much difference between us and them."

"Touching the minds of dragons was always a terrible ordeal," said Phoenix. "Many went mad when they tried."

"Right," said Cait. "So let's stay well away."

"But don't you see?" said Lugg. "Everything is coming together like I said. We have to do this. We have to go there. We have to head north to find her. The undain won't be able to follow us. When we're ready we can fly to the White City and destroy them all. It's our fate."

"I don't believe in fate," she said. "We can do what we like. It's a free country."

"Actually, it isn't," said Nox. "It really isn't."

"You know what I mean," she shot back at him.

Lugg looked thoughtful for a moment, then seemed to come to a decision. "I'm sorry, but I'm going to take the

Wyrm Way north and find Xoster. I have to."

"It's insane, Lugg. You won't stand a chance. You haven't even got any tattoos, just a few bleeding scratches. The riders had them all over their bodies to protect themselves."

Lugg shrugged and actually grinned. "True. But I think it's what I have to do. And it's what I want to do. I'll be no use to you in the White City. I'll be no use to you anywhere much. But perhaps I can find Xoster. And perhaps I can survive the meeting and, somehow, be able to help you. Be able to do *something*."

She could see it was useless to argue with him. He reminded her a little of Danny in that moment. The same boyish idiocy. She looked away, down at the map, not wanting to think about Danny. "What is this *Wyrm Way*?"

"The path the riders of old took to reach the dragons," said Phoenix.

"Here, see," said Lugg. "This line heading north from Caer D'nar. It's faint now, but just visible if you look closely. A wyrm road leading into the mountains."

She studied the map. "I don't see the other end of it. It just fades out."

"That's because no one ever knew where it led," said Phoenix. "The riders who used it – those that came back – were sworn to secrecy. All we know is that somewhere in the far, frozen north there were dragons. And a wyrm road leading to them. Some said the dragons dwelt in a place of perpetual night. Others said that the sun never set there. But none really knew. The place might not even have been on this world at all."

"And you think you can go there?" she asked Lugg.

"Don't know. I think I can try."

She turned to Ran. "And will you go with him?"

She didn't need to be able to see into the dragonrider's mind to know that he wanted to. That he yearned to go north with Lugg to seek this Xoster. For once he seemed undecided. He didn't reply for several seconds.

In the end he said, in stumbling English, "No. I am sworn to protect you, Cait."

His assumption that she needed protecting riled her, but she said nothing. In truth she couldn't help feeling relieved. She needed all the help she could get. She really didn't fancy the idea of heading to the An alone. And without Ran they had no chance. He was the only one who could open the wyrm roads.

"And you, Nox?"

He shrugged. "I guess I'll go with you, too. I'm a city person. Quests for mythical dragons aren't really my thing."

"We have to head east," she said to Lugg. "We can't afford a diversion into the mountains. I'm sorry."

He shrugged. "Probably best I go alone anyway."

She peered at the map once more. She hated to lose Lugg but there appeared to be no choice. "Then the three of us should leave at once. Perhaps if we go the undain will leave Caer D'nar in peace."

"Perhaps," said Phoenix. "And perhaps they won't. I don't think Menhroth will let things lie. He's not really the forgiving type."

"Then, I'm sorry," said Cait. "We had no choice, but maybe we shouldn't have come here."

Phoenix shook his head. "I'm glad you did. We all are. It's time for us to do something. But what of you, Cait? Are you up to travelling? A vision like that can take its toll. Sometimes my head throbs so badly all I can do is lie in a shuttered room for days."

"I'm fine," she said, sounding surer than she felt. "We'll head to the archway, try and get there before Charis marches north from the river. Then we only have the small problem of Fiveways. Somehow we have to fight our way through the undain to the other arch. Although I don't see how that's possible."

"Actually, we may be able to help there," said Phoenix. A smile deepened the wrinkles on his face. "Like I said, it's time we did something. It's time we stopped smouldering and *burned*."

They said goodbye to Lugg an hour later. Phoenix and the rest of the Smouldering Fire had equipped him as best they could for a journey into the unknown north. Ran had spent most of the time deep in conversation with the boy, desperately trying to compress a lifetime's knowledge and lore into one hour. Lugg listened and nodded his head again and again. She could feel the emotions churning within him without having to burrow into his mind. Excitement, fear, awe. Most of all, relief. He'd thought his life would be worthless. Empty. And now he had this purpose, this meaning. It made sense of everything. He might die, but at least he knew there was a *point*.

She shook her head. The idiot. What was the point of being brave if it meant going and getting yourself killed? She'd done all she could to stop him. She still blamed herself, but there was nothing she could do.

"Goodbye, Cait," he said, coming to meet her. "Thank you for everything." Awkwardly, unsure of his reception, he held out his arms to her.

She took hold of him and hugged him hard. "I didn't do anything. I blacked out, and they carried me to your house. Big deal."

"No. You've changed everything. It's all different because of you. I told you."

She let go and looked at him. The chances were she would never see him again. Why did that keep happening? "Lugg, you will be careful, won't you? Don't take any stupid chances. I mean, don't take too many stupid chances. What I said about Xoster was true. She's seriously deranged."

"I'll be careful," he said. "You should be worrying about yourself. You're the one trying to reach the White City. I'd rather face Xoster than Menhroth."

She thought about those unblinking red eyes and didn't

reply. Lugg released her and turned to go, hefting a leather sack onto his back.

"Lugg," she called after him. "I should have told you. I did do something. Sort of. When your cart crashed and you lost all that Spirit, it was our fault. We were there, hiding behind the bank. We spooked the undain. I'm sorry."

Lugg considered for a moment then looked amused. "See? I said you changed everything. I thought it was the end of my life at the time, but crashing that cart was the best thing that ever happened to me."

He turned to pick his way up a snaking path into the mountains, and didn't look back.

Within the hour Cait and the others were leaving, too. Phoenix and five of the Smouldering Fire accompanied them as they retraced their steps southward. Others had gone ahead to scout the land. More than one chough flapped south or returned north, bearing some message.

"Anything from the river?" she asked Phoenix. Caer D'nar was already disappearing behind them, nestling back among the mountain peaks. In front of them lay the wide plain strewn with shattered boulders and knife-sharp shards of rock she remembered. The day was bright and clear, the sky blue and cold. There was no sign of any mist just as there was no undain horde thundering across the plain toward them. Not yet, anyway.

"They still haven't crossed, last we heard," said Phoenix. "But flying creatures have been spotted on the southern bank. There are boats on the water, too. Barges and rafts being built to carry the army. It won't be long."

"If they cross now will they reach the archway before us?"

"Yes, well before. We have to hope they don't move yet. They may not expect us to return to the wyrm road. If they think we're going to stay in the mountains to defend Caer D'nar, they'll wait a little longer, build up their forces first."

"And will you?"

"Will we what?"

"Defend Caer D'nar?"

Phoenix plodded along two, three, four paces before replying. "We'll try. That's all we can do, isn't it?"

She glanced around, making sure no one else was near. Nox was some way away, lost in his own thoughts. Ran, unusually for him, brought up the rear, looking back again and again to the mountains. Their Smouldering Fire escort was fanned out in a circle ahead of them.

"I suppose," she said. "It all seems pretty hopeless, though, doesn't it? I don't think we really have much chance of succeeding."

"You underestimate yourself."

"And you sound like my gran."

"Well, she's right," said Phoenix. "Look how far you've come in such a short time. A little over a week ago you didn't know about any of this. Now you're at the centre of it. Do you think that's coincidence? And do you think it's chance that magic is frost and ice with you? The world is turning cold, the weather is changing. The An is going to freeze. And here you are, just at the right time. A witch who is only going to get stronger as the winter deepens."

"What, now *you're* saying it's my fate to be here as well?"

"You don't think it is?"

"No! I don't want to be some sort of stupid *chosen one*. My gran also told me to be my own woman, not waste my life trying to live up to the expectations of others."

"Of course," said Phoenix. "And again she's right. You must do what you see fit. But here's the world as it is, and here you are. Call that what you like."

Cait sighed as they plodded along. "I just wish I had more of a clue what to do. I don't understand half the things that happen."

"We have a little time now. It isn't much, but perhaps I

can answer a few of your questions."

The problem was she didn't know where to start. Even if they could reach the An, how were they going to find the book? And how were they going to cross the river? That was, like, famously impossible. And if, by some miracle, they did all those things, what difference would it make? Her world was still under the thumb of Genera. The undain army was still going to invade Andar. A lot of people were going to die. And worse.

"I don't know where to start. It all seems so big."

"Then start with the little things."

"I mean, don't I need to know about, you know, pentagrams and arcane symbols and mystic stuff?"

Phoenix looked a little amused. "Not really. Some of those things can help. A focus. The problem is people think they're powerful or significant on their own. That all you have to do is draw the right shape and assemble the right components and the magic will work. Which is coming at it completely the wrong way."

"OK."

"Anything else? There must have been much that didn't make sense in the past week."

"OK, so why is it at all ice and frost with me when I work magic?"

"Sometimes there's no reason for the way magic works. Maybe when your mind was trying to come to terms with what you could do it latched onto that as a way of understanding and stuck with it. Or maybe some magical forebear of yours came from somewhere cold. Or maybe you took to ice because you were afraid of its elemental opposite, fire. Or perhaps it's a bit of all those things."

They walked in silence for a few moments while she thought about his words. One other thing had been puzzling her. It was insignificant in the grand scheme of things, but Phoenix might know the answer. "OK, then tell me this. My gran told me about paying the price for magic. I get that. But at Greygyle's palace it seemed to work the other way round. I felt really ill and it hurt like hell but that was before I worked any spells. Then I had this sort of moment of clarity when my senses expanded. But it was like I paid for it beforehand."

Phoenix nodded, as if that all made sense. "It can be like that for the powerful ones. Because you're more in touch with the flow of magic, so the books say."

"So is it ever like that for you?"

"Me? No, never."

"And will it happen like that again?"

"Perhaps. It's different for everyone. Wasn't Bethany able to explain?"

"Not really. She sort of comes and goes. Sometimes she's clear, but quite often she's very faint."

"I've known her for a long time," said Phoenix. "She's always been like that. Some days a laughing child, some days an old woman, sullen and withdrawn."

It was strange to think of this man communicating with people from back home all this time. "How long have you known her?"

"Since I was a boy. At first she was one of many voices that came to me through the aether. It took me years to work out who they all were, where they lived. Some I still can't identify."

"And you spoke to her?"

"I listened, mostly. She was already quite old by that time, being dead and all. But we've conversed on occasion, when the aether allows. There's a lot of fear in her. Anger, too. But I expect you know that."

Cait thought back to the rider who'd attacked her at Empire Towers. The way Bethany and the other ghosts had swarmed around him and *through* him. The rider's screams. "Yes. You won't tell anyone about her, will you? It's good to know I'm not alone, whatever else happens."

"I won't mention her. And she teaches you about the craft? About working magic?"

"Some."

"Good. You need all the help we can give you."

"You could say that. It's been pretty crazy."

Phoenix looked thoughtful for a moment as they walked side-by-side. "Actually, there may be another way I can assist. A small thing, but perhaps it will make a difference."

"What is it?"

"The gift of voices."

"I don't know what that is, either."

"Something people like me have. I think it's because we're so used to hearing people's underlying thoughts as well as what they say out loud. We quickly learn to connect the two."

"That's … that's how you can understand me? How you can speak English?"

"English and a lot of other languages."

"And you're saying you can give this ability to me?"

"With Bethany's help. If it worked you'd be able to understand what people say here in Angere. And Andar, if you ever get there."

"Do you know French, too?"

He looked puzzled at her question, lifting one eyebrow. "Yes, as a matter of fact. There are covens in Paris and many other French cities."

"Then it's a shame you couldn't do this earlier. I might have done a whole lot better in my exams."

"So you want me to try?"

"If Bethany's willing."

She was aware, dimly, of Phoenix and Bethany conversing. It was weird hearing a whole conversation inside her head, a conversation she wasn't part of. She decided to let them get on with it. It reminded her of being at home in her bedroom, hearing the muffled sound of the TV through the walls as her mum watched one of her endless soaps. Phoenix and Bethany talked backward and forward for a long time. Cait soon forgot about them and plodded along in silence, her stomach fizzing with anxiety as if electricity buzzed through her.

They camped that night on the open plain. They set up a ring of six fires and slept within. Cait didn't see any sign of spectral mists, but as the darkness gathered and the smoke drifted, she found herself reaching out nervously into the gloom, searching for the aether creature. She got nothing. The call of some night-time beast, like a shriek of agony, was the only sound over the crackle of the fires and the murmur of voices.

"We'll post guards tonight," said Phoenix, kneeling beside her. "We'll wake you if anything comes. You should try and get some sleep while you can."

She smiled at him and lay on the hard ground. She was weary to her bones from walking. Still she couldn't sleep, fears over what she faced filling her. She lay on her back, gazing at the unfamiliar stars in the black sky. Was one of those glimmers her own sun? Was that how it worked? Or wasn't she even in the same universe? There was no Milky Way to be seen, for one thing. She tried to get her head around it all but failed.

She thought about Danny. The tears that came made the bright stars blur into smudges. She closed her eyes and, eventually, drifted into troubled slumber. The stars became bobbing werelights that she had to follow, even though there were so many and she couldn't hope to reach any of them, however hard she tried.

The archway came within sight late the following morning. The sun was bright ahead of them, blinding, making details hard to pick out. Two Smouldering Fire scouts, swathed in grey to match the rocks, popped up to report no sign of any undain in the area. There was also no word of them crossing the river. Still, Cait and the others approached warily, expecting a trap. Nothing happened. The day stayed calm and quiet as they approached the ancient stones. A faint wind rattled the clumps of dry, scrubby grass that grew here and there.

Phoenix stood with her in front of the dark archway of the ruined watchtower. "We'll go in alone. Best you stand well back. If this goes wrong it will destroy the building and the archway and everything else in this whole area."

"Is it that dangerous?"

"Yes. Wyrmfire is enormously explosive, at least by the standards of this world. The dragons used to eat a few grains of it. We've got a whole cart-load in there."

"What were you planning to do with it?"

"There are stockpiles at all the watchtowers. We've tunnelled for generations beneath Caer D'nar to amass it all. The plan was always to ignite it if the undain attacked. There are hidden caches between the river and Caer D'nar, too."

"But how do you set it off?"

"Someone has to light the fuse. A desperate measure, but one we're prepared to undertake, if we have to."

"And yet you abandoned this stockpile."

"We used to watch this archway, long before I came here. But then, as our numbers dwindled, we had to concentrate on the Dragon's Tongue. It seemed unlikely the archway would ever be used again, and it was too dangerous to move the wyrmfire, so we left it here."

"And there's a chance it will explode by being moved?"

"A good chance. It's unstable, especially in large quantities."

"Great."

"If we do manage to get it through the archway and ignite it, it's going to level Fiveways completely. Even the undain won't survive. It'll give you the chance you need. You can go through before they can reinforce."

Cait caught Ran's glance as he strode up to them. Of course it had to be him. He was the only one the archway would open for. He would haul the cart through, light the fuse, then fling himself back before the detonation blew everyone and everything for five hundred yards to pieces.

Ran nodded to her, saying he was ready. She wondered

if he was afraid. He didn't look afraid. She wanted to tell him he didn't have to do this. But she couldn't because, the truth was, he did.

Nox stood a few yards away, wary of coming too near. "We'll shelter behind those boulders over there. No point in us all being killed if that stuff goes off."

He was right, of course. He didn't have to sound so calm about it. Not replying, she turned and made her way to the outcrop of grey rocks.

She and Nox watched as the members of the Smouldering Fire manoeuvred the creaking wooden cart from the shadows of the ruined building. It lurched as it moved, as if its sagging axles would collapse at any moment. How long had it been left there, rotting away? Phoenix directed from the front of the cart, waving his arms, calling out instructions. He and the rest of the Smouldering Fire could be blown to pieces at any moment. She tried not to think about it.

The cart got stuck in a rut and refused to budge. They had to rock it backward and forward to move it on. She watched as Ran ran to the back of the cart to add his muscle to the effort. The cart nodded to and fro more and more violently.

Cait found she was gritting her teeth tightly. "We should go and help."

"No, we should stay right where we are," said Nox, beside her. "Think, Cait. How would it help if we got killed too?"

"At least we'd feel we'd done something."

"We wouldn't feel anything. Because we'd be dead."

With a shout, they managed to get the cart moving again. The pile of rocks in the back slipped visibly, sending up a plume of dust. Cait closed her eyes, expecting the detonation. None came.

When she looked again the cart was trundling unevenly toward the archway. Phoenix and Ran walked to the front, where ropes had been attached. Phoenix gave Ran some last instructions, pointing at the cart, and then he and the rest of the Smouldering Fire ran for the cover of the boulders.

"He told us he could tow the whole thing the rest of the way," said Phoenix as he arrived, breathing hard. "It's incredible."

When everyone was safe, Ran laid the ropes over his shoulders and, leaning forward, hauled on the cart. It moved an inch or two. The effort required was clearly enormous; she could almost feel his straining muscles. Once or twice he slipped to his knees, but each time he stood up, took a fresh grip on the ropes, and resumed the battle.

Finally he reached the ground between the pillars of the arch. For a moment she thought the wyrm road wasn't going to open, that Charis had worked some magic to stop it from functioning. But then, as Ran heaved forward one more step, half of him disappeared from view. Then he was all gone, and the ropes from the cart dangled in mid-air. Step by step the whole of the cart edged through until, eventually, it vanished completely.

In the silence that followed, Cait said, "How do we know if the wyrmfire has exploded?"

"We don't," said Phoenix. "It's too far away to hear. Only Ran can tell us."

"And if Ran leaps through as it's exploding, won't it hit us too?"

"It might. This isn't something we've tried before."

"Great."

"We're going to launch barges laden with more wyrmfire from the northern bank of the Dragon's Tongue, too. They might think we're attacking on all fronts and, with a bit of luck, not know you've sneaked through here."

They waited in silence. A single black bird flapped through the sky, high overhead, although whether it was a chough heading for Caer D'nar, a crow in the service of Menhroth, or a normal bird, Cait couldn't tell.

"Why hasn't he come back yet?" she asked. "It shouldn't be taking this long."

"Perhaps he's having trouble getting the fuse to light," said Phoenix.

"But the undain aren't just going to stand around waiting for him to blow them to pieces."

"No," said Phoenix. "It's possible they've captured him. He knew that when he went."

"If that happens, they have the wyrmfire, too," said Nox. "We've basically handed them a weapon."

"A weapon that's very dangerous to the wielder," said Phoenix.

Cait didn't take her eyes off the archway, willing Ran to return. Still nothing happened. It had been far too long since he'd gone through.

"He's not coming back, is he?" said Cait. "Something's gone wrong."

"He may have been caught in the blast," said Nox. "He may have succeeded."

"But without him to open the wyrm road we can't go and see," she said. "It's too far by land. And the undain army is between us."

"Perhaps it was a mistake to let Lugg go north," said Nox. "He might have attempted the crossing."

"I could hardly stop him going off into the mountains if he wanted to."

"Couldn't you?" said Nox.

"What's that supposed to mean?"

"Oh, come on, Cait. You must have seen how he looked at you. You're probably the first girl his age he's seen in years."

"If that was true he wouldn't have run off into the mountains."

"Really? You don't think he might have been trying to impress you?"

She ignored him. She was in no mood for this conversation.

"Phoenix?" said Cait. "Is there any other way to reach Fiveways? Any way at all?"

Phoenix didn't reply. She turned round, wondering why he wasn't speaking. The old man lay on the ground, slumped in a heap. She was about to berate him when she saw his eyes were white, his pupils rolled back into his head, alarming to see.

"Phoenix," she called, kneeling. "Phoenix, what is it?"

His eyes flickered and the muscles in his body trembled and shook. His feet shuffled as if, in his head, he was trying to flee some pursuer. She looked around to the others, not knowing what to do. "Phoenix!"

Demara kneeled, putting her hands on Phoenix's shoulders. "A vision. It takes him like this sometimes. We can only make sure he doesn't harm himself."

Phoenix bucked and writhed as Demara held him. Others came to assist. Phoenix convulsed so strongly they couldn't hold him. His violent movements reached a crescendo – and then stopped. His body went limp as he sank back to the ground. For a moment Cait thought he was dead. But then his eyes flickered open. After licking his lips a few times he whispered something to her.

She couldn't hear his words. She put her ear close to his mouth. His breath was warm on her neck.

"A vision," he said. "One came to me, too."

"What did you see?"

"Across the aether. All the way to your world, Cait."

Dread like icy water dripped through her. There was something troubling in his voice, something he was struggling to say. She glanced at the archway. Still no sign of Ran. If he was gone they were trapped in the frozen north, far from the An. She had the clear sensation of events spinning out of control, slipping through her grasp. It was suddenly all going wrong. Lugg, Ran and now this. Perhaps it was another moment of insight.

"What did you see?" she asked him again.

"I'm sorry, Cait," he whispered. "I saw her. I was with

her. The undain all around on the green hillside and the grey walls fading. I was there in your world as she died. There was nothing at all I could do."

14 – MR. SHANKLY

Mount Öræfajökull, Iceland

Six days earlier

"**C**ait!"

Fer cried out as Cait, Ran and the man from Genera fell into the lava-pit. The shock on Cait's face as she disappeared from view was terrible to see. For some reason she'd jumped – jumped or fallen – before Fiona, her mother, could take her hand.

Fer, along with Johnny, Fiona and Cait's grandmother, Catherine, scrambled to the edge of the pit. The heat coming off the lava was intense, prickling Fer's eyes. The red pool of molten rock looked alive, moving and breathing, little plumes of molten rock flicking off it. There was no sign of Cait or the others. They'd fallen: either into the lava or across the aether into Angere. Fer wasn't sure which was the worse fate.

Catherine slipped her arm around Fiona, holding her grown-up daughter tight, as she must have done many times when Fiona was a girl. Still no one spoke. Everyone's face was stark with shock. Even the minstrel, Johnny, who normally grinned and laughed through everything, looked as if he had been struck.

Without Fiona, what chance would Cait have in Angere? Fer could tell Fiona wanted to follow, jump after her daughter. But it was impossible. The bookwyrm had been clear. This portal would open only once in six months. Cait and the two men were alone in Angere.

Fer touched Fiona on the shoulder. Hard as it was they had to keep moving. If the undain or Genera came, there would be nowhere to escape to. There would be time later to worry and lament. They had the book, so unexpectedly given to them by Nox. Somehow they had to keep that out of Genera's hands and take it to Andar, or many other daughters and sons would be lost as well. Perhaps it was futile now, but they had to try. They had to fight.

Catherine nodded in understanding at Fer's touch. She spoke to Fiona while Johnny interpreted.

"The bookwyrm said the lava-pit becomes a lesser portal once it's been used to get to Angere. It should take us elsewhere in this world."

"Do we know where?" asked Fer.

"Not a clue. Fiona thinks somewhere in Manchester is likely because we're so close to the other shadow path, the one that brought us here. They'll be *entwined*. Does that make any sense?"

She had no idea. Hopping between the worlds was not something she was used to. "Perhaps. But they'll be watching the shadow paths," said Fer. "They'll be waiting for us."

Johnny shrugged. "You know, it doesn't seem like the undain have much clue about where these wormholes really lead, otherwise they'd have been here waiting for us. Maybe Nox really did keep them in the dark. Besides it's, like, use the portal or traipse across the frozen mountains of Iceland for a week."

He was right. Genera would stop at nothing to retrieve the book, just as they'd stop at nothing to retrieve their precious blood. They'd be scouring the world for her, Fiona and Catherine. And if Nox really had defected then perhaps Genera would be in confusion for a time. Perhaps if she and the others carried on running, Angere wouldn't notice Cait was gone for a few days. It was the only thing they could do.

While the two older women conversed, Fer stepped outside the cave. She needed to breathe fresh air. She wanted to be sure their pursuers weren't coming after them.

Outside an icy twilight awaited. The western sky glowed pink and orange, but overhead it was fully night. There was no sign of pursuit. Nothing moved. She looked up at the unfamiliar stars of this world, their odd arrangements and shapes. Did the people here give them names, too, see faces and creatures as they did in Andar? A pathway shone directly overhead, like a sparkling road. It was incredibly beautiful. They had nothing like that in the skies of Andar. She stood beneath different stars.

Johnny walked up to stand beside her. He didn't speak as he admired the view.

"This musical instrument of yours," said Fer. "This guitar. *Mr. Shankly*. We have to find that first? In order to open the shadow path back to Andar?"

"There's no other way," said Johnny. "I don't really know how I worked the spookiness the first time, but if I can get my old guitar back maybe I'll be able to weave the spell again. Or whatever it was I did."

"And you're sure you can't use some other guitar?"

He looked at her like she'd asked the stupidest question in the world. "It has to be Mr. Shankly. I mean, sure, I can get a tune on other instruments. I can *play* them. But I can only make music with Mr. Shankly. It's hard to explain."

"This guitar of yours is alive in some way? Like your boat?"

"No, no. Nothing like that." But then he paused and considered for a moment, running his hands through his straggly hair. "Except, maybe, yeah. Not *actually* alive. But that's kind of how it feels when I'm playing him. It's like we're talking or singing together or something. We're *one*. Strange, huh?"

She liked Johnny. It was hard not to. His fear burned brightly within him, close to the surface, but he refused to let it control him. "Strange? That's one of the few things I've heard in this world that makes sense. But how can we be sure your guitar is still here? You've been away for a long time."

Johnny shrugged. He held the small black triangle that Danny had given him. The *guitar pick*. He twirled it through his fingers like someone fretting with worry-beads. "We can't be sure. But Cait said it had been auctioned off as part of some charity gig. Chances are whoever bought it would look after it, I guess."

"Then how do we find it?"

"Get back to civilization and trawl the internet. See what we can find."

"Won't they see us doing that? Genera?"

"Maybe. Just have to hope they don't put two and two together."

"The archaeon has taken up residence on this *internet*. Perhaps it can help us? Or hide what we're doing?"

"Maybe. But first we need to find WiFi."

"Who is that?"

"It's a thing, not a person," said Johnny. "It's kinda like the aether, but with more pictures of cats."

She had no idea what he was talking about. But they weren't going to get far if she made him explain everything in this strange world.

"Then we'd better go and find this mysterious *WiFi*," she said.

Back inside, the four of them stood around the lip of the lava-pit, staring at the seething pool of orange-red.

Cait's grandmother spoke. Fer was already picking up a few words of the language, although Johnny had to translate a lot.

"Are we absolutely sure about this?" said Catherine. "You're sure the little dragon said this would become a Lesser Portal once it had been used, and not, say, a pool of molten rock?"

"That's what it said," replied Fiona. "You were there, too. Let me go first. Hopefully you'll see me disappear before I hit the lava."

"*Hopefully?* Well that's encouraging," said her mother.

"What choice do we have? Follow me if it seems to work. Otherwise, you'll have to head for civilisation and hope Genera doesn't find you first."

"And why are you going to be the one to jump?" asked her mother.

"Because, I don't want *you* to be the one if it is a lava-pit."

"Well," said Catherine, "you'll have to get used to not getting your own way, won't you?" And before anyone could stop her she stepped off the edge and tipped forward into the chasm.

"No!" shouted Fiona.

Fer managed to grasp hold of her arm and stop her. They watched as Cait's gran plummeted toward the lava. At the last moment, as it seemed inevitable she would plunge into the burning rock, she winked out of existence.

Fiona looked at Fer and Johnny, relief mixed with a questioning look on her face. *Were they ready for this?* Fer nodded, although she wasn't at all sure she was.

Holding on to each other, the three of them fell into the searing flame.

Fer expected to thump painfully into the ground, but she found herself standing upon a round, metal grid in a narrow alleyway between high stone walls. The others were there, too, gazes casting around as they tried to work out where they were. They certainly seemed to be back in the city, or *a* city at least. Cars roared past the mouth of the alleyway, punctuating the deep background note that hummed from the buildings. The sky glowed orange even though it appeared to be night. A light drizzle hung in the air, soaking her face. A little way above them, in one of the walls, was a single square window, dark and grimy. There didn't appear to be anyone looking through it.

"One of the ginnels off Deansgate," said Fiona, Johnny still translating. "We're back in Manchester. Follow me."

"Where are we going?" asked Fer. "And what's a *ginnel*?"

"It's a sort of narrow passageway between two buildings that follows the route of an ancient pathway. Manchester's riddled with them, a bit like portals running between the big streets. And we're going somewhere they won't find us."

"Where? The grove on that *roundabout* Cait described?"

"No, that's too far. Somewhere nearer. There's still safe ground to be found in the city centre if you know where to look."

Fer followed, trying not to resent Fiona's assumption she would simply do as she was told. Now wasn't the time.

They emerged from the twisting, narrow passageway onto a busy, blaring street that blazed with flashing, zooming lights. Moving in a line, they weaved their way through the crowds, following Fiona. Once again, cars clogged the road, sometimes sitting with their engines rattling, sometimes roaring forward and then stopping suddenly as lights in front of them turned red. One or two people crossed the road between the lines of moving cars. She couldn't watch, still couldn't see how it was they didn't get killed.

"Does anyone have any cash?" asked Johnny as they hurried past a row of brightly-lit shops that were selling a dazzling array of items, most of which Fer couldn't begin to guess the function of.

"What are you buying?" she asked. "We need to get off the streets."

All the undain that had surrounded them on their way through to Iceland had to be somewhere near. And it wasn't just the people. She was beginning to understand that there were machines watching, too. Storing the pictures they saw and even, so Johnny had explained, identifying individuals from their faces. Tracking them. How did the people here put up with it?

"We need a new SIM in case there's no WiFi. So we can surf the interweb without being traced, yeah?" said Johnny.

"Of course," said Fer.

He took some of the paper they used as money from Fiona and disappeared inside the shop. Fer, Fiona and Catherine pretended to study the contents of the window so their faces couldn't be seen from the road. Fer studied her own pale reflection overlaid on the dazzling array of *things* for sale. She expected attack at any moment. Glancing over her shoulder, she watched as a long white car drifted by, windows blackened so those inside couldn't be seen. Undain? Perhaps. She was still learning how to see the creatures. See the absence where their glow should be. Something Cait seemed to be able to do instinctively.

When Johnny emerged they hurried on. Fer tried to keep her head down, not catch anyone's eye. It was easy to do; everyone on the street seemed to be locked in their own little world. Some had wires in their ears, listening to music, so Johnny explained. One or two talked to themselves, although no one appeared to think this strange.

Fifteen minutes later they arrived at a large, ornate building with tall, beautiful windows and a clock tower reaching into the sky. The windows were unlit. A welcome circle of greenery surrounded the place, as if to keep the roads and buildings at bay.

"The Cathedral," said Johnny.

"I don't know the word," said Fer.

"It's, like, a place people go to sing and worship gods."

"And Fiona worships these gods? She thinks they can help us?"

Johnny shook his head. "From what I can tell this is another ancient grovey place. Down underground. When this god came the followers built their first church on top of it."

"Why?"

"To claim the place. To draw on its power. To cleanse it. Who knows? It's what always happens."

"And we can get down to the old levels. Beneath the building?"

"Apparently there are arcane *ways* if you know how to find them. There's a crypt. And then natural tunnels below that."

Fiona walked to a tall wooden door. It looked to be locked, but with a casual wave of her hand it clicked open. One by one they filed inside. Fer was aware of standing in a large, airy space, faint lights from the city filtering through the windows. Stone pillars supported the roof and, between them, were rows and rows of wooden seats.

"We have to go underground," said Fiona. She lit a faint light. "The doorway only reveals itself when the clock reaches a certain time."

"Midnight, I'll bet," said Johnny.

"That's maybe what it should be, but actually, no. 11:37. No one knows why."

In the crypt, bricked-up archways of something like an ancient bridge were visible in one of the walls, a remnant from part of the city now submerged beneath the ground.

Fiona stood by one of the archways and glanced at her watch. "We go through there. The way should open in a few minutes. At least, it did last time I was here, although that was many years ago. I'll have to dismiss the light; it only opens if there is absolute darkness. Hold my hand and I'll lead us in."

They stood together for long minutes, no one speaking, Fer holding one of Fiona's hands and also one of Johnny's.

Eventually Fiona squeezed her hand and pulled her forward. They made their way past the point where the solid stones of the wall should have been. The ground beneath Fer's feet became uneven. They kept moving. The air grew heavier with damp and, dimly, Fer sensed the rush of water. Although whether a river was nearby, or below them, or above, she couldn't tell.

Finally, Fiona lit another light to reveal a long, natural cave that stretched into shadows. They appeared to be deep underground. Water dripped and babbled from somewhere nearby. "We'll be safe here while we decide what to do. I doubt they know about this place, but even if they do it will be hard for them to get inside."

"We'll need food," said Johnny. "Soft pillows and TV would be good, too."

"Fiona and I will go for supplies," said Cait's gran. "Sandwiches and cups of tea at least. Probably *not* TV and comfortable beds. We can work a glamour or two to alter our appearance."

"How will you get back in?" Fer asked.

"I can hold the doorway open for a short while," said Fiona. "When we return I'll seal it again. The book will stay here in case we're spotted and chased."

"I'll come back up, too," said Johnny. "No signal down here."

"Stay out of sight," said Fiona. "If someone spots a famously dead rock singer hanging around in the shadows of the Cathedral making phone calls, we'll never hear the end of it."

Johnny grinned. "Got it."

When they were gone, Fer stood alone in the underground space. A rough circle of square stones dotted the interior of the cave, although whether they'd been deliberately placed or were natural, she couldn't tell. She sat on one and breathed deeply, trying to clear her mind. She'd barely had time to think since arriving in this confusing, terrible world.

She caught a flicker of movement in the shadows, movement that disappeared when she turned to look at it. She didn't need to see the indistinct figures to know what they were. She'd felt their presence more and more, and it was immediately stronger below the ground. Ghosts. Faint, faint wraiths all about her, many of them little more than children when they'd died. She sensed confusion, longing, loss seeping from the stone walls. Centuries of them it seemed. What had been done to them? Once there had been much death here. Hard lives, barely lived before they'd ended, buried away beneath those bright, pretty lights on the surface.

Cait had been in touch with them, too. Fer had sensed something hidden in her, some memory or indistinct presence. She hadn't liked to pry. Perhaps any witch living in Manchester would be in contact with the ghosts of the place. Genera and its machinery had been there a long time.

But Fer was beginning to see her true purpose for coming, beyond retrieving the vile book, beyond attempting to avert the disaster about to overwhelm her home. This world needed help. Oh, it was a place of wonders and marvels. Most of the people appeared to be like those in Andar: warm and daft and flawed and loving.

But this terrible thing had been done to them. Genera's machines drained their Spirit each day: marring them, reducing them, without them knowing. She thought about the container-loads of bones shipped through the portal to the White City. The scale of it was horrifying: the harvest of wars and poverty and disease. And her world was to blame. Not Andar, perhaps, but the undain and Genera. The monsters of Angere were parasites sucking the life out of this world.

Perhaps she wouldn't be able to do much, but she could do *something*. Count herself on the right side of the balance. The side of life. That was what she would do. Help some of the lost souls find rest.

She'd been so resentful of Hellen and the rest of them on Islagray, their rules and covens. The way they gave up freedoms for the strength of the group. It seemed a petty concern now. The evil done here was on a different scale.

She sat with her arms around her knees, trying to hear the quiet voices in the shadows. Communing with them if she could, although many were too far gone. Occasionally a face formed in the air before her, nothing more than a brief blur, a flash of sombre eyes or the laugh of a giggling child. She tried to reach out to them, touch them, but they fled in alarm each time.

She was still there fifteen minutes later when Johnny returned. The pale ghosts dissolved into the darkness as he stepped into the cavern. She wished she could have had longer, given them more time to come to her. Perhaps there would be a chance later.

"I found it," said Johnny, the glow from the screen lighting up his face. "My guitar."

"Did the archaeon assist?"

"Nah. I asked it, but it told me to do my own search and stop bothering it."

"And where's the guitar?"

"Well, the bad news is it's currently in New York."

"That's a long way?"

"A long way. A flight across the ocean."

"Flying over water is difficult," said Fer.

"Not with an aeroplane it isn't," said Johnny. "But it doesn't matter. Because the guitar's coming here in five days."

"The guitar is coming *here*? I don't understand."

"Screaming Machinery, my old band. They're on the road. *The Glastonbury Tour.* They bought the guitar back and they're in London in two days' time, then up here before moving on to Glasgow. And they're using Mr. Shankly in the show."

"Can we afford to wait that long?"

"We'll have to. It's too good a chance to miss." He was

filled with excitement. "There's this song, you see, *Beyond the Veil*. Kind of our signature tune, used to close our shows with it. And they've got this robotic me playing it. See, there's video footage. All this darkness and smoke and then I – I mean it – appear from above, descending on a shaft of light. It's all programmed to replicate how I used to play the song. Even has a few random variations thrown in so it's different each night."

"That seems pretty ... inappropriate," said Fer. "They think you're dead don't they?"

Johnny shrugged. "It seems pretty cool to me. Plus it means the guitar will be here. We can use this."

"You mean, talk to the rest of this band of yours? Ask them to give you the instrument?"

A frown played across Johnny's features. "They would, for sure. I mean, it would be a majorly weird conversation, but they'd do it. But then Genera would find out, right? There's no way we could keep them in the dark. Genera must know who I am. They'll have eyes and ears inside the band, just in case I get in touch."

"Eyes and ears?" she said. What evil magic did Genera have at their disposal? "How would they do that?"

"Not *literally*. I mean they'll have spies or they'll be monitoring texts and social networking or something. News would leak out one way or another."

"Perhaps we could take the guitar from them between shows. When the band is travelling around?"

"The security would be too tight. The guitar is well-guarded."

He continued to examine the pictures he'd found on the phone, swiping his finger across the machine's glassy surface. Then the frown on his face faded to be replaced by his familiar grin.

"Hey," he said.

"What is it? What have you thought of?"

"It's obvious," said Johnny. "How I get to the guitar. They give it to this robot to play, right?"

"I don't know what that means," said Fer.

"It's, like, a machine that resembles me."

"OK, but I don't…"

"So I replace the robot. We sneak inside the venue, I take the place of the machine, and they'll just give me the guitar. Plus, I'll get to play with the guys again. One song only, but think how cool that would be."

"You think that might work?"

Johnny considered for a moment. "Dunno. But I think it's damn-well worth a try."

15 – BEYOND THE VEIL

They camped in the cold cave below the Cathedral crypt for five days, venturing outside as little as possible, waiting for the arrival of the Screaming Machinery tour.

The wait took its toll on all of them, but it was worse for Cait's mother and gran. Fer didn't need to be a witch to see the anxiety gnawing at them. They were filled with worry for Cait, frustrated at not being able to do anything to help her. Guilt blazed its grim light in their minds: guilt at letting Cait go so unprepared.

When one of them did sneak onto the streets to buy more food, they reported more and more Genera activity: riders on the roads around the Cathedral and also a great many uniformed security guards, more like soldiers than the police who were supposed to keep the peace in this world.

Fer couldn't be sure, but it appeared Genera suspected they were hiding in the area. Although perhaps it was the same in all the other towns and cities.

Or perhaps the soldiers were there in reaction to the increasing trouble. On the second day, Cait's mother returned looking flustered.

"What is it?" said Fer. "Did they see you?"

"No, I don't think so. There's just … something like a riot going on up there. I managed to avoid it, but there were gangs of people, youths and older people, breaking shop windows and turning cars over."

"And that's unusual?" asked Fer.

"Of course." Fiona sat on one of the rocks while Catherine poured her a cup of tea from a flask. "I mean, we've had problems before from time to time, but this is all so sudden. It was scary. Their faces were covered as they threw bricks and firebombs."

"It's Genera," said Catherine. "Has to be. They must have turned up those machines of theirs, sucking the hope from people, turning them angry."

"Why?" said Fer. "Are they doing it to find us? Flush us out?"

"No, I don't think so," said Fiona, sipping at her steaming tea and trying to brush her hair into some sort of order with her fingers. "I think there's more to it than that. It must be the invasion of Andar. The undain army needs powering. Things are coming to a head. The time is drawing near as the An freezes over."

And what damage would be done to this world by the undain machines? What harm would be done to the *people*? Fer was filled with anxieties of her own. Not just for Cait but for everyone she knew. Here and back home. Her family, the friends she'd grown up with, how many of them would survive when the undain came? Any of them?

Her own guilt at leaving Andar ate away at her, too. She spent her quiet moments seeking the shadows for lost ghosts, offering what peace and reassurance she could. In truth, it probably helped her more than it did them.

When the day of the concert came they sat together in a circle to discuss their plans.

"I'll go with Johnny," said Fer.

Fiona looked doubtful. "We should all go. Who knows

what dangers we'll face? Genera will be watching the concert. They may not suspect we'll try this stunt with the guitar, but they'll be *there*."

"Someone should stay here and guard the book," said Fer. "Besides, you've been taking all the risks. It's time we did something."

"Plus it will look a lot more believable if it's just the two of us," said Johnny. "No offence, but you're not typical Screaming Machinery concert-goers."

"As a matter of fact, young man, I'm quite a fan," said Catherine. "Cait played me several tracks. Very ... exhilarating. Think I'm too old, do you?"

Johnny looked mortified. "No. Hell, no. We loved fans of any age, trust me. I just figured the two of us would stand out less. People might think we're a couple." He threw an apologetic glance at Fer. "We'll sneak in, grab the guitar, then come back here. Lie low for a couple of days until the heat dies down then slip off to Glasto."

A look passed between Fiona and her mother.

"I don't like it," said Fiona. "Too much could go wrong."

Fer said, "Too much could go wrong whatever we do. This is the best way. I can work a glamour to hide our appearances as well as you can. You two can guard the book and let us back inside when we have the guitar."

Fiona hesitated, partly, no doubt, because she didn't want to let Fer head off alone just as Cait had.

"And will you be able to play this song?" Fiona asked Johnny. "You haven't been able to practice since coming here."

Johnny flexed his fingers. "No problems there. Some songs become second nature after a while. Once I pick up Mr. Shankly the magic will happen."

"Very well," said Fiona. "But stay hidden. If they pursue you, try to put them off the trail so they don't know where we are. If you can't shake them, get away, out of the city, and we'll contact you later."

"We should talk to the bookwyrm too," said Johnny. "Perhaps it will be able to disrupt Genera's communications."

"Worth a try," said Fiona. "And what about tickets to get in?"

"I can handle that if the archaeon can't," said Fer. "A few simple illusions in the minds of the guards and we'll get inside."

"You can do that?" said Johnny.

"I don't see why not."

"Cool. Would have saved me a bucketful of money over the years. We'll need back-stage passes, too. So I can replace the robot thing."

"Show me what I need to do when we get there."

"And if that all works, we just have to figure out how to get to Glastonbury unseen, yeah?" said Johnny.

"We'll cross that bridge when we come to it," said Fiona. "First we need this guitar of yours. Then we'll worry about the rest."

It was dark when Fer and Johnny took the passageway into the Cathedral crypt and onto the streets of Manchester. An icy wind whipped around the old stones of the building. She was glad of it; it would probably do more than anything else to keep the mob off the streets. Cars whooshed by on the nearby roads, but no one appeared to be watching them.

"Let's talk to the wyrm," said Johnny. "Security is going to be tight with all this panic on the streets."

Fer watched as he touched the little picture of the sleeping dragon on his phone. At first she thought it was going to ignore him. Then the colourful little creature appeared, strutting across the screen, even huffing out sketches of red flame.

Johnny held the phone close to his mouth so he could whisper to the dragon. "Hello again, noble Archaeon. We really need your help this time."

"Is that correct?" The voice from the little machine was tinny but clear if she listened carefully. "You're sure you're not just incapable of using a website like last time?"

"No, this is something more suited to your skills," said Johnny. "Trust me. We're facing a difficult situation and only you can help us." He winked at Fer, grinning.

"Is that so?" said the archaeon. "Then I suppose you'd better explain what you need. Oh, and I *can* see you winking through your phone's camera, you know."

"Ah, right," said Johnny. "OK. Sorry. So here's the situation."

Half an hour later they stood together in the queue for the concert. They were at the building they'd arrived beneath when first coming to Manchester. Its wide, curved front arched over them, a white clock in its middle showing them they had half an hour before the concert began.

Feeling exposed now that they were outside, Fer concentrated on the spell she was maintaining to alter their appearance. It would fool most people glancing at them, but she knew a higher undain wouldn't be deceived. There would be cameras on them, too, watching them, capturing their images. Would her magic still work when it passed through the machines? She didn't know. They'd seen quite a few police cars on the roads, and here at the concert, there were security guards in gaudy orange tops, watching the crowds with blank expressions. But so far, no one had paid them any attention.

She glanced at Johnny. The whole situation had to be strange for him. What would happen if the people around them knew who he really was? She saw his true appearance and, overlaying him, the version of him she'd fashioned. Roughly the same height, short hair, a very different face. She'd modelled him on a lad from back home, Arik, whom she'd admired from afar. A fact which Johnny didn't have to know anything about.

"You're sure this is going to work?" she asked. "You

just show them the tickets on your phone and they'll get us in?"

"So the wyrm said. VIP passes too. Stupidly expensive but apparently the dragon's acquired quite a hoard of gold trading on the internet."

When they reached the front of the line, a guard eyed them suspiciously but waved them through when the tickets checked out. Inside, a large crowd already filled the cavernous space. Many of them sipped at drinks as they milled around or sat on the floor in little groups. Crashing music blared from somewhere, although no one was playing on the distant stage. One or two figures in black fiddled with the various bits of machinery the band would presumably use once they started. The crowds were denser toward the front; the people there standing crammed together rather than sitting. Everyone seemed to be in a good mood. She could feel the anticipation coming off them like a glow.

Johnny led her through the throng to another line of security guards near the stage. After more expressionless glares they were admitted into the inner sanctum of the *VIP area*. This was much less crowded. Soft seats lined the walls, and food and drink were freely available. She should have been hungry but couldn't face the thought of eating.

"OK," said Johnny. "Time to work your voodoo and get us backstage." The archaeon hadn't been able to acquire these tickets as, apparently, they had to be on paper.

She could see the guard studying them as they approached. Other people she'd seen wore brightly-coloured necklaces. These, she assumed, were needed to grant access to the mysterious *backstage*, like some artefact with magical properties. In truth she couldn't conjure such things easily, especially as she didn't understand any of the words written upon the necklaces. But people she could work with. All she had to do was convince the guard they were supposed to have the necklaces and all would be well.

She strode up to him. Looking like you belonged, that you didn't expect to be turned away, was half the battle. Maintaining the glamour that hid both of them as well as working this new magic would cost her, although she wouldn't admit it to anyone.

With a blink of her eyes, she reached gently into the guard's mind and whispered quiet suggestions to him about the thoughts he really *should* be thinking.

For a moment, the briefest moment, she thought he wasn't going to respond, that his mind was too severe, all hard surfaces. Or that some magic or machinery protected him. Then he stirred into life. Not looking at her, he reached into a brown box beside him and picked out two of the colourful necklaces for them to take.

Resisting the temptation to thank him in the tongue of Andar, Fer nodded and took a necklace, slipping it over her head. Behind her, Johnny did the same.

Once inside, they made their way down narrow corridors around the back of the stage, past machines and lights and enough ropes to rig a hundred of the coasters that sailed in the shallows of the An.

At one point, they brushed past a group of four people dressed for the stage in bright colours and exaggerated make-up. They had to be Johnny's band mates. Fer tried not to catch their eyes. One, a woman, stopped and frowned as they hurried by, her eyes on Johnny. Had she seen something? Sensed something? The glamour was still in place but the woman must have known Johnny well. After a moment, she shrugged and moved on.

The robot Johnny stood on a platform at one side of the backstage area, its head slumped forward as if asleep. Up close it was clearly a machine, clever cogs and metal rods and wires making up its body. It looked like it could move its head and arms but that was about it. The legs were simple metal columns attached to a small platform. The hands, through, were as complex and jointed as real ones, designed to perform the intricate movements required for playing the guitar. The machine's face, lifeless and rubbery, nevertheless bore a striking similarity to Johnny.

"Hey, now that's one good looking robot," said Johnny.

"But where's the guitar?" said Fer.

"They'll tune it and bring it out when they're ready. Can you do the hocus pocus thing to make me look like that?"

She couldn't follow the complexity of those hands. "I doubt it. Not so it looks believable."

"So, we wait for the robot to be set up with Mr. Shankly and then do the switch. I'll bet there'll be a guard so you'll have to spoof them. Send them to a happy place while I take the place of the Terminator."

She thought she understood. "I can probably do that. So long as the guard isn't some undain lord."

"Nah. Probably won't be. Come on, let's lurk in the shadows until it's time. I'll show you where you can watch the gig." He looked at her, suddenly troubled by something. "You know, back in Andar, we don't really have music like this. Nothing so *loud* for one thing. Are you going to cope?"

"Don't worry about me. Just make sure you get the guitar."

She remembered his words with some bitterness when the concert finally started. It wasn't simply loud, it was deafening: a huge sound like solid rocks hurled through the air as the lights blazed into life. Instinctively she covered her ears. A passing man in black, one of those setting up the instruments, handed her something, a grin on his face. Protectors for her ears, ridiculous looking yellow hemispheres like two halves of some piece of fruit. She slipped them over her head, and the sound was immediately muffled. She stood, trying not to get in anyone's way, fascinated and intrigued, while song after song crashed over the audience.

When the concert finished and the band came off stage, Johnny, now harnessed onto the little platform in place of the robot and holding Mr. Shankly, still hadn't moved. The guard she'd bewitched stood in front of him, occasionally muttering into a little machine in his chest. She was confused. Were they not going to do this special song after all? She removed the protectors from her ears. The audience was chanting and cheering, roaring for the band to come back. People stood around waiting, expecting something to happen. It was like they knew the band would return and it was all a game. Or a part of the ceremony of the thing. She'd have to ask Johnny about it.

Then the little platform was suddenly pulled upward, and the band members reappeared. Fer decided to try without the ear protectors. The noise would be huge and terrifying, but she'd found she was starting to enjoy it, too. It vibrated in her rib cage, shook her whole body, but there was something thrilling about it. It moved her in ways she wasn't used to music moving her.

The lights went back up, and the woman who'd half-noticed Johnny earlier spoke to the crowd.

"Thank you. I honestly can't tell you how much that means. We'd like to play one more song. You probably know what it is. You may also know we used to have a guitarist called Johnny, who's no longer with us. It's strange though, sometimes I think I can feel him nearby. Maybe, who knows, if we all shout loud enough, he'll appear during this song. Let's give it a try. This one's called *Beyond the Veil*."

And they were off again, the sound a solid wall of noise blasting into the audience. Half-way through, at some pre-arranged signal Fer didn't see, the noise cut out. Everyone in the audience clearly knew what to expect. A sea of faces peered upward into the darkness.

There was the briefest moment of absolute quiet. Watching from the side of the stage she could feel the excitement, the anticipation, coming off them like something solid in the air.

Then lights lanced down, as bright as the sun through gaps in clouds. And there was Johnny, high up, seemingly floating in the air. More lights picked him out, making him glow.

And he began to play, so loud it made Fer jump, although the sound was sweet and clean, notes as clear as birdsong. His left hand ran up and down the neck of his guitar like some great spider as he played faster and faster. How did he remember all the notes, the movements? It was dazzling. He held her, held them all, rapt.

Fer, glancing across the stage at the other band members, saw something else, too. *They knew*. They stared in clear amazement, glances of confusion and delight passing between them. They could tell when it was the machine, the robot, pretending to be Johnny, and they could tell the real thing. Here he was. The long-lost, presumed-dead guitar player of Screaming Machinery, impossibly restored to them and playing the guitar, his guitar, in the air above them. For a minute or more the band were at one with the crowd. Awestruck.

Johnny descended as he played, the lights and wires cleverly arranged so that he seemed to be walking down the white beam of a spotlight. He passed directly over the audience, playing all the time. A round platform had been set up at the back of the crowd, on top of the fenced-off area where people sat pressing buttons and watching screens, presumably controlling all the dazzling lights and smoke and noise. People in the crowd reached up to try and touch him as he floated over their heads, still playing.

He touched down, struck the final few screaming notes of his solo, and then the rest of the band came crashing in, drums and more guitars and singing, all a vast roaring din as lights blazed on the stage once more.

Fer couldn't stop herself from covering her ears, but everyone else waved their arms or jumped up and down. Even one or two of the security guards. They shouted and laughed their delight even though their voices couldn't be heard. There was a sense of something unexpected coming from them: beyond joy or adulation. A sense of being part of something. Something wonderful. Something bigger than they were.

This world continued to amaze her. Odd delights turned up in surprising places. That sense of togetherness, of submerging yourself into the greater whole. She recognized it. It was something she'd always been wary of, although now she understood something of the joy and power of it. Because the only word she could really find to describe what she was witnessing was *coven*.

She was tempted to stay, enjoy the moment. But it was time to leave. She slipped past the security guards protecting the backstage area from invaders, through the VIP area, and out into the crowd. It was easy enough to weave down the side of the room with everyone pushing forward to be near the stage or Johnny's platform.

Johnny was facing the crowd and stage as he continued to play *Beyond the Veil*. Fer watched as he took his hand from the guitar during a pause and waved to them all. Simply waved. And she knew without needing to be told that the robot he'd replaced never did this. Couldn't do this. This was Johnny saying to them all, *Hi, yes, it's me. Here I am*. And also, because she knew what was coming, *thanks* and *goodbye*.

Then the song ended in a huge crescendo and the lights cut out. The roar from the crowd swelled to fill the void. Fer pushed to the back of the fenced-off area, where more guards stood to keep people away. The crowd was sparse here because the stage wasn't visible. She only had a moment before Johnny appeared.

Closing her eyes to summon the magic, she reworked the glamour on his appearance, altering him before anyone saw him coming down. She was weary from the sustained effort of it, grateful for the blank expression she needed to reproduce. Believable faces were the hardest part of this spell. Nevertheless, between the new magic and maintaining her own appearance, she experienced a moment of dizziness and nausea. The floor lurched sideways and threatened to tip her off. She tried to ignore it. This was how it was when she worked magic. But everything depended on her getting this right.

Johnny appeared. She saw him clearly as he really was: the daft grin on his face, the straggly hair. The look of pure joy in his eyes. But she also saw the form she'd given him: one more security guard, powerfully-built, grim-faced. Across his back, where the guitar was really, a black backpack. She'd done it. Now they only had to creep away and get back to the Cathedral.

The hand that grasped her arm from behind was iron-cruel. "Don't move, little witch-bitch. Or I will eat you alive."

16 – THE LIZARD KING

Fer twisted around, desperate to pull herself free from the undain that had seized her. There could be no doubt this was a horror from Angere come to this world. Its mind was an emptiness where it should have glowed with light, and the sense of malign *wrongness* coming from the creature made her sick. It was a walking corpse, a devourer of others' lives. And it had hold of her.

For a moment, the crowds, the guards, Johnny, everything faded. There was only her and the creature. She met its gaze, and recognition flashed through her. She knew this undain. She had met it before. That same handsome face and raven-black hair. On the banks of the An one bright morning, walking north with the spice merchant Merdoc. Memories she'd blotted out, partly from the pain she'd experienced, partly from something else. Hellen had asked her more than once to try and recall what had happened, how it was she'd killed the flying undain. The memories she'd buried since then rushed back bright and clear...

The undain horror approached Andar after its long, impossible flight over the waters. It was clearly exhausted, its movements broken and ragged. Between each pained beat of its wings it dropped farther and farther from the sky. For a moment she thought it wasn't going to make it; that the waters of the An would swallow it, sweep the horror away and leave Andar untainted. But with one desperate effort, the creature lunged for the wooded bank. Coming, so it seemed to Fer, directly for her. She stepped back into the shadows of the boughs. She would have to face the nightmare. There was no one else. The winged creature was half-dead, but the undain on its back, the rider, watched her with cold malevolence. A tall, raven-haired man, impossibly beautiful, one hand on the flying beast's reins, another held aloft as if preparing some magic to hurl at her.

Unbidden, unexpected, words whispered to Fer as a girl rose to her lips. Her family's secret. A story, or a guilty truth, or a nonsense rhyme. No one knew which. Words she'd repeated until she knew them by heart. Words that made no sense to her, alien sounds in an alien tongue. Their meaning had been lost over the centuries even if their importance wasn't. A secret passed down through the generations, whispered in the darkness from mother to daughter, father to son. *Remember this. Tell no one else.*

Had she spoken the words purely out of fear and shock? Or had she known, somehow, that they needed to be said? That here, finally, was the moment?

The creature crashed to the bank, half of its bony grey body still in the water. It still lived, its jaws a gaping hole of serrated bone teeth, snapping at her. The syllables tasted like iron spikes in Fer's mouth as she hurled them at the clashing, snarling horror.

The cost to her was great. There was strong magic to the words, magic of a sort she didn't understand, magic far removed from the gentle coaxings and persuasions the witches used. Pain tore through her and she screamed, terrified she had done some fatal damage to herself. The creature screamed too, an agonized, mindless roar of despair.

The world faded as Fer lost consciousness, her mind fleeing the pain. Dimly she was aware of the rider, the undain lord, leaping from the stricken creature's back and hurrying away, leaving the winged beast to its fate. She couldn't let either escape into Andar. She had to slay both of the nightmares before they could sully the land she loved.

She tried to fight off the fog engulfing her. Pursue the rider. Protect Merdoc. Protect everyone. But it was no use. The terrible words had exacted their price. The undain lord, its shape already altering into something smaller and hunched, disappeared into the trees toward Merdoc and his cart. The winged creature, with one final clash of its sawed-bone jaws, crashed to the ground and died. And Fer fell to the ground with it…

The undain in the concert hall spoke again, its grip on Fer's arm tightening. "We meet again, witch whore spawn of Ilminion. If I'd known who you were when we met last time you wouldn't be alive now. You'd be strung from a hook in the dungeons of the White City, holy blood dripping from your carcass."

Did the undain know what she'd done to the winged creature on the bank? What magic she'd wrought? The words rose to her lips once again. She had no other weapon. In desperation, she spat the syllables at the creature, careless of the cost to herself. A tearing pain cut through her, but she wouldn't relent.

The shock on the face of the undain was clear. It thought she'd worked some mundane magic by the river, some weak witch's incantation. It didn't think she could do it any real harm. Didn't know about the family secret passed down to Fer from her distant forebears.

The undain screamed. It struggled as if she had it pinned down. It tried to resist the magic she'd thrown. This undain was far more powerful. It wavered and writhed, its features fluid for a moment.

"Vile abomination," it rasped, its voice rough. "You'll pay for that."

The creature's human appearance was reasserting itself. She knew what she had to do. The family secret wasn't just the words. There was another element. *The blood. Our blood.* Ignoring the pain of it, Fer bit into the soft inside of her own cheek. The metallic taste filled her mouth. She spat her blood at the undain's face, then threw the foul words at it for a second time.

This time the effect was immediate. With an agonized scream, the creature faltered and began to melt. The hard features it had adopted sank into formless grey flesh. It collapsed to the ground, writhing in its agony. For a moment she saw the dog-like animal Cait had described, then the man again, then a broken mess of bone and muscle and ancient, string-like sinews. After a moment it was still.

Fer's world turned to darkness, but this time she didn't pass out. She half-fell to the floor. The roaring of the crowd came back to her, washing over her. She had defeated it. The words had defeated it. She'd always known there was power in them. Because the family secret also whispered *where* the words had come from. Set down in antiquity by Ilminion and passed down the line, carried in a locket by a baby girl from the ruins of Angere. Some dire curse or death-spell. Fer hoped she'd never have to utter them again.

She crouched there, panting, waiting for the pain of what she'd done to overwhelm her. Instead a glorious rush of euphoria flooded through her body, lifting her up. She felt suddenly strong, invincible. What was happening? She felt she could do anything, defeat all the undain in the city. The sensation was glorious.

Johnny emerged from the shadows. It took her a moment to realise he looked like he really was. The tall, long-haired Johnny Electric. She'd let the glamours slip fighting the undain. Anyone looking at them would see them as they really were. It didn't matter now. She could destroy them all.

She was about to stand, preparing to unleash more magic, when something stopped her. This power she felt, it wasn't her power. It had rushed into her after defeating the undain, some hideous effect of the necromancy. It was corrupt, stolen magic. If she used it she was no better than any of them. The temptation was huge, she could do so much good with such power, but she knew it would change her, eat away at her.

She made the decision in a moment. She placed a hand to the stone ground and, with a wrenching effort, let the power ebb from her. She wouldn't have it. She would remain weak and scared. She would remain herself.

When she was sure it was all gone, she tried to place the illusions back over her and Johnny. It was too much for her. She was spent. Her weakness made her feel good about herself.

Johnny hauled her upright. "Come on. We've got to get out of this place."

The effort of limping from the concert hall onto the cobbles outside nearly finished her. There were more guards there, but they appeared to be normal people, unaware of what had happened.

"Too much to drink," Johnny said to them, as they staggered forward. The guards grinned their understanding.

She wouldn't be able to get far. Certainly not all the way across the city centre to the sanctuary beneath the Cathedral.

"You go," she said to him. "Take the guitar to Andar. Only, tell Hellen. How I killed the undain. The family secret. Tell her that. It's important."

Stooping, Johnny placed his shoulder under her arm and more or less carried her. "Tell her yourself when we get there."

"No. I won't make it."

"Blah, blah," said Johnny. "Be quiet and put all your energy into walking, OK?"

They were nearly at the road that ran around the hall when a vehicle pulled up. An expensive, silver car with blacked-out windows. It had to be Genera. She knew she couldn't fight them.

The window of the car slid down and a man she recognized peered out. A man with tattoos on his hands, arms and neck. Images of chameleons and iguanas peeped at her. The wise man. The Lizard King who'd served them food in the Golden Palace the day they'd arrived.

"Get in," he said. Johnny pulled the door open and pushed Fer inside. She lay on the back seat, panting like a wounded animal, holding her chest and stomach tight.

"I saw you," the Lizard King said as he made the machine surge away from the concert hall. "Saw what you were doing. Are you mad? How did you think you were going to get away?"

"We figured we'd walk back to the Cathedral and hide out," said Johnny.

"You thought the undain would just let the two of you stroll across the city?"

"I guess it does seem badly thought out if you put it like that."

"We have to get the others," said Fer. It was painful to breathe let alone talk. "Cait's mother and grandmother."

"We're going there now," said the Lizard King. "Then we have to leave. Get far away from Manchester."

"Glastonbury," said Johnny. "That's the plan."

"I know. I told you, I see what other's see."

"I thought you could only watch, not act?" said Johnny.

"I can't do any other magic. I can drive a getaway car as well as anyone."

They streaked down a long, straight road, the one they'd walked down the day they'd jumped back to the city. It was late, but there were still plenty of cars about.

The Lizard King weaved through the traffic. Weren't they supposed to stop at the red lights? Fer closed her eyes, shutting it all out.

"I've told the others to be ready," he said. "Fiona and Catherine. We can't wait around. Genera will throw everything at us."

At the Cathedral they barely even stopped. Cait's mother and grandmother climbed inside and they sped into the night, tyres screaming.

Fiona, in the front seat, turned to study them with concern on her face. "What happened? Did you have to fight?"

"There was an undain there," said Johnny. "Looked like a lord. It caught Fer, but she killed it."

"She *killed* it? How is that possible?" There was clear surprise in the older witch's eyes.

"Dunno," said Johnny. "Worked some special move to defeat the end-of-level boss."

Both Fiona and Catherine looked to Fer to explain. But now wasn't the time. She barely understood what she'd done herself.

"How far to this Glastonbury?" she asked.

The Lizard King glanced into his little square mirror at her. At the same moment, the tattooed lizard that curled around his neck like a scarf opened its eye to study her.

"Three, four hours if we take the motorways," said the Lizard King. Lights flashed by the windows as they sped along the city streets.

"They'll follow us," she said. "Come for us. They must know where we're going."

"They'll only have a vague idea," said Fiona. "They know Johnny disappeared the day after playing the Glastonbury festival but not where he was when the portal opened."

The Lizard King swerved to avoid a slower-moving car. "They can't do much to us if we stick to the bigger roads."

"But at the other end," said Catherine. "We'll have to

stop."

"Let's worry about that then," said Fiona.

Fer nodded, happy for the moment to succumb to sleep, despite the unpleasant lurching of the car as it swerved and veered.

"Have you seen anything of Cait?" Fiona asked the wise man. Her voice was as brittle as glass. "Is there any news from the other world at all?"

"I have been granted … glimpses," said the Lizard King, pausing as he concentrated on the road. "Nothing more. The aether is turbulent at the moment, like trying to see through a storm. You will understand why."

Fer knew well. The aethernal. She'd given it a home, let it consume the Tanglewood built in the aether. She still had nightmares about the creature's all-consuming hunger. She'd unleashed it, and it had swelled in moments to consume the clearing, the trees, presumably the whole of that island-world in the aether. She had given it that, *fed* it that. And who knew what the effects would be? But she'd had no choice.

"What have you seen?" asked Fiona. "Is Cait still alive?"

"I know she made it to the other world. There was a moment five days ago when I saw something through her eyes. A fleeting glimpse of her standing on a straight road between black trees. A flying monster attacked her, a terrible creature. Something like a dragon, perhaps, but broken and … undain. Cait fought back, but the vision stopped abruptly. I thought perhaps she'd died. But then three days ago, as I was about to seek you out to tell you, I caught sight of her again. Or the world through her eyes. She was riding at huge speed across a sea of mist and moonlight."

"I don't understand," said Catherine.

"I don't either. That was how it looked. She was rising up and down, as if on a boat. She was being pursued, I knew, but she seemed calm in the moment, and there were others with her. Friends. I caught nothing else, and again the bond was lost. I know nothing more. Except…"

"What?" said Fiona. "Go on."

"There is another in that world I sometimes connect with. There are few there, very few, who aren't of the undain, but he is one. An old man, living in the mountains of the high north. A group of renegades. I've been trying to reach him, converse with him, but it's been difficult. Except, early this morning, my mind touched his briefly. He was in a room with several others, studying a map. And I think … I'm sure … Cait was there with him. She collapsed and the old man went to help her."

"Was she wounded? Or ill?"

"I couldn't tell. I'm sorry."

"Would you be able to talk to them? To Cait or this man?"

"I can try. It's like throwing a message in a bottle into the ocean."

There was silence in the car after that. The thought that Cait had still been alive that morning was welcome and wonderful. But it wasn't enough. Who knew what she'd faced? Whether she was still alive? If only there was something they could do. But there was nothing.

Dimly, Fer was aware of a wave of undain and Genera soldiers pursuing them, shadowing them. On the roads, in the air. She wasn't free. She hadn't escaped. But just for the moment she didn't care. Like Cait on her mysterious sea, Fer was glad simply to be safe for a time.

Gratefully, she let herself sink into the numbness of slumber.

17 – DEATH OF A WITCH

Fer watched nervously as Johnny plucked at his guitar. He was holding it close to his ear, tuning its six strings.

"It's not very loud," said Fer.

"It's an *electric* guitar. Not a lot of opportunity for massive amplification on top of a hill in Somerset."

"So will it work?"

"Did last time. I can still *play*. Just quietly."

"And you're sure this is the right spot?"

"I'm sure. Look at it. It's like Avalon down there."

She didn't recognize the name, but she thought she understood what he meant. A sea of early-morning mist, delicate as a dream, washed over the flat, green land all around them. Here and there, the tops of round hills or the peaks of spires peeped through. The sun, rising in the east, touched everything to gold. They stood with their backs to a stone keep on top of a conical hill rising out of the flat landscape. Glastonbury Tor.

It barely looked natural to Fer. An ancient place, Fiona had said, one of the points where the worlds were close together and vision or passage was sometimes possible. Standing there she could believe it. It might have been early morning in Andar.

Apart, that was, from the flying machines clattering toward them, the ranks of soldiers she could sense without being able to see in the mists. The Lizard King had brought them to Glastonbury unassailed, helped in part by the archaeon doing its best to disrupt Genera's communications, send them off the trail. But the bookwyrm couldn't hide their progress completely. Unmanned flying machines like huge buzzing dragonflies had found them and trailed them.

"So hack into them," Johnny had said. "Send them haywire. Tell them we've gone to Wales or something."

"Not possible," the archaeon had replied from Johnny's phone. "They're using private networks, high levels of encryption."

"I thought you could do anything. I thought you, like, owned the internet now."

"Yes, yes. But they aren't on the internet, didn't I just say? They must have realised their other communications were compromised. I've done all I can."

"Great," said Johnny.

"Thank you, noble archaeon," said Fiona. "We appreciate it."

They'd abandoned the car and climbed the hillside as quickly as they could, Cait's gran occasionally grumbling about *her old knees* and *cups of tea*. Fer had looked around every few steps, aware of the forces closing in on them, but they'd made it to the top unassailed. Now, they all stood over Johnny: Fer and Fiona and Catherine and the Lizard King.

"Take the book," Fiona said to Johnny when he'd tuned Mr. Shankly to his satisfaction. "Don't let go of it, whatever happens."

"Wait, wait," said Johnny, translating for Fer's benefit once he'd spoken to Cait's mother and grandmother. "That's actually a good question. How do I even bring the evil tome with me? Last time I was obviously holding onto

Mr. Shankly but I still left him behind."

"You said there was a moment of decision," said Fer. "A point when you consciously took the road to Andar. Do you recall thinking you'd leave the guitar behind?"

"I don't know. It's kinda weird when you slip through the cracks between the worlds like that. You get all spaced out. It was like my mind, everything I knew, was dissipating, fading away. I remember I didn't want to vanish completely from this world, felt bad about going without saying anything. Maybe leaving the guitar was a way of telling people I'd be back. Or maybe I just forgot to bring it."

"Then, this time," said Fiona, "when you get to that point, make sure you concentrate. And make sure you take the book. This is our only chance."

Johnny nodded his head in consent. "I'll do what I can."

"We'll hold them off while you play," said Fiona. She glanced to Fer and Catherine, a questioning look on her face. "The three of us have combined before, at the refinery. I think we can work a circle to protect Johnny for a while."

Catherine nodded, determination clear on her lined face. Fer, after a moment, nodded too. *Do what has to be done.* They would put everything into this. Fiona, Catherine and herself, although she was still so sore and weak from slaying the undain.

"And Johnny?" said Fiona.

"Huh?"

"When you get there, you tell Hellen to save my girl. Use the book, do whatever she damn well has to do, but save my girl. Or Hellen's no kind of witch worth the name."

Johnny nodded for a second time.

Fiona turned to the Lizard King. "I know you won't be able to contribute to the circle. Your powers lie elsewhere. Will you try and reach Hellen, tell her what we are attempting?"

"I will."

"And Cait in Angere? Or the man you mentioned?"

"I will do what I can."

"Very well. Let's begin."

Johnny strummed chords on Mr. Shankly, waiting for the moment of inspiration, the sensation of being picked up and carried away by the music. There was nothing. He ran through some simple twelve-bar blues, then the trickier chord progressions from *Beyond The Veil*, hoping something might kick off. Still nothing.

The three witches stood with their backs to him as he sat against the old stones of the tower. They would defend him to the death, sacrifice everything so he could do this thing. But what if he couldn't? More troublingly, what if he didn't want to?

Andar was going to be overrun. Did he really want to go back there? This world, his world, was broken and troubled but at least *he* might survive. If Genera let him live, he could rejoin the band, have a damn good time of it, even. He glanced down at the red leather book in his lap. If he handed that over to them, traded it, would they let him go? Would all this be over, for him at least?

He shook his head, flicking the hair from his eyes. Bad thoughts. Unworthy thoughts. He'd never live with himself. After what the girl had done, Cait, it was the least he could do to play his part. Cait and Danny and the whole lot of them.

The truth was he couldn't actually achieve very much. The others could zap baddies with their mind-powers or fight like Ran. All he could do was tag along and play guitar. He'd thought music mattered more than the world to him, but he'd come to understand that the world, the *worlds*, mattered more than anything. The undain had to be stopped. There was no song of Angere, he was willing to bet. That was the difference right there.

Problem was, what if his subconscious didn't want to play ball? What if some survival instinct kicked in and he simply couldn't get the damned Song of Andar walking-between-the-worlds thing to work?

Angry with himself he played a little harder, a little faster, trying not to follow tunes he already knew, trying to let his fingers find their own way. He thought about the day he'd sat in the Songroom on Islagray, listening to the singers. The weird cadences had seemed random at first, endlessly variable. But as he'd listened he'd picked up patterns and melodies. Melodies he couldn't recall now, couldn't reduce to chord patterns. But if he could somehow get near them, resonate with them, the magic might work.

"They're coming," he heard Fiona say. "Up the hillside, surrounding us. Lend me your strength. I will form the grey walls around us."

The fear on the women's faces was clear as they glanced at each other. The Lizard King came to sit near Johnny. He buried his head in his hands as if lost to despair, but Johnny knew he was throwing everything he had into reaching the other world. This man, a restaurant waiter, had sacrificed everything, too. He probably knew he wasn't going to get out of this.

Johnny tried again, trying to set aside the buzzing fear in his brain. Everything else was right. A beautiful morning on Glastonbury Tor. Mr. Shankly. Even the slightly unreal sense of detachment that came from not getting enough sleep. But last time there'd been no pressure. Last time there'd been no army of slavering horrors coming to suck out his brains, no trio of women prepared to die to protect him. Stuff like that could put you right off.

He strummed, not looking at the guitar, not looking at anything. Had he shut his eyes last time? Maybe. Worth a try. If he could just find an echo of the tune he could follow it, coax it into life.

Still it wouldn't come.

A scream from Fer shook him from his thoughts. The girl was on her knees, hands held up as if fending off invisible blows. Beyond her was the wall of fog. Indistinct shapes moved in it. Hulking, inhuman shapes coming through, only yards away.

He shut his eyes again. *Just play the damn guitar, Johnny. That's what you do. That's all you can do.*

There were many sorts of magic in the world, he'd come to understand. There wasn't just the hocus-pocus, eye-of-newt-and-wing-of-bat stuff. Put him in front of a crowd like the night before and *something* happened. To the people watching he become something else. Not just a person, but larger, glorious. It wasn't *him* of course. It was being on the stage, the lighting, the amplified sound, all of it. But he became, briefly, something transformed, divine. It was the only sort of magic he'd ever been able to work. Sounds in the air that had an effect on the world.

And *there*, he felt it. A thrill in his gut. A tingle in his fingers. The melody was like a series of shifting shapes in his mind, indistinct, hard to follow. His fingers made chord shapes he couldn't actually name as he tried to play along with the song. The Song of Andar. His fingers strummed and plucked, faster and faster, and he, Johnny Electric, became merely an onlooker. A part of the audience himself.

He lost himself in the music. Here was another of his superpowers. Everything else, the whole world, could fall away and there'd be just him and the song. A happy place. A place he reached now. His playing joined with the greater music. He was one of the countermelodies, part of the whole but separate, too. A new riff, a new theme he introduced to the song.

While his fingers worked he opened his eyes again.

He remembered the endless grey of this place. A

universe of fog. He was between the worlds. His own private shadow path, like a ginnel between one land and the other. A tiny universe all of his own, details on the ground blurring to scribbles, to nothingness as they stretched away. Up ahead, a light awaited. He knew what it was. That was where the music was coming from. The music he'd picked up on, joined in with. Andar.

He stood. Behind him was something like a window or a door. A square, in any case. That was the way he'd come. No sounds reached him from back there, but he could see through, like looking through a telescope the wrong way. Two of the women lay on the ground, spent or dead. Fer and Cait's gran. Fiona, the last, stood alone, the grey closing around her. The undain emerged through the walls: claws and swords and fangs slashing into the clear light as they battered and battled through the magical fog. Fiona was weakening. She glanced back to him, a look of pain and alarm on her face. She shouted words he couldn't hear, telling him something, something hugely important. But what? He was already through, already safe.

By his feet, two items lay on the ground. Or two outlines of items. A guitar and a book. They were, he knew, really on the ground back on the Tor. These were only the ideas of the real objects. He could take them if he wanted. Here was the moment of decision. And the items were both important, weren't they? The guitar, especially. And now people back there, his bandmates, knew he was alive. This time he could take Mr. Shankly with him. He picked the guitar up, the outlines becoming smooth wood in his hand as he reached.

The book, too. Should he take that? He tried to remember. It was so hard to concentrate. The book was important. Terribly important. Was it important he left it behind or took it with him? He couldn't recall.

The window back to the old world was shrinking, as if moving away from him. Fiona was on her knees, still fighting, still struggling. Why was she defending him when he was safe? She shouted something again. One of the words on her lips, he thought, was *Cait*. Then Fiona threw her arms wide and worked some huge magic, the blaze of it blinding even to him in the aether. It burned red as if she'd unleashed some long-suppressed rage. A blaze of fury blasted from her, scattering the monsters who thronged around her, blowing them backward.

Fiona fell to the ground to join the other two. Her eyes, he saw, were closed even as she slumped.

More undain began to appear. There were too many of them. Fiona had bought him moments but no more than that.

He had to get away, let the portal close. He had to make sure the monsters couldn't follow him through to Andar.

The book still lay at his feet. Standing alone on the shadow path between the worlds, Johnny Electric tried to recall what it was he was supposed to do with it.

18 – WYRMFIRE

Angere

Cait crouched beside Phoenix, trying to understand his words. Who was dead? Fer was in the other world, of course, along with her mum and gran. "Who, Phoenix? Who has died?"

"I'm sorry," said Phoenix. "She was fighting the undain, working magic to protect the others. But they were too strong for her. She blazed like a great light at the end, but they were too strong for her. She knew I was there and she shouted to me, shouted to *you*, telling you to race for the safety of Andar. Then she went. Your mother, Cait. Your mother is dead."

For a moment Cait couldn't take in his words. "No. That can't be right. My mother's *powerful*. I mean she was lost, and broken, but she's back now. She's herself again. I saw what she did outside the factory."

"I'm sorry. They were too much for her."

"But ... but you said yourself the visions are vague. How can you be sure?"

"I'm sure, Cait. I felt it. I felt her go."

"And the others?"

"I don't know. Your grandmother was there at the

start. And Fer and the singer. I saw it all through the eyes of the wise man of that world. Fer and your grandmother fell. But then the light was so bright I couldn't see anything properly any more. I didn't feel the others die, but I couldn't feel that they were alive either. Perhaps they made it through to Andar. I don't know."

Cait looked at those around her. Even Nox looked sombre. The stones of the ground were sharp beneath her knees. She hadn't noticed the pain. She ignored it.

Her mother as well as her father. And Danny. She was losing everyone. Everyone and everything was falling away from her, slipping through her fingers. The old certainties of her life, the solid ground she'd walked on, had turned to shifting mud, sucking her down.

She stood, not knowing what to say. How did they ever think they could defeat the Witch King? Why had they even tried?

"Cait." It was Nox, putting a hand on her shoulder.

She shrugged it off. "Leave me alone. I don't want to hear it."

"Cait, look," said Nox. "Over there."

Tears had filled her eyes, blurring her vision. She wiped them clear and looked to where Nox was pointing.

The archway. A plume of dust or smoke billowed from it and a figure was staggering through. Smoke curled off him as he lurched forward a few steps then slumped to the ground. Ran. Ran had made it back after all.

The others sprinted for the archway, and Cait ran with them, overtaking them as they crossed the rough, stony ground. She was glad to escape into the moment, set aside thinking about her mother. She clung to the simple fact that somehow, impossibly, Ran had survived.

The dragonrider was climbing to his feet, his features twisted with pain. The closer she got the more clearly she could see how hurt he was. His clothes were singed through in places, revealing his tattooed flesh. Livid burns ran across his arms and one side of his face. Half his hair was gone, seared away. The smell of smoke and acrid chemicals coming from him was sharp, prickling the back of her throat.

He took a step forward and then collapsed again. The sight of it was terrible to see. Ran was always strong. Now he could barely stand.

When she reached him she kneeled beside him, too. His eyes were open, his gaze darting from side to side. She put a hand on his shoulder. He grimaced with pain at her touch.

"I'm sorry!" she said. "Ran, I'm sorry! What can I do? I…" The smoke in her throat made her words trail off into a rough cough.

Ran tried to rise again, panting heavily with the effort of it, teeth gritted. He refused to give in. He held out a blackened and blistered hand to her. Holding him as gently as she could, she helped him to his feet so he could face the others as they arrived.

Phoenix was at the back, coming as quickly as he could, walking with Demara's help. The others parted to let him through. "You lit the wyrmfire, Ran? You were so long we thought it had failed, or you'd been caught in the blast."

"I ignited it all," said Ran. With Phoenix's gift of voices and Bethany's help Cait found she could understand his words perfectly. It took her a few moments to even notice Ran was speaking in the language of Andar. "There were many undain there. An army. Charis was among them. The moment I went through they came for me. They saw the wyrmfire and must have known what it was but still they attacked. I had to fight them off before I could light the fuse. Even as it exploded they had me. They very nearly held me back but I managed to break free and jump."

"You're badly injured," said Phoenix. "Can you walk?"

"If I have to," Ran replied.

"Don't be insane, he can't go anywhere," said Cait. "Look at him."

"Cait, he has no choice. Whatever the cost he has to go

back through the archway." It was Nox, telling them all what to do. Again.

"Don't be ridiculous," said Cait. "He's half dead. It's amazing he's even talking."

"Cait, he's right." This time it was Phoenix, his voice sadder. "He has to go back through, so you can go with him. Even if he can't make it much farther he has to do this one last thing. The undain will know what has happened. In moments they'll flood into Fiveways and only Ran can open the wyrm roads."

Ran's legs were unsteady, but he turned back to the archway, ready to make the return journey. They were right, of course. They had to go now. She suddenly wasn't ready. She need to talk to Phoenix, go over what he'd seen back home. She needed to think. But there was no time.

Nox put an arm under one of Ran's shoulders, supporting him, and they limped their way to the archway, Ran grunting with the pain of it.

"Cait, come on," Nox called back to her. "We're leaving now."

She cast one final glance around the Smouldering Fire, at Phoenix, wondering if she would see any of them again. There was much she wanted to say and no chance to say it. Turning, she followed Nox and Ran.

Holding hands as they had in Iceland, Cait, Ran and Nox stepped together through the smoking ruins of the archway.

The devastation at Fiveways was absolute. The shattered remains of hundreds or thousands of the undain lay around, their remains scattered in a wide circle that stretched beyond the stone archways. There was no sign of the cart that had borne the wyrmfire; the explosion had completely incinerated it. Only a blackened circle on the ground, the only spot free of sundered body parts, marked the place. Even some of the ancient archways had succumbed to the blast, their stone pillars thrown outward by the force of the explosion. The smoke was thick, stinging Cait's eyes.

Incredibly, some of the undain were moving. All around, limbs flailed and writhed. Some of the creatures moaned or snarled as they tried to rise, even though their arms or legs were gone, torn off by the blast. Their programming compelled them. She watched as, only a few yards away, an undain soldier with two legs, a single arm, but no head, lurched itself upright and turned as if it could smell them. It carried a sword in its remaining hand.

"Run," said Nox. Half hauling Ran along, he picked his way across the field of broken undain in the direction of the other archway they needed to take. The one that would throw them across Angere to the White City.

Cait followed, hopping over and around the mangled remains, trying to find ground rather than undain to step on. She didn't always succeed. In places the ground was a swamp of red and purple, the blood and entrails of the undain.

Ran fell again and again as he tripped or slipped. More than once he cried out but still he refused to give in. Each time they hauled him to his feet and the three of them set off again for the archway.

Horns blasts filled the air. More undain arriving. Cait didn't dare stop to see how close. The shattered stone archway was only a few yards away. Through it, the sea of ruined undain bodies continued. Once again it seemed impossible that crossing between the pillars would take Cait and the others anywhere. Surely the explosion had dealt the old stones too much damage? This one had been a complete archway, but now it was just two columns of stone, one noticeably higher than the other. The great rocks that had formed its arch lay on the ground on the other side where they'd been thrown, bodies of the undain crushed beneath them.

Cait tried to focus, concentrate on forming magic. If the wyrm road didn't open they would soon be surrounded. Something in the sickening smell of smoke made it hard to find the cold fury within her.

The horns sounded again, much nearer, their blaring sound angry. She thought she could hear footsteps, too, thundering across the ground, louder and louder.

She was a pace away from the archway when a hand seized her ankle, sending her sprawling. She landed in something wet and sticky. The hand on her shin tightened its grip, slithering her backward over the slippery earth. One of the undain soldiers had her. It was little more than an arm protruding from an unidentifiable mass of organs and guts, but its grasp was iron.

Shrieking with revulsion, Cait kicked and kicked at her captor. It was no use. She was aware of Ran trying to pull her to the archway, but he was too weak.

Without thinking, she unleashed a stream of cold magic at the creature who held her. Sharp pain prickled across her back, but she paid it no attention. It was nothing. She had to get away from this terrible place. She threw everything into the effort. A rain of cold blasted from her hand, freezing everything in its path. She kicked again, and this time the arm holding her shattered into icy shards.

She lurched to her feet and, before she could be caught again, dived for the remains of the archway. She still had Ran's hand in hers. She couldn't see if Nox had Ran's other hand. All she could think about was getting away. A horn blasted, suddenly very near, but then it cut abruptly out and was silent.

Twilight engulfed them and soft grass covered the ground where they landed. For a moment she thought she must have lost consciousness, lost more hours, but then she understood. They were farther east. Here, the night was already drawing on. They had escaped. For now.

Ran and Nox were with her. The dragonrider rolled on the ground in clear agony from this latest fall, but he pushed himself to his hands and knees and then to his feet.

He drew his sword with a silvery metallic scrape. The tip of it wavered in the air, describing little circles, as he tried to hold it steady. Even now he would defend her. He looked like he could collapse at any moment.

Nox's gaze darted around in alarm as he tried to work out where in Angere they were, the fear in him burning clear.

There was no sign of the White City, or of any undain, or of anything other than trees. Once more they were in woods. A whispering hush filled the world. Some leaves lay strewn on the ground, but most were still on the trees. Winter had barely begun here. At least they hadn't landed in the middle of the Holy Court.

Whether they were in the middle of some endless forest, or a mere clump on top of a hill, she couldn't say. There was no sign of an archway, or anything to mark this end of the wyrm road. That was good. Very good. There was a chance the undain didn't know where they were.

The problem was, she didn't know either. The air was much warmer, so they must be farther south. Had they come far enough? Or perhaps the wyrm road, untethered by an archway, had brought them too far. How many miles away was the White City?

If only her phone worked. She could try using magic but didn't dare for fear of being spotted. She could feel *something* in the air, though. A deep, murmuring roar underneath the quiet, just beyond hearing. There was a sense of unstoppable power to it. The An. It had to be the An. Wherever they were, they had reached the river.

With a thump, saying nothing, Ran slumped to the ground behind her, the effort of standing finally too much. He was lucky not to land on his sword. When she got to him his eyes were closed, and he didn't respond when she called his name. Tendrils of smoke coiled from his clothes and hair. She stroked his face, careful to avoid the burns. His flesh felt hot, as if some of the wyrmfire still raged inside him. Perhaps he had inhaled too much smoke, or too many fumes. His skin was greasy. Was it just the leaves overhead or did his face have a green tinge to it? It was incredible he had got this far, opened up the two wyrm roads so they could escape the north. The cost to him had been terrible.

Nox came to stand over her. "He doesn't look good."

"He needs rest. I don't know, medicines and bandages."

"Can't you work some healing magic? Or is it just the pretty lights and the snow thing?"

"It isn't that simple, you know." In truth, she had no idea where to start. She knew such magic was possible; Fer had said there were witches in Andar who could mend broken bones and lift fevers. Cait had quizzed Bethany about it more than once, but the witch-girl had been no use. She'd been taught none of the healing arts as a girl, and, being dead, hadn't needed to learn any since.

Cait could at least try. Closing her eyes, she touch the exposed skin of Ran's shoulder with the tips of her fingers. She could sense the damage, the deep hurt, almost as if the wounds and burns were on her own body. Perhaps that was the key. She turned her attention to the raw, screaming pains down his back. Perhaps she could simply will his tissues to heal, visualize them healed as she visualized the ice before unleashing it. Was that what you did?

The sharp pain that flashed across her own back as she began to work the magic made her scream in agony. She stopped trying to work the spell. It felt like a flame had been taken to her flesh. As if she was healing his wounds by taking them on herself. Was that what they did, those witches back there in Andar? Was that how it worked? The thought filled her with horror.

The pain subsided in her back. She'd cut off the magic before doing any real damage. She looked up at Nox and shook her head.

"We should leave him here," said Nox. "We have to keep moving. There must be undain everywhere."

"What?"

"He can't walk and we can't carry him. Think, Cait."

"He could die if we leave him here, Nox."

"Then what difference does it make if we're with him? Don't be stupid. The longer we wait, the more chance there is they'll find us. They'll work out where the wyrm road leads, or simply track us down. They must be scouring all of Angere."

"No. We can't just leave him lying here like an injured animal."

"He might be out for hours. Days. There isn't time for this, Cait."

"No," she replied. "We won't leave him. We wait."

He was going to say something else, but instead he turned and stomped off, heading for the trees.

"Where are you going?" she called after him.

"I'm going to scout around. Find out where we are. Do something *useful.*"

"And you're good at scouting are you? That was a skill you used a lot as a company executive?"

"Oh, you'd be surprised," he said and disappeared into the gloom between the trees.

Putting Nox out of her mind she turned her attention to Ran. What were you supposed to do with injuries? Bind them up? Let them breathe? She had no idea. There was so much she didn't know. Washing his wounds seemed like a good start. Cold water might cool him down at least. It was the only thing she could think of.

Rising, she headed for the An, knowing which way it lay without really thinking about it. The rushing power of it grew stronger as she approached. She expected the trees to thin out as she reached the bank, but they grew right to the edge. The river was eroding the land here, scraping its way inland inch by inch. Tree roots writhed out of the bank where the waters had eaten into the ground, and more than one of the great trunks leaned over at a crazy angle, ready to crash into the water.

She took a moment to stare across the An. It was beautiful, the waters like blue glass. And it was *vast*. She'd imagined some great river like those back home. Like the Amazon in TV documentaries about the rainforest. But this was more like the sea.

She couldn't see far up or downstream because of the curve of the bank. There was no sign of a shore on the other side. No sign of anything save for water stretching off into the distance. But it was definitely running water. She could see the slow glide of its flow as it rolled by. Not too far out, a black stick floated along, looking like the snout of a crocodile as it headed south. It moved with some speed. She wasn't a great swimmer. She *really* didn't want to fall in.

At some point on the journey to Iceland, Johnny translating, Fer had told her there had once been a bridge leading to Andar. How was that even possible? It had to be a myth. Some old story parents told their children. They couldn't construct a bridge that long back home, let alone here. Perhaps magic had been used. If so, who could have performed such a feat? It was surely beyond anything the witches could work.

Grasping hold of the firmest-looking bough she could find, she reached down into the waters to fill one of the flexible leather bottles Phoenix had provided. She expected the water to be warm, but it was icy cold. When the bottle was full she drank, hoping it would wash away the acrid prickling in the back of her throat. Then she filled the bottle again and retraced her steps to Ran.

He had a small knife in his boot, and she used it to cut away the tattered remains of his shirt. Then she washed his wounds as best she could. It would have been better to turn him over, clean up his back too, but she wasn't strong enough. As she worked, she revealed more of his tattoos, the swirling blue lines all across his chest and the muscles of his stomach. She could see the suggestion of a dragon clearly. A rearing, roaring dragon winding its way around his body. On a whim, she lifted the seeing stone to her eye, to reveal how the tattooed lines looked close up.

The blue lines became immediately vivid, almost electrical in their intensity. Between them though she could see nothing, like peering at one of the undain. Somehow the tattoos prevented her from seeing him as he really was. Absorbed or deflected the magic to shield him. Pretty cool, really.

Low down, on the muscled flat beside his hip-bone, some of the blue lines overlaid a tiny set of darker lines, purple or even black. The outline of a complete dragon inked onto his skin. Looking at him without the stone, they were completely covered up by the blue, but through the stone they were quite clear. An older tattoo, perhaps, there before the blue ones were added. The dragon lay asleep, and appeared to be lying on something hidden beneath the waistband of his trousers. She decided not to investigate farther down. His legs hadn't been burned and she really didn't want to hear Nox's sarcasm if she stripped Ran completely.

Instead, she dribbled water into Ran's mouth, hoping he'd swallow at least some of it. He remained unconscious throughout, occasionally muttering something about his *kin* or *king* that she couldn't understand. She had to resist the temptation to delve into his mind. Perhaps, now that he was asleep, his thoughts would be open to her. But, no. She wouldn't intrude.

When she was done, she found a spot where the sun was on her face and sat with her back against one of the trees. Ran's tattooed chest rose and fell slowly, as if on each breath he deliberated whether to give up living or carry on. Each inhalation a decision to take one more lungful. She found herself willing him to keep breathing, keep breathing.

In that moment of calm, birds twittering in the treetops, the nearby waters chortling against the banks, she thought about her mother. It was still too much to take in.

It was like some great ball of darkness she kept approaching, trying to understand, but from which she fled in alarm. It pulled on her mind, a black hole sucking at her. Danny was there and now her mother too, the loss of them both tangled up inside her. She didn't know which to think about first.

It wasn't *fair*. This wasn't how it was supposed to happen. Danny had nothing to do with this. He'd come along because she'd gone round to his house. And as for her mother: she'd only just come back to her and now she was gone forever. How was that possible? They hadn't even said goodbye, not properly. Cait couldn't even remember what her mother's last words had been.

There were all these unfinished conversations and unanswered questions. Things she'd meant to say to them both *one day*. Things left unspoken because the time wasn't right or she couldn't find the right words or because she was mad with one of them. And now they could never be said. Or not heard, at least.

The tears, when they came, wracked her whole body as if someone were shaking her. She sat with her head in her hands and let them flow, wondering how this had happened, how her life could unravel so completely in a few days. She sobbed uncontrollably for long minutes, only the unconscious Ran for company.

After a while she was aware, dimly, of Bethany, too. That distant presence offering comfort. But not intruding, leaving her to her grief. Cait was grateful of the witch-girl more than ever just then. She couldn't remember feeling so alone, so lost.

When the sobbing had subsided, Cait spoke to her.

Bethany?

I'm here.

Can I ask you something?

Yes.

Why is it you're still here? Even though you're dead, I mean? How is that possible?

Bethany didn't reply, and Cait thought she wasn't going to. She sounded reluctant when she did speak. *You're hoping your mother isn't gone. That she still exists somewhere.*

It's possible isn't it? said Cait. *I mean, I'm talking to you and you've been dead for, like, hundreds of years.*

It's rare, Cait. We remained in Manchester because of what was done to us. The injustice of it. Our whole lives denied. We lingered because we had a score to settle. It's possible that could happen with your mother, I suppose. Because of you and her need to protect you. But she may be gone. That's what usually happens. From what Phoenix said, she may have used up all her life protecting your gran and the others. I'm sorry.

Cait didn't reply. She couldn't help herself from reaching into the aether, not knowing what she was doing but hoping, somehow, to catch an echo of her mother.

There was nothing.

They waited there the rest of that day, and all of the next. Ran didn't rouse from his coma. Nox grew angrier and angrier, spending more and more time away from her, ranging farther and farther afield.

On the morning of the third day, he came back from his travels carrying an armful of bruised fruit. They were something like misshapen apples, orange and red in colour. He dropped them to the ground and handed one to Cait. "Windfalls. Don't worry, they're not poisonous. I've eaten three and survived."

Cait took the fruit and ate, picking her way between the bruises. The flesh was sweet and juicy. "Did you find anything else?" she asked. "Have you worked out where we are yet?"

"We're south of the White City. We're lucky. All the undain will be north, either looking for us, or heading that way anyway as the waters start to freeze."

"Did you see anyone?"

"Only a few slaves on the road. These woods run along the river bank for several miles. There's a road on the other edge but no one was using it."

"Good."

"Cait, we can't sit here forever. We have to move."

He was right. She'd been sitting there earlier when a wind had picked up, sending many of the leaves whirling to the ground. Autumn was underway. Winter would be creeping south, inch by inch. And Ran still hadn't moved. Perhaps he wasn't going to.

"So how are we going to do it?" she asked.

"Do what?"

"Any of it, Nox. Get into the White City. Find this fabulously precious book. Escape without being seen. Reach Andar by some miracle. How are we going to do any of that?"

"I thought you were in charge, Cait. Don't you know?" He seemed amused by her doubt. Right then she really didn't care. She didn't reply.

"Tell me, Cait," he said. "How powerful are you really? I've seen you work some magic and, I'll be honest, you keep surprising me. But what are you really capable of?"

Good question. She had no idea. Phoenix had said she was going to get more powerful as the winter wore on. But where that would take her, what it would *make* her, she had no idea. She wasn't even sure she wanted to get more powerful. Her mother had been very strong and look what had happened.

"Why do you ask?"

He shrugged. "I'm assessing our situation. Working out our options. What we face is like any business problem. We have resources, and we have competitors. We need to decide an optimal strategy and then carry it out."

"Really?"

"Of course. So I need to know. If it comes to it, if we're surrounded, can you unleash that ice magic? Can you send our enemies screaming in horror? Can you save us?"

Could she? If it was one or two people, then maybe. Even one or two of the undain if she was lucky. But there had to be hundreds of the monsters in the city. Thousands. She couldn't hope to fight them all. But she also wasn't going to admit that to Nox.

"I can try."

He studied her for a moment, weighing her up. He was plotting again. Scheming. She could see it in his eyes,

"OK, Nox. So what's your *optimal strategy* so far?"

"It would help if I could show you. We can leave Ran alone for an hour or so. He's not going anywhere."

She was reluctant to leave him, but she had to do something. She nodded and stood to follow Nox through the trees. They shadowed the line of the bank but always stayed out of sight of river or road. She kept imagining movement in the distance, but she could sense nothing other than birds and small, scurrying creatures. It was just the shifting shadow of the woods.

After an hour or so, Nox cut right toward the bank. They reached a small headland jutting into the river, its sides cliffs of mud as the waters worked away at them. Nox kneeled and crawled to the water's edge. Feeling ridiculous, Cait followed. She soon saw what he wanted to show her.

A mile or so upstream, the bank curved in a gentle arch, and there, dazzling in the golden glare of the sun, was the White City. It stretched into a hazy distance, towers and domes and walls arrayed along the bank like something from a fairy tale. And it was *beautiful*. She had to remind herself what it was. What it was built from. What it meant.

"Why?" she said.

"Why what?"

"Why is it so vast? Who do they need all this? What's it for?"

Nox snorted. He spoke quietly, as if they might be heard even from this distance. "Need? It has nothing to do with need. They've built all this because they *can*. Because the worlds are their playground and no one can stop them.

They build because it's fun."

"Fun?" She could hear the excitement in her voice as he spoke. "But it's hideous. All that death. It's nothing but pointless, insatiable greed. Cruelty and greed."

He laughed, but didn't reply. Despite what the undain had done to him he clearly admired the place. But she didn't want to go anywhere near it. It was a city of death. A city of ghosts. But going near it was exactly what they had to do.

"So, can you get us inside?" she asked.

"Actually that's the easy part. We walk in."

"Walk in? Are you mad?"

"Sure. You can see how big it is. It's not defended; the undain have no enemies in Angere. There are a thousand ways in. You can walk into the White City unnoticed as easily as you could walk into Manchester unnoticed."

"But they'll sense us. They'll see we're not like them."

"Perhaps. We have to hope Phoenix and his rabble are keeping Menhroth distracted in the north. The undain won't be looking this way. The ancient bridgehead where the archway used to be is that way, too."

"Still, we don't look like undain. We look a mess."

"No, no," said Nox. "You've seen the nobles and the soldiers, but most of the undain aren't like that. Most of them are drones and grunts, shuffling around in rags, building and cleaning. Keeping their heads down and not talking."

"You think I can pass for one of those?"

"Have you looked in a mirror recently?"

"Bastard. And what about you?"

"I can pass for one of them, too. But Ran would be too obvious. Another reason to leave him behind."

"But they'll be able to sense we're alive."

"Only if they're looking. And I've been trained to close my mind off, as you've found out. You're going to have to do the same. Can you do that?"

"Maybe." Bethany had been teaching her. She thought

she was getting better at it.

She thought about everything that could go wrong with the plan. In many ways it was completely crazy. But what else could they do? And perhaps doing something unexpected made sense. "But, OK, the book. How do we get that? We won't be able to just walk up and ask to borrow it."

"No. That's the hard part. The Grimoire is kept in the Cathedral of the Moon in the heart of the Six Palaces. It's well guarded. Very, very well guarded. A ring of dragonriders stand guard around it thirty-six hours a day."

"*Thirty-six?*"

"That's how many they have here."

"And did you ever see it?"

"Several times. They like to show it off to impress visitors."

"So is there any way to get in there and steal it?"

"Not sure," said Nox. "Still weighing up options."

"Meaning you don't have a clue."

"Meaning I haven't decided the best strategy yet."

"And if we can somehow steal this book and somehow escape, there's still the river. I had no idea it was so vast. We have to get across somehow."

"That thing you do with the ice," said Nox. "Can you sustain it?"

"I don't know what you mean."

"Don't they teach you long words in school these days? I mean can you keep doing it? Could you freeze us a path right across the water so we could walk to Andar?"

"No! It's miles. How would that ever work? I told you, magic hurts. I'd be dead before I got anywhere."

"OK, so you can't do that either. So, we find a boat, float across. Can you row?"

"No," she said. "Can you?"

"I really don't know."

"What do you mean you don't know?"

"I mean I've never tried. I generally find you can do

anything if you put your mind to it."

"But we'd be swept away. We'd end up, I don't know, hundreds of miles downstream. And then there are the monsters."

"The monsters."

"In the river. Fer told me about them. They destroy anything that tries to cross, right?"

"The river serpents. Yes, they do. We'd just have to hope they didn't spot us."

"That's your optimal strategy? Hope they don't spot us?"

She thought he was going to come up with another insult, but his voice was unusually subdued as he replied. "I think that's the best we can hope for. If we get that far and the serpents take us, they'll take the Grimoire too. Then at least we'll have destroyed it, stopped Menhroth using it."

"But we'll be dead, Nox."

"Yes. I think that was pretty inevitable the moment we came here. Did you think something else, Cait? Did you think this was all some fun school trip?"

He was being serious for once. Not sarcastic, not rude. Possibly she was seeing the real him, just for a moment. He expected to die but he'd come because he wanted revenge on those who had cast him out. She studied him for a moment, but he didn't look at her.

"Let's check on Ran one more time," she said. "Do what we can for him. Then we'd better go hadn't we?"

"Yes," said Nox. "We better had."

19 – THE WHITE CITY

Ran hadn't moved when they returned to him. Sometimes he thrashed around, animated by nightmares, but now he was still, chest rising and falling slowly but steadily. She dribbled a little more water into his mouth, feeling bad at what they were about to do. Ran was always ready to leap to her defence, protect her, and now they were going to abandon him. She consoled herself with the thought he was safer out here in the woods than marching with them into the White City. He at least might survive living in the wilds. Perhaps he could make his way back north, return to Caer D'nar. If it still stood. He'd be shocked when he came round and found they'd gone, when he realised he could no longer fulfil his vow to protect her. But there was nothing she could do. Perhaps he'd understand. He had brought them this far, done all he could.

She took one of the plain silver chains from her neck and placed it around his, next to his string of dragonrider memory stones. He'd asked her about the jewellery she wore more than once, imagining it had some great meaning or significance to her. But the necklace was just a cheap chain from *Bling Thing*. The precious seeing stone her gran had given her was still around her neck. But Ran would know the gift was from her. That was what mattered.

As they left she glanced back, hoping he'd wake up miraculously and come running to join them. That was what would happen in a movie or a book. But he didn't move and soon he was lost to sight behind the boughs of the trees. Now there were only two of them. Her and Nox. Three if you included Bethany.

They reached the northern edge of the woods two hours later. The White City stood clear before them, the road snaking toward two ornate towers forming a gateway. As Nox had described, there were many other roads arriving from all directions. None of the entrances looked to be guarded. Several teams of undain slaves worked along the roads, hauling carts to and from the city. Supplies of Spirit presumably. Troops of soldiers marched at speed from the south. They didn't appear to be searching for anyone.

"Come on," said Nox. "Follow me."

Before she could object, he pulled the hood of the cloak Phoenix had given him over his head and set off for the road. One of the creaking wooden carts was lumbering nearby, pulled by a team of eight or ten undain. There were two of the creatures on each of the cart's giant wheels as well, hauling on the spokes to make the wheels turn.

Cait set off after Nox, pulling her own hood over her head, feeling exposed as she left the eaves of the trees.

Nox hurried to the back of the cart and pretended to join in with the effort of pushing it forward. None of the undain objected. Cait joined him. "Why haven't they noticed us? Why don't they say anything?"

"Because they haven't been told to. They're here to work, not think. It's an excellent system."

Cait studied the nearest undain, who was heaving one of the wheels forward as if he were steering a vast sailing ship. The creature was skin stretched over bones, his sinews sharp lines as he strained forward. His gaze was vacant when she looked at his face. She wondered who he was, whether he had come from back home. She tried to touch his mind, but there was only the familiar void with no light illuminating it. The empty churns in the cart clanked as they bumped along.

They passed through the archway half an hour later and found themselves on a rutted road with tall, ornately-decorated walls on either side. And everything, everything carved from bone. The smell of the place made Cait gag. It wasn't just the miasma of death. There was a chemical tang in the air, too. All around, undain slaves were scrubbing and polishing the floors and walls with cleaning fluid. It masked the underlying scent of decay, which somehow made it worse.

A deep sense of dread had filled Cait as they approached but now that they were inside the walls it redoubled. And it wasn't simply her own fear churning away. It was in the air. She could *feel* it. A background roar of rage and fury coming at her from every angle. It made her weak to taste it. The combined auras of all the undain.

How many were there around her? Many, many thousands. And what would they do if they knew she was there, the one they sought, calmly walking though the gates? She tried not to think about it.

A few yards farther, the undain hauling the cart stopped and wheeled the vehicle around to point toward another archway up a steep hill. A number of carts stood waiting in a line.

Nox touched her on the shoulder. "This is where we leave them. We need to carry on up the main road." He indicated the direction with a nod of his head. The thoroughfare opened into a wide square and in the middle, like a vast moored ship, stood a single huge building, all steeples and spikes and arches.

"The Grimoire's kept in there?"

"No, no. That's just one of the minor cathedrals."

"So they have cathedrals here? They worship gods?"

"What need do they have for gods when they've made themselves immortal? Menhroth is their god as well as their king. He is their creator. He raised them all up with his necromancy."

"So where is the book?"

"The Cathedral of the Moon is near Menhroth's palace, several miles farther on."

"Several *miles*?" It seemed impossible they could get that far without being noticed, especially now that they didn't have the cart to hide behind.

The streets were already busier than back by the gate. Undain slaves shuffling by and, more and more, those who were clearly *not* slaves: richly dressed nobles, some walking, some being carried on golden seats. There were more cartloads of Spirit being wheeled north, too. Supplies for the army, perhaps.

"Keep your head down and keep moving," said Nox. "Once we're past this cathedral we'll take to the back streets that only the slaves use."

"OK."

They skirted around the vast building, sticking to the shadows as much as possible. Its richly decorated towers reached high into the sky. She'd seen similar buildings back home: huge gothic constructions that must have taken decades, *centuries* to build. She couldn't help stare in wonder at the intricate carving.

Movement caught her eye part-way up the wall. Above a large doorway, a line of archways was arrayed, in each of which was placed a statue of a skeleton. Except, as she looked on, she could see they weren't statues. They were actual bone, still somehow animated, writhing and reaching into the air but unable to escape. Locked into place in their alcoves. Ragged black birds like the dead crow she'd seen were perched on many of their heads, as if to taunt the skeletons. Occasionally one of the skeletons lifted a bony arm to scare a bird away, but the crows simply flapped in a little circle and settled back where they were.

Were the skeletons alive and aware of their fate? She didn't like to think about it. It was hideous. The whole place was hideous.

"Cait. Come on," whispered Nox, the anger in his voice clear. "You look like a tourist."

They moved out of the square, Nox leading her into a narrow alleyway between two buildings with more carved, arched windows. It was darker in the alleyway, the walls too high to let in much sunlight. Cait felt a little safer in the shadows.

She tried not to catch anyone's eye, tried to keep her mind blank as if she, too, were one of the undain. Lines of slaves shuffled along, and she shuffled with them, glad of the anonymity.

The alleyway opened onto a broad road running alongside a canal. She expected the waters to be blood-red but it was just water, some tributary of the An. Many bridges spanned the stream. The nearest, directly ahead, arched across the river in a gentle curve, a cradle of white struts holding it in the air. Lamps had been set up along it, lamps held by more skeletons. These at least weren't moving. Perhaps they were just dead bone. She hoped so.

"Do we have to cross?" she asked.

"It's that or swim. What's the problem?"

They'd be exposed on the bridge, visible all around. She thought back to the pursuit across Manchester, when she and Danny had crossed the old canal and Nox had seen them from his bridge. The memory brought with it a pang of pain. Danny, whom she'd led to his death.

"Nothing," she said, "Come on. Let's get this over with."

The wind gusted as they crossed the bridge. She kept her head down, shoulders slumped, eyes on the water visible between the bridge's slats. On the other side, the bone-cobbled road was wide, no shadows to hide in, the sunlight glaring off the endless white. She wished she had sunglasses with her.

There were more and more statues too: men and women in heroic poses, as well as an endless variety of fantastical creatures with bat wings or dagger fangs or monstrous heads. The statues troubled her more than the undain. Something in the unblinking gaze of their blank white eyes gave her the creeps. She couldn't shake the feeling they were watching her. There were more of the black birds, too, perched on the statues, in archways, around the tops of the buildings. Eyeing her.

They skirted the curving walls of some round tower. One of the nobles being carried on a golden throne passed by, twelve undain slaves supporting his weight. Not thinking, Cait glanced at the noble and there was a moment, the briefest moment, when their gazes met. Quickly Cait lowered her head to stare at the floor. She expected to hear cries and shouts. Surely he would see she wasn't one of them?

No calls came. She didn't dare look back as they joined an even wider, straight road that led into the heart of the city. It fell and rose slightly so that she could see it was thronged with undain. Slaves, soldiers, nobles, many more carts.

They'd only walked a few yards when she heard running footsteps from behind. A great many footsteps, urgent, clattering on the ground, coming nearer. The undain were coming for her, she knew it with sudden certainty. The noble had recognized her, alerted the army. The crows or the statues had raised the alarm. Why did she think she could creep unnoticed into the enemy city? It was insane.

Well. She wouldn't go down without a fight. Perhaps it wouldn't make much difference, but it was all she could do. She began to summon the storm of ice in her mind. It didn't matter if she worked magic now.

"Cait!" Nox pulled her roughly to the side of the road, slamming her against the wall of the building. His voice was an urgent hiss. "What are you doing? Get out of the way."

A troop of soldiers pounded by, feet stamping, armour clanking. They were racing for the city centre. Not coming for her. She closed her eyes and tried to calm the fury whipping inside her. Her heart thundered and she wondered how it was no one could hear it. The wall behind her was polished smooth against her hands.

When the soldiers were gone, she and Nox set off once more. Five minutes later, Nox turned sharply to the right and led her off the busy road into the hush of a courtyard. There were no undain to be seen. The courtyard was lined on all four sides by ornate pillars, between which ran delicately carved screens of bone. Each was an intricate lattice-work of tiny holes. Holes, she saw, in the shape of so many skulls. Someone had really worked hard to goth the place up. Low benches ran around the edge of the courtyard. In the centre stood a white statue, twice normal size, of a man standing triumphantly upon a mound of lolling dead bodies, all carved from bone. He held aloft a bone crown. Menhroth, presumably.

"Wait here," said Nox. "This is one of the cloisters of the Holy Court. Stay out of sight." He indicated the benches beside the entranceway. She would be invisible from the road there. No one would see her unless they came into the courtyard.

"What if someone comes?"

"Say nothing. It won't seem strange; there's no talking here; it's a place for contemplation."

"Where are you going?"

"To scout around. We need to find out what's going on. With the army mobilising, Menhroth and the rest of the Holy Court will be preoccupied. There's a chance they'll have taken the Grimoire out of protection to carry it north with the army."

"I don't see why they would."

"Think, Cait. Because there's a chance the other half of

the book has reached Andar. If *we* know that, they must know that. The undain might plan to take the book with them when they cross the ice so they can reunite the two halves. That might be our chance. Give me an hour. Don't move. If I don't get back then you're on your own, OK?"

"OK," she said. Although it really wasn't.

He slipped away, and Cait hid herself out of sight of the road, sitting on the bench. Its surface was worn almost to glass by the countless thousands who'd sat there over the centuries. She shut her eyes, trying to force herself to breathe more slowly. Her heart was still racing. She had to suppress the desire to run, flee this hideous place and never come back.

The grim aura she'd sensed earlier rushed into her mind. She had to learn to block it. She sat in silent effort for ten, twenty minutes trying to build walls of fog around her mind. Walls others couldn't pierce. Once again Bethany guided her, showed her how to go about it. The problem was Cait couldn't tell if she was managing it or not. She needed someone to see if they could overcome her defences, and there was no one she could trust to try.

The sound of more running feet on the roadway came to her. More soldiers racing north to join the mobilisation. She pushed herself back against the screen, making sure there was no chance she could be seen.

The running feet stopped. She heard metallic clinks and scrapes. The sounds of swords being drawn. Alarm thumped in her stomach. She made herself remain seated. Maintain the pretence. She covered her head with the cowl of her cloak and lowered her gaze to the ground, as if lost in contemplation.

"You can get up now, Cait."

It was Nox's voice. Something in his voice sent a chill through her. There was a note of delight. A note of *triumph*. She looked up. Nox stood before her. Around him were ten or more of the giant dragonriders with their weird transparent skin. It was clear Nox wasn't their prisoner.

Thoughts tumbled incoherently through her brain as she tried to make sense of it. "You ... you told them? After everything, you're still with them?"

"Obviously. You really are stupid, aren't you? I kept *telling* you you were stupid, but you were too stupid to believe me. I mean, I actually led you into the White City and you just followed me."

"But they cast you out. At Greygyle's palace Charis laughed at you when you tried to betray me."

Nox shrugged. "Charis was a setback. But they already had you then, so they thought. I wasn't offering them anything. When I talked to them here, said I could hand them the spawn of Ilminion, I was in a much stronger bargaining position."

"They took you back?"

"They forgave my sins in return for your blood."

"So now you're one of them again? Just like that?"

"Just like that, Cait. Oh, it was fun travelling with you. I've enjoyed our time together, I really have. And I've learned a lot. But now I've had this better offer so I'm switching sides. Always best to choose the side that's going to win, don't you find? Soon Andar and Angere will be reunited under the rule of King Menhroth. The cloven land and the cloven book will be reformed and the undain's dominance will be assured."

"You bastard, Nox. You utter bastard."

"Yes. True. But at least I'm not about to be slaughtered by the undain, so I think, on balance, I can live with it."

Fury mounted within her at the sight of his self-satisfied smile. She began to work magic, reawakening the swirling storm of ice. But before she could unleash it, before she could do anything, the riders moved, blindingly fast. One raised his hand to strike her with a mailed fist.

There was the briefest thump of pain, and then only darkness.

Eight undain dragonriders flanked Cait as they marched

her through the impossibly huge palace of Menhroth. Her head throbbed from the blow she'd received, from the terror hammering through her, from the all-pervading stench of the place. There was nothing she could do. If she stumbled the riders picked her up and pushed her forward.

Nox had betrayed her. The magic had fled her. Bethany had fled her. Danny and her mum were dead. She was walking to meet the Witch King alone. How had it come to this? She wanted to curl up in a ball. She wanted to wake up from the nightmare she was in. But she couldn't.

After what seemed like hours they reached an archway across from the vault, the second or third they'd passed beneath. Moving in harmony the dragonriders sank to the ground and began to crawl. One pulled her leg, instructing her to do the same. The touch of the undain awoke her anger. She was damned if she would. She was sick of the fear, sick of running from them. What more could they do to her?

She walked forward, striding from the squirming wyrm lords behind her. She was trapped and lost, but she wouldn't crawl on her stomach before this so-called King. What the hell made him a king anyway? An accident of birth. She was damned if she'd bow to him.

One of the riders scrambled forward, grabbing her foot, intending to pull her to the ground. She kicked at the hand holding her but couldn't break free.

"Let her be." The distant voice from the far end of the hallway boomed in the great hall. "The heir of Ilminion can be allowed to walk the rest of the way. The rest of you may leave."

A surprisingly young voice. She'd expected another Charis, another ancient horror.

The grip on her foot let go immediately. She strode forward, eyes on the distant figure who had spoken. The Witch King. The god the undain worshipped. A man dressed in white and gold sitting upon a ridiculously ornate throne, a spiky crown upon his head. He was handsome, too, no doubt about it. That was almost the creepiest thing of all. He was, what, over five hundred years old? Tubes like those she'd seen Greygyle use snaked from his chair directly into his neck, pumping raw Spirit into him. She fancied she could hear the countless tiny screams of all the individuals he was consuming. The sight of him made her stomach heave with sickness and fizz with terror at the same time. His eyes were pure black, hard as polished glass.

She stopped in front of him but refused to bow or curtsey or whatever it was she was supposed to do.

"Cait Weerd," he said. "It is good to meet you at last."

"What do you want with me?" she said, trying to sound angry, trying to sound brave. She couldn't stop her voice quavering. "Why am I here?"

"You know why you're here," said Menhroth. "We have unfinished business. Rituals begun five centuries before you were even born need to be completed. Sealing syllables for so long left unsaid need to be uttered. Now we have the blood and soon we will have the book, and at last, it will be done."

"Half of the book has been returned to Andar," said Cait. "They will never let you have it. They'll destroy it first." She didn't actually know if that was true. For all she was aware, Genera had retrieved the book before it could be taken to safety.

"No," said Menhroth. "They'll cling to the desperate belief your little mission here will succeed. That by some series of impossible miracles you'll retrieve this half of the Grimoire and carry it to Andar. So long as they think you're still alive, Hellen Meggenwar and the rest of them will do nothing, muttering ineffectual spells into the night. And while they're doing that we'll sweep across Andar and kill them before they realise what's happening."

Menhroth's reply sent the tiniest thrill of hope through her. It appeared they didn't have the book from her world. Someone had carried it through the portal to Andar, or had avoided capture at least. "You won't win," she said. The words sounded hollow even to her. "Someone will stop you. Sooner or later someone will stop you. All you can think about is death. You're sick, all of you. You're perverts. You're disgusting."

The king held up a hand to stop her. He laughed, the sound golden and sweet. She wanted to ignore him, carry on shouting, but she could think of no more insults to fling.

"You talk of death," said Menhroth, smiling down at her from his throne. "Shall I tell you the central truth of your existence? Shall I tell you the fact so huge and terrible that you aren't even consciously aware of it most of the time?"

She didn't want to play his game, but she had no answer for him. She shrugged, as if she didn't care what he had to say.

"It is simply this," said Menhroth. "You are aware of your own mortality. You all are. You know you are going to die. Every moment of your life that terrible little thought is there, loud or quiet but never disappearing, always there to torture you. Always a clock ticks in your heads. It's quiet when you're young, perhaps, but slowly it gets louder. You are the ones obsessed with death, not us. We don't die. We don't die because we've already died."

"And yet you've spent the last five hundred years trying to get your hands on the Grimoire. If you're so powerful why do you need it?"

The king nodded his head, as if she'd made an interesting point. "The unfinished ritual is an inconvenience, nothing more. Thanks to the generous supplies of Spirit from your world we thrive as we are. Our armies are unstoppable. But with the book and the blood, we will be ten times more powerful. Yes, we have hunted you and your ancestors all this time, sought that which was stolen from us. But you can see for yourself how well we have survived." He waved a hand in the air to indicate the splendours of the palace.

Was that true? Her gran had explained how the ritual Ilminion performed on Menhroth remained unfinished in some way. How the undain were incomplete and, as a result, in need of vast supplies of Spirit to sustain them. Despite his words, it was clear Menhroth did desire the book. Desired it very much.

"But they didn't steal the book from you, did they?" she said. "They took it for safekeeping. To stop you from using it."

"Is that how they tell the story? No. The truth is they stole Ilminion's book. Took what wasn't theirs and carried it across the bridge to Andar. And that wasn't all they stole."

"What do you mean? What else was taken?"

"They kept that from you? Did you imagine your ancestor bravely fighting alongside the riders as they fled across the bridge? Because it wasn't like that at all. They took a baby girl, too. Weyerd, Ilminion's daughter, your ancestor. They ripped her from her home in Angere and carried her to Andar. Took her without her consent because they knew how important she'd be. But the blood calls, even all this time later. And here you are, Cait. The last of your line come back to Angere where you belong."

"That isn't what's going on here."

"Are you sure of that?"

"Yes."

He smiled his handsome smile. "If you say so. And tell me, what of Ran? You entered the city with only Nox. Did the brave rider die of his burns?"

Perhaps if they thought Ran was dead they wouldn't hunt for him. Nox would surely tell them the truth sooner or later, but perhaps she could buy Ran a little time.

"Yes. He brought us here with the last of his strength. He died where the wyrm road left us, on the banks of the An."

"Ah. That explains it. It does seem people keep dying

around you doesn't it? First your father and now your mother. Then the boy Lugg heads off alone into the mountains on a doomed mission to confront an insane dragon. Now Ran, too. Death stalks you, Cait Weerd. The blood of Ilminion is strong in you."

So Nox had told Menhroth everything. Xoster, the Smouldering Fire, everything.

"My blood is my own," she said. "It's just blood. I'm nothing like that necromancer. Nothing."

"So you keep insisting. Well, it matters little. The ritual can be completed whatever objections you raise. A shame. You might have been as great as he was. I can see it in you. You could have become one of us."

"I'd rather die."

"Given what's going to happen that's just as well."

In desperation, she wondered if she could send a message across the An, tell the witches she was imprisoned, tell them there was no hope. Then at least Hellen could destroy the half of the book they possessed, if indeed it had been returned to Andar. There'd been talk of the witches using the Grimoire, turning the necromancy against the undain. That clearly wasn't going to happen now. Destroying the book was all that was left to them.

"What will you do with me?" she asked. "How long do I have?"

"You've a while to live yet. Once we've reunited the Grimoire we can complete the Ritual of the Seven Ascensions. You can keep your blood until then. You can spend the intervening time in the dungeons. You should be pleased, we have very little need of the lower levels these days, and they are vast and impressive. There are vaults down there as great as this hall, all echoing and empty. You will have a palace in the dark all to yourself. Almost all to yourself, anyway."

As much as she wanted to get away from Menhroth, the thought of being hurled into an underground dungeon seemed worse. She kept on talking. "And where is Nox in all this? What is his reward?"

"He is being allowed to live. His gift has bought him that much."

"You do know what he did, don't you?" she said. "You do know he took the Andar half of the book from Genera and gave it to my mother. It's because of him you lost it."

Menhroth regarded her. For a moment, a look flashing across his eyes, he was the ancient, malevolent monster she'd expected. Then his ready smile returned. "I know what Nox is, have no fear. I have always known. He can be trusted to do what is in his own interests, nothing less and nothing more."

"So now he's one of you again?"

"He has earned our thanks. That is all. Whether he will ever become *one of us* is a matter of debate. We shall see in time. We'll think about it for a few decades. We have all the time we need, even if he does not."

"He hates you. I saw it in him."

"He is free to hate me. So long as he fears me more what does it matter? Now go. The guards will escort you to your subterranean palace. We will meet again, Cait Weerd. But only once more, at the end, when we are ready to complete the ritual."

She wanted to object, scream, attack. But she couldn't. She was utterly powerless in the face of him. She stepped backward, some compulsion forcing her from his presence. There was nothing she could do. She strode the length of the hall, back to the doorway.

Back outside, in the dazzling brilliance of the White City, she stood blinded and blinking for a moment. The river was visible in the distance. They were higher up here, but there was still no sign of a far shore. The water stretched forever. In the distance, downstream to the south, she could see the woods they'd hidden within. A short way north, jutting into the water, the ruins of an ancient bridge. Perhaps the old stories were true after all.

More guards came for her as she stood dazzled in the

bright light. She could do nothing but follow them.

They led her down a long flight of steps, undain slaves scrubbing and cleaning them part-way down. They passed a tall gate, through which she glimpsed an archway standing alone in the middle of a wide square. This one was no ruin. Something large was coming through it. A container. A container of bones from back home. Here was the other end of the portal she had seen from the refinery.

They hurried on, crossing a circular space toward a domed building that housed a flight of steps leading into the ground. The smell of mildew and age breathing up at her almost made her faint. The riders led her down, the glow from their bodies illuminating the way. The stairs wound so that the sky was soon lost to sight. Down they descended, hundreds and hundreds of steps. They had to be at the river level, perhaps even lower. The air felt damp on her face. Still they descended, until finally reaching an iron gate, ornately decorated with flying dragons. It squealed as they pushed it open, as if angry at being interrupted from its long slumber.

They pushed her inside. Another squeal was followed by a metallic scraping as locks turned. Then, saying nothing, the glowing dragonriders climbed the stairs, leaving her to the darkness.

Fingers of cold seemed to envelop her. Water dripped from the roof with hard *tap* sounds. She shuffled forward in the darkness, arms outstretched in case she hit a wall. She tripped on something on the floor, and fell to the damp ground. She reached out, horrified at what she might find. It was only a slimy cone of rock. Was that a stalagmite or a stalactite? She hadn't paid enough attention in school to know. She regretted it, although it made no difference now.

She tried to work a werelight but none would come. She was too weak, too lost. She lifted the seeing stone to her eye, glad of its presence, its simple weight in her hand.

But even that was no help. It was just a stone, and the darkness remained absolute. She suddenly didn't remember where the gate was that she'd come through. She shuffled forward again in a random direction, feeling with her feet as well as her hands. Eventually she found a wall, slick with water or slime.

She sat with her back against it, put her head in her hands, and lost herself to misery and self-pity.

Some time later, shuffling sounds from nearby made her heart leap. What had Menhroth said? *Almost all to yourself.* There was something in the dungeon with her. In her mind's eye she was surrounded by ancient horrors left to rot down there for centuries, reaching for her with clammy fingers. The sound came closer, hesitant, feeling its way toward her.

In her panic, she found the strength to work a light. It flared in front of her eyes, blinding her momentarily. She sent it toward the rustling, shuffling thing.

It wasn't a *thing*, wasn't an undain. It was a filthy, ragged, blinking human crouching on the ground. It cowered from the light, but she saw immediately who it was. Her heart rang like a bell.

"Danny?"

20 – THE DESTRUCTION OF ANDAR

Andar

They made good progress down the An, *Smoke on the Water* finding fast currents on the great river, picking its way among them like a weaver working a loom. At times they strayed so far out into the sparkling waters that Ashen lost sight of the bank completely. The first time in his life he'd truly left the soil of Andar behind. Terror filled him each time. He didn't need to be as powerful as his mother to sense the voracious minds of the river serpents, bellowing and clashing in the deeps of the An.

On more than one occasion the waters swirled and boiled as one neared the surface. Once he caught a flash of grey flesh as one of the creatures surfaced. *Smoke on the Water* turned and sped for the safety of the shallows before a tentacle could reach out for them.

Over the days Ashen grew to trust the ancient mancer whose spirit inhabited the miraculous boat. On the first night of their journey, sweeping down the wide waters, Ashen had lain awake, heart hammering at each new splash and call in the darkness. In his imagination, the undain were out there as well as the serpents, threatening to loom out of the darkness at any moment. But the following morning had dawned bright and clear, and they'd survived unscathed.

By the next night, unable to keep his weary eyes open, he'd slept. The boat, however, never slumbered. The mind controlling it had been human once, but now it was something else. The craft's timbers were oak, hard as iron, and something of that indomitability had taken root in the mancer's mind. A refusal to break or yield. *Smoke on the Water* ploughed onward, day and night, cutting through the waters with rushing speed.

After six days of relentless southward travel they reached the mouth of the Meander. Turning east to run upstream, their progress slowed, the tributary moving with a wide, steady flow against *Smoke on the Water's* bows, splashing repeatedly over the golden figurehead. The boat rocked and bucked like a horse as they cut through the currents.

Wide grassy plains lay on both banks, clumped here and there with copses of ancient wood. Good land, it looked, land to grow wheat and apples, graze cattle and sheep. Farms and homesteads ran along the banks, horses and oxen working the fields, harvesting this year's crop or ploughing in readiness for the next. The tang of roasting hops mingled with the sweeter scent of wood smoke in the air. Sometimes laughing children raced him, waving and calling. They were a glad sight. It was hard to believe that they, that all of this, could ever be destroyed. Hard to believe that any shadow threatened these fertile, sunny lands. But the darkness gathering in the west was already moving, and time was running out.

In the distance the mounds and peaks of the Azend mountains picked themselves off the eastern horizon and sidled closer. Ashen had a telescope of brass and glass with him, one of those used to observe the snowlines on the northern mountains to predict the coming winter. He scanned the land ahead, searching for a hill with a stone keep on its top.

The sight of the peaks made him think of his father. He had no memory of the dragonrider Borrn, although his mother had told him he'd lived with them for the entire first year of Ashen's life, away from Islagray in his mother's home village. Then his rider duties had taken him into the wilds and the mountains, to the far north, and they never heard of him again. More than once over the years Ashen had cast the incantations to seek for Borrn through the aether, but there was never anything. His father was long dead.

The thought left Ashen strangely untroubled. He should have felt worse than he did. But *Borrn* was just a name; a person he had no recollection of. The most he knew of his father was the far-away look in his mother's eyes whenever the subject was raised. A look that spoke of love and loss. He often wondered what kind of man his father had been, to capture the heart of Hellen Meggenwar.

But his mother, now, there was no doubt *she* was still full of life. Still running everyone's lives, still squabbling with his beloved aunty Ariane. Still plotting and planning, and sharing as little as she could get away with. He regretted staying away so long, now. He remembered the day he'd told her of his plans to travel north to Guilden and seek apprenticeship with the mancers. He'd expected her scowl, the raise of an eyebrow that was all she had to do to make her displeasure ice-clear.

There were warlocks on Islagray and he had some talent for the craft. He could have stayed and learned the old ways. But instead of arguing with him she'd nodded, accepting his decision, then held him close and told him to make sure he came back to visit, or else she'd unleash some terrible plague on him. When she let him go there were tears in her eyes, the only time he'd ever seen his mother cry.

He'd never been able to work out how she became the Hellen that most people saw. The Hellen that wasn't his mother, the Hellen that arranged everything and everyone around her to suit her plans. The Hellen that led. There was some trick to it he didn't possess. His mother had only to utter a few suggestions and people simply carried them out. She never ordered anyone to do anything, but they always obeyed.

There were many sorts of magic in the world. Islagray was the beating heart of Andar and his mother, he often thought, was the spirit of Islagray. The witches and the mancers had their differences over the rights and wrongs of spellmaking. There were plenty in the north who dismissed the witches of Islagray as doddering old midwives, lost in their ancient superstitions. But Ashen knew the truth of it. When it came to it, Andar depended on Islagray. On the Song.

On his mother.

He only hoped he could play his part in the defence of the land and the people he loved. He wasn't his mother, the eldest of Islagray, and he wasn't his father, a dragonrider of Angere. He wasn't anything much. An apprentice mancer. An acolyte struggling to twist his tongue around the simplest spells. But he would do what he could. This message for the girl from the other world was a start. A vital task. But there would be more to do before the end. Much more.

Slowly, the land on the banks of the Meander rose into rougher scrub, uncultivated, cropped by flocks of shaggy brown-black creatures that were either sheep or goats. Buildings became scarcer and he stopped seeing people. He wished he'd stopped sand asked some of those laughing children if they knew of the Blind Mapmaker. But the boat had swept onward, meeting the oncoming waters with an outpouring of determined, magical strength that Ashen didn't dare interrupt.

The light was fading from the world, darkness seeming

to roll down from the slopes of the mountains, when he glimpsed the keep in the distance, appearing around a bend in the stream. It was a simple stone tower, three or four floors high, atop a perfectly round hill. Ashen, closing his eyes, clutching the gems around his neck in which he'd stored a few shreds of magical strength, murmured the spell of a seeking incantation. He reached into the darkness toward the keep, searching for a presence.

It took time, and in the end the echo was faint, as if the man were close to death. But he was there: a solitary mind within the walls.

Smoke on the Water saw the keep or sensed the presence, too. Without a word from Ashen it heeled to starboard and headed for the bank. It beached itself on a tiny shingle cove to let Ashen off. Even as he stepped ashore, the solid ground feeling strangely fluid beneath his feet, the boat's eyes shut as if the mancer, finally, was allowing himself to rest. Clutching a flaming torch to light his way, Ashen scrambled up the muddy bank and climbed to the keep.

Twenty minutes later, he stood at the base of the tower, peering up at the stone walls silhouetted against the starry sky. From afar the building had looked deserted, no sounds to be heard, no lights in the arched windows. But what use did a blind man have for lights? Now Ashen was up close he could see a small garden and pens for animals around the stone walls, all well-maintained. A large animal, a pig perhaps, snuffled inside one of the low stone huts. Someone was living there, or had recently.

A solid wooden door barred his way. He strode up to it and knocked, the hollow sound loud in the cold darkness. Nothing in the night moved. In the distance, moonlight glinting off its surface, the river was a ribbon of silver in the night.

Ashen shivered in the cold air while he waited for a reply, huddling his robes around him. No response came. He rapped again, louder, hard enough to skin his knuckles. When this, too, went unanswered, he twisted the iron ring that latched the door. To his surprise it turned easily, and the door swung inward.

The wavering flame from his torch revealed a round room that filled the entire lower level of the keep. The walls were bare stone. A collection of muddy leather boots and well-used garden implements lined the walls, each carefully placed so their owner would know precisely where they were. A central stone staircase spiralled upward. Closing the door behind him, and holding his torch forward, Ashen climbed.

On the next floor, shelves had been built from floor to ceiling. They were filled with rolls of parchment, piled high in some places. The characters of some language he didn't know were carved into the shelves, cataloguing the thousands of maps. He wished he had time to study them. If this man could see through the aether clearly enough to draw the lands he glimpsed through borrowed eyes, there would be maps of many worlds, many impossibly distant places. Places Ashen had only heard about in myth and fairy-story. What wonders were sketched on these parchments?

But there was no time to find out. He climbed past two more levels, on each of which the walls were covered by more shelves piled high with scrolls. The smell of old paper filled the air. Still no one called to him or tried to stop him. He was beginning to think the keep was abandoned, that he'd been mistaken in sensing the Mapmaker's presence. Wasn't it strange he'd been allowed to walk in there with all the precious maps lying around? Perhaps he'd arrived too late after all. Perhaps the Mapmaker had been dying even as Ashen quested for him from the river. Perhaps, despite all *Smoke on the Water's* efforts, he was a few minutes too late. It was a grim thought. If they couldn't get a message through to Cait, what hope was there for any of them?

The thought struck him that there might be another undain there. That some skulking horror had flown across the An and made its way to the tower to kill the Mapmaker. The old man had to know things about Angere. Had to know about the massing of armies and their plans. He may even have heard Menhroth giving his orders. If the undain knew about the Mapmaker, they might come here to destroy all record of what had been glimpsed. And if so, if the murder had only just happened, the monster would still be there, lurking in the darkness, waiting to attack.

Perhaps leaping from the shadows even now…

The temptation to flee was almost overwhelming. Ashen had to force himself to carry on. His heart raced in his chest, his pulse pounding in his ears. He stepped warily up to the next floor, torch held forward, listening for any movement. The winding stairs stopped a few steps up. If there was an undain, this was where it would be. He clutched the gems around his neck again, preparing to work a spell of fire if he was attacked. He was no match for an undain lord. At least he could die fighting.

"Ashen Meggenwar, mancer of Guilden. Welcome to my ruin."

The voice was an old man's, weak, little more than a croak. Surely not one of the undain. Ashen climbed to the top of the stairwell, still wary. The Mapmaker appeared to be expecting him. Perhaps that was why Ashen had been able to enter the tower so easily. If the old man had wanted to keep him out, he would simply have locked his door.

Scraps of torn parchment lay in drifts on the floor, as if someone had torn and shredded the maps in a fit of fury. In the guttering torchlight, Ashen picked out fragments of detail here and there. The curve of some unknown coastline. The towers of an unnamed city. Had one of the undain come here after all? Had the old man fought it, defeated it?

Ashen search the darkness for the Mapmaker. "Are you injured? Were you attacked?"

A dry chuckling from the shadows told Ashen where the old man was. Ashen crossed warily toward the sound, kicking through mounds of tattered parchment. Something crunched and snapped beneath his boot. Shards of glass scattered the floor, too. Ashen thought he knew what they must be. The seeing sphere, smashed into pieces.

"Attacked?" the man said. "No, no. You're the first visitor I've had in many years."

"Then, who did this? Who destroyed all your maps?"

Ashen's torch revealed the shape of a man slumped against the shelves, as if he were too drunk to move. There could be no doubt this was the Blind Mapmaker. An old man, skin lined and grey like the bark of a tree, his silver hair straggly and wild. His eyes were a piercing green, but it was clear from the angle of his gaze that he didn't see Ashen. Instead, he stared into the distance as he spoke. "This, Ashen? Isn't it obvious? I did this."

Ashen kneeled beside the man, looking for wounds or some sign of injury. "But why? Why would you do such a thing? All these maps. Your life's work…"

"Because they're useless!" said the old man, a sudden fury rising within him. "Don't you see? When the undain come they'll all be wrong. They'll have to be drawn again. All those names, all those villages and towns and cities, will have to be erased."

"You can see the future?" asked Ashen.

"No, no. I can see people's *minds*. See what they see. Know what they know. I have seen the undain preparing on the far bank of the An. Glimpsed what they are up to on other worlds, too. I know what is coming."

"And what have you seen?" Ashen couldn't stop himself asking even though he knew what the answer would be. He had already seen the certainty of it himself, in the snows on Howl Hill.

"The destruction of Andar," said the Mapmaker. "The end of everything." He picked up a handful of scraps and threw them into the air, a flurry falling like snow to the ground.

"It may not be like that."

"You haven't seen what I have seen. The *number* of them. The scale. They will cross the An like an unstoppable tide. Like another flood."

"So you have seen Angere? You can converse with people there?"

"There are no *people* there."

"There are some," said Ashen. "One or two at least."

The Mapmaker turned his head to Ashen then, as if he could finally see him. "I know why you're here. You want me to send a message to this girl. This lost, weak girl. What is the point? What is the use?"

"So you know of her? You have seen her? She's still alive?"

"I've seen glimpses. Scraps. Enough to know she is powerless to do anything. That there was never any hope. She should never have been sent. Your mother and her plans: what is the worth of any of them?"

Ashen persisted. He had come too far to give up now. "Perhaps you're right. But you have to try. Everything depends on it."

"Nothing depends on it. It will make no difference."

"Please."

The old man seemed to sag into himself, as if the air had left him. "No. The girl is lost. I could see little enough of her at the best of times but certainly not now."

Dread clutched at Ashen's insides. "Then, she is dead?"

The old man didn't reply for a moment, as if he were peering into the aether there and then, seeking answers. "Dead? No, not yet I don't think. They will prepare for the rites. But it won't be long. They have her you see, the undain have her. She lies lost in the dungeons of the White City, and her mind is closed to me."

Ashen didn't know what to say. He had the sensation of falling. For some reason he thought of the children who'd run along the banks of the river, shouting and laughing. They were damned now. They were all damned.

"And my mother? And Ariane?"

"They are lost to me, too. They walked together into the underworld and faded from my sight."

Ashen slumped beside the old man, the hard edges of a wooden shelf digging into his back. He paid it no attention. "There … there must be someone in Angere you can reach. Others went with the girl. What of them?"

"It's pointless."

"Then there is nothing to be lost by trying."

The old man scowled, shook his head. He picked up another handful of scraps, let them fall. "There is one I might reach. One I can talk to. But it will make no difference even if I can find him. He is far from the girl and as powerless as she is."

"But perhaps, somehow, the message will get through and Cait will hear it."

"And perhaps we'll simply feel a little better about ourselves for having made the effort, though it is a waste of time."

"So you'll do it?"

The Mapmaker sighed. "I can try. For what it's worth."

"Thank you," said Ashen. "The message…"

"I know what the message is. Just because I choose not to open my mind to your mother doesn't mean I'm blind to what occurs on Islagray. *The bridgehead.* I will do what I can. Not for you, mancer, and not for your mother. But for Andar. Then at the end I can console myself that I did all I could."

"Thank you."

Ashen opened the leather bag he'd carried on his back. The bag containing the old maps his mother had given him as a gift. "You probably know already that I brought you these old maps from Islagray. We thought you could add them to your collection."

There was the briefest spark of interest on the face of the old man. For a moment Ashen thought he was going to take them, run his fingers over them, feel their lines. But then he looked away. "They are as useless as all the others. The world is about to be redrawn. The old maps are all wrong now."

After a few moments, Ashen rose. There didn't appear to be more to say. It would be fully night outside, but he didn't want to stay in the keep any longer than he had to. The sooner he left, the sooner he would be back at Islagray.

At the stairs, though, he paused and looked back to where the Mapmaker lay in the shadows. "You could come back with me."

"With you?"

"To Islagray. We could load up the boat with all the maps that remain. We could store them underground with the old books."

"And you think they will be safe there?"

"They'll be safer there than anywhere else. *You* will be safer there than anywhere else. They will come for you here."

"They will come for us wherever we are."

The old man didn't say any more, didn't move.

After a moment of silence, Ashen turned and climbed down the steps to the foot of the keep.

21 – THE ENDLESS DARK

Ariane stopped by the entrance to the caves beneath Islagray. "Will we need the spiders in our hair again?"

A large, iron cage hung from a hook beside the door. Inside was a dark, rustling mass of leaves and cobwebs and the purple legs of the archive's spiders. The creatures knew the endless, twisting tunnels intimately. If Ariane or Hellen took one with them it would play out a gossamer thread they could follow back to the entrance if they got lost. A thread that wasn't really there: a shimmering line of magical light.

Hellen poked a finger through the bars to stroke one of the creatures. It stamped a striped leg as if waving at her.

"No," she said. "Where we're going is beyond even their knowledge. They'd be as lost as we'll be."

"Well, that sounds promising," said Ariane. "And where exactly are we going? As so often you have completely failed to tell me what you're planning."

Hellen stood for a moment, trying to remember the route they had to find. It had been many, many years since she'd taken this road. The deep hum of the Song, reverberating through the rock from the Songroom, had a clear edge of alarm to it now. Occasional pauses too, as if the song of the land was sputtering out. She tried to ignore it and set off at a brisk walk, taking the leftmost of the five tunnels that descended beneath the Witches' Isle.

"That's because I don't fully know what I'm planning myself," Hellen called over her shoulder. "Despite what you may think I don't have all the answers either."

Ariane muttered something to herself about *daft old women* and hurried to catch up. "But you know a far sight more than you're telling me, Hellen Meggenwar, eldest and supposedly wisest of Islagray. How will burrowing down here help Cait? You heard what her mother said, we have to help her."

"I agree, we do."

"Then tell me what's going on. Assuming Ashen manages to get word through to Angere, and assuming by some miracle Cait gets the message *and* is able to do as you instruct, how are we going to get there to rescue her? And what's in the archive that will help?"

"There's nothing in the archive that will help," said Hellen. "We're going much farther. Didn't I once tell you the caves go on forever? Well, maybe they do and maybe they don't. But they go a long way, that's for sure. And if you know the path to take, they lead to other tunnels, other secret ways."

"Secret ways going where?"

"To the Island in the An."

"What?"

"Don't pretend to be deaf."

"But that's just an old story," said Ariane.

"And you're just an old woman, but here you are. Just because a story's old doesn't mean it isn't true. There's an island in the middle of the An, invisible from either shore, and that's where we have to go."

"How do you know?"

"I read about it. There was someone who glimpsed it from the bridge."

Ariane tramped along in silence beside Hellen, her brow furrowed. "But how do you know it's possible to get there? Have you been? Is this another adventure you neglected to tell me about?"

"No," said Hellen, pausing to study the carving of an oak leaf above one of the doorways. "No, I've never been there. I tried once, many years ago, but I failed."

"Wonderful," said Ariane. "Well that puts my mind completely at rest."

Hellen smiled at her old friend. Ariane was nervous, worried, and this bickering was how she coped. How they both coped, truth be told. Could Hellen find the way to the ancient tunnels beneath the river? Perhaps. That was the problem with old books. She'd once thought she could rely on them. Their words didn't change as stories passed by word of mouth changed. That was the whole point of writing: an account written a thousand years ago could be read unchanged today. It was miraculous, magical in its own way. But it wasn't so simple. The words on the page or the parchment stayed the same but the people reading them didn't. Language altered. Thoughts set down long ago barely made sense any more. Words were lost. Or, worse, hung around but changed their meaning. Sometimes subtly, sometimes becoming the opposite of what they'd once meant. How could you be sure what the ancient writings truly said now?

Not for the first time she wished she'd coaxed the archaeon into more of the books. The bookwyrm was ancient and wise, spoke all languages and all versions of those languages. It would have been able to tell her in a moment the true meaning of the words she'd unearthed in the old scroll. A scroll written, unless Hellen was completely mistaken, on the hide of an actual dragon. But somehow she'd never got round to it.

What had she been *doing* all the years and decades? She'd been busy, she knew that, but she'd left so much undone. Ariane was right, she was an old fool. Part of the problem was that she'd never thought reaching the mythical island was important. Intriguing, certainly, but not day-to-day, making things better for people important. But that was another thing Cait had changed by throwing herself into Angere. Everything was different now.

"Hellen?"

"Hmm?"

"You've done that thing where you wander off into your own thoughts. Tell me what you know, woman. I might be able to help. I'm not completely useless."

"No. Sorry. Yes. You're right. In truth I don't know much." She stopped at another doorway. This one had a lizard carved into the rock above it, long tail curled in a crescent. Not this one. An hour's walk down there and you hit a dead end. "We're looking for a locked door."

"Locked by whom?"

"I don't know."

"And do you know where this door even is?"

"I know in … broad terms."

"Fine. So do you have the key for this door?"

"No. Wouldn't help much if I did."

"Why?"

Hellen stopped. They were approaching the last of the torches. Beyond the flickering, honey light was only darkness and the slow, quiet age of the ancient tunnels. She tried to put the notion that it was patiently waiting for them out of her mind. "Because there's no keyhole on this side. Whoever locked the door did so from the other side. To keep us out."

It took them half a day of wandering and backtracking to find the locked iron door. It was rusty and ancient, coated with a patina of green, but it was solid when they pounded on it. Just as Hellen remembered, there was no keyhole, no handle, no way at all of opening it.

"What did you try last time?" said Ariane, running a hand over the metal.

"Everything I could think of, obviously. All the unfastening and unfurling spells. All the rust and decay charms. I tried knocking it flat with brute force, and I tried politely knocking. I even tried bellowing out the magical words the mancers go around shouting. Nothing had any effect."

Ariane set down her backpack and studied the door, as if she might find answers written upon it. "And what makes you think we'll have any more success this time?"

"Last time I was here because I'd read about the door and wondered what was on the other side. This time we have to get through it. The future of Andar may depend on it. The future of Cait certainly does."

"Well, if everything you tried failed, perhaps you were trying the wrong things," said Ariane.

"Why do you think I brought you down here? To put up with your prattling all this time?"

"Nice to know you've admitted your limitations for once," said Ariane. "Now, stand back and let me take a look." She struck an orange werelight and let it play slowly across the whole surface of the door, looking for any marks that might give her a clue. Her eyes were narrowed in concentration as she peered close, almost as if she were sniffing the ancient metal.

After a few minutes she stepped back. "No marks or signs. Not even a draught coming from underneath. Are you sure this is a door?"

"You can see it's a door," said Hellen. "Is your eyesight that bad?"

"I can see it looks like one. But how do you know it leads anywhere? Perhaps someone set it against the mother rock to fool people like you, make them think something lay beyond."

"Perhaps," said Hellen. "I thought about that. But you can sense the strength of the warding spells woven into the iron. Someone went to a lot of trouble to keep this door closed. Why would they do that if it was nothing more than a joke?"

Ariane nodded, deep in thought. "So this scroll you found. Do you have it with you?"

"Obviously. It's not much help. It's very old, from long before the Cleaving." Hellen pulled the ancient scroll from her own backpack. It crackled as she gently unfurled it.

Ariane's lips moved as she tried to read the old words, tracing her fingertip across the parchment. The writing was clear still, vivid letters of purple, but the words, the sense of them, were all but lost.

"This talks about someone a witch went to meet." said Ariane. "Does that say *guardian*? And here again, it talks about *An* as if it was a person, not a place. Who, Hellen? Who did they go to meet? Who lives on this island?"

"Isn't it obvious? Do I have to sit you down and recount all the old fireside stories?"

Understanding dawned on her old friend's face. "You mean Hyrn. You actually think Hyrn lives on this island. Or did all that time ago."

"I do," said Hellen. "The guardian of An. The spirit in the wood and the water. The Green Man. The one who walked these lands when there was no one else to walk beside him. Hyrn, yes. He was there when the land was cleaved in two. He was part of it, and from what I've read he took up residence on this island afterward. It was his escape, his refuge."

"But we can't rely on a myth to step from the mists and save us. If Hyrn is real, why isn't he helping us? Why is he making things so difficult for us?"

"I don't know. I think, perhaps, we don't really understand who or what he is. How he is connected to the land."

"But the sagas say he *made* An. Raised the two lands from an endless sea to form the river, flowing in its eternal circle. If that's true, why would he allow the undain to become what they have?"

"Good question," said Hellen. "Just because there is

knowledge in some of the old tales doesn't mean we have to believe all of them. From what I've read I think it was the other way round. An created *him*. He's the spirit of the land, the essence, the voice, given human form."

"Like the Song."

"Something like the Song, yes. And the Song is faltering and breaking. You've heard it. It occurred to me that Hyrn, too, may be fading. He's not the all-powerful being some of the stories describe, dreaming the sky into being and all that nonsense. I think maybe he's dying because the land is dying. And that's why he's not helping us."

Ariane didn't speak for long moments. It was a lot to grasp, Hellen knew. It had taken her years of reading and thinking to get that far.

"Then we have to help him," said Ariane finally. "Help him to help ourselves."

"Yes," said Hellen, quietly, smiling at her old friend. "We do. And that means opening this door."

They stayed there for two or three days, although in truth it was hard to be sure of the passing of time when there was no moon or sun or stars. They'd brought supplies with them: food and blankets and candles, as if setting off for a long trek across country. It was just as well they had. They camped by the door for one sleep, and then another, while they tried and failed to open the entrance.

Some time in the middle of the third night – if it was night – Hellen was awoken by Ariane's gasp.

"Sorry," said Ariane as she regained herself. "A dream. A vivid dream."

"Ah. You must tell me all about it. In the morning."

"No, Hellen, I think I have tell you now."

An urgency in Ariane's voice made it clear Hellen had to listen. She pushed herself up, her hips stiff and sore from lying on the hard stone. Ariane struck a werelight, bathing the two of them in its pallid, shifting glow.

"Go on then if you must," said Hellen.

"I saw him," said Ariane. "Hyrn. He had antlers on his head, and he prowled through the dapple of the woods, disappearing into the shadows again and again. I tried to reach him, follow him, but he sped away each time I got close."

"Probably very sensible of him."

"Hush. For some reason I had to reach him. And then I saw the trail of blood on the ground. He was wounded and I caught him, put my hand on his arm. He turned to face me, but he was old and weak and exhausted. His tongue lolled purple from his mouth. He fell at my feet and lay there panting like a wounded animal. He looked up at me, wary, as if afraid I was going to kill him."

"Which tells us nothing, except that your tired old mind is capable of weaving everything we've talked about into dream nonsense."

"No. I think I've understood something."

"And what would that be?"

"That we've been doing it all wrong," said Ariane. "Trying to blast the door down and force it to open. He needed my help. He's injured. It's what you said about him being the land given body. Don't you understand?"

"I understand you're making no sense."

"I think what you said was right for once," said Ariane. "And maybe it works the other way round, too. Hyrn is the land and the land is Hyrn. In which case, perhaps this mysterious doorway is a part of him. A way into his being, his heart. Perhaps it's his … connection to Andar. All you've been doing is inflicting more damage, pursuing him, making him defend himself. He needs healing, Hellen, not attacking."

Enthusiasm burned bright in Ariane's voice. But that was often how it was when you woke from dreams. It didn't mean the visions were true once the lights were back on. But Hellen also thought about a recent dream of her own, back in her room on Islagray. The day Fer turned up and everything started. Booming, metallic voices had chased her, making her run in terror. There'd been truth in that dream, in a way.

"Go on," she said. "Tell me what you have in mind."

"We need to approach this place as we would an injured person. With care and love. We need to try and bring healing."

"How?" said Hellen. "How would you do that?"

"I don't know. But I think it's what we have to try."

Ten minutes later, Hellen watched as Ariane sat beside the door, hands laid flat upon it. She'd seen her old friend do something similar often enough at the infirmary. Pour her own spirit into the sick and injured to bring them back to life.

"There is pain there," Ariane whispered. "Pain and confusion. And huge guilt, too. I can feel it. Beyond the door but also within it."

Hellen nodded but didn't interrupt. Perhaps the pain Ariane was tapping into was the same thing Hellen had heard in the Song. The whole land crying out in its distress. She lit a werelight of her own so Ariane could focus on the door and settled down to watch.

Ariane's eyes were closed as she expended a great magical effort. She scowled and winced with the pangs of it again and again as she sought for what was broken. Here was a skill Hellen had never really acquired. She could blunder around and fix a broken bone, maybe, but anything beyond that escaped her. Ariane, on the other hand, was an artist.

They sat together for an hour, Ariane working, Hellen keeping vigil, wishing she could be of more use. At some point she must have drifted to sleep because a shriek from Ariane awoke her, sending her heart pounding in alarm.

It was utterly dark. The werelight had faded when Hellen had fallen asleep. She kindled it again to reveal the scene in front of her. Ariane lay sprawled on the floor. Her eyes were closed, but she groaned and writhed as if wracked by cruel pains.

And in front of her the iron door stood open, the endless dark beyond waiting for them.

22 – HYRN

Hellen half-supported Ariane as they stood at the top of a flight of stone steps leading into an unknown darkness.

"How far down do they go?" asked Ariane in a whisper. The effort she'd expended on opening the door had drained her badly. She walked with a limp when previously there'd been none. She'd said nothing, but Hellen knew what the magic had cost her friend.

"Let's see." Hellen sparked a second werelight and sent it bobbing down the stairs. As it descended, lighting up a patch of grey stone steps, grey stone walls, it dimmed. She made it burn brighter for a time, hoping to see the bottom, but all the light revealed were more and more steps. "A long way. We should sleep here and continue tomorrow."

"No," said Ariane. "We can't afford the time. Who knows where the girl is now? We're no use to anyone if we reach the bridgehead a day late."

"And if we fall and break our necks? You need to rest. We'll wait an hour and then descend."

"Is that an order, old woman?"

"It is."

Ariane nodded and sank to the ground. "Very well. Just

this once I'll do as you say. So long as you don't tell anyone."

An hour later, Ariane insisted on going first in case she slipped. *No point in us both falling is there?* The stairs were cracked and loose in places, forever threatening to tip them forward into the deep. There were no handholds, only the circle of darkness beneath, forever receding. The scuffing of their feet echoed off the narrow stone walls. Hellen had the strange sensation they were burrowing into Hyrn's mind as well as the earth and rock of Andar.

They descended for a long time, hours it seemed. Hellen counted the stairs, but she got as far as five hundred and gave up. Besides, she needed to think. She had no idea what they were about to face. She needed to watch Ariane, too. Her friend was stubborn and proud and wouldn't call a halt even if she needed it. With each step, Hellen worried Ariane might collapse, slip and fall to tumble down the endless stairs. And what if they didn't lead anywhere? What if Hyrn – fading, broken, Hyrn – had slipped into madness and the stairs went on forever?

But an age later they stepped forward and found there were no more steps. A wide, stone level stretched into the darkness. Hellen flared her light, making it burn as brightly as she could, but she could see no walls, no roof, no detail at all except for the grey stone floor and the sheer wall through which the steps emerged.

Shadows gathered on Ariane's face by the yellow glow of the light. "Which way do you think?" she spoke in a half-whisper. The silence around them seemed to swallow her words as soon as she uttered them.

"West toward the An," Hellen replied. "These caverns must pass right beneath the waters."

"But which way is this island? Upstream or down?"

"The account I read said it was south of the bridge, so it must be somewhere north of here." She should have visited the Blind Mapmaker herself, found out for certain. Another thing she'd failed to do.

"Can you tell which way is west?"

Hellen nodded into the darkness. "Somewhere that way there must be stairs back up."

"Well," said Ariane. "The sooner we start the sooner we'll find them."

"You need to rest."

"True. But I'm not going to. Now stop fussing and walk."

Hellen soon stopped trying to illuminate the ceiling or the walls. They seemed to be crossing a vast, limitless space, crawling across it like ants. Strange to think of this void down here all this time beneath the trees and grass and soil. Or perhaps it hadn't always been here. Perhaps it was part of the sickness, Andar rotting away into nothingness. Or were they below the An itself by now? The thought of that enormous body of water above their heads was unsettling.

She wondered if anything lived down here. There were bats in the caves beneath Islagray, although she'd never worked out how they flew in and out. Pale, eyeless fish in some of the pools, too. She couldn't feel anything nearby with her mind, apart from Ariane beside her. But perhaps she wouldn't. If, somehow, they were walking through the mind of Hyrn, who knew what nightmares might be lurking in the darkness? She tried not to think about it.

Dimly, as she grew more used to it, she did begin to perceive the positions of the moon and sun in the unseen sky far above them. It was a comfort, although in her mind's eye the sun blazed with a cold grey light rather than its usual red or gold. But she'd spent her whole life aware of their presence, knowing where they were in the sky even when they couldn't be seen. They anchored her to the real world. Perhaps this was only a cave after all. A void in the ground, nothing more.

The passage of the sun acrross the sky allowed her to track the time. Three days they spent marching in silence, heading west. Three nights they slept, eating the bread and fruit they'd brought, then lying wearily on blankets and the unyielding rock. At least it was warm in the cavern: a constant, low warmth, indifferent to summer or winter in the world above.

She almost walked flat into the far wall when they finally reached it. It rose vertically, another sheer cliff of rock, with no sign of any way up or through.

Ariane put a hand to it, as if she could discern secrets hidden within. "We could split up. Take opposite directions to find the stairs."

If they even exist, Hellen added in her mind. The thought had troubled her more and more as they'd crossed. And if there was no way out, could they find their way back across the void to the stairs they'd come down? Or were they doomed to spend the rest of their days fumbling around in the darkness, lost to the world?

"No," she said. "Let's stay together. I'm not sure I trust this place. I don't think these walls are quite so solid as they pretend. If we get separated we might never find each other again."

"Then which way?"

"I think we need to go farther north. If we find nothing we can always double back."

Ariane took a shard of stone from the floor and scratched something into the rock face. Their names, *Ariane* and *Hellen*. "Then at least we'll know when we're back where we started," said Ariane.

They set off, keeping the rock face to their left. Hellen glanced back at their carved names. She had the unsettling sensation of the darkness rushing in to read the words. Devour them. *Erase* them. She tried to ignore it. The place played tricks on the mind.

They tramped along for the whole of another day, following the wall. They came across no doorways or staircases.

As they sat together to eat Ariane said, "So. Do we turn back and try in the other direction tomorrow?"

"We might find the steps at any moment," said Hellen.

"Or we might not. If we were above ground we would have reached Forness by now."

"I know. But let's carry on a little longer. Otherwise we'll spend the last of our days walking backward and forward along this wall. This cliff seems to run in a straight line, but for all we know it's curling around to confuse us."

"Very well, if you insist," said Ariane. She lay down to sleep, exhausted by the day's walk. Hellen sat watching over her for a time, worrying she'd made some wrong turn, trying to see a way out of the endless darkness. She could think of nothing. In the end she slept beside her old friend, nestling next to her for warmth.

They found the doorway half way through the next day. They'd nearly decided to turn back when a low archway came into sight in the rock face. When they reached it they saw it framed a flight of stone steps leading upward.

"You're sure these aren't the same steps?" said Ariane. "You're sure we aren't going round in circles down here?"

"Of course we aren't," Hellen replied, although in truth she wasn't quite as convinced as she sounded. She wished she'd scratched something into the rock when they'd first arrived. "Somewhere up there is the island in the An. Are you ready for the climb?"

"I'm ready," said Ariane. "It's your ancient legs I'm worried about." Something of her friend's humour had returned as she recovered from her ordeal at the door. It was good to hear.

The climb up to the world took the best part of a day, and several times they had to stop and sit on the steps while their laboured breathing slowed.

"Perhaps they go on forever," said Ariane at one of their stops. "Some magic we're not aware of keeping us from the island."

"Perhaps," said Hellen. "Or perhaps you're making excuses for being so slow. Let me know when you're ready and we'll resume."

"When I'm ready?" said Ariane. "I'm waiting for you."

Another three hours of relentless climbing later, of hauling themselves up step by step, Ariane stopped again. She stood still as if listening for something. Hellen paused, too. She was glad of the rest; her knees and thighs burned.

"The air is changing," said Ariane. "Can you smell it?"

Hellen drew in a deep breath. Ariane was right. Distantly she caught the tang of water and fresh air and growing things. "We must be getting near."

"Put out that little light you're maintaining, and let's see if the exit is visible."

They stood in the darkness for several minutes while their eyes adjusted. Finally Ariane said, "I think there's something. A smudge of grey."

"You're imagining it," said Hellen. "I see nothing."

"That's because you've ruined your eyes reading all those books. It's there, believe me."

"I think we've climbed through most of the night," said Hellen. "The sun will be rising soon."

"Then let's rise to meet it," said Ariane, setting off again.

It soon became clear she was right. A circle of shadow ahead lightened to grey, to purple, and finally to blue. The clean air blowing on Hellen's face was a joy, lifting her spirits. For a moment she forgot about the screaming pains in her knees.

Half an hour later, they stumbled over the last step and fell onto a little clearing of grass. Rustling trees, blown by a steady wind, whispered around them. The sun, gloriously warm, sparkled through swaying branches. Neither of them spoke for several minutes, while breath and strength returned.

"Well," said Ariane. "If Hyrn really is here, he'd better be prepared to sail us back to Andar. I'm not making that journey again."

Hellen pushed herself to her feet. Some days she felt all

of her one hundred and fifty years. She offered Ariane a hand and hauled her upright.

They wove their way between the ash-grey boughs of tall trees and soon found the island's edge and the waters of the An. They were looking north. Filaments of mist drifted across the water, hiding everything. Neither bank was visible. They weren't in Andar any more, nor were they in Angere. This was a place between and apart.

Hellen crouched and scooped up a handful of water to drink. It had never tasted so good.

They circled the island. The interior was a mass of trees, leaves fading to browns and yellows, but a lip of green grass ran around the edge of the island, as if it were a well-travelled path. At one point they found a sagging wooden jetty jutting into the water, a small rowing boat moored to it, its timbers green with decay. It looked like it hadn't been used for a long time.

"He was here at some point, then," said Hellen.

"Someone was, at least," Ariane replied. "Look, is that a path into the woods?"

"It's badly overgrown. Let's see where it takes us."

The path snaked between the trees, climbing as it wound around the sides of a low rise in the ground. Birds whistled from the treetops as Hellen and Ariane worked their way through the undergrowth. It was strange to think that birds had been coming here all this time, flying from Andar. Or did they stay there, close to Hyrn? The island was, perhaps, the centre of everything. The heart of the land. The navel.

They had to push through bushes repeatedly as the path twisted around the hill. Eventually it opened onto a flat, wide top. In the centre stood a small, round building with open archways, the trees crowning the hill hiding it from view. Within, beneath a curved canopy, stood a plain, oblong stone block. Upon it lay the body of an old man. Ivy trailed across the little building, climbing the sides of the altar as if it intended to cover the figure, too.

Deep lines riddled the man's face. His skin was so grey that Hellen might have mistaken him for a statue if not for his straggly hair flowing to the floor. It must have been black or brown once, but now it was pale grey and white, all colour leeched from it. Two wounds on his forehead marked the place where the horned man's antlers might once have been attached.

It could only be Hyrn.

"Tell me," said Hellen. "Back at the door. What did you feel? What did you do?"

"I felt *him*," said Ariane. "Hyrn. Ancient and terrible, but wounded and fading. He'd sealed himself away to protect himself, like an injured deer hiding in the woods."

"But he opened up to your touch?"

"Reluctantly. I had the feeling he was wary of me coming any closer."

"But he is alive?"

Ariane placed a hand on the stone-grey skin of his forehead. "Barely. The life inside him ebbs."

"As it must have for a long time."

"And you really think he can help us, Hellen?"

"If he can't, no one can. The river is his domain. It is because of him the An may not be crossed. I think he pours what remains of his strength into it, keeping Angere and Andar apart. And what he keeps apart he may, perhaps, allow together. For a time."

"There is madness within him, too," said Ariane, frowning as she touched his mind with hers. "It's as if there are two voices in his mind rather than one. Two voices that argue and shout."

"What he did tore him in two, just as it tore the land in two," said Hellen. "Perhaps his mind is broken as well. We must be wary of him. But if we can get through to him he might be persuaded to help. You said there was guilt in him?"

"Guilt. Regret. Loss. Yes, all that."

"He blames himself for what was done to the land five hundred years ago. The undain devoured half his domain, like a body eaten by a canker. He could only watch in despair as more and more of his children died. Deliberately sought out death. The land cloven is sick. It is like a lover forever separated from the one they love. It pines and fades, joyless and infertile, torn in two. So it is with him."

"He has gone very deep," said Ariane, frowning. "The cold creeps across his mind just as the ice freezes the An. I fear he may be beyond my powers of healing, Hellen. The effort of trying to bring him back would be … terrible."

"Will you try?" asked Hellen. They both knew what she meant, without having to spell it out. A look passed between them.

"So now you're asking me, not telling me?" said Ariane.

"Neither, old friend. What you do must be your choice."

Ariane knelt beside the prone figure of Hyrn and laid her hands upon him.

"I've lived a long and happy life," she said at last, looking up at Hellen. "My only hope now is that others, the young and those yet to be born, have the chance to do the same. I will do what I can for him."

Hellen nodded but couldn't reply.

"But there's a condition," said Ariane.

"Anything."

"Whatever happens, promise me you'll stop those abominations. Stop them eating the whole world. Promise me, that Hellen."

"I will try," said Hellen. She stooped to kiss the grey hairs on her old friend's head. "I will. I promise you that."

23 – A HUNDRED MILLION VOICES

Angere

Cait dreamed again. She stood beside the cool waters of the mountain lake, the ring of peaks around her. Bethany stood half-emerged in the centre of the pool, the water streaming off her hair and hands. The witch-girl drifted closer, eyes closed, skin blue.

Cait dreamed, but she was also aware she was dreaming. This place was inside her mind, so Bethany had said. But was that right? Perhaps it was a real place, an island in the aether that she travelled to. Whichever, she knew that outside, elsewhere, her shivering body lay next to Danny's in the endless dark of the dungeons of the White City, and that there was no hope.

She turned to Danny's spirit, standing beside her, holding her hand. Here he looked like his old self. Not the ragged, terrified boy she lay beside, but the amused, grinning lad from back home.

"So," he said, "this is what the inside of your mind looks like?"

"Yes. I think so."

"And the witchy water-girl floating toward us?"

"Bethany."

"Bethany, yes. She's your long-dead relative whose soul inhabits yours?"

It sounded a bit weird when he put it like that. "I met her at Empire Towers. You remember the rider who grabbed me? She saved me. She and the others. She talks to me sometimes. Explains things."

"Pretty cool. You didn't feel the need to mention it at the time?"

"Not really the sort of thing you can easily drop into the conversation."

"I guess. But if this is a dream of yours, how come I'm here? Are you dreaming about me or am I dreaming about you?"

"I don't know. I don't know how any of this stuff works. I guess your spirit's here inside my mind even though I'm asleep. If I *am* asleep." In the long hours of darkness they'd huddled together it was hard to know where wakefulness and sleep met.

Bethany stopped at the lip of the lake, the water up to her waist. "This is Danny?" She opened her eyes and studied him, unblinking, eyes wide. As ever she clutched her tattered rag doll to her chest. "The one who you thought was dead?"

"Yes," said Cait. "They brought him here because they thought he'd know our plans, know where we were going. In the end he wasn't able to tell them much so they threw him into the dungeons." Whether they planned to use him to lure her there, or whether they'd just forgotten about him, she had no idea. Greygyle had said he was dead. Maybe he'd believed that, or maybe he'd just said it to hurt her. She'd probably never know. She didn't care. The joy at finding Danny alive was a glowing, wonderful light inside her. Danny wasn't dead because of what she'd done. Danny wasn't dead at all. And grim as their situation was, at least they'd had this brief time together.

She'd thought he'd hate her, blame her for everything.

Amazingly, he'd been overjoyed to see her. Being trapped together in the infinite darkness of a city of undead nightmares was hardly a dream date, but more than she could have hoped for.

"Hello, Danny," said Bethany.

"Um, hi," he replied. "Nice … lake you've got here."

Bethany giggled. "He's a good looking boy. I can see why you have all these fantasies about him."

It was clearly going to be hard to keep secrets from anyone when they were living inside her mind. "You're not seeing him as he really is right now," said Cait, keen to change the subject.

"Actually, I think I am," said Bethany. "He's pretty."

"I, er, I am actually here listening to this," said Danny.

Was it possible to be jealous of a long-dead forebear hitting on your boyfriend? Maybe it was, but it didn't make much sense. And what difference did it make now? They were trapped and awaiting the end. There could be no escape. They'd tried more than once to find a way out but had found only more echoing caverns, a maze of them, seemingly endless. Once they'd found their way back to the iron gates, but they were sealed with more than just locks and chains, and refused to open.

"I wondered whether our spirits could escape even if our bodies can't," said Cait. "If we could become like you, Bethany."

"You mean dead?"

"I was hoping not *actually* dead. More sort of … free to float away." She was so weak, so useless. It was the only way out she could see.

For a moment, Bethany stopped being the giggling girl and became the sombre woman. The lost soul. "Life is far too precious to throw away. Believe me, I should know."

"But there's no other hope," said Cait. "We can't stop the undain. At least if I was dead they couldn't carry out their stupid ritual."

"There is always hope," said Bethany. "We simply need

some help."

"Help from where?" said Danny. "There is no one. The rest of them are stuck on the far side of the river or through the portal. We're on our own here. By the sound of it the Smouldering Fire aren't up to much."

"You're wrong," said Bethany. "There are many here who will assist us. A very great many."

"Who?" said Cait.

"Them."

Bethany pointed upward. All around, as if responding to a call, figures were scrambling and sliding down the mountain slopes. Hundreds of them. Thousands. Women, men, children. More and more each moment, thronging over the tops to scramble down the slopes to the mountain pool.

"Who are they?" asked Cait, staring in amazement and alarm. But even as she voiced the question, she knew the answer. Greygyle had called it the *City of Ghosts*. The huge sense of anger and dread she'd felt ever since arriving: she'd thought it was the undain. But no. It was the dead. It was the bones of the city calling into the aether. So much confusion and rage. They were like Bethany's ragged troop of urchins back in Manchester, except there were *millions* of them.

"They will help us?" asked Cait. "They're on our side?"

"I called them," said Bethany. "Lost and broken in the darkness, I called them. Some had no understanding of who or where they were. Many burned with rage. Yes, they will help us. Individually they are weak but together they're strong. Very strong indeed."

A crowd of indistinct, shifting ghosts gathered around the lake, more and more each moment. They overlapped each other, moved through one another. Cait caught glimpses of a face here, the flash of an arm there. She could feel their combined fury mounting like a deep thrumming in the air, like some roaring machine approaching.

"So what do we do?" said Cait.

"I will take their fury and give it to you," said Bethany.

"You can do that?"

"Yes. But it will be hard on you, Cait. The spirits clamour for release and it will take all your self-control to hold them back. You have to wait for the right moment. Can you do that?"

Could she? She had to try. "I guess."

"They can be very destructive. You saw a glimpse of what they can do back in Manchester. This many would be very different. They could bring the ceiling of your dungeon crashing down on top of you. And if you set them free at the wrong moment then try to contain them, the damage to you would be terrible. The pain alone would kill you."

"I understand. Anything's better than being down here. When do we start?"

Bethany smiled, like it was some wonderful game she'd devised. "Now. Wake up and we can begin."

The damp ground was cold on her cheek as Cait woke. As ever, utter darkness engulfed her, so complete that opening her eyes made no difference. She lay curled in a ball. Danny stirred, his arm around her. They always slept like that, huddled together for whatever warmth they could give each other.

"Come on," she said. "Time to try what Bethany said."

"Huh?" His breath was warm on the back of her neck. He sounded confused. For a moment she thought he had no idea what she was talking about. She had dreamed the whole thing with Bethany; it was nothing but a stupid fantasy she'd made up to make their situation more bearable.

Then he said: "Bethany, right. The storm cloud. Yeah."

He had been in her mind. It was real. He was just waking up, that was all. It always took a minute or two for him to start making sense.

"Storm cloud?" she said.

"Over those mountains. Purple and orange, like you see before the lightning strikes and the torrential downpour comes."

"That was how you saw it?"

She felt his shrug. "Sure. How else?"

"I saw a great crowd of people. So many of them. I don't know, *millions* of them. But I get what you mean. A storm cloud is kind of how they felt."

"And you can do this? Do what Bethany said, channel all that fury?"

"Don't know. Maybe."

They stood. The ball of rage seethed within her, threatening to ignite, spill out at any moment. Bethany was there too, cradling it, holding it. Offering it. Cait struck a light, something she did from time to time when the darkness got to her, or she heard scuffling sounds nearby. Usually all she managed to work was a hesitant flame that brought more shadow than illumination. This time it was different. A great, sun-like ball of light flared into life above her head with a sharp *crack*. It blinded her. Alarmed, she struggled to make the light dimmer, stem the outpouring of anger. She had to learn to control the power being given her.

She opened her eyes again. The light was bright but bearable. Danny looked like a startled animal caught in a car's headlights, hair plastered to his head, face filthy. He'd looked better, but she didn't like to *think* about her own appearance. The hall stretched into the distance, pillars receding seemingly forever. The bones of the walls, with no one to scrub and clean them, were yellow and sepia, stained and rotting. This swas what the White City was built upon. This was the decay at its heart. Somehow, though, she almost preferred the dungeons to the shining glory of the buildings on the surface. They were more honest.

"Let's get that gate open," she said. "Get out of here before they come for us."

"Won't they know what we're doing?" asked Danny. "Won't they be able to tell?"

"I think it's going to be pretty obvious to everyone soon. I can't hold the storm back much longer." She felt like she was wading through water. Electricity seemed to crackle in the air around her. At the gates she deliberately took it slowly, careful not to unleash all the power at once. The gates creaked backward but stayed shut. Some warding charm worked into the ironwork resisted her. She pushed at it, struggling to contain the flood of rage. The gates buckled and squealed but refused to yield. Unable to stop herself, suddenly impatient, Cait hurled a bolt of fury. The gates exploded outward, crashing against the stairwell in a tangled, twisted mass of metal like the mangled ribs of an animal.

Together, Cait and Danny raced toward the light, desperate to be away from the dungeon. How long had she been trapped down there? She had no idea. Days, weeks. Maybe it was all too late and Andar had already fallen. The air grew warmer as they clattered up the stairs. Perhaps it would have been better to escape at night, when the darkness could hide them, but right then she didn't care. She wanted to feel the warmth of the sun on her face. Her limbs felt as cold as lead, as if the dripping water had seeped inside her bones and turned them to ice.

On the surface, she looked around, confused and half-blinded by the light. The ground shook with the fury of the ghosts. The high walls of the White City seemed to shiver and ripple as if the bones were desperate to twist themselves free, break the shackles of their carved shapes. The city sang its pain.

From one of the high, delicate towers a cracked bell rang, tolling an alarm. Thundering footsteps came running, hundreds of them. Before Cait and Danny could flee, undain soldiers and dragonrider giants flooded into the square. Seeing the two of them, they charged forward at crazy speed, rapidly forming an impenetrable ring.

And Cait, closing her eyes, set the terrible rage boiling inside her free.

The fury of what she unleashed threw her and Danny to the ground. A wall of seething red blasted outward. The whole world shook, rattling her skull. The raging red engulfed the undain, hurling them backward, scattering them like leaves in a gale. She glimpsed the occasional form of an individual ghost amid the fury, swooping with glee, but mostly there was only a single cloud, removing everything in its path.

Exultation roared through Cait. She laughed as the power flowed through her. It was glorious. She was unstoppable. All this magic and it hadn't cost her anything. There was no pain, no price to pay. She could destroy them all. Kill the undain. The white walls of the palace, struck by the force of the explosion, buckled and fell, crushing the undain beneath them. Cait laughed at that, too.

"Cait, come on. We have to get away." It was Danny, somewhere beside her, his voice distant.

He looked so small, so frightened. Couldn't he see what she was doing? Why should she run? Why shouldn't she bring the whole city down? She understood now why the undain did what they did. To wield such force. It was wonderful, intoxicating. She never wanted to stop. And she wasn't like *them* was she? She hadn't stolen any of this power. It had been given to her. Given freely. It was hers to use as she saw fit. That made it OK.

Across the square, a high tower buckled, crumpled and crashed to the ground. The great bell it had housed bounced and rolled with deafening clangs, crushing more of the undain.

Danny put a hand on her arm. "Cait. Stop. You're getting scary now. What you're doing is amazing, but you're going to get us killed if you carry on."

The look on Danny's face made her pause. She saw something in his eyes. Fear. He was afraid of her. Afraid of what she'd do. A part of her wanted to laugh at him, cast him aside. With an effort she pushed away the impulse. She wouldn't be that person. She didn't ever want Danny to be afraid of her. And she was wrong. The magic wasn't hers to do as she wished with. It had only been lent. She and Bethany has set the ghosts free, released them, but the dead of the city could do what they wanted. Howl and rage at the undain or fade into the aether. It was up to them, not her.

Cait sagged and seemed to shrink. Once again she was on Danny's level.

"Sorry," she whispered. "Went a bit crazy there. Kind of hard to stop when you start. It's a bit, you know, *just one more go!*"

"Can we please get out of here?" asked Danny. Beneath his grinning exterior, she could see how everything had taken its toll on him. His features were pinched and he shook as he stood there, though the sun on their faces was warm. Perhaps, she thought, he would never be that carefree boy again, worrying about exams and homework. She was sorrier about that than almost anything.

"Where is there to go?" she said.

"The portal back home. The refinery. It's our only hope. Maybe we can sneak through in the chaos."

The ground lurched as they raced for the archway. There were still many undain, but all were under attack, swatting uselessly at the angry spirits. Cait watched as one of the giant dragonriders scythed her great sword in a circle. It achieved nothing. The ghosts swirled, faster and faster, and then shot at the rider, directly through her head. The undain collapsed to the ground with a shriek, just as the rider had back at the tower blocks in Manchester.

Cait and Danny dodged around mounds of white rubble where the walls and towers had fallen. They raced across a wide white square toward the portal that would return them home. She tasted dusty grit in her mouth and tried not to think about what it might be. Flocks of the black birds boiled overhead, calling raucously.

Distantly she was aware of more undain coming. Many, many more: summoned to repel an attack on the White City. In her mind she caught a glimpse of Menhroth too, the king's fury amid the chaos. The touch of his thoughts sent a shiver through Cait. But she sensed confusion there as well. Menhroth didn't fully understand what was happening. An attack from Andar? From Cait's own world? For a moment he didn't know. He sought answers but saw only the raging ghosts. They were no threat to him; he swatted them away as if they were flies. But his private guard had fallen and he was unsure how many other undain had been destroyed. It wouldn't take long for him to find out the truth, but for a few minutes there was confusion. It might be their chance to escape.

The archway that housed this end of the portal still stood, unmoved by the tumbling buildings. A great beast's skull, a dragon maybe, had been set on the top. They had only to step beneath it, and they'd be back home.

But the gateway repelled them when they tried to push through. Danny glanced nervously at her. The sounds of shrieking and the *crumps* of collapsing walls were dying away. The ghosts, the fury expended, were fading. They didn't have much time.

Cait closed her eyes and pushed with all her strength against the magical walls of the archway. This time the effort of it did cost her, a spiky pain in her stomach that sent electric tingles down her arms. She didn't relent. She thought about Charis, the guardian of the portals. What incomprehensible, ancient magic had he woven here to prevent anyone going through without his knowledge?

She tried again, hurling herself against the barrier, screaming out loud with the agonizing price she paid. But it did no good. The portal resisted and remained closed. Perhaps if Bethany could summon the ghosts again, combine them, they could batter down the barrier, blast a way through the aether. It was the only thing she could think of.

"Cait. Someone's coming."

She turned. A figure was hurrying across the square. There were still ghosts swirling around, picking off the remaining undain, but the newcomer strode through them, immune to their attacks.

"Is it Charis?" asked Danny.

The square was so vast that she couldn't tell. She held the seeing stone to her eye and immediately saw the familiar pattern of colours. They'd sent *him* to recapture her?

"No. Not Charis. It's Nox."

She turned to the portal. They had to punch through before Nox stopped her or gloated or whatever the hell it was he intended to do. Cait threw everything she had at it. The oblong of the portal flickered briefly then snapped back to grey, her efforts resisted. She stepped back, clutching her stomach.

Nox was only a few yards away. "You took your time. I've been waiting days for you to do something."

She turned, ready to strike him dead if she could. He wore the flowing cloak of an undain lord, not his black leather jacket.

"What?" she said.

"Still," he continued, "it was impressive when it came. I was worried you didn't have it in you."

What was he saying? "You were waiting for me to do this?"

"Obviously."

"You're saying you're not with *them*?"

"Cait, do we have to keep having this conversation? It's extremely boring. This was all a feint to get close to the Grimoire. Why do you think the ghosts didn't attack me?"

"Because you have some powerful defence against them."

"Because they know I'm on your side. Surely if they can work it out you can?"

"But you handed me over to them."

"There's no time for this, Cait. The army has been recalled from its march north up the An. The first legions will be here within minutes. We have to get away now."

"Just explain yourself," said Cait. "I need to understand. I need to know what's going on."

The irritation on his face was clear as he replied. "When I left you to scout around I was recognized. I had to improvise. Handing you over in return for winning back some of their trust was the only sensible option."

"Plus you hedged your bets," said Danny. "If Cait *didn't* manage to do all this you'd be back in with the undain."

Nox nodded his head in assent. "That too. The best way to succeed is to make sure you win either way."

"Why should I believe you?" she said

"You know, I'm getting a sense of déjà vu here," he said. "You have real trust issues, you know that? Perhaps this will help." He pulled something from inside his flowing cloak. She recognized the red leather of the cover immediately. "I keep doing this for you, don't I? Taking the Grimoire from under the noses of the undain. The other half at the refinery and now this. What would you do without me, Cait?"

"You took the book?" said Danny.

"That's what I just said. They'll never really trust me again, and I want my revenge. No ascension for me now. I got close enough to it by *pretending* to betray you. Then when the walls began to fall and the ghosts took out the book's dragonrider guards, I picked it up and ran."

"Just like that?"

"There were certain magical wards as well. As it happens I learned long ago how to circumvent them. Just in case I ever needed to."

"But how did you know we'd be here?"

"It seemed the obvious place."

Either that or he intended to escape with the book alone. She let it go. They could argue later.

"So," said Nox. "We head through the portal back to Genera? That should be an amusing surprise for Ms. Sweetley."

"I can't open it," said Cait.

"Then try harder."

"I did! It won't open. Charis must have sealed it."

Nox looked genuinely worried for a moment. He hadn't planned on this. He waved a hand at the scene around them. "So you can do all this, set off an undead *bomb* in the city centre, but you can't open a door? What kind of witch are you?"

"The kind who can't open portals sealed by creepy ancient dead guys."

He studied her for a moment. She could see his mind whirring as he tried to come up with a strategy. "Well that's brilliant," he said. "Just wonderful."

She didn't need to be a genius to work out what he'd come up with. Turn them in. Hand the book back to Menhroth and say he'd been protecting it. She glanced at Danny and saw from his eyes he'd come to the same conclusion.

She turned back to Nox. She'd kill him first.

In the distance, from parts of the city unharmed by the ghosts, more bells rang out. A crashing, discordant cacophony filled the air.

"What's that?" said Cait. "What's going on?"

"It's the undain army," said Nox. "They've been sighted. Tell me, do you happen to have any more ghost armies at your command?"

Cait shook her head but didn't reply.

24 – ITS BEAK DIPPED IN BLOOD

Nox stepped forward. Did he still have his gun? She prepared to face him, just as her mother had done. She was exhausted and bruised all over, but she would fight him if she had to. They studied each other for a moment, weighing each other up. Nox held the book. He didn't hand it over this time.

One of the black birds landed on the white ground beside them. It strutted around, head cocked as it peered at them through a shining black eye. Something about it caught Cait's attention. Trying to watch Nox, she threw a glance at the bird. It cawed in a harsh croak and flapped its wings but didn't fly off.

She saw what had distracted her. The bird wasn't dead. It wasn't one of the tattered bags of feathers and bones. And its beak was bright red. *As if dipped in blood.* Around its neck was a small silver chain. It watched her, waiting for her.

Ignoring Nox she knelt and held out her hand to the bird, just as she'd seen Phoenix do at Caer D'nar. The bird appeared to look from her to Nox and Danny, as if deciding which of them it could trust. Cait kept her hand held flat. The cracked ringing of the bells cut out suddenly, and the world went silent. No one moved, although she could sense Nox's impatience.

The bird hopped forward and jumped onto Cait's hand. Its claws were like sharp twigs on her skin.

Moving slowly, Cait felt for the chain. A simple clasp on the back held it together. She worked it loose and took the tiny message capsule. The bird, released of its burden, flapped its wings once and then, with another croak, took to the skies. It climbed over the roofs of the city, heading for the north.

"A message?" said Nox.

"Obviously," said Cait as she tried to open the slim metal capsule.

"A message you were expecting?"

No point telling him the truth. "You're not the only one with the clever plans, you know."

By twisting one end of the tube she found she could remove a little cap. She pulled out a tightly-curled strip of paper with her fingernails.

"Who's it from?" asked Danny.

"Phoenix."

"What does it say?" asked Nox.

Cait read what was written there. She stood and looked them both in the eye. "It says we have to get to the river."

"What?" said Nox. "Why?"

"Because we do."

"But that's madness," said Nox. "There's nothing there. Just the first hundred yards of a bridge that used to be a hundred *miles* long."

"And that's where we have to go," said Cait. "That's where Danny and I *are* going. Come if you like, or stay here and try and explain everything to the undain. But we're going, and we're taking the book, whether you give it to us freely or not."

Quite how they'd take the book from him if he refused she hadn't worked out yet. More calculations whirred in Nox's brain. He didn't know what she was really capable of but he'd seen the fury she'd unleashed on the city.

Finally he relented. "I should have had you killed and resurrected as a mindless slave the day I first saw you at the library. It would have saved me a lot of hassle. This plan of yours had better be *good*, Cait Weerd."

She only wished she knew what the plan was. The note from Phoenix contained only two words. *The bridgehead*, it said, scrawled in ink, hard to read as if written in a great hurry.

"Do we have to keep having this conversation, Nox?" she said. "It's extremely boring. Do you know a quick way to the river?"

Nox considered for a moment. "There's an old flight of steps that leads down there. Very narrow and steep; doesn't get used much these days."

"We'll try it," said Cait.

Running together, the three of them fled from the portal.

The staircase cut between two glittering palaces, the entrance so low and narrow she probably wouldn't have noticed it. The steps were worn smooth, making it easy to slip. She couldn't see where they led; it was dark in the narrow canyon between the two high walls, and the alley cut repeatedly around corners. But it always led steeply downward, and soon a cooler, damper wind brushed their faces.

"What are these steps?" she said. "Why aren't they guarded?"

"Guarded from who?" said Nox. "No one can attack from the river. No one can attack from anywhere. This is one of the oldest parts of the city, used hundreds of years ago to carry up boat-loads of bones for the building work."

Cait peered at the high walls, the thin strip of blue sky above her. "If we're attacked here there'll be no way out." Was it possible Nox was leading them into another trap?

"True," said Nox. "But I told you, they don't come this

way. They'll flood all the wide, grand staircases with soldiers, but they won't think to look here. Not immediately anyway. The king spends his days thinking such big thoughts he sometimes misses the little details. It's a failing."

"Told him that have you?" said Danny.

"The opportunity never arose."

For once Nox seemed to be telling them the truth. The steps ended in a low archway where a road, cobbled with bones, led across a flat area to the edge of the An. Some ancient carving topped the archway, but the detail was too worn to see. There were no undain in sight. The ground was churned up as if thousands of pairs of feet had recently marched across it. Deep wheel ruts ran in lines, perhaps from the cartloads of Spirit the army would have to take with it. Bells were ringing out in the city above them once more, echoing off the walls so that it was impossible to work out which way they were coming from. Great as the destruction of the ghosts had been, it was clear most of the buildings stood unscathed.

"Let's go," said Cait, running for the An. They'd be visible from all sides, but there was no alternative. If they could get to the water then maybe, somehow, they'd be safe.

The bridgehead was little more than a line of worn stone columns striding into the An, the crumbling remains of stone archways connecting them. A hundred yards or so out the bridge stopped completely. The whole thing looked like a weird, mediaeval pier at some seaside resort. She liked piers though, liked the sense of being able to leave the land behind, stride off over the surface of the sea. She'd visited many of them with her parents on family holidays. There were always fun things at the ends of piers: shows or rides or amusements. And people behaved differently, too, as if they were freed from the ties of normal life.

Still, getting onto the bridge wasn't going to be easy.

The end was little more than a pile of rubble, many of the great blocks of stone lying in the water where they'd tumbled down the banks. The remains of the bridge looked just about passable, although there were gaps where some of the stones making up the deck had crumbled into the water. Gaps they'd have to leap over, but with luck they'd be able to get to the end. And what then? What miracle was going to occur to rescue them? She wished she knew. Most likely there would be no salvation, and a leap into the fast-moving waters would be the only way out.

She didn't need to look behind her to know time was running out. The undain horde was close, streaming south in its fury. Once they returned they would surround the bridgehead in ranks a thousand deep. There were no angry ghosts to come to the rescue now. There was only a scrap of paper plucked form the neck of a bird. Two scrawled words upon which she was risking everything. *The bridgehead.* Well, here they were.

She climbed, scrambling up blocks of stone the size of a small car to get to the floor of the bridge. Danny followed her. After a moment so did Nox.

A short way along the bridge was a section where only a single width of stones remained in place. Gaping holes on either side revealed the drop down to the waters of the An. Cait went first, keeping her eyes forward as she walked. The single stone was as wide as a pavement, but something about the gaping drop, the flowing water beneath, made it difficult to manage the feat of walking in a straight line. Thankfully she made it across without wobbling or falling in.

She turned to watch Danny come across – and there was the undain army. It filled the wide plain beside the river, countless ranks of them. Most of them looked like normal people: soldiers with swords and spears, clad in shining armour. Others crouched on all fours, more beast than human, and some were giants wielding clubs huge enough to bring down a house. Steam rose off them from the speed of their rush south. A group of glowing dragonriders and a single robed figure stood at their head, watching or awaiting instructions.

Cait stepped back. "Let's get to the end."

"And then what?" said Nox, stepping calmly along the narrow section after Danny. "What exactly happens when we get to the end of the bridge?"

"You'll see," said Cait.

The wind was keener at the end of the bridge, blowing from the north, a cold edge to it. Four feet below, the waters of the An swept by. There was nothing to be seen but the wide waters and, some way out, thick mists hanging in veils. Down the coast, Cait could see the woods they'd hidden in. Upstream, there were only more of the undain, the banks black with rows of them answering the summons from the city.

"So?" said Nox.

"Wait," said Cait. She didn't look at him.

Danny, catching her gaze, looked troubled but grinned. He believed in her at least. She wasn't sure she did.

"They're coming," said Nox. "Now would be a good time to zap us out of here."

A group of undain soldiers were moving at the other end of the bridge. The robed figure waved them onward. They were being cautious, still afraid she could unleash more furious spirits. She really, really wished she could.

She could take out one or two of them, at least. Reveal their true selves to them to turn them mad. Blast them with ice. Freeze the blood in their veins. *Something.* It clearly wouldn't be enough, but they couldn't just give in.

As they waited, to her surprise, Nox handed her the book. "Take it."

"What? Why?"

"So you can destroy it. Burn it or shred it with magic if this mysterious miracle of yours doesn't occur. Can you do that?"

"I can try."

"Good."

The first undain soldier leaped onto the bridge in a single bound. The creature was powerfully built. It didn't have a sword; instead, the bones of its right arm were horribly extended, stretching from its flesh to form a long, jagged cleaver. The undain practised a few slashing strokes before stomping forward.

It had reached the narrow section when another figure appeared, climbing upward from beneath the bridge. A shorter man than the hulking undain, but armed with a snaking sword. She saw immediately who it was.

"Ran!" She called his name, but he paid no attention. He stood on the narrow stone pathway to fight the undain. The undain swung, but Ran jumped over the blow, slashing his sword at the same time. There was a crunch of metal on bone and the undain, roaring, toppled sideways into the water, its arm severed.

For a moment she thought Ran was going to follow as he landed awkwardly, but he regained his balance and stood waiting for the next attacker.

"He'll fight them all, one by one," said Danny, something like awe in his voice.

"Don't be ridiculous," said Nox. "Look at him, he's barely standing."

Another undain soldier stepped forward, carrying a metal sword. This one was shorter, more Ran's height. He was nimbler, too. He stepped across the narrow stones where the first had lumbered. Cait couldn't follow the blur of blades that followed. Each seemed to strike the other repeatedly but neither fell. Somehow they remained standing on the thin strip of stone.

Ran, under pressure from a flurry of blows, stepped backward. If he was pressed too far the undain queuing up behind could cross to surround him. Then it would all be over.

Ran seemed to stumble, overbalancing, his sword held wide as he tried to stay on his feet. The undain saw its chance and lunged, going directly for Ran's exposed chest. Cait cried out.

The undain's sword never reached Ran. In a single, flowing movement, Ran crouched beneath the blow, bringing his own sword in and up to impale the shocked undain. There was a harsh cry and a spray of blood. The second undain fell, and once again the An swallowed it.

"Incredible," said Danny.

"It makes no sense," said Nox. "Why are they doing this? They could flood across. They could leap over him if they wanted."

"The bridge," said Cait. "Perhaps the ancient stone prevents them somehow. This isn't Angere any more. This is the An. We're between the two lands. Perhaps that affects the undain."

Nox looked extremely doubtful. "News to me if it does."

A third undain squared up to Ran. The sunlight glinted off their raised blades and then once again there was a whirl of blows and counterblows. Ran adopted a different strategy this time, striding forward to push his opponent, overwhelming the creature with the sheer speed of his sword strokes. The undain stepped backward, desperately defending itself. In a few moments, it, too, fell into the waiting waters.

"They're not going to let this continue," said Nox. "Here they come."

On the bank, the group of glowing dragonriders, eight of them, moved. In unison, they leaped onto the bridge. Huge swords in hands, they simply stepped over the gaps in the bridge's stonework. Ran, seeing them coming, fell back. He knew he couldn't defeat them. He glanced at Cait and the rest, retreating toward them all the time.

The undain let him go, happy to corral him with the rest at the end of the bridge. Ran edged away. But then, unexpectedly, he charged, throwing himself at the undain in the middle. It was a doomed attack. The undain's sword met Ran's, and Ran was hurled onto the floor of the bridge. He tried to rise but couldn't. Instead he scrabbled backward from his huge attacker, trying to get away.

With another blur of movement, the undain reached Ran. He held his great sword high, preparing to deliver the killing blow.

25 – THE COLD WATERS OF THE AN

Ran scrambled backward from the blow. The undain let him go, as if it enjoyed toying with him. Cait ran toward them. The undain watched her warily but didn't step closer. She lent Ran a hand to haul him up. His bare, muscled skin was wet from sweat and the waters of the An.

"Ran. You're alive. I'm sorry we left you. We had no choice."

His burns were healing a little, but he still looked terrible, his face pale and drawn. Fresh wounds on his arms showed he hadn't escaped unscathed defending the bridge. She supported him as best she could as they made their way to Danny and Nox.

"You did the right thing," he said. "Waiting was too dangerous."

"How did you find us?"

"Tracked you. I saw you running to the bridgehead. Swam beneath the bridge so they wouldn't see me."

"It's amazing you made it."

He grunted as he limped along with her. "What is happening? Why are we here? Is help coming?"

"Perhaps. I hope so."

"From where? Tell me the plan and I can help."

She wished she could tell him, she really did. They reached Danny and Nox. The four of them stood at the lip of the shattered bridge. Thirty yards away, the eight undain dragonriders edged forward in a line, swords held ready.

"You don't have a plan do you?" said Nox. "No one's coming to rescue us are they?"

"Is that what you think?" she asked.

"That's what I think."

But even as he spoke, a chill wind swept from the river, forceful enough to make the four of them stagger and sprawl to the ground. For a moment they were engulfed by a thick, freezing mist that streamed off the water. When it passed, the bright sun returned. But now the undain, and beyond them all of Angere, were obscured by a solid wall of grey. The stones of the bridge appeared to stop thirty yards away. They were on a tiny island of their own in the An.

Puzzled, Cait reached into the mist with her mind. She thought it might be the aether creature, that somehow it had followed them. She soon saw the truth. There was magic at work. This was a natural mist, but magic was controlling it. A *person* was controlling it.

"Cait. Look." Danny pointed the other way, out onto the waters.

A small wooden boat floated toward them. This far away it was little more than a black smudge upon the shining waters. It was a sketch of a boat, two oars dipping in and out of the water and two stick figures inside. One, the rower, sat head bowed with the effort. The other, a woman with long hair, stood at the prow. With each stroke the boat inched nearer.

Nox looked at Cait, surprise clear on his face.

"Who are they?" said Ran. "How can they be out there in a boat?"

Cait didn't reply. One of the figures – the standing woman – she thought she knew. It could only be Hellen

Meggenwar, the Andar witch Fer had told her about. Fer had said she was a weatherworker. The gale and the fog had to be her work. Maybe she was powerful enough to keep the undain at bay for a time, too.

As to the other, Cait had no idea. When she held the seeing stone to her eye the light blazing from him was blinding, like staring into the sun. His aura was a deep green. Yet, without the stone, he was a hunched old man, his head bald, his grey beard long and ragged.

The boat nudged the stone pillar of the bridge and still the undain hadn't attacked, hadn't appeared from the mists. Distantly, Cait was aware of the desperate magical struggle taking place in the air around her as the fog was maintained. It couldn't last for long. More and more power was being thrown at the wall as the undain tried to punch through.

The old woman threw a rope for them to catch. "Come on. I can't maintain it forever, can I? Into the boat. You have the book?"

Ran climbed down to stand perfectly balanced in the centre of the boat, holding it tight to the stones of the bridge. Cait followed. The boat swayed alarmingly as she stepped inside. She sat down on a wooden plank that ran across the craft, cradling the book in her lap. Danny climbed in beside her, clearly not quite able to believe what was happening. The old man, the rower, sat opposite them. His eyes were all but invisible beneath his shaggy eyebrows, but he was watching her. Studying her. His long beard flowed down to his legs. He had two little round wounds on his forehead, one on each side, both scabbed over.

"And what about him?" said Hellen, indicating Nox with a nod of her head. "Does he come to Andar or does he stay here with his old friends? What do you say, Cait?"

Nox, she could see, was calculating even now, deciding which option was most to his advantage. She couldn't escape the impression that Hellen was doing precisely the same thing.

"It's up to him," said Cait. "Let him choose which side he's on."

"Do you trust him?" Hellen asked.

Did she? He'd given them the book, it was true. Given them both halves of the book and risked a lot to do it. Still, she couldn't forget the look of glee on his face when he'd turned her over to the undain. They could trust him only to do what was in his own best interests. She tried to ignore the fact that Menhroth had said almost exactly the same thing.

"Let him come," she said. "The undain will tear him to pieces if he stays."

Hellen nodded, as if she approved of her answer. "Come on, Nox. We're leaving Angere now."

Nox climbed down. Cait thought he was going to thank her but instead he said, "Get us out of here, witch. Even you can't fight them."

Hellen studied him, amusement on her lined face. "Really? I seem to be managing it so far."

Ran pushed them off and the old man brought them about. He began to row, moving them away from Angere with strong pulls on the oars. He muttered some continuous babble of syllables to himself, although whether it was the words of some spell, or he was crazy, she couldn't tell.

Cait couldn't be sure but the fog seemed to follow them over the waters as they crept eastward. In a few moments, the ancient stones of the bridge disappeared. Hellen sat down, breathing rapidly from the magic she'd worked.

"Well," she said. "That's that. I am pleased to meet you, Cait Weerd. And you, too, Danny. You've been through a lot, both of you. More than we had any right to ask."

"Are we safe now?" said Cait. "Can they reach us?"

"Not out here. No one sails on the An, didn't you

know?"

The fact that they were on the An didn't appear to trouble her. "But the flying undain," said Cait. "Can't they come for us? Fer said one made it all the way to Andar."

"It did. But no more. There will be no more undain in Andar until the waters freeze and they can march across. We've made sure of that, at least." Hellen glanced at the old man, who didn't respond. He maintained the rhythmic surges of his oar strokes. He looked ancient, little more than bone and sinew, although his movements were sure and strong.

"But the serpents," said Nox. "They'll destroy us out here."

"No," said Hellen. "They will not. The beasts of the deep are really in *his* mind, you see." She indicated the silent rower with a nod of her head. "In many ways they are him. They'll let us cross safely enough. But if the undain put out in boats to follow it will be a different story."

Nox's mouth opened and closed a few times, fish-like, before he replied. "Who is he?"

"He is called Hyrn. You know the name?"

Nox nodded. The astonishment on his face was satisfying to see. He clearly did know the name, although it was new to Cait.

"When did you know?" Nox said to Cait. "Why didn't you tell me he was involved?"

"It was too dangerous to tell anyone else," said Cait. "We couldn't risk the undain finding out, could we?" She caught the look of amusement in Hellen's eye, but the old witch didn't comment. Instead she changed the subject.

"What you've done, what all of you have done, is a wonder. You've given us a chance. Your grandmother was right about you, Cait. And your mother."

"My mother? You've spoken to her?"

"Only to your grandmother. But they both knew what you had in you. Both wanted to protect you, too, shield you from … all this. Maybe that was the right thing to do and maybe it wasn't. But here you are."

"My mother…" said Cait.

Hellen put a hand on hers. "I know, child. I know what she did. At the end I don't think she was trying to save your world, or mine, or anything else. I think she was doing what she could for you. She knew the book might help us, but she wanted only to protect her beloved daughter, that's all. And that's exactly as it should be."

"You saw what happened? Through the aether?"

"No. Johnny told us. Johnny brought the other half of the book through with him."

"And my gran? And Fer?"

"Johnny was alone. He doesn't know what happened to them. I'm sorry."

They moved in silence for a time after that, each lost in their own thoughts. Cait dipped her hand in the cold waters of the An. She could feel the chill of ice in it. The only sounds were the slap and fizz of the oars, the creak of the boat's old timbers. They skimmed along in a bubble of clear water surrounded by mist. There was no magic being used, though. These were the An's own veils. The waters grew rougher, the little boat dipping and raising its head as it cut eastward. Once, Cait thought she saw the hulking grey shape of a river serpent in the fog, the flash of a vast eye peering down at her. It vanished as quickly as it came.

"So what happens now?" she asked.

Hellen was staring into the mist, lost in her own thoughts. She turned to Cait and smiled. There was something, Cait thought, of her gran about the old witch. Something that refused to be beaten.

"Now? We have both halves of the Shadow Grimoire. Perhaps we see about using it. Perhaps we destroy it. We have, at least, deprived Menhroth of it. We've dealt him a blow, and he'll be furious. But it isn't a fatal blow. At best we've slowed him down, bought ourselves a little time. The days grow shorter and the light is fading. The ice creeps down the An and soon they will be able to cross. We have a struggle ahead of us. A grim struggle in which much will be lost."

"So how do we fight them?" said Danny. "What plan do you have?"

Hellen laughed. "Plans? Ariane used to say I spent too much time scheming. *Pots and pans before plots and plans.* You deserve the truth. I truly don't know, everything is moving too quickly. There is much here I didn't foresee: you, Hyrn, Nox for that matter. I'm only a foolish old woman, as Ariane also liked to remind me. We will return us to Forness. Then we must get to Islagray and hear your story. And then we will see what's what."

"Wait," said Cait, "what happened to Ariane? Fer told me she healed her. You speak as if she's no longer alive."

"Yes. Ariane died too, I'm afraid," said Hellen. "Died fighting those *things* in her own way. That's a story I will tell you. But I miss her more than I can say."

"So is there any hope?" said Cait. "For Andar? For our world? Angere. Genera. They seem so powerful and we're so weak."

"Tell me, Cait," said Hellen. "Were there moments when you lost hope? When you thought you'd never make it to Andar?"

"I guess."

"And yet here you are, safe for the moment, sitting in a boat surrounded by friends. There is always hope. We've got this far. Now, somehow, we have to see about the rest. That's all we can do, isn't it?"

Cait nodded. She huddled with Danny, arm in arm, glad of the warmth from his body, happy to be alive and safe. For that moment, it was enough.

She closed her eyes and let the rhythmic surging of Hyrn's rowing rock her to a welcome sleep.

The travels of Cait and Fer conclude in *Witch King.*

Witch King – The Cloven Land Trilogy, Book 3

The war for Andar begins...

The mighty river An freezes from shore to shore, and the army of horrors from Angere marches across to devour peaceful and beautiful Andar. Cait, Hellen and the others head north, hoping to slow the invasion. At Islagray, Ashen battles to make sense of the reunited Shadow Grimoire, seeking a way to turn the undain's necromancy against itself. Fighting dark magic with dark magic is a grim and dangerous road.

Meanwhile, in our world, Fer evades Genera and the undain as she undertakes a desperate mission to sever the supply of Spirit fuelling the armies of Angere.

Unlikely friends rise to the skies, and hidden enemies wait to betray Cait and Fer. With every defeat, Andar fades. And at Islagray, the heart of the land, the last free place, the Song can barely be heard over the rising tide of war.

https://simonkewin.co.uk/witch-king

Hyrn – a Cloven Land Trilogy prequel

Some wounds are too wide to heal...

The world changes one bright morning in spring. The ageing king of Angere turns to necromancy to prolong his existence, and the price of dark magic is paid in innocent lives. The land descends into chaos as loyalties are tested and friends become bitter foes.

For Black Meg, eldest witch of Angere, time is desperately short. She receives a vision from Hyrn, the horned man of the woods. The future is worse than anything she could have imagined. But Hyrn also shows her an answer, a way out.

It's a terrible and desperate path. But the free people of Angere have no choice but to take it.

Free to download.

https://simonkewin.co.uk/hyrn

ABOUT THE AUTHOR

Simon Kewin was born on the misty Isle of Man but now lives deep in the English countryside. He writes fantasy, science fiction and some things that can't make their minds up. He is the author of over 100 published short stories as well as a growing number of novels.

To find out about his other books, go to:

www.simonkewin.co.uk

Sign up for his newsletter and you'll be the first to know when he has new books out. There are some fine sci/fi and fantasy books to download for free as thanks

www.ingramcontent.com/pod-product-compliance
Lightning Source LLC
Chambersburg PA
CBHW050615170726
48283CB00001B/259